By Royal Appointment

REBECCA WINTERS
NICOLA MARSH
CARA COLTER

MILLS &
BOON

Published in Great Britain 2013
by Mills & Boon, an imprint of Harlequin (UK) Limited,
Eton House, 18-24 Paradise Road, Richmond, Surrey TW9 1SR

BY ROYAL APPOINTMENT
© by Harlequin Enterprises II B.V./S.à.r.l 2013

The Bride of Montefalco, Princess Australia and *Her Royal Wedding Wish* were first published in Great Britain by Harlequin (UK) Limited.

The Bride of Montefalco © Rebecca Winters 2006
Princess Australia © Nicola Marsh 2007
Her Royal Wedding Wish © Cara Colter 2008

ISBN: 978 0 263 90565 6
ebook ISBN: 978 1 472 00138 2

05-0913

Harlequin (UK) policy is to use papers that are natural, renewable and recyclable products and made from wood grown in sustainable forests. The logging and manufacturing processes conform to the legal environmental regulations of the country of origin.

Printed and bound in Spain
by Blackprint CPI, Barcelona

THE BRIDE OF MONTEFALCO

BY
REBECCA WINTERS

Rebecca Winters, whose family of four children has now swelled to include three beautiful grandchildren, lives in Salt Lake City, Utah, in the land of the Rocky Mountains. With canyons and high alpine meadows full of wild flowers, she never runs out of places to explore, and they—along with her favorite vacation spots in Europe—often end up as backgrounds for her novels. Writing is her passion, along with her family and church. Rebecca loves to hear from her readers. If you wish to e-mail her, please visit her website at www.rebeccawinters-author.com.

CHAPTER ONE

"LIEUTENANT DAVIS?"

The Portland police detective looked up from his computer.

"I'm glad you got here so fast, Mrs. Parker."

"Your message indicated it was urgent."

"It is," he said in a solemn tone. "Come in and sit down."

Ally took a chair opposite his desk.

"I take it there's been a new development in the case."

"Major." He nodded. "The woman who died in the car accident with your husband four months ago has finally been identified through dental records and a DNA match-up."

Though Ally had buried her husband two months ago, she'd needed this day to come if she were ever to find closure. Yet at the same time she'd been dreading it because it meant getting painful facts instead of wallowing in useless conjecture.

"Who was she?"

"A thirty-four-year-old married female from Italy named Donata Di Montefalco."

Finally the woman had a name and a background.

"The Italian authorities have informed me she was the wife of the Duc Di Montefalco, a very wealthy, prominent aristocrat from a town of the same name near Rome. According to the police investigating the case, her husband has had his own people searching for her all these months."

"Naturally," Ally whispered. Had he been in love with his wife? Or had his marriage been unraveling like Ally's?

Though the detective had never said the words, she knew he suspected her husband of having been unfaithful. So had Ally who'd known her marriage was breaking down but hadn't wanted to believe it.

Jim had changed so much from the seemingly devoted family man she'd first married, she'd slowly fallen out of love with him though she wasn't able to pinpoint the exact moment it happened.

During the latter part of their two and half year marriage she'd seen signs that something was wrong. The long absenses from home because of his work, the lack of passion in his lovemaking when he did come home, his disinterest in her life when he made brief, unsatisfactory phone calls home, his desire to put off starting a family until he was making more money.

Despite the fact that there was still no definitive proof of an affair, this news gave added credence to her suspicions.

A fresh stab of pain assailed her. She needed to get out of his office to grieve in private.

Though she'd already had two months to absorb the fact that he hadn't died alone, a part of her had hoped the other woman would have been middle-aged. Possibly an older woman he'd given a lift to because of the storm. But this latest information put that myth to rest. It increased her turmoil that she hadn't loved him as much as she should have, otherwise why hadn't she confronted him before it was too late?

"Thank you for calling me in, Lieutenant." Any second now and she was going to lose control. Living in denial was the worst thing she could have done. Her guilt worsened to recognize she hadn't fought harder to recapture the love that had brought them together in the first place.

"I appreciate what you've done to help me."

She got up to leave. He walked her to the door of his office.

"I'm sorry I had to call you in and remind you of your loss all over again. But I promised to let you know when I had any more information.

"Here's hoping that in the months to come, you'll be able to put this behind you and move on."

Move on? a voice inside her cried hysterically.

How did you do that when your husband had died at the lowest ebb in your marriage?

How did you function when your dreams for a happy life with him were permanently shattered?

The detective eyed her with compassion. "Would you like me to walk you out to your car?"

"No thank you," she murmured. "I'll be all right."

She hurried out of his office and down the hall to the front door of the police station.

Dear God—how was it possible things had ended like this? *Nothing* was resolved. If anything, she was riddled with new questions.

Her thoughts darted to the woman's husband. He would have only just learned his wife's body had been found and identified. Besides months of suffering since her disappearance and now this loss, he had to be wondering about Jim's importance in Donata's life.

Wherever the Duc Di Montefalco was at this moment, Ally knew he was in hell.

She could relate…

"Uncle Gino? How come we're going to stay at your farm for a while?"

Rudolfo Giannino Fioretto Di Montefalco, known only to his family and a few close friends as Gino, eyed his eleven-year-old niece through the rearview mirror. The girl sat next to Marcello, Gino's elder brother.

"Because it's summer. I thought you and your father would enjoy getting out in nature instead of being cooped up in the palazzo."

"But what if Mama comes back and we're not there?"

Gino braced himself. The dreaded moment had come.

He pulled up to the side of the farmhouse. In the dying rays of the sun, the cypress trees formed spokes across the yellowed exterior.

He turned in his seat to make certain Sofia was holding her father's hand. Since Marcello had been stricken with Alzheimer's and could no longer talk, it was one of the ways she could express her love and hope to feel his in return.

"I have something to tell you, sweetheart."

A full minute passed. In that amount of time the color had drained from his niece's face. "What is it?" she asked in a tremulous voice. The strain of going months without knowing anything about her mother had robbed Sofia of any joie de vivre.

"Sofia, I have some bad news. Your mama, she was in a car accident, and…she died."

Four months ago in fact, but Gino had only been informed of her death last night. Today he'd been making preparations for Sofia's move to the country with Marcello.

The details surrounding the tragedy were something neither she nor the trusted staff both at the palazzo and the farmhouse needed to know about.

His gaze took in Sofia's pain-filled expression. When his news computed, he heard the sobs of an already heartbroken girl who buried her dark brown head against her father's shoulder.

Marcello looked down at her, not comprehending, not able to comfort his daughter.

Gino felt her sobs from the front seat. Tears welled in his throat. Now that Donata's body had been found and identified, the nightmare of her disappearance was over. But another one had just begun…

His motherless, already introverted niece was going to need more love and understanding than ever.

As for Gino, once he'd arranged with the priest for a private memorial service away from prying eyes so Sofia could say goodbye to her mother in private, he needed to increase security to protect his family from the press.

Carlo Santi, the region's top police inspector and one of their family's best friends was doing his best to stop information from the police department leaking to the various newspapers and media in Rome and elsewhere. But there were those rabid, insatiable vultures from the tabloids who invaded without mercy, always lurking to find something juicy on Gino and his family. It was the price they paid for their title and wealth.

If it weren't for Carlo running interference for him all these months, the situation could have gotten uglier much sooner.

With the sudden debilitating onset of Marcello's disease two years ago, Donata's selfish streak had created havoc in his brother's marriage, and had damaged their daughter irreparably. In Gino's opinion, Donata had to have been one of the world's most insensitive, neglectful wives and mothers on record.

He'd fought hard to protect his brother and niece from the worst of her flaws.

As a result he'd been forced to guard the family secrets with a certain ruthlessness that Donata enjoyed publicizing to anyone who would listen. Her indiscriminate venting had made its way to the press, casting a pall over all their lives, Gino's in particular. Through innuendo she'd made him out to be the grasping, jealous brother-in-law who wanted her and the title for himself.

The only thing Donata hadn't ever considered was her own death.

Once the media got wind of the accident that took her life, everything Gino had done to keep family matters private was about to become a public scandal. The fact that an American man close to Donata's age had been driving the car when they'd been killed provided the kind of fodder to cause a paparazzi frenzy. This kind of story would sell millions of papers with far reaching consequences for Sofia. His niece could be destroyed by the facts, let alone the malicious rumors surrounding them.

Aside from physically removing the two in the back seat to a protected place away from media invasion, there didn't seem to be a thing in hell he could do about unscrupulous journalists digging up old lies on him in order to sell more newspapers. Since his teens, battling the press had been the story of his life. Now it was about to be the story of Sofia's, but not if he could help it!

The orchestra conductor put down his baton. "Take a ten minute break. Then we'll pick up the Brahms at bar 20."

Thankful for the respite, Ally placed her violin on the seat and filed out of the music hall behind the other members of the string section.

She walked down the corridor where she could be alone and reached in her purse for her cell phone.

She was expecting a call back from her doctor. After the meeting with the detective yesterday, she'd developed a migraine that still hadn't gone away. To her dismay there was no message from the doctor. Maybe he'd tried her house phone and had left one.

Sure enough when she retrieved her messages, she learned his nurse had called in a prescription for the pain. If she could just get some relief…

Right now nothing seemed real. The hurt of her failed marriage and the circumstances surrounding Jim's death had gone too deep.

There was one more message, but she'd wait until she got home because the throbbing at the base of her skull refused to let up.

"Ally?" Carol called to her. "Are you all right?"

"I-it's a migraine giving me grief. Do me a favor and tell the maestro I had to go home, but I'll be here in the morning for rehearsal."

The Portland Philharmonic Orchestra's end of May concert was the day after tomorrow.

"I will. Don't worry about your violin. I'll take it home with me and bring it back tomorrow."

"You're an angel."

After getting a drink from the fountain, Ally found the strength to leave the building and head for her car.

Once she'd stopped at the pharmacy where she'd taken one of her pills on the spot, she drove straight home and went to bed with an ice bag across her forehead.

An hour passed before she started to feel a little better. But there was no pill to stop the questions that wouldn't leave her alone.

For one thing, she wanted to see the place where Jim had died. Her mother hadn't thought it a good idea because visiting the scene of the accident would be too painful.

But Ally couldn't be in any more pain than she was right now. She needed to look at the bridge where Jim's car had skidded on ice into the river. It had happened during a blizzard outside St. Moritz, Switzerland.

She also felt a compulsion to see Donata's family home, maybe even commiserate with the Duc on the phone after she arrived in Montefalco. He wouldn't be human if he didn't have questions, too. Maybe talking together would help both of them cope a little better with the tragedy.

Filled with a sense of purpose she hadn't felt in months, she reached for her cell to phone the airlines. Using her credit card she booked a flight out of Portland for the next day. She would fly to Switzerland, then Italy.

By midafternoon she felt well enough to drive to the bank for traveler's checks. The decision to do something concrete about her situation was probably more therapeutic than taking pills because she found the energy to get packed and arrange for her neighbor to bring in her mail while she was gone.

Once she'd showered, she took another pill and went to bed. When she awakened the next morning she felt considerably better.

With her car safely parked in the garage, all she had left to do was phone for a taxi. While she waited for it to come, Ally listened to the message that had been on her home phone since yesterday morning.

"Hey, Jim! This is Troy at the Golden Arm Gym. Since new management is taking over, we've been cleaning out the lockers. I found something pretty valuable of yours. I don't have a phone number or address on you, so I've been calling all the J., Jim or James Parkers in the city trying to find you. Call me back either way so I can cross you off the list. If you're that Jim, drop by within twenty-four hours or it'll be gone."

Ally had buried her husband two months ago. Just hearing someone ask to speak to him today of all days sent a chill through her body. This call was like a ghost from the past.

Since Jim had never joined a gym, she phoned the number to let them know.

"Golden Arm Gym."

"Is Troy there?"

"Speaking."

"You're the person who called my house yesterday morning. I'm Mrs. James Parker, but I'm afraid you have the wrong Jim Parker."

"Okay. The Jim I'm looking for works in Europe a lot, and he doesn't have a wife. Thanks for letting me know."

He clicked off, but Ally's fingers tightened around the receiver. Much as she wanted to dismiss his words, she couldn't. Too often in her marriage she'd ignored little signs because she hadn't wanted to believe anything could be wrong.

But those days were over. She was no longer the naïve idealist he'd married.

Once the taxi arrived, she instructed the driver to stop by the gym. It was on the other side of Portland near the freeway leading to the airport. There was no time to lose.

The driver waited while she hurried inside the gym.

When she entered, there were several people already working out. The trainer at the counter flashed her a look of male interest.

"Hi!"

"Hello. Are you Troy?"

"That's right."

"I'm Mrs. Parker, the woman you spoke to this morning."

He squinted at her. "I thought you told me I had the wrong person."

"Something you said forced me to reconsider. Did this Jim tell you what kind of work he did in Europe?"

"Yeah. He sells ski wear. In fact we worked out a deal. I gave him free workouts in exchange for his top of the line ski equipment."

She took a fortifying breath. "Then that was my husband."

He blinked. "What do you mean 'was'?"

"Jim died four months ago."

"You're kidding. So that's why I haven't seen him around. What happened?"

"He died in a car accident."

Had there been other women before Donata, and she'd happened to be the unlucky one who'd gone off the bridge with him?

"I'm sorry, Mrs. Parker. Maybe I misunderstood about him not being married."

She shook her head. "No. I'm quite sure you didn't. When did he join this club?"

"About a year ago."

A whole year?

Struggling to remain composed, she pulled the wallet from her purse. Inside was a little photo holder. She showed him the one of Jim.

The other man stared at it, then nodded. "Just a sec and I'll get what he left here."

Half a minute later he came out of his office with an unfamiliar looking silver laptop. The power cord had been taped to it.

He tore the attached slip in half. "Sign here."

Ally complied, trying her best not to tremble.

"Thank you for the call, Troy. I'm anxious to keep anything that belonged to my husband."

"Of course. I'm glad you came when you did, otherwise we'd have sold it. I really am sorry about your husband."

"So am I," she muttered in a dull voice.

She'd known nothing about the purchase of this laptop. Jim's company had supplied him with the one he'd always used to do business.

The only reason for this computer to exist meant he'd had something to hide.

She would have to take it to Europe with her. She didn't have time to go back home. After she returned to the States, she'd look inside. If she discovered painful secrets, hopefully by then she'd be better able to handle them.

After going out to the cab, she packed the laptop in her suitcase then told the driver to step on it.

As she sat back in the seat, she shuddered to realize that her husband had been working out in a gym for eight months, and she'd had no knowledge of his activities. He must have stopped by either coming or going to Switzerland on business.

It was one thing to recognize that the two of them had drifted apart, but quite another to realize he'd been living a separate and secret life. How humiliating to be confronted by the truth in front of Troy, a total stranger to her.

Oh, Jim. What happened to the man I married? Did I ever really know you?

Ally was beginning to wonder….

With the aid of the staff, Gino helped his grieving Sofia and her father into the limo outside the local parish church. They'd just buried Donata in the adjacent cemetery. It had all been carried out in secret while word of her death had finally been announced by the media.

One day when the furor had died down, he would have her remains removed and buried on the grounds of the Montefalco estate in the family plot.

"I'll join you at the farm in a few minutes, sweetheart."

Sofia's face was ravaged by fresh tears. "Don't take too long."

"I promise. I just want to say goodbye to a few people and thank the priest."

She nodded before the farmhouse caretaker Paolo drove the car away.

Vastly relieved this part was over, he turned swiftly to Carlo whom he'd asked to wait until they could talk in private.

"The onslaught has started in earnest, Carlo."

"What's going on?"

"One of the security guards at the palazzo just left a message that a woman claiming to be Mrs. James Parker tried to get in to see Marcello a few minutes ago. It's another ploy on the part of the paparazzi to ruin my family."

The other man pursed his lips. "I must say I'm surprised they'd be audacious enough to imperson-ate the wife of the deceased."

Gino grimaced. "Nothing surprises me anymore. She came in a taxi. As a precaution, the guard wrote down the license plate number."

Carlo's brows lifted. "Want me to track her down and have her vetted?"

Gino was way ahead of him.

"If you could locate her, I'd like to do the interrogating for a change."

"What's your plan?"

"How long could she be held at the jail?"

"Only twelve hours. If you can't make the charges stick, then we'd have to release her."

Gino's eyes glittered. "Don't worry about that. She's going to wish she'd never ventured into my territory."

Carlo pulled out his pocket notepad. "Give me the plate number. I'll alert the desk sergeant at the jail to cooperate with you."

"As usual, I'm indebted to you."

"Our families have been close for years. I'm not about to see you and Sofia destroyed."

Those words meant more to Gino than his friend would ever know.

"*Grazie*, Carlo."

There was a jarring knock on the bedroom door.

"Signora Parker?"

Ally had only been in bed an hour and groaned in disbelief. Her long connecting flights from Oregon to Switzerland, then Rome, had been bad enough. But it was the horrendous day she'd spent on a hot, overcrowded train to reach the hilltop town of Montefalco that had done her in.

To compound her troubles, every hotel in the

town had been booked months in advance for some festival. If her taxi driver hadn't taken pity on her and brought her to his sister's house to sleep, she would have been forced to return to Rome for the night. Perish the thought!

The rapping grew louder.

"Signora!"

Ally couldn't work out what was happening.

"Just a moment!"

She sat up, unconsciously running a hand through her short, blond curls. They made her look younger than her twenty-eight years.

Grabbing her robe lying across the end of the bed, she slipped it on, then hurried over to the door and opened it.

The elderly woman looked tired. Ally thought she sounded out of breath.

"Quickly! You must get dressed! A car from the Palazzo Di Montefalco has come for you."

Ally's green eyes widened. "But that's impossible!"

Earlier in the day she'd been turned away from the palace gates by armed guards. No one knew where she'd gone after she'd gotten back in the taxi.

"You have to be a very important person for the Duc Di Montefalco himself to send for you. Hurry! You must not keep the driver waiting,"

"I'll be out as soon as I can. Thank you."

Unless one of the guards had followed the taxi here, Ally was mystified as to how he'd known where to find her.

But that didn't matter now. In a few minutes she was finally going to meet with the man she'd flown thousands of miles to see. After her futile attempts to reach him by phone from Rome before boarding the train, and then the fiasco that took place earlier in front of the palace, she'd almost given up hope.

She shut the door and reached for her suitcase. In a few minutes she'd donned fresh jeans and a green print blouse. At one-thirty in the morning she didn't feel like dressing in the suit she'd brought.

Once she'd put on her sneakers, she finished the little packing she had to do. Before leaving the room, she found her purse and left two hundred dollars on the dresser.

One more look around to make sure she hadn't left anything behind and she joined the older woman who stood in the foyer waiting.

Ally rushed up to her. "I'm so sorry you had to be wakened at this late hour because of me. Especially after you were kind enough to take me in. I've left money on the dresser for you and your brother. Thank you again for everything, including the delicious meal and the chance to shower. Please tell your brother thank you, too. I don't know what I would have done without your help."

The other woman nodded impatiently. "I'll tell him. Now you must go!"

She opened the door onto an ancient narrow alley. The woman's house was one of several built at street level. Yet all Ally could see was a gleaming black sedan parked right outside the door.

The light from the foyer illuminated the gold falcon insignia of the Montefalco crest emblazoned on the hood.

As Ally ventured over the threshold, a man dressed in black like the palace security guards stepped away from the stone wall connecting the houses.

Since Ally was only five foot five, she was immediately aware of a tall, solidly built male with hair black as night. Something about his imposing demeanor and the almost hawkish features that distinguished him from so many other Italian male faces she'd seen today sent a little shiver of alarm through her body.

With breathtaking economy of movement he relieved her of her purse and suitcase.

"Give that back!" she cried. Ally tried to wrest the suitcase from his hand, but it was no use. She was no match for him. Besides, he'd already stashed everything in the trunk.

She felt his glance mock her before he opened the rear door.

The interior light revealed a broad shouldered

man of unquestionable strength. The sun had darkened his natural olive toned skin. He was more than conventionally handsome. The words splendid and fierce came to Ally's mind before she climbed in the back seat.

Following that thought she wondered if she wasn't crazy to let a total stranger whisk her away from her only place of refuge in this foreign country. She didn't know a soul here except the taxi driver and his sister.

Worse, she'd somehow lost her cell phone during the train ride, so she couldn't call for help. Someone had probably pilfered it.

The premonition that she might need a phone to the outside world was growing stronger as he climbed in behind the wheel and set the locks.

After he turned on the engine, they shot down the empty alley to the main road. Three blocks later and Ally sensed she was in trouble.

Instead of climbing to the top of the hill, the driver drove them through the lower streets of the town. He appeared to have a destination in mind that wasn't anywhere near the ochre-colored ducal palace clinging to the side of the cliff.

Rather than leave the old woman's protection at such an unorthodox hour, Ally should have obeyed her instincts and stayed in her room until morning.

She leaned forward in the leather seat. "This isn't the way to the palace." She'd said it in as steady a voice as she could muster.

"Please take me back to that woman's house."

The enigmatic guard ignored her demand and kept driving until they entered another alley behind some municipal buildings.

"Where are you taking me?"

"All in good time, *signora*." The first words out of his mouth were spoken in impeccable English with only a slight trace of accent.

He pulled in front of a steel door with a single light shining overhead. In the next instant he'd come around to her side of the car and opened the door for her.

"After you, *signora*."

She lifted her proud chin, refusing to budge. "Where have you brought me?"

His heavily lashed eyes looked like smoldering black fires.

"The Montefalco police station."

Police? "I don't understand."

"Earlier this evening you asked to speak to the Duc Di Montefalco, did you not?"

"Yes. Are you telling me I didn't have the right?"

"Let's just say he doesn't grant interviews."

"I didn't want an interview. I've flown a long way to talk to him in private."

He shifted his weight, drawing her attention to the play of raw muscle power in his arms and chest.

"Anyone who wants to make contact with him has to go through me."

That explained why she could never get anywhere on the phone or in front of the security guards.

Ally couldn't prevent her gaze from traveling over his distinctive masculine features. Those piercing eyes were framed by startlingly black brows. Never had she looked into such an arresting face.

"Are you a police officer who doubles as one of his bodyguards or something?"

A dangerous smile curled the corners of his mocking mouth. "That's one way of describing me."

CHAPTER TWO

A STRANGE CHILL rippled across Ally's skin. "How did you know where to find me?"

"The guards took down the license plate of your taxi. A simple phone call to the driver told me what I needed to know."

As easy as that.

"I told the palace guards who I was. They didn't even try to help me."

His lips twisted unpleasantly. "Any woman could claim to be Mrs. James Parker."

"But that's who I am! I have my passport to prove it."

"Passports are a dime a dozen. I believe that's the American expression."

She shook her head in exasperation. "Why are you being so hateful to me? I came to Italy expressly to meet with Mr. Montefalco for very personal reasons. You act like I've committed some crime."

"Trespassing *is* a crime," he muttered just loud enough to heighten her anxiety.

"This is impossible! I demand you call the American Embassy and let me talk to someone in charge."

His mouth formed a contemptuous line.

"No one there will be available before morning."

"In America you're innocent until proven guilty!" she flung at him, starting to feel desperate.

"Then you should have stayed there, or wherever you really came from, *signora*," he retorted in a voice of ice.

Trapped and painfully tired, Ally made the decision not to fight him. He was too formidable an adversary. This was all a terrible mistake, the kind you were supposed to be able to laugh about after you'd returned home from being abroad.

Once this man went through her belongings and found out the truth of her identity, she didn't expect an apology. However she could hope for a quick release and the chance to talk to Mr. Montefalco before too much more time passed.

Wrapping her dignity around her like a cloak, she got out of the car and waited for him to open the door.

He pressed a button on the wall of the building. In a minute the door swung open electronically.

She'd never been inside a jail of any kind. In the small reception area there were two armed police officers, one of them seated at a desk.

They nodded to her captor.

After an exchange in Italian she couldn't possibly understand, he left her in their charge and disappeared out the door.

"Wait—" she called out to no avail.

At that point she was photographed, fingerprinted and escorted down a passageway to a tiny room with a cot and a chair.

The door closed behind her, leaving her to her own devices.

The whole situation was so surreal, she wondered if she was hallucinating on the painkiller she'd taken before going to bed. It had been a preventive measure to ward off another sick headache.

Suddenly she heard the click of the electronic lock and the door opened. She swung around in time to see the driver who'd abducted her step inside. The door shut behind him, enclosing her in this tiny closet of a holding cell with a man who could overpower her before she took her next breath. He'd brought her purse with him.

"During your interrogation you have your choice of the chair or the bed, *signora*."

She was feeling pretty hysterical about now.

"I'd rather stand."

"So be it."

He opened her purse. After examining the contents including her wallet and bottle of medication, he pulled out her passport.

She watched him study the picture that had been

taken three years earlier. At that point in time she'd been a radiant fiancée with long blond hair and sparkling green eyes, anticipating a skiing honeymoon in the French Alps with Jim.

Ally could no longer relate to that person.

The stranger's enigmatic gaze flicked to her face and hair. He scrutinized her as if trying and failing to find the woman in the photo.

He put the passport in his pocket, then tossed her purse with its contents on the cot next to the pathetic looking lump that was supposed to be a pillow.

Only now did she realize her suitcase was still in his car.

"I'd like my luggage. There are things I need," she explained. "I have to have it, you know? Like clean clothes?"

"First things first, *signora*. Until I get the answers I'm looking for, we'll be at this all night. Since you already appear unsteady on your feet—no doubt from fear that you've been caught in the act—I suggest you sit down before you pass out."

"In the act of what?" Ally questioned, totally shocked by his assumption she'd done something wrong.

"We both know you're one of the unscrupulous paparazzi, willing to do anything for an exclusive. But I'm warning you now. After trying to impersonate someone else, you're facing a prison sentence unless you start talking."

"I *am* Mrs. James Parker."

"Just tell me the name of the tabloid that sent you on this story."

Heat swept through her body into her face. "You're crazy!" she blurted in exasperation. "My name is Allyson Cummings Parker. I'm an American citizen from Portland, Oregon. I only arrived in Rome from Switzerland this afternoon, or—or yesterday afternoon. I'm all mixed up now about the time. But I'm the widow of James Parker. He was a ski clothes salesman who worked for an American manufacturing company called Slippery Slopes of Portland. He died in a car accident outside St. Moritz, Switzerland, with Mr. Montefalco's wife four months ago!"

"Of course you are," he said in a sarcastic aside that made her hackles rise.

Her breathing grew shallow.

"Since you tracked me down through the taxi driver, he'll tell you he picked me up at the train station, and had to do all the translating while I tried to find a room because I don't speak Italian."

Her captor nodded. "He admitted you put on a convincing performance. That is…until you gave yourself away by asking him to drive you to the palazzo. That was your fatal mistake."

Her hands curled into fists. "How else was I supposed to talk to Mr. Montefalco? He doesn't list his phone number. When I reached Rome, I was on the phone with an Italian operator for half an hour trying to get a number for him."

"He doesn't talk to strangers. If you were an innocent tourist who didn't have a place to spend the night, you would have been much more concerned about that than brazenly attempting to ramrod your way into the ducal palace that has always been off limits to the public."

"But I didn't know that!"

"You're a good liar, I'll grant you that, but it was a dangerous act of idiocy on your part no matter how greedy you are for money. It's the one credential you sleazy members of the media carry every time you trespass on sacred ground for a story. You have no decency or thought for the precariousness of the situation. None of your kind has a conscience."

He folded his arms, eyeing her with chilling menace.

"As you're going to find out, I don't have one, either. So you can start talking now, or look forward to being incarcerated here indefinitely."

Her mouth had gone dry. "You're going to be sorry you're treating me like this," she warned him with a mutinous expression. "When Mr. Montefalco finds out I'm here anxious to talk to him, you'll be lucky if it's only your job you lose."

His black eyes felt like lasers, scanning beneath the surface for any abnormalities.

"Who sent you to do their dirty work?" he rapped out as if she hadn't spoken. "Tell me now and I'll use my influence with the judge to get you off with a light sentence."

A pulse throbbed at the corner of his hard jaw. He was in deadly earnest. That made the situation so much worse for Ally.

She spread her hands. "Look—there's been a huge misunderstanding here. If you think my passport and driver's license are doctored, then look at my airline tickets again. It proves I just flew here from Portland, with a stopover in Switzerland to see where my husband's accident happened."

His gaze searched hers relentlessly. "You call that proof when you could have flown from Italy to Oregon on your tabloid's money to begin your impersonation? You're wasting my time."

He pressed a button above the door, no doubt sending a signal that he was ready to leave. This was a nightmare!

"No—don't go yet—" she begged as the door swung outward.

He paused in the aperture, almost filling it with his tall, powerful body.

"Please—" she beseeched him. "There's someone you could call who will vouch for me. His name is L—"

She broke off talking because she suddenly realized she didn't want him to talk to Lieutenant

Davis. She would be too embarrassed for the detective to know she'd flown here to satisfy her curiosity about Donata. It was a private matter she'd rather no one else knew about. Until she talked to Mr. Montefalco, it was absolutely crucial her activities and whereabouts remain a secret to everyone including her mother. Ally's mom thought she was spending the weekend with friends from the orchestra. If she knew the truth, there would have been a battle Ally couldn't have handled.

"Yes?" her adversary mocked again. "You were saying?"

He stood still as a tree trunk. By now she was so beside herself she felt light-headed. Her ears started to buzz.

Out of self-preservation she sank down on the end of the cot and lowered her head so she wouldn't faint.

"Anything you'd like to confess before lights out, *signora*?" he asked without an ounce of concern or compassion.

His voice sounded far away. Ally had to wait until the worst of her weakness had passed before she could talk.

By then, he'd gone…

Vaguely disturbed by the woman's insistence that she really was the wife of Donata's last lover, Gino sped faster than was prudent through the dark streets toward his family home at the top of the mount. He wanted total privacy before searching the woman's suitcase. En route he phoned Carlo.

"Thank you for helping me carry out my plan. The suspect is in her cell, but I realize we won't be able to hold her for long. I asked the desk sergeant to run her passport through the scanner for verification, then report to you. Do me a favor and let me know what he finds out. When we've learned it's counterfeit, I'll expose her in my own way so she never gets another job. I'm sick of the media."

Once they'd hung up, he used his remote to enter the estate.

After slipping in a private side entrance to the palazzo with his prisoner's luggage, he entered Marcello's study and set it on one of the damask couches.

Upon opening it, he was surprised to see how lightly she traveled. The interior was redolent of her flowery scent. There were only a few changes of outfits and feminine underclothing, all modest and for the most part American brands.

Frowning because he couldn't find a camera or film, in fact nothing that sent up a red flag, his hands dug deeper.

"What's this?"

He felt something solid, wrapped in a towel.

"I knew it!" he whispered fiercely as he pulled out a silver laptop.

No wonder she'd wanted to hold on to her luggage.

He carried it over to the desk and plugged it into the wall adaptor.

"You and your paper are about to be exposed. Believe me, *signora*, you're going to pay—"

He turned it on, then sat down in the leather chair and waited to see what flashed on the screen.

He was ready to seize on anything that linked her to one of the tabloids.

Her home page popped up. He immediately clicked on her favorite pictures icon. Before long he came face-to-face with photos of Donata.

Gino let out a curse. He counted thirty pictures showing his sister-in-law in various stages of dress and undress. The outdoor pictures had been taken in Prague. He recognized the landmarks.

How in the hell had that impossibly green-eyed imposter gotten hold of these?

Donata, Donata.

He gritted his teeth. If these were to make it onto the streets… If Sofia were ever to see them…

He felt his gut twist in reaction.

There was only one reason why the champagne-blonde with the voluptuous curves locked up in the cell hadn't gone public with them yet. Perhaps she'd decided to approach Marcello first to extort more money from him than her paper would pay out.

Sick to the depth of his being because he knew these photos were only the tip of the iceberg, he packed up the laptop, closed her suitcase and carried both out to the truck he kept on the estate.

Leaving by a hidden road that came out on a side street, he headed for the jail.

Later at the farmhouse when he had the luxury of time, he'd delve into the e-mails and other secrets of the computer's hard drive. Until then, Gino would break her down until she was grist.

He wanted the name of the tabloid she worked for, how many more photos existed and the length of time she'd been on Donata's trail in order to obtain those particular photos.

Ally heard the door open. When she saw a tall dark figure coming toward her before it closed again, she let out a bloodcurdling scream and pulled the sheet over her head. "Nightmares, *signora*?" sounded the devilish voice of her captor. "With the kinds of things you have on your conscience, I can't say I'm surprised."

"Get out!" she shouted into the darkness. "The only person I'll speak to is a diplomat from the American Embassy. Do you understand me?"

"I'm afraid you're going to have a long wait."

She heard something scrape against the cement floor. She shivered to realize he'd pulled the chair next to her bed and had sat down.

"What you're doing is against the law!"

He gave a caustic laugh.

Fear of a sort she'd never known before embold-ened her to say the first thing that came into her mind.

"What a tragedy that such a lovely, beautiful town produces monsters like you."

The rhythm of his breathing changed, letting her know she'd struck a nerve. Good!

"For someone in your kind of trouble," he began in a frighteningly silky voice, "I'd advise you to stop fantasizing and tell me everything before the chief prosecutor of the region gets here and you're arraigned before the magistrate."

She sat up on the cot and pressed herself into the corner of the wall, as far away from him as possible.

"Whether you believe me or not, I'm Mrs. James Parker. So far, all you've told me is that I trespassed. But I don't see how I did that when the guards wouldn't let me past the gate."

She heard him shift in the chair.

"If you're telling the truth, and you really are the hapless wife who was the last person to know what your husband was up to, explain what those pictures are doing in your laptop."

Pictures? Ally rubbed her bloodshot eyes with her palms. She was so desperately tired, maybe she was dreaming this horror story.

"I asked you a question, *signora*."

No—she wasn't dreaming. He was sitting there next to her, intimidating her by his very presence.

All two hundred pounds of him, hard as steel physically and every other way.

"It's my husband's laptop. I don't know anything about any pictures."

She heard a sharp intake of breath.

"So you carried his laptop with you all the way to Montefalco for no particular reason?"

"I didn't say that!" she protested. "I told you earlier that I came to have a private talk with Mr. Montefalco and no one else."

"In order to show him the photographs and extort thousands of dollars in the process."

Thousands of dollars? What pictures would be worth that kind of money? She took a deep breath, scared of what she might discover.

"If there are pictures, I haven't seen them."

At her hotel in St. Mortiz, Ally would have looked inside the laptop, but she hadn't brought an adaptor to fit in the foreign outlet and figured she would have to wait until she returned to Portland. Part of her knew that was just an excuse. She didn't want to know.

"I planned to talk to him about things that aren't your business or anyone else's."

After a pause, he said, "You can tell me. I have his ear."

"Prove it! For all I know you're just a lowly policeman pretending to be Mr. Montefalco's bodyguard."

Suddenly he was on his feet. She could feel his

rage as he pushed the chair away. She hid her face behind the sheet even though it was dark in the room.

Still bristling she said, "Now *you* know how it feels to be told you're a liar and a sleazy con artist out to cash in on someone's private tragedy. I repeat." Her voice throbbed. "I'm *not* saying another word until I can speak to someone from the Embassy."

While she waited for his response, the door opened, then slammed shut.

The next thing she knew the light in her cell went on.

She checked her watch, which she'd changed to Italian time on the train. It said 7:30 a.m.

How long were they going to leave her in here before allowing her to freshen up?

In desperation she dragged the chair over to the door so she could push the button he'd pressed earlier.

Suddenly the door swung open, almost causing her to fall.

A guard she didn't recognize waited for her to climb down, then ordered her to follow him.

She grabbed her purse and trailed him down the hall and around the corner to the bathroom. There was no sign of her captor. She sincerely hoped she would never have to see or talk to him again.

After brushing her hair and putting on some lipstick, she felt a little more human. When she emerged minutes later, the guard escorted her back to her cell where a tray of food was waiting on the chair.

Just looking at the chair reminded her how her interrogator had shoved it across the room in a fit of anger.

In spite of the precariousness of her situation, the fact that she'd been able to infuriate him caused her to smile.

The guard noted it before disappearing.

Locked in once more, her gaze fell on the sparse continental breakfast. Rolls and coffee. But she wasn't about to complain. It might be a long time before she was allowed to eat again, so she consumed everything in short order.

She kept thinking about those pictures he'd mentioned. Jim had evidently stored some in one of his files. Maybe they were photos of all the women he'd had affairs with in Europe. At this juncture she didn't put anything past him. Her husband had truly lived a double life.

Ally let out a sound of abnegation.

What a fool she'd been not to have confronted him when she'd first suspected there was another woman.

Her abductor's words stung more than ever.

If you're telling the truth, and you really are the hapless wife who was the last person to know what your husband was up to, explain what those pictures are doing in your laptop.

Ally hadn't been hapless. It was a case of not wanting to admit something was wrong and have her mother say, "I told you so. A man with good looks and knows it can't be satisfied with one woman."

Ally didn't believe that. She knew too many attractive couples who had wonderful marriages.

Hers had started out that way, but when she saw changes happening, she should have questioned him point-blank. But she'd been scared. They could have talked things out and maybe salvaged their marriage. Now it was too late. There was no use wishing she'd acted on her suspicions a long time ago.

She looked around her claustrophobic cell. What she needed to do was get out of here.

Her abductor was waiting for her to cooperate. Maybe if she made up a lie, he'd believe her and allow her to go free with a slap on the wrist.

Without hesitation she pushed the chair over to the door and climbed up to press the button.

While she waited for a response, she put it back against the wall.

In a minute the door swung open to reveal the guard who'd brought her breakfast.

"*Signora?*"

"I hate it in here and I'm ready to talk."

He took the tray off her bed and started out the door.

"Did you hear me?" she cried. "I'm ready to confess!"

He shot her an oblique glance before the door closed.

"Ooh—" She pounded her fists against it. "What kind of a lunatic place is this?" she shouted.

When she realized she was only hurting herself, she gave it up and walked around her cell, trying to rub the pain from the sides of her hands.

Five minutes later she experienced déjà vu to hear the door open and see her captor enter the room. When she glimpsed the forbidding look in those fiery black eyes, she backed away from him.

"You're ready to tell the truth, *signora*?"

"Yes, but not in here. I can't abide enclosed places."

He gave an elegant shrug, reminding her what an amazing physique he had.

"It's either in here, or not at all."

"Oh all right!" She took a deep breath. "It's true I pretended to be Mrs. Parker to get the duc's attention.

"I do freelance stories for a local magazine in Portland. One of my boyfriends works for the police department and once in a while he tells me something interesting.

"A couple of months ago he told me his boss was working on a missing persons case involving a married man from Portland and another woman who died with him in Europe. Just the other day he mentioned that they'd finally identified the woman and had pictures of her.

"I asked him if he would let me see them. He did, so I scanned them and downloaded them to my laptop.

"All I wanted to do was talk to the woman's husband and ask if I could do an exclusive story on him. In case he didn't believe I was serious, I planned to show him the pictures. But I wouldn't have allowed them to be published, or have bribed him for money. I just wanted to write about his heart-wrenching ordeal. Americans love stories about wealthy, titled people with problems. It makes them feel better about their own less glorious lives.

"So now that you know the truth, please let me go. All I want is my passport and suitcase back. If you'll send for a taxi, the driver will take me to the train.

How about it? You let me out of here and I'll go straight home to Portland."

His eyes held a frightening gleam.

"You're lying through your pearly-white teeth, *signora*, but I give you credit for your amazing resourcefulness."

His wintry smile daunted her. "As it happens, I never told you the nature of those photos. If you'd known what they contained, you wouldn't have placed your source's job in jeopardy. All you've done is convince me you're a liar."

He was bluffing…

"How typical," she mocked. "If I were a man, you would have said 'good try.' But since I'm a woman, I can't be trusted."

One black brow quirked.

"Aren't you? So far you've told me two diametrically opposing lies, none of which hold water. While I'm still here, want to try for a third? I have nothing more important to do for the moment."

"Okay." She felt all the stuffing go out of her. "I'll make a deal with you. I'll give you a hundred dollars if you'll let me go. No one will need to know."

"If it were a hundred thousand dollars, I wouldn't take it."

He was impossible!

"Look— All I wanted to do was speak to Mr. Montefalco. This is between him and me, no one else."

He pursed his lips. "Why is that, *signora*?"

She lifted solemn eyes to his.

"Because it's very sad and very personal."

He put his hands on hips, the picture of the ultimate male. "I'm his closest confidant. You can tell me anything. If it will make you feel any better, you can whisper it to me. I promise it will remain sacrosanct."

Something in his tone had her halfway believing him, but it didn't matter.

"How do I know you're not wearing a listening device?"

"You don't," he clipped out. "You'll have to trust me."

She leaned close to him. "Sorry, but I have to talk to him alone."

* * *

The nearness of her heart-shaped mouth and the flowery scent her body gave off, stunned him as much as the words that fell from those enticing lips underlining her intransigence.

She couldn't be Mrs. James Parker. Any man married to her wouldn't have felt the urge to turn to Donata or any other woman for that matter.

"If you won't let me out of here," she continued in a low voice, "then bring Mr. Montefalco to me. I want to talk to him, and I believe he'll be anxious to talk to me. We might find we're a comfort to each other."

With his body still reacting to the warmth of her breath on his ear, Gino found himself reluctant to put distance between them. But he had to no matter how much the imploring look in her eyes and the haunting appeal in her voice persuaded him to believe she was finally telling him the truth.

He'd just stepped away, rubbing the back of his neck in an unconscious gesture of frustration when the door opened to reveal one of the guards. He informed Gino that Inspector Santi wanted him on the phone.

Without saying a word to her, he strode down the hall to the office, hardening himself against her sound of protest. In truth he was oddly reticent to find out she was the beautiful dust of the enemy.

He picked up the receiver, then turned his back toward the desk sergeant.

Knowing the jail phone was tapped he said, "Inspector? I'll call you back on my phone." After replacing the receiver, Gino pulled out his cell and rang him on the other man's private line.

Keeping his voice low he said, "Carlo? What did you find out?"

"She *is* Mrs. Parker, Gino."

While his thoughts took off in a dozen directions, Carlo kept talking. "I guess I'm not surprised. She's a widow grieving for her husband."

Gino had proof of that. He'd just come from her cell. She'd claimed that she'd sought out Marcello in the hope of giving and receiving comfort. But if that was true, how did she explain the laptop? Something didn't ring true.

"She said she'd been in St. Moritz to visit the scene of the accident," Gino murmured.

"It's unfortunate she chose this time to come to Italy when the press is just waiting for anything they can do to sensationalize this case. She's the last person *you* should be seen with."

Gino agreed. All it would take was a photo of the two of them together caught by one of the lurking paparazzi, and the hellish situation would escalate overnight.

"You need to leave the jail and let me handle this, Gino. I'll instruct the sergeant to free her. One of the guards will escort her to Rome by train and put her on the next plane for the States."

Gino grunted a response as he listened to his

friend. Though Carlo made a lot of sense, Gino couldn't forget that Mrs. Parker had come all this way with that laptop to see Marcello for a specific reason. Since she'd put herself in jeopardy to accomplish her objective, Gino couldn't let her go until he'd found out what was so important she'd risked everything, even jail, to make contact.

"I'm sure you're right, Carlo. I'll leave it up to you."

"That's good. You need to stay as far removed from her as possible."

He would as soon as he'd had time to talk to her away from other people. "*Grazie*, Carlo. It seems that's all I ever say to you."

"Forget it. *Ciao*, Gino."

Ally had been sitting on the cot wondering what was going on when the door flew open.

It was the same guard as before.

"Come, *signora*. You've been released. Please to follow me."

Hardly able to believe it, she grabbed her purse and started after him.

"What about my suitcase?"

"It is here," he said once they'd reached the reception area of the jail.

Convinced her abductor had confiscated the laptop, she leaned over to open the catches and sure enough, she discovered it was gone.

For some inexplicable reason, which was absurd considering her circumstances, she wished he were still here so that in front of his colleagues, she could accuse him of absconding with it.

She shut the lid and lifted her head. "What about my passport?"

"You'll be given it after you board your flight for the U.S."

She almost blurted that she couldn't leave Montefalco yet, but she stopped herself in time. All she needed was to make that mistake and then be shuffled back to her cell for defying him.

She took a deep breath to calm down. When she boarded her jet, she would claim to be ill and ask to be put on a later flight. Once she found a hotel room in Rome, she would figure out another plan to reach Mr. Montefalco.

"Very well. I'm ready whenever you are."

The jail door swung open. Another guard stood outside in front of a white police car and held the rear door open for her. Unlike her captor, he didn't help her with her luggage. No doubt he considered her a lowlife reporter who didn't deserve common courtesy.

She pushed her case across the seat and climbed in.

When their car emerged from the alley, throngs of tourists filled the walkways. The guard wound his way through the charming streets for the short ride to the depot.

She hated the thought of another hot train ride, but there was no help for it.

"Come, *signora*."

The guard had parked the car in a VIP zone. He escorted her through the crowded station and out to the quay.

After a brief talk with one of the conductors, he boarded the train with her and put her in a second class compartment already filled except for one seat in the middle. She had to put her suitcase on the shelf above without his assistance.

"I'll be in the corridor until we reach Rome, *signora*." The warning that she shouldn't try anything to escape was implicit.

Her cheeks hot with anger, she sat down, trying to avoid the interested stares of the other passengers.

No sooner had the guard stepped out of the compartment and disappeared than the train began to inch forward.

Ally was so exhausted after spending a wretched night in that jail cell, she rested her head against the back of the seat. Dispirited by everything that had happened, she closed her eyes for a few minutes, needing sleep. The first thing she would do when she could finally be alone in a hotel room was to crash.

Soon she lost track of time and was almost out for the count when she felt a hand on her arm.

"Signora?" sounded a deep male voice with a vaguely familiar timbre.

She came awake with a cry of alarm.

When she saw her striking captor still dressed in black, standing there bigger than life carrying her suitcase, the breath rushed from her lungs. She blinked up at him, wondering if he was real, or if she was dreaming.

"W-what's going on?"

His hooded eyes played over her features, awakening her senses in spite of her fatigue, or maybe because of it.

"I relieved the other guard. We're getting off at the next stop. Come with me."

Though she felt so groggy she didn't know how she'd be able to walk, she realized this man was her only chance to get Jim's laptop back, and maybe find an entrée to Mr. Montefalco.

Clutching her purse, she got up and followed him out of the compartment and down the corridor. The train had already begun to slow down.

When it came to a stop, several people were waiting to climb on board. But he stepped off the stairs first, and held out his hand to help her. Feeling distinctly light-headed from sleep deprivation, she found his strong grasp oddly reassuring.

To her surprise he kept hold of it as he led her out of the small station to a truck parked along the road.

It wasn't anything like the black sedan from the palazzo she'd ridden in last night.

Heavens—was it only last night? Ally felt all mixed up and confused. She had to be confused to be happy this enigmatic stranger had rescued her from that awful train.

"Where are you taking me?" she asked once he'd turned on the engine.

"To a place where you can eat and sleep in that order."

That sounded so wonderful, she wanted to cry.

"Why would you do that for me when you had me jailed for false credentials, trespassing and impersonating someone else?" her voice trembled.

His hands tightened on the steering wheel. She could tell because his knuckles went white.

"I've found out you're who you said you were."

She jerked her head away from him so he wouldn't see her eyes smarting.

"You mean you now believe I'm Mrs. Parker…"

"Yes."

"I see. So now that you know my name, what does Mr. Montefalco call *you*?"

There was a curious silence, then, "Gino."

She stirred restlessly in the seat.

"Which may or may not be your real name, but at least it's something to call you."

"Besides bastard you mean?" he interjected in a wry tone.

Caught off guard, Ally laughed softly. She couldn't help it.

"Actually that's what I felt like calling the guard when he wouldn't help me with my suitcase on the train. Even at your worst, you were more of a gentleman."

She heard him draw in what sounded like a tortured breath. "I owe you an apology."

She flicked him a covert glance. "If I ever get to meet your employer, I'll be able to vouch for your fierce loyalty to him. It's no wonder he keeps you on his payroll. Every man who's a target should have such a trusted bodyguard."

By now they'd left the little village of Remo and were driving through fields of sunflowers with a hot Italian sun shining down.

"How do you know so much about him?"

She studied her hands. "I know very little apart from the obvious facts."

"Which are?" he prodded.

"He's rich, titled and has lost his wife. If he loved her desperately, then my heart goes out to him."

"What about your heart?" he whispered.

"If you're asking if it was shattered by my husband's death, then yes." *If you're wondering if his probable infidelity has wounded me, then yes.* But because she'd waited too long to try to fix what was wrong between them, Jim's unexpected death had brought on guilt she couldn't seem to throw off.

Gino drove along the maze of country roads with what appeared to be long accustomed practice and expertise.

Once upon a time she would have loved traveling through the countryside, but right now she was numb to the world around her.

The next time he stopped, her bleary eyes took in a yellowed, three-story farmhouse that looked quite ancient.

"Where are we?"

"My home," he announced before helping her from the car.

He carried her suitcase and told her to follow him. She didn't question him as they entered the foyer and climbed some stairs to the next floor.

He opened a door on his left. "You'll be comfortable in here, Mrs. Parker. The en suite bathroom is through that door. I'll ask my housekeeper Bianca to bring you a tray. Sleep well. We'll talk later."

"Yes, we will. I'd like my husband's laptop back."

"All in good time."

As she was coming to find out, it was his favorite saying.

He placed her suitcase on the aged hardwood floor, then left and shut the door behind him.

Straight ahead of her was a four-poster double bed with a comfy looking white quilt. She was so tired, she removed her outer clothes and climbed under the covers. Ally didn't remember her head touching the pillow.

CHAPTER THREE

ON GINO'S way down to the kitchen, Sofia met him in the dining room. "Who's that lady you brought home with you, Uncle Gino?"

Gino had to think fast. "An acquaintance of mine who wanted to see the farm. She's flown all the way from the States, and is so tired, I told her to sleep before I introduced her to you."

"Oh."

"Where's Bianca?"

"Out on the back terrace with Luigi and papa."

That was just as well. He tousled Sofia's hair. "Our guest needs food. Do you want to help me fix it?"

"Yes."

She started walking to the kitchen with him.

"What does she like?"

"Can you imagine her not liking anything Bianca cooks?"

"I guess not."

His morose niece needed her friends. Now that

he was home, he would arrange for it. Together they made a plate of ham, fresh bread, salad, fruit and hot tea.

"Can I go with you to take it to her?"

"Of course."

"What's her name?"

"Signora Parker."

"Does she speak Italian?"

"No." Not according to the taxi driver. "It will give you a chance to practice your excellent English with her."

"Is she a farmer, too?"

Gino was equally curious about the wife of Donata's lover. "Why don't you ask her later?" It would be interesting to hear her answer.

They went up the stairs. He tapped on the door. *"Signora?"*

"I'll peek," Sofia offered and opened the door a crack. After tiptoeing inside, she came back out again.

"She's sound asleep."

Gino wasn't surprised. "We'll fix her another plate later."

Once back in the kitchen, they worked together to clean things up while he devoured the meal meant for the intriguing woman sleeping beneath his roof.

"She has pretty hair. It looks like the color of fairy wings."

That was as good a description of gossamer as you could get. He eyed his brunette niece he loved.

"Not many people we know have hair that particular shade do they?"

"I don't know any," she declared.

Neither did Gino.

"What do you say we call Anna's mother and see if your friend can stay over with us for a few days."

"She likes me to play at her house."

He frowned. "Why not at yours?"

"I don't know."

He put a hand on her shoulder. "I think you do. Tell me what's wrong?"

Her eyes filled with tears. "I think she's scared of Papa."

Pain shot through him. "Did she tell you that?"

"No. But the last time she came to the palazzo, Papa suddenly started walking around the rooms. He kept doing it over and over again, and—" Sofia couldn't finish.

Gino crushed her in his arms, absorbing her sobs while he let her cry her heart out. Deep inside he cried with her to think of the brother he idolized reduced to this state so early in his life. But even worse, to realize Sofia had been robbed of a normal childhood. God give him the strength to help his precious niece find some happiness before her childhood was gone.

"Would you like me to drive you to Anna's?"

"No. I don't want to go anywhere. I just want to stay with you."

That's what Gino had been afraid of. Sofia was crawling deeper and deeper inside her impenetrable shell. It was up to Gino not to let that happen. But how to prevent it when he was having trouble enough holding body and soul together?

When Ally first woke up, it took a minute for her to remember where she was.

She checked her watch. It was almost 8:00 p.m. She'd slept nine hours!

Someone must have just come in the room and brought her a tray of food. She was so grateful, and so ravenous, she ate every crumb, then drained the cup of hot tea in one go.

Her suitcase was still where Gino had left it. She carried it to the bed and got out clean clothes before hurrying into the bathroom to shower.

When she walked in the bedroom ten minutes later freshly shampooed and dressed in a clean pair of jeans and a blue cotton top, she felt a little more human again.

Delighted with her cheerful yellow room, she opened the green shutters to look outside. In the twilight she could see fields of flowers under cultivation. Incredible.

After brushing her damp hair until it formed

natural curls, she applied lipstick, then left the room and went downstairs in search of her host.

A tall, slender girl about eleven or twelve with long brown hair and large, sad brown eyes met her at the bottom of the stairs. Gino's daughter?

Ally slowed down. Of course he would have a family. Why would she even question it?

"Hello."

"Hello, Mrs. Parker," the girl said.

Ally was charmed by her manners. "What's your name?"

"Sofia."

"I *love* it."

"You do?"

"Yes. There was once a very important queen ahead of her time with that name."

The girl eyed her solemnly. "What's yours?"

"It's Ally. But I like yours much better."

"What does your name mean?"

"I don't think it means anything, but I got teased a lot because of it."

"How come?"

"Do you know what a cat is?"

"Yes. Uncle Gino got me one a couple of months ago. It's black with white feet."

Uncle Gino. That explained the superficial likeness to him.

"Lucky you. What's its name?"

"Rudolfo."

"That sounds quite magnificent."

"It's Uncle Gino's real name."

How apropos. He more than fulfilled the expectation of such a name.

"I see. Well, in my case the kids called me 'alley cat'."

"What's that?"

"A cat that lives on the streets because it doesn't have a home."

"But you had a home." She sounded worried.

"Yes, darling." The endearment just slipped out. There was a wistfulness about the girl that caught at Ally's heart strings.

"Where do you live in America?"

"Portland, Oregon. Have you heard of it?"

"I think so. Uncle Gino said you came to see his farm. Are you a farmer?"

That was as good an explanation as any for Ally's presence in the home of Mr. Montefalco's bodyguard.

"Not exactly, Sofia. But my grandparents used to have a small farm at the base of Mount Hood in Oregon. It's an old volcano."

"We have volcanoes here," Sofia confided.

"I know. Very famous ones. Someday I'd like to see them."

"Is the one by your grandparents' alive?"

"I guess they can all come alive, but Mount Hood has been quiet for many years. The soil is perfect for growing lavender.

"That's one of the flowers Uncle Gino grows."

"I noticed. That's the reason I stopped by. The flower fields reminded me that my grandmother used to keep a garden and would give lavender away for gifts. One of my favorite memories was helping her separate it into bundles."

"I wish I could do that."

"Don't you get to help your aunt and uncle on the farm?"

"Uncle Gino's not married. He says girlfriends are much better."

At least Gino was honest. Bluntly so.

Having witnessed several sides of him already, she couldn't say she was surprised by his philosophy. It reminded her of her mother's attitude about handsome men making bad husbands. Maybe Gino and her mother had the right answer after all.

Ally moved closer. "Since you're family, I bet Gino would give you a special farm job to do if you asked him."

"Maybe I will." Sofia looked up at Ally with fresh interest. Do you want to meet my father? He hasn't gone to bed yet."

"I'd love to. What's his name?"

"Marcello."

"That's another wonderful name. What's your mother's?"

Her face closed up. "Donata."

Donata?

But that meant—that meant—

Fresh pain knifed through Ally.

Dear God—

Just then Gino emerged from the shadows of the corridor.

Ally wondered how long he'd been standing there. How much had he heard of her conversation with Sofia?

Their eyes met for an instant. As he hugged his niece to his side, she registered anguish in those black depths.

Ally leaned over and grasped the girl's hands.

"Gino told me about your mother, Sofia. I'm so sorry." Her voice shook.

I despise you, Jim Parker, for your part in depriving this child of her mother.

How was it possible Donata hadn't cherished her daughter and husband enough that she would go on vacation to Switzerland without them? It made reason stare and brought a different kind of ache to Ally's heart.

She had to clear her throat before she could speak again.

"My father died a few years ago. No matter how young or old you are, I know how much it hurts."

What had hurt Ally was to learn that her father had passed away, and she'd never once met him.

Tears trickled down the girl's pale cheeks. "Uncle

Gino says I have to wait until I go to heaven to see her again."

Over the last four months Ally had thought she'd cried all the tears inside her. But in the face of seeing this child's suffering, she could feel new ones threatening.

"You and your father are going to need each other more than ever. Where is he?"

"In the kitchen with Luigi drinking his tea."

"Is Luigi your brother?"

"No. I don't have any brothers or sisters. Luigi is one of the nurses who takes care of papa."

Takes care of him?

Ally darted Gino another questioning glance. She discovered a mixture of sorrow and bleakness.

"My brother was diagnosed with Alzheimer's two years ago. His was a very rare case because it hit so hard and fast."

Ally gasped. There'd been too many painful revelations at once.

She cupped Sofia's wet cheeks. "I'd love to be introduced to your father. Can he talk at all?"

"No, but sometimes he squeezes my hand. Come with me."

She grasped one of Ally's hands and led her through the spacious dining room off the foyer to the kitchen. Ally was aware of Gino's hard-muscled body following them at a short distance.

One glimpse of the black-haired fiftyish looking

man seated at the oak table, and she saw the strong resemblance between the two brothers.

As they drew closer, she noticed that Sofia had inherited her father's brown eyes and widow's peak.

Two immensely attractive men in one family. How tragic that one of them had to be stricken in the prime of life.

His attentive nurse, an auburn-haired man who looked to be in his mid-thirties like Gino, kept his patient perfectly groomed.

The Duc Di Montefalco was dressed in an elegant robe and slippers, quietly drinking tea from a mug. Sofia's cat did a big stretch at the base of his chair, as if letting Ally know he was guarding Sofia's father, so be warned.

The girl drew Ally over to him.

"Papa? This is Mrs. Parker from America."

Her father took no notice. He just kept taking sips of the hot liquid.

It killed Ally to realize that this darling girl wouldn't be able to derive the kind of love and comfort she needed from her father.

The moment was so emotional for Ally, she let go of Sofia's hand long enough to clasp Marcello's arm for a brief moment.

"How do you do, Mr. Montefalco. It's an honor to meet you," she said in a tremulous voice.

Luigi smiled. "He's very happy to meet you too, *signora*. Isn't that right, Sofia."

"Yes. He likes company."

The nurse placed a hand on Sofia's shoulder. "Do you want to help me put him to bed? I think he's still tired after our big day yesterday."

"I know he is. His eyelids are drooping." Sofia sounded way too adult for a girl her age.

Ally watched Gino kiss his niece on the cheek. "While you say good night to him, I'll be outside with Mrs. Parker. Come and find us when you're through."

"I will."

By tacit agreement Ally left the kitchen with the man she no longer thought of as her captor. Thankful he'd suggested going outside, she stepped over the threshold into the warm, fragrant night where she could breathe in fortifying gulps of air.

Gino watched her through veiled eyes. She met his glance. "Why was yesterday especially tiring for your brother?"

His features took on a hardened cast.

"The priest conducted funeral services for Donata at the church. I don't know if Marcello had any comprehension of what was going on, but Sofia insisted he did."

A sob got trapped in Ally's throat. "She's had too much grief to deal with."

"Tell me about it," he ground out. "Sofia needs her father."

Just then she heard the agony in his voice and sensed he was grieving for the loss of his brother.

Any man in Gino's position would be feeling over-whelmed right now. But as she was coming to find out, Gino was no ordinary man. He had strengths she admired more than he would ever know.

Tears glazed her eyes, moistening her silky lashes. "Throughout my life I've been able to forgive those who've hurt me. But for my husband and Donata to have hurt an innocent child... Right now I'm *really* struggling."

He moved closer. "Donata was far too concerned for herself to ever consider other people's feelings, least of all her daughter's."

Ally bit her lip, realizing this man was carrying an extra heavy load now that Sofia didn't have a mother.

"I was an only child. I would have loved a sister or brother."

"Marcello and I were best friends," he whispered. "To protect him and Sofia, I've brought them to the farm where I have heavy security in place around the clock. We're safe here. No one gets in or out without my knowing about it. When the news of Donata's death is publicized, the media's going to turn it into the scandal of the decade."

Ally shuddered. Her thoughts flashed back to the night she'd spent at the jail because he'd thought she was a journalist.

"Has it always been this terrible for you?"

He nodded grimly. "Since my brother and I were old enough to go out in public with our parents, the paparazzi has dogged us. The only time I found peace or anonymity was to escape to the countryside.

"When I was away at college in England where Marcello had attended, I couldn't even look at another woman without some salacious headline showing up in the paper the next day. My every move was cataloged. The European press billed me the playboy of the decade. Perhaps some of it was deserved, but not all…

"After graduation I knew I had to end the nightmare or go a little mad. About that time tragedy struck when our parents were killed in a light plane accident.

"Marcello inherited the title, and I was left free to become a flower farmer, something I'd always wanted to do with my mother's blessing.

"So I bought property and this farmhouse. Instead of going by the name Rudolfo Di Montefalco, I became Gino Fioretto, It's an old family name on my mother's side. Until my brother became ill, I was able to live in relative obscurity. But with Donata's disappearance and death, all hell has broken loose. I moved Marcello and Sofia out of the palazzo as fast as possible.

"You'll notice I don't have TV, radio or newspapers here."

"I don't blame you—" she cried out. "If Sofia had any idea…"

Gino studied her horrified expression. "Then we understand each other?"

"Of course."

"You forgive me for my callous treatment of you at the jail?"

"Under the circumstances, I don't know how you kept any control at all."

As she lifted her tortured gaze to him, they heard Sofia call out, "Uncle Gino?"

"We're by the fountain."

Sofia came running to her uncle. He swept her up in his powerful arms.

Ally could hear Sofia denying that she was tired. It was understandable the girl didn't want to go to bed. She was in too much pain and needed her uncle. Gino was the girl's sole source of love and safety now. They needed time to themselves.

"Gino?" Ally said. "Before it gets any later, I need to make a phone call. If you two will excuse me?"

"By all means." His sober mood hadn't altered.

She smiled at his niece to break the tension the girl must be sensing. "Good night, Sofia. I'm very happy to have met you."

"Me, too. You're not going away yet are you?" The question was so unexpected, it caught Ally off guard.

"Of course she isn't," Gino answered before she could, sounding the absolute authority. "She's here to tour the farm. That could take some time."

Ally trembled at the inferred warning that she shouldn't be planning to leave anytime soon.

"Can I come with you tomorrow?" The girl's brown eyes implored him.

"The three of us will do it together," Gino declared as if it were already a fait accompli.

"Maybe we could take Papa, too?" Sofia added.

"I'm sure your father would love it," Ally stated before Gino could say anything else. "Even if he can't talk, deep inside I'm sure he'll enjoy getting out in the sunshine with his beautiful daughter."

"I'm not beautiful."

Ally winked at her. "Then you haven't looked in a mirror lately." She kissed her cheek.

"Good night," she whispered before hurrying across the courtyard to the farmhouse entrance, away from Gino's enigmatic gaze.

Once she reached her room, she picked up the receiver of the house phone and made a credit card call to her mother.

"Mom?"

"Ally, honey— The caller ID said this was an out of area call. I was hoping it was you."

"Forgive me for phoning this early. Did I waken you or Aunt Edna?"

Ally's mother had been helping her widowed sister who'd come home from the hospital with a hip replacement.

"Heavens no. Edna and I have already had breakfast."

"That's good."

"How's the headache by now?"

"It's gone." As for Ally's emotional state, that was another matter entirely.

"Where are you and your friends staying?"

Ally bowed her head. It was time to tell the truth.

"That's what I'm phoning you about. I decided to take the doctor's advice and get away for a while by myself."

"I hate the thought of you being alone. Have you cleared it with the maestro?"

"I didn't need to. We have the month of June off, remember?"

"Of course. So where are you?"

"I'm staying at a bed and breakfast on a lavender farm."

"You always did love it at Mom and Dad's. I wish they were still alive so we could all be together."

"So do I, Mom."

"I'm sure the change will do you good. Where is it exactly?"

Her hand tightened on the cord. "In Italy, not far from Rome.

"Mom—" Ally spoke before her mother's shock translated into words. "Let me explain. Detective Davis told me the woman who died with Jim has been identified. She was Italian, so I flew to Switzerland, and now I'm in Italy to talk to the authorities."

"Oh, honey, you must be in terrible pain."

Ally had been in excruciating pain for months, but right now another emotion dominated her feelings. The compassion she felt for Gino and Sofia superseded all else.

"I need closure. This seems to be the best way to achieve it."

To prevent her mother from asking the burning question about Jim's involvement with Donata, Ally said, "This shouldn't take too long."

"I hope not. When you get back we'll find you another place to live that doesn't remind you of Jim."

No matter where Ally lived, she would always be haunted by two people's treachery to an innocent Italian girl who only asked to be loved.

"Mom? Will you do me a favor and call Carol? Since I couldn't make the concert because of my headache, she still has my violin. Tell her to keep it until I get back."

"I'll do better than that. Edna and I will drive over to her house and get it."

"Thank you. Please give Aunt Edna my love. I promise to keep you posted and I'll call you soon."

She hung up before her mother asked for a phone number where Ally could be reached in case of an emergency. That was the way Ally wanted it right now.

Too restless to sit still, she wandered over to the open window and looked out. If Gino and his niece were still walking, she couldn't see them.

"Signora Parker ?"

At the sound of Gino's low male voice, she whirled around to discover him in the aperture. By now she ought to be used to him appearing as silently as a cat.

"I—I didn't realize you were there." Her voice caught.

"I knocked, but you were deep in thought."

So she was…

"Has Sofia gone to her room?"

"No. To her father's. If it's her only comfort right now, I'm not about to deny her. But as she's expecting me to join them, I'll say good night."

Ally had seen Gino at his most forbidding. But his tenderness toward his brother and niece revealed a side of him she found rather exceptional.

"Thank you for your hospitality, Gino. When I came to Italy, I had no idea I would end up here. Please know you can trust me with what you've told me."

"If I didn't, you'd be back in Portland right now," he ground out. "Sleep well."

He studied her for an overly long moment before disappearing.

Part of her wanted to call him back and ask him to return the laptop. If he had an adaptor, then she could see the pictures and read any e-mails Jim hadn't planned on her knowing about. But another part resisted because she knew Gino had too much on his mind to deal with anything else tonight. They'd only buried Donata yesterday. Tomorrow would be soon enough to ask for her property back.

This family needed sleep to help assuage their deep sorrow. As for Ally, she turned once more to the open window. After sleeping all day, she was wide-awake.

A slight breeze carrying a divine fragrance ruffled her curls. She rested her head against the frame, feeling herself suspended in a kind of limbo. It was almost as if she was standing outside herself, not belonging in the past or in an unknown future, but somewhere in between—a flowered fantasyland where she felt the unconditional love of one man for his family. In light of the tragedies that had befallen the Montefalco clan, Gino's devotion to those he loved touched her so deeply, she couldn't put it in words.

She finally went to bed with her mind full of new images. No matter the setting or situation, they all contained Gino…

"Where's Signora Parker?" Sofia asked Gino without even saying good morning. "We've been waiting for her."

For Sofia to be interested in a stranger she'd only met for a few minutes last night, it meant that Signora Parker had made a strong impression on his niece. It wasn't that surprising since Gino couldn't seem to put the American woman out of his mind, either.

He kissed her forehead. "I guess she's still asleep."

"But she slept all day yesterday."

Gino had a hunch Jim Parker's widow had lain awake most of the night just like Gino, and hadn't fallen asleep until dawn.

He knew she'd already had several months to grieve deeply, but he feared she could be in mourning for a long time to come. Why that knowledge bothered him he couldn't answer yet. He only knew that it did.

"I'll go upstairs and see if she's awake."

Before Gino could blink, Sofia ran out of the kitchen. His first inclination was to stop his niece from bothering their guest. But since he, too, had been looking forward to spending the day with her, he decided he was glad Sofia had taken the initiative.

In a few seconds his niece came running back. Her anxious expression disturbed him. "She's not in her room! I thought she came to see the farm. We were going to go around it together. Where did she go, Uncle Gino?"

The alarm in her voice echoed inside him.

He turned to Bianca who was pouring coffee into Marcello's cup. "Have you seen Signora Parker this morning?"

"No. Maybe she's outside taking a walk."

Gino jumped up from his chair. "I'll go look for her."

"I'll come with you," Sofia cried.

No sooner had they left through the side door off the kitchen than they spotted her in the distance. She was leaning over one of the rows in the special herb garden he'd grown expressly for Bianca.

It pleased Gino no end that she appeared to be intrigued by the various plants.

Sofia ran over to her. Ally raised a smiling face to his niece and put out an arm to hug her. The spontaneous gesture came naturally to her. She had a warmth that drew Sofia like a bee to the flowers growing on his farm.

"Good morning, *signora*."

Their eyes met. Hers shimmered like green jewels.

"This garden is fabulous, Gino."

"He made it for Bianca," Sofia exclaimed. "She likes everything fresh."

"Well isn't she lucky that the owner of this farm appreciates her so much."

He chuckled. "I'm the lucky one. You'll see why when you eat one of her meals."

"I'm looking forward to it."

"Come on, Ally. She has breakfast ready for us."

"I'm coming."

Gino watched her straighten. Dressed in a skirt and a peach top her curvaceous figure did wonders for, Gino found himself staring at her.

Hopefully his niece was oblivious as she pulled their lovely houseguest along. Gino hardly recognized Sofia in light of her affection for Ally whom she was already treating like an old friend.

A minute later they were all assembled at the table with Bianca fussing over them.

"I tell you what, Sofia," Gino spoke up. "On our ride we'll drop by the Rossinis'. You've never met my farm manager, Dizo. He and his wife Maria have two daughters. One of them, Leonora, is your exact age. She's a very nice girl who has been asking to meet you. You'll like her."

"Do we have to do that today? I just want to be with you and Ally."

His niece was transparent. For months she'd been so unhappy, he'd been at a loss how to help her. Now suddenly Ally Parker had come into their lives. When was the last time any of them had experienced any happiness?

Gino had to think back twelve years when both brothers had been in their prime, their parents had still been alive and all was well with their world. Until the advent of Donata…

He peeled an orange and gave a couple of sections to Marcello who automatically ate them. Gino was still incredulous that his brother would never be normal again, would never be able to make his daughter laugh and feel secure again.

In the past Marcello could always make things right for Sofia no matter how her mother neglected her. Everyone loved Marcello, especially Gino.

Sometimes like now, the pain of loss was unbearable. He could only imagine how much his niece suffered. Yet this morning she wasn't showing any signs of heartache.

"Tell you what, Sofia. I'll run over to the Rossinis' to check on business, then come back and we'll all go swimming at the river. How does that sound?"

Ally was bent over her food and didn't make eye contact with him.

"I can't wait! Don't take too long, Uncle Gino."

Maybe Leonora would return with him so the girls could meet. He left the kitchen and went outside to start up the truck.

A few minutes later he pulled to a stop in the parking area surrounding the covered stands. The usual crowd of customers kept the staff busy. He looked around to see if Leonora was helping her mother.

Maria was in charge of the workers who ran Gino's flower market called Fioretto's. What wasn't shipped from his farm to different areas of the country by train and a fleet of trucks was sold as overflow to the local businesses who sent their buyers to his farm.

Several of the staff recognized him and waved. He reciprocated as he moved past basket after basket of flowers that would all be sold by three in the afternoon.

"Ah, Gino— Over here!" Maria called to him. She was surrounded by customers. Once she was free they talked business for a few minutes.

"Is there anything I can do for you before you go?" she asked at last.

"I need two bunches of lavender."

"Coming up." She wrapped them in paper and handed them to him. "Is Leonora around?"

"No. She's home tending the baby who has a cold."

"I was hoping she could come over and meet my niece."

Maria's eyes rounded. "She would love it! Maybe tomorrow. I could ask Dizo to drive her."

"That would be fine, Maria. I'll arrange to have her driven back later in the day. *Ciao*."

"*Ciao*, Gino."

He hurried out to his truck anxious to get back to the farmhouse. To Ally. Since finding her in the herb garden this morning, he was still so mesmerized by her femininity and shapely figure, he almost climbed into the cab of another truck before he realized what he was doing.

In point of fact, Ally Parker shouldn't be here. She shouldn't be anywhere in Italy where the paparazzi could find her. Carlo would have a coronary if he knew. But Gino couldn't think about that right now.

She was here under his roof. That's where he wanted her to stay.

He'd admired the fight she'd put up at the jail.

She never once acted like a victim. Signora Parker had fire and guts, the kind you didn't often see in a man or a woman.

Jim Parker hadn't deserved a wife like her any more than Marcello had deserved Donata…

Gino gritted his teeth to think of the pain Donata had caused, but by the time he returned to the farm and saw Ally out in front with Sofia, his dark thoughts evaporated.

No sooner did he stop his truck than they walked up to him. He jumped down and handed them their gifts.

"What's this?" Ally stared at him.

"Open it and find out."

Sofia actually giggled in delight. Gino put a hand on her arm. "Why don't you take yours inside and open it with your father?"

"I will! Thank you, Uncle Gino." She kissed his cheek, then ran across the courtyard to the house.

The woman at his side was busy opening hers. "Oh, Gino— Fresh lavender. It's wonderful!"

"So are you."

She quickly lowered her eyes as a subtle blush filled her cheeks.

"Your presence has made Sofia happy. She needs people around who care about her. An outing with you is exactly what the doctor ordered."

"No child should have to live through a nightmare like this."

"I agree, Signora Parker. That's why I'm indebted to you for staying with us."

"Please don't keep calling me Signora Parker. It makes me feel old. My name is Ally."

"I've thought of you as Ally for quite a while, but was waiting for your permission to use it."

She finally looked up at him. "Well you have it. If you'll excuse me, I'll just run these flowers in the house, then come right back."

She took a few steps then paused. "I'm afraid I didn't bring a swimsuit with me."

"No problem. I'll run you and Sofia into Remo to shop. After Sofia's growth spurt this last year, she needs a new one."

"All right. Then I'll see you in a minute."

"*Bene.*" The Italian word slipped out of his mouth as he watched her walk away carrying the lavender in the crook of her arm. Like a bride approaching the altar with her sheaf…

Once again he was struck by how incredibly attractive she was. If he were her husband…

CHAPTER FOUR

WITH her heart pounding, Ally found Bianca and asked her to get a vase for the flowers she could take to her room.

The unexpected gift had whipped up her sense of excitement which was way out of proportion to the situation. The reason being that Gino was an incredible man.

Her friend Carol would call him drop dead gorgeous.

He was. But he was a lot more than that.

He had character and nobility along with those striking looks. Somehow Ally needed to forget what the combination was doing to her, how he made her feel when they were together.

Something was wrong with her to have these feelings over a man she barely knew when she'd only come here to talk to Donata's husband. It didn't make sense. She needed to get her head on straight.

But the second she walked back outside with

Sofia and felt Gino's eyes assessing her with an intimacy that made her legs go weak, she realized she was in serious trouble.

His niece ran up to him. "Papa loves the lavender. He just keeps smelling it. Bianca loves it, too. She says it's been too long since there were fresh flowers in the house."

Ally shot Gino a teasing glance. "And you, a flower farmer. Shame on you."

He broke into a full-bodied smile, turning him into the most attractive man she'd ever seen in her life. The European tabloids must have made a fortune just following him around snapping pictures.

Her heart kept rolling over on itself.

"Mea culpa. It takes a woman to civilize a man's abode."

"What's an abode, Uncle Gino?"

"A house. Come on. Up you go." He'd opened the truck door to help her inside.

Ally had purposely waited so she wouldn't have to sit next to him. But by making that decision, she'd left herself open to more scrutiny while he assisted her.

Careful to keep her skirt from riding up her thigh, she climbed in, aware of his appraising glance as she swung her legs to the floor. He seemed to pause before shutting the door.

When he finally walked around and got in behind the wheel, she exhaled the breath she'd been holding.

"Bianca has packed us a picnic lunch and some towels," he informed them. "Paolo will bring everything when he drives Luigi and Marcello to the river."

Ally eyed the girl seated next to her.

"Do you like to swim, Sofia?"

"I used to when Papa swam with me at the palazzo."

Gino's gaze met Ally's with the implicit message that his niece gauged all her happiness before Marcello had been afflicted.

Ally had no words. All she could do was put her arm around Sofia and pull her close.

An hour later while Gino and Luigi helped Marcello swim, Ally and Sofia sat huddled in huge beach towels beneath a shade tree to watch.

The river was more like a stream that broadened in parts. Near the tree it was deep enough to come up to Ally's neck. On such a hot day, the refreshing water couldn't have been more welcome.

Thankful Gino had been too occupied helping his brother to pay much attention to Ally, she and Sofia had played in the water for a while. When Ally thought it was safe from Gino's all-seeing glance she'd scrambled out, but not before he'd caught her attempting to cover her bikini clad figure with the towel. Warmth still filled her cheeks, the kind she couldn't blame on the sun.

Sofia sat next to her, eating a roll and cheese.

"I think your father is enjoying himself, don't you?"

Sofia nodded. "I wish Uncle Gino could be with us all the time, but I know he can't. He has to do Papa's business and run the farm, too."

"That's too much for any man," Ally declared. She munched on a ripe plum and looked all around them. "This is a heavenly place. I could stay here forever."

"I love it, too! But Mama would never let me come."

"Why not?"

"She said she didn't think Uncle Gino liked her very much so she preferred I stay at the palazzo. I told her Uncle Gino liked everyone and was my favorite person next to her and Papa. But she wouldn't talk about it."

Ally moaned inwardly. "Maybe your mama was a city girl."

Sofia looked at her. "Are you a city girl?"

"I like the city, but to be honest, I preferred my grandparents' farm. Unfortunately when they died, my mother and her older sister sold it so they would have money to live."

"Why didn't you all just live there?"

"Because Aunt Edna got married, and my mother was divorced. She had to raise me on her own, and she didn't like farming."

"What *did* she like?"

"Her talent was music. She could play the piano so well she gave lessons. It would have been hard to find enough students in the country, so we lived in Portland."

"Did she teach you to play?"

"Yes. Do you play an instrument?"

"I started the piano, but I wasn't very good and quit."

Ally chuckled. "I didn't like it, either, but my mother said I had to learn to play something, so I started on the violin."

"Did you like it?"

"I loved it so much, I play in the Portland symphony orchestra. It's how I earn my living, but right now the orchestra is on vacation, so I decided to come here for a holiday."

It wasn't a complete lie.

Sofia's eyes lit up. "I've been to the symphony a lot with my papa and Gino. Do you have to wear black?"

"On performance night, yes."

The girl sighed. "I wish I were good at something."

"I'm sure you're good at a lot of things. You just haven't discovered all of them yet. My husband hated piano lessons but he became an expert skier."

The observation had just slipped out.

Sofia studied her for a moment. "How come he didn't come with you?"

The question Ally had been waiting for...

"He died a while ago."

The girl looked wounded. "Do you have children?"

A pain seared Ally. "We weren't married long enough for that to happen. I always wanted a son or a daughter like you. But I have my mother and aunt, and you have your father and your uncle."

Sofia sighed. "I'm glad they're both alive."

"You're very lucky to have them."

"After we tour the farm, do you want to see where my mother is buried?"

"If you'd like me to."

"We don't have a headstone yet. Uncle Gino told me I should decide what to have engraved on it since I'm the Duchess Di Montefalco now. But I don't know what to put."

A duchess at eleven years of age. So much responsibility for a young girl. What Jim would have given…

On Ally's honeymoon he'd admitted wanting more from life than a stable job with a steady income. She heard his resentment when he spoke of people who'd been born to a life of privilege and wealth, and he hadn't.

She'd thought he was like most people who had their dream of winning the lottery or something, so she didn't place any stock in it. But over time Jim began to change into someone restless and ambitious. Before long he was willing to spend more and more time apart from her in order to get financially ahead, as he put it.

That *did* alarm her since she'd wanted to start a family.

The marriage that should have lasted a lifetime began to fall apart. Though she'd longed to have a baby, knowing what she knew now, Ally was thankful it hadn't happened.

She glanced at Gino's niece, feeling a bond with her that made her want to protect her every bit as fiercely as Gino did.

"Do you happen to know your mother's full name?"

"Yes. It's Donata Ricci-Cagliostro Di Montefalco."

"What a beautiful name. Since you know it you could say 'In memory of our beloved wife and mother,' then put her full name, and the dates."

Sofia pondered the suggestion for a minute. "I think that's perfect. I'm going to tell Uncle Gino right now."

She threw off her towel and ran toward the edge of the river where the men were just getting out.

The girl's voice carried in the light breeze.

Gino drew closer to the picnic blanket. His black eyes sought Ally's with such impact, she could hardly breathe.

"What do you girls say we go back to the farmhouse to change, then I'll drive you and Sofia around the farm."

Bemused by his unexpected aura of contentment and his blatant masculine appeal, Ally averted her eyes. The sight of Gino was too much. He put the sun god Apollo to shame.

"Let me gather up the remains of this delicious picnic first."

The rest of the afternoon turned out to be magical.

Dressed in jeans and T-shirts, Ally and Sofia rode in the back of Gino's truck. To Sofia's delight, he drove them through the colorful flower fields where they waved at the workers. She wondered which ones were the security guards Gino had posted to watch over his domain.

At different times he pulled to a stop and the three of them walked on the rich earth enjoying the fragrant air beneath a sunny sky.

A last stop at the cemetery to put some fresh flowers on Donata's grave, and they drove back to the farmhouse for dinner.

"Can we do this again tomorrow?" Sofia pled with Gino.

"Tomorrow I've arranged for Leonora to come over."

"But I don't know her. I'd rather be with you and Ally."

Gino patted her hand. "I have to do some work tomorrow, sweetheart."

Ally decided the two of them needed to be alone. While they'd been driving around, she realized it was time to separate herself from Gino and Sofia who, like her uncle, had already become too important to her.

Without hesitation Ally got up from the table. "If you will excuse me, I have to go upstairs and pack."

Two pairs of eyes swerved to hers in an instant. Sofia's were already full of tears. Gino's expression bordered on anger.

"I wasn't aware you were leaving to go anywhere," he muttered with barely concealed impatience.

"I put off my flight a day in order to spend it with you. Now that I've toured your farm, I—I have to return to Rome first thing in the morning," she stammered. "My flight to Portland leaves in the afternoon."

She hurried out of the kitchen and headed for the guest room upstairs. Ally couldn't stay here any longer. Today there'd been moments when it had felt like the three of them were a family. Sofia had already endeared herself to Ally. As for Gino…

With every second she spent in his thrilling company, she was losing her objectivity. To stay in Italy any longer would be playing with fire. She'd come to Italy to talk to Marcello, but his illness made that impossible. She had no excuse to stay any longer. She would only be intruding on Gino's personal life.

Ally hadn't missed Sofia's aside when the housekeeper told Gino that Merlina had dropped by the farmhouse while they'd been out.

"Merlina is one of Uncle Gino's girlfriends.

Sometimes she used to come to the palazzo to talk to Mama about him." Hearing those words, Ally had actually experienced a stab of jealousy! Everything was getting far too complicated. She needed to go home and leave temptation behind. Back in Portland she would find herself another place to live. Keeping busy would prevent her from thinking too much. Fantasizing too much about impossible dreams.

To stay here any longer would be disastrous.

By the time she reached the bedroom, she heard footsteps behind her and wheeled around to discover Gino had followed her. With his rock-hard body filling the aperture, it prevented her from shutting the door. She had no choice but to back away from him.

"Earlier today," he began in a neutral tone of voice she couldn't help but envy, "Sofia and I had a conversation. Before you get carried away with plans, how would you like the job of teaching her the violin for the summer?"

Ally let out a soft cry of surprise. In the semidarkness his eyes glowed like hot coals. "Sofia told me that's how you earn your living. I had no idea you were an accomplished violinist. She begged me to ask you to teach her the fundamentals.

"You've sparked something in my niece I didn't know was possible. I'm indebted to you, Ally, and I'll make it worth your time financially to stay here."

Ally was stunned.

More than anything in the world she wanted to say yes, but she didn't dare. Another night under his roof and she feared she'd want to stay forever, not just for a summer.

Trying to catch her breath she said, "I'm sorry, Gino, but I can't."

I can't. Don't ask me.

"I'm under contract with the symphony. We start rehearsing again in July."

His expression darkened. "You want me to tell that to a young girl downstairs who today had her first taste of happiness in over two years?"

"That's not fair—" she cried.

His black brows furrowed. "Nothing about this situation has been fair—" he bit out.

"Even so, Gino, I—"

"Even so nothing," he cut her off without apology. "Every contract has a clause that exempts a person under extraordinary circumstances. When you explain what you've been going through, I can guarantee they'll allow you whatever time you need."

Ally knew it was true, but that wasn't what concerned her the most.

He cocked his dark head. "I don't expect you to be a babysitter, if that's what's worrying you. All I ask is that you give her an hour a day. You two can work out the time that's most convenient for you. The rest of the time you'll be free to do whatever you want.

"The farmhouse has rooms rarely used. You could choose any one of them to practice in. "You can use one of my trucks so you can drive where you want. When you don't choose to eat out, Bianca will prepare your meals."

She put up her hands. "Stop, Gino. You're making it difficult for me to refuse."

Lines marred his features. "As the acting Duc Di Montefalco, I plan to make it so damn hard, you wouldn't dare."

Acting Duc… No wonder he was given such preferential treatment everywhere he went. It explained his being able to take over at the jail as if he were in charge.

She had trouble swallowing.

"You don't understand."

"No, I don't, not after Mrs. James Parker spent a brutal night in jail insisting she needed to meet in private with the Duc Di Montefalco and no one else. That woman never once backed down.

"Your courage, like your beauty, is the talk of the Montefalco police department."

Her breathing grew shallow. "You must be talking about someone else."

"No," his voice grated. "I was there, remember? If you need reminding, take the advice you gave Sofia and look in the mirror. It will remove all doubt."

Maybe she was mistaken to think she saw a brief flash of desire in his eyes.

When she thought of the women he'd known in the past—no doubt beautiful women who'd do anything to be seen and loved by him—

All she knew was that it found an answering chord in her. She couldn't help wondering how it would feel to be kissed by him. Thoroughly kissed. Just imagining it made her so unsteady, she weaved and had to hold on to the corner of the dresser for support.

"After Leonora goes home tomorrow, I'll drive you and Sofia into town. You can pick out violins and anything else you need to get her started. Think about it. If necessary, make any phone calls you need to. Then come downstairs and give me your answer."

He disappeared too fast for her to call him back. She couldn't.

With her senses as alive as a red-hot wire, she couldn't muster a coherent thought, let alone talk.

Four months ago she couldn't have conceived of a time when she would be so attracted to another man, she would consider staying with him. Especially when she knew she was already in emotional jeopardy.

Uncle Gino prefers his girlfriends.

Such were Sofia's words.

As if thinking about the girl conjured her up, Gino's niece tapped on the open door.

"Hi," Ally said in a shaky voice.

"Hello. Is it all right if I come in?"

"Please do." Ally tried to sound normal, but it was difficult because Sofia's unexpected visit to the bedroom had thrown her.

"Did Uncle Gino tell you I'd like to take violin lessons?"

Ally nodded.

"I know this is the country, but if you gave lessons to my friend Anna, and maybe to Leonora and her sister, that would make four students. It would give you more money. I could pay for my lessons from the allowance Uncle Gino gives me."

Ally let out a heaving sigh. "It's not the money, Sofia. I—I just wouldn't feel right about staying here at your uncle's."

"You could stay at the palazzo. Nobody's there but the staff. Paolo would drive me for my lessons."

She smothered a groan. "Your uncle wants you and your father with him for the summer. He can't be worried about you going back and forth."

They couldn't risk Ally being seen by journalists just waiting for an opportunity.

Sofia studied her. "I thought you liked it here."

"I do," she rushed to assure her. More than Sofia would ever know. But—

"This is a big farmhouse," Sofia kept talking. "And Uncle Gino has to be gone a lot. He says you can stay as long as you want."

"That's very generous of him."

"He says if you agree, he's got a special surprise planned for us."

Ally could feel her defenses crumbling. "What kind of surprise?"

Suddenly Gino appeared in the doorway again looking devilishly handsome.

"You'll have to wait and see," he answered for his niece. "I promise it will be something neither of you will want to miss."

Ally had run out of excuses. With both of them imploring her to say yes, she couldn't take the pull on her heart any longer. Sofia needed love. As for Gino, she realized he needed someone to lean on. If she could help him through this transition with his niece, why not. Part of her felt she owed them.

"I tell you what. For the next few weeks I'd be happy to get you started on the violin. But when my vacation is over at the end of June, I'll have to go home."

I'll *have* to.

Gino put his hands on Sofia's shoulders. "We'll accept that arrangement, won't we, sweetheart."

Sofia was beaming. "Yes."

His eyes held a strange glitter of satisfaction. "Then let's say good night to our guest. In the morning we'll make our plans over breakfast."

"Good night, Ally," Sofia murmured. "I can't wait till tomorrow."

At this point Ally was a mass of jumbled

emotions. Avoiding Gino's probing gaze she said, "I'm looking forward to it, too."

"We all are." As Gino closed the door, the silky timbre of his parting words almost caused her legs to buckle.

She'd done it now. There was no going back or it would crush Sofia. Even Ally could see the girl was fragile.

But no more so than Ally who would be worse off when she eventually left Italy. At least Sofia would still have Gino.

When Gino's cell phone went off the next morning, he was already up and shaved. Knowing Ally Parker was in his house, and wouldn't be leaving Italy anytime soon, had to be the reason he'd awakened with a sense of exhilaration he hadn't experienced in years.

He left the bathroom and went back to his room where he'd left the phone on the dresser.

He checked the caller ID, then clicked on.

"*Buon giorno*, Maria."

"*Buon giorno*, Gino."

"Is Dizo bringing Leonora, or do you want me to come and get her?"

"I'm calling because the children are sick. They've all come down with colds. Leonora is running a temperature. I'm so sorry, Gino. She's very upset that I won't let her leave the house."

"It's all right, Maria."

It was better than all right. She'd just given him the excuse to spend the morning with Ally and Sofia.

"Tell Leonora we'll look forward to seeing her when she's better. *Ciao*."

A few minutes later he went downstairs where he could hear female voices drifting through the rooms. The animation in Sofia's chatter when she never chattered was like a balm to his soul.

The sight of their blond guest at the breakfast table dressed in a soft yellow blouse and white skirt, was more intoxicating than his first breath of fresh air when he opened his bedroom window at sunup.

Bianca had outdone herself to make an American breakfast. She buzzed around the kitchen with new energy. Marcello appeared to have a healthy appetite. His eggs and fruit juice were disappearing fast.

As Gino and Roberto, the other nurse, exchanged a silent greeting of amusement, Sofia cried, "We thought you'd never come down, Uncle Gino."

Was she speaking for their guest, too?

His gaze flicked to Ally's. Her eyes reflected a lush spring-green in the morning light coming through the windows. With glowing skin and diaphanous hair, she didn't look a day over twenty-two.

"I had a phone call from Maria," he explained taking his place at the table across from Ally. "She told me her children are sick with colds. Leonora is running a fever and can't come over today. Maybe tomorrow."

"That's okay." Sofia didn't sound at all bothered by the change in plan. "Will you take us to get our violins this morning? Then you can do your work."

Gino chuckled. So did Ally. His niece was definitely an organizer.

"I don't see why not."

Her brown eyes sparkled, another first in several years. He saw the promise of a lovely woman inside the girl who reminded him so much of Marcello, it brought a pang to his chest.

"Ally said we should rent them and practice for a few days to see if we like them first."

His gaze trapped Ally's.

"You're the expert, so we'll bow to your judgment." Anything to prevent her from changing her mind and leaving.

His good mood had made him ravenous. He ate a double helping of everything.

After he'd praised Bianca for her cooking, he suggested they get going.

On the way out to the truck, Sofia caught hold of his arm. Ally hadn't joined them yet.

"I think we should practice in the living room because there's a piano. Is that all right with you?"

"I can't think of a better place."

"Good. Did you know Ally can play the piano,

too? She says when I've learned a few songs, she can accompany me."

"That doesn't surprise me a bit, sweetheart. Signora Parker is a woman of many parts."

Gino wouldn't be satisfied until he knew all of them...

CHAPTER FIVE

ALLY climbed in the truck with an eagerness she was hard-pressed to conceal. It was because of the black-haired man at the wheel. He looked fantastic this morning in a navy polo shirt and cream trousers. Ally decided that Italian men just looked better in their clothes. Of course she'd seen him at the river yesterday when all he'd been wearing were his black trunks. The truth was, he needed no embellishment.

She'd only known him a short while, but so far she could find no fault with him.

That was the scary part. She felt she was under some sort of spell.

To be recently widowed and yet this happy when she was living on borrowed time, defied logic.

They reached Remo in no time at all. "Here we are. I made inquiries and learned that Petelli's should have everything you need."

They'd pulled up alongside an arcade with shops that had been built the century before.

Sofia followed Ally out of the truck, then ran ahead to view the instruments displayed in the front window of the music store.

Ally glimpsed a guitar, harp, cello, viola and violin. She was no more immune to the sight of a beautifully crafted instrument than Sofia who grasped her arm.

"Let's go inside."

Gino held the door open for them. Ally's arm brushed against his chest as she trailed Sofia. The contact caused her to gasp softly.

Fearing Gino had heard her, she rushed over to the counter where a man probably in his late seventies smiled at them. She had a feeling he was the owner.

"Good morning," Ally greeted him. He nodded. "Do you speak English?"

"A little. Your husband can translate, *si*?"

"Yes," Gino responded, drawing up next to her.

She gave him a covert glance and noticed his eyes were smiling.

While heat crept into Ally's cheeks, Sofia said something to the man in Italian.

"Ah…she's the professor."

"Yes," Ally exclaimed. "We would like to rent two violins."

"For the little one and her father?"

Once again Sofia came to the rescue, obviously to Gino's delight because a rumble of laughter came out of him, deep and full bodied. The attractive sound reverberated through Ally's nervous system.

The owner eyed her with curiosity. "No violin for the little one's papa?"

The man was a huge tease. She couldn't help smiling at him. "No."

"*You* are the professor, and you need a violin?"

"Yes. I left mine in America."

"Are you good?"

"I try."

"*Momento.*" He turned behind him and reached in the case for one of the violins. Then he found her a bow from the drawer.

After tuning the instrument, he placed both items on the counter in front of her. "Play something by Tchaikovsky. Then I know which violin is for you."

Ally was more nervous than the time she had to audition in front of the maestro and the concert master. But her adrenaline wasn't surging because of the owner. She wanted to perform her best for Gino and his niece.

Once she'd fit the violin under her chin, she reached for the bow and began playing the final movement of Tchaikovsky's violin concerto.

Normally when Ally played, she receded into another world. But this was one time she couldn't forget her surroundings. With Gino's black eyes riveted on her, all she could think about was him, how loving he was to Sofia, how tenderly he treated his brother. What she couldn't tell him in words, she found herself compelled to say to him through her music. She wanted to ease the pain and suffering of this wonderful, selfless man.

"Stop—stop—" the owner cried.

Ally turned to him, surprised and confused. She saw him wiping his eyes.

"Give me the violin."

Ally handed it to him. He put it back in the case, then unlocked another one.

"Here. This is a Stradivari. Now finish, please."

Whether it was an authentic Stadivarius, or a model of one copied from the master violin maker in Cremona, Italy, Ally trembled as she fit it beneath her chin and finished the Tchaikovsky.

The difference in instruments made such a difference in the sound, she could have wept for the beauty of it. When she'd come to the end, there was silence, then a burst of applause from several people who'd come into the shop without her being aware of it.

While Gino and Sofia stared at her mesmerized, the owner clapped his hands.

"Bravo, *signora*. Bravo, Bravo."

Ally handed the violin and bow back to him. "Thank you for the privilege of being allowed to play it," she said to him.

Sofia's eyes had filled.

"I'll never be able to play like you."

Ally leaned over and kissed her forehead. "You never know until you try. Once upon a time, I was just like you. I'd never even held a violin in my hand."

She raised up and looked at the owner. "Let's fit her with one her size. I'll rent the violin you first gave me to try. We'll need a music stand, and some beginner books."

Before Ally could say she would pay for her own rental, Gino gave the other man a credit card.

As they gathered up their purchases and went back out to the truck, Gino was oddly silent. For that matter, so was Sofia. That is until they arrived at the farmhouse where she glimpsed an unfamiliar car parked near the fountain.

Roberto, another nurse she'd been introduced to, was taking Marcello for a walk in the courtyard.

The second Ally climbed down so Sofia could get out, the girl ran over to show them her violin case. "Bring Papa in the house, Roberto. He's going to love hearing Ally play. He'll think he's at the symphony again!"

While Ally watched the three of them head for the front door, she heard footsteps behind her. The next thing she knew Gino had turned her around by the shoulders.

His features solemn, he grasped both her hands and kissed her fingertips. She thought his breathing sounded labored.

"Sometimes there aren't words. Today was one of those times." His black eyes streamed into hers. "How in God's name could your husband have done what he did?"

His comment made her realize that some if not all of those pictures in the laptop were of Donata. It verified beyond any doubt that Jim had betrayed Ally. Now it meant Gino was party to her secret *and* her humiliation. Since he knew the truth, there was nothing to hide. She could be frank with him.

"That's what I ask myself about Donata every time I look into the face of her precious daughter. She's so blessed to have you to look after her and love her."

"Ally—" Gino whispered huskily before they both heard footsteps and saw Bianca hurrying toward them. Ally pulled her hands away from him in a self-conscious gesture.

The housekeeper ran up to him and said something in rapid Italian.

Though the spiel was unintelligible, Ally heard the name Merlina.

After Bianca went back to the farmhouse Gino said, "It appears I have a visitor."

"I recognized the name." The same woman had come by the day before.

Not wanting Gino to know how upset she was, Ally started for the back of the truck to get her violin.

In a few strides he'd joined her.

"How do you know about her?"

"Sofia told me she's your girlfriend."

"Was," his voice grated. "I ended it with her before Donata's disappearance."

His personal life was his own affair, yet the news set her pulse racing.

He reached in the truck bed for her instrument case and the other purchases.

"Let's go inside. While I talk to her in the study, you and Sofia can get started in the living room."

"I'll need to freshen up first." She ran ahead of him, but once again he caught up to her and held the front door open for her.

She dashed inside the foyer and up the stairs. On the way she caught sight of a lovely redheaded woman who'd come out into the hall.

Though Ally believed Gino when he said his relationship with this Merlina was over, she wished she hadn't seen her.

The presence of a former girlfriend in his house served as a wake-up call to remind Ally he preferred his single status. He could have any woman he wanted. It hardly made sense that he would be seriously interested in a twenty-eight-year-old widow who hadn't been able to keep her husband from straying.

Only one reason would bring the striking Italian woman here two days in a row. She'd come to pay her respects because she loved Gino and couldn't bear to think their relationship had ended.

It made Ally realize how futile it would be to fall in love with him.

If Ally's mother knew she'd agreed to stay with him until July, she would say her daughter was an even greater fool than before. Ally would never hear the end of it.

"It's been all over the news for the last two days," Merlina exclaimed the minute Gino ushered her back into his study. "The police are saying that the accident that killed Donata and that American man might not have been an accident. According to them the brakes might have been tampered with and you've been named their prime suspect."

Thanks to Carlo who'd phoned him night before last, Gino already knew the worst of the lies.

"It's the usual malicious propaganda put out to sell papers, Merlina. You've wasted a trip to come and tell me something I've been dealing with for a score of years now. The media will say or do anything to create a story out of nothing. It's the way they work. If they couldn't print distortions, there would be no news anyone would want to read."

"But Gino—this time it's different because Donata was killed! Don't forget she wasn't just a local. She was the Duchess Di Montefalco."

Gino heard the envy in Merlina's voice.

"I know you could never have hurt her or anyone else. It isn't in you. But in this case you have to take this seriously."

His jaw hardened. "I don't have to do anything, Merlina."

"Please don't get angry with me. You know how I feel about you, how I've always felt. I love you, and I'm afraid for you."

"There's no need to be. This is a nine day wonder that'll pass just like all the other scandalous lies made up to try to ruin my family's happiness."

"It's so unfair to you." She pushed her hair behind her ear. "I don't have to be back in Gubbio before tomorrow. Why don't we go someplace and I'll help you get your mind off things."

He folded his arms, resting his body against the closed door. There was only one woman who could accomplish that miracle. She was living beneath his roof.

"I'm gratified by your faith in me, Merlina. Your concern means a great deal. But to take up where we left off isn't possible. Whatever we had was over a long time ago. To pretend otherwise wouldn't be fair to either of us."

Her face closed up. "What happened to your feelings for me, Gino?"

He pursed his lips. "We've been over this ground before. We shared some good times, but that's all they were."

Her eyes grew suspiciously bright. "I was hoping if I stayed away for a while, you'd be excited to see me again."

He hated to be cruel, but she was asking for it. "I'm only sorry you made this trip for nothing."

"There's someone else, isn't there."

The salvo shot straight to his gut.

"Whatever is going on in my life is my business, Merlina. If you don't mind, I have a busy day ahead of me so I'll see you out."

"Who's that blond woman who came in with you a few minutes ago?"

Gino was stunned by her aggressiveness.

"You saw the violin cases. She's a teacher who has come to help Sofia focus on something constructive."

Merlina shook her head, causing her red hair to swish. "I saw her go up the stairs. I've never heard of you allowing another woman to live in your house."

"These aren't ordinary circumstances. Sofia just buried her mother. She's grieving."

"And you actually expect me to believe this woman has nowhere else to live while she instructs your niece? Can she actually play?"

Even as she asked the mocking question, they both heard the sounds of the Tchaikovsky. Sofia must have begged Ally to play for Marcello, and she'd chosen the first movement.

Ally didn't need the Stradivari to make her violin sing. She had the touch of an angel.

Merlina looked shocked. "Who is she?"

Time to get rid of her before she learned Ally's identity.

"Someone helping Sofia find a reason to go on living."

He unfolded his arms and opened the door. "After you, Merlina."

For a minute he thought she was going to create a scene. Finally she said, "I'm leaving."

Thank God.

He walked her to the front door and watched her drive out of the courtyard.

The difference between the women he'd known and Ally was so great, the normal comparisons didn't apply.

He moved to the doorway of the living room to listen.

Roberto and Bianca were understandably awestruck. But it was Marcello who sat in the recliner, his whole body in an attitude of being spellbound. Normally nothing going on around him fazed him.

This was different. Just by the way Marcello's hands gripped the arm rests, Gino could tell how happy it made him.

The Montefalco family had been concertgoers for years. Having heard great music before, his brother's soul recognized it.

As for Sofia, she sat on the couch, entranced.

Thankful for Ally who'd managed to captivate his

entire family, Gino decided this was the best time to get a little farming business done. The sooner he got things out of the way, the sooner he'd be home to spend the evening with Ally.

One of the hardest things he had to do was tear himself away when all he wanted was to get her to himself so they could concentrate on each other. His gut instinct told him that besides her affection for Sofia, Ally didn't dislike him, even if she'd only recently buried her husband. What he needed was time to prove there was an attraction between them, even if she was fighting it. Tonight couldn't come soon enough.

Ally learned that in most Italian households, the family didn't eat supper until eight or later.

At 6:20 Gino still hadn't come home. Ally had an idea it wasn't all farm business that detained him. Even if he'd ended it with Merlina months ago, the other woman lived in denial. Ally knew all about that dangerous state of mind and was living proof of her own weakness where that was concerned.

Evidently Merlina still had the same lesson to learn and had come by Gino's house to try to stir up the old spark. Ally felt a stab of pain to think maybe it hadn't been that difficult to entice Gino after all.

Thankfully Ally had a job to do teaching Sofia about the violin. There was a lot to learn first about the various parts, how to string it and tune it.

Once immersed in showing her the proper technique of using the bow, Ally was able to separate her thoughts about Gino long enough to concentrate on her delightful student.

The girl was eager to learn. Because she'd taken piano lessons, Sofia was able to read notes which was a big help. If she could maintain this enthusiasm, she would see great results.

Before Ally knew it, the day had gone. Sofia didn't want to stop. Ally chuckled and gave her a hug.

"We've done enough for one day, but I bet your father would love to see the progress you've made."

With that suggestion, the girl ran from the room with her violin and bow.

Ally took a little walk outside to stretch her muscles.

Gino's truck was parked in the courtyard, but there was no sign of him or Merlina's car.

Deciding she wasn't about to hang around waiting for him to return from wherever, she went back in the farmhouse to find the housekeeper. Bianca was in the kitchen preparing food.

"I need to go into Remo, so I won't be eating dinner. Gino said I could use one of the trucks."

The other woman nodded. "Take his. The keys are in the ignition."

"He won't mind?"

"No, no. Before he left he said you should use it if you needed to."

Gino thought of everything.

"Thank you, Bianca. If Sofia should ask, tell her I had some errands to run."

The housekeeper smiled her assent. "She's a good student, yes?"

"Very good. In another week she'll be able to play tunes for her father."

She left the house and hurried out to the truck. Glad it wasn't dark yet, Ally started it up and headed away from the farmhouse. It gave her a secret thrill to put her hands on the steering wheel where his hands had been earlier today. Everything about him thrilled her. That was the problem. She didn't want to be like Merlina who couldn't stay away from him.

Ally pressed on the accelerator. She had no particular destination in mind. All she knew was that he wouldn't find her watching breathlessly for him when he decided to come home.

With her mind made up to be gone for a few hours, she found her way into the small town of Remo. En route she memorized certain signposts so she wouldn't have any trouble driving back home later in the dark.

When she'd been in town with Gino, he'd pointed out various landmarks and items of interest, among them a movie theater.

It was playing an Arnold Schwarzenegger film. Ally had seen a few of them and decided it would be fascinating to watch one in Italian.

After parking the truck along the side of the street like everyone else did, she went inside and bought a ticket.

Distracted by the amount of goodies in the concession stand, she decided to try some Italian chocolate. With her choice made, she walked inside the theater. The film couldn't have been going more than ten minutes.

She found a seat in the middle of the back row where no one was sitting, then sat down to watch the screen.

There was something about the Austrian born actor trying to teach the kids in his classroom that made Ally chuckle. When he spoke in Italian, it was even funnier. She found herself laughing out loud, something she hadn't done in ages.

"Scusi, signora." An attractive guy, beautifully dressed, who looked to be about her age, sat down next to her, bumping her arm.

He'd done it on purpose of course. In fact he could have had his pick of seats in the semifull room, but he'd claimed one next to her.

He said something else to her in Italian.

She said, *"Scusi, signore.* No Italian."

If he didn't move in about one second, she would.

Naturally he refused to budge. "You are from America. *Si*?" What an incredibly bad idea it had been to sit alone.

"You dance with me after?"

Ally started to get up when another man sat down on her other side. She panicked when he put his arm around her shoulders.

"Sorry I'm late," he spoke into her ear.

She jerked her head around, assailed by the familiar scent clinging to his skin.

"Gino—"

She'd never been so happy to see anyone in her life.

"I've missed you, too, *bellissima*," he whispered against her lips before capturing her mouth.

He drew her close like a lover who'd been anticipating this moment and could no longer hold back.

Ally had been so caught off guard, her mouth opened to the urgent pressure of his and she found herself kissing him back in a slow, languorous giving and taking she'd never experienced in her life.

The background laughter of the crowd faded. All Ally was cognizant of was the throbbing of her heart against his solid male chest. The armrest between them might as well have been nonexistent.

Incredulous when she realized the moaning sounds she heard were coming from her own throat, she finally tore her lips from his and sat back in her seat, completely breathless and ashamed she'd gotten so carried away.

"That other man has gone. Thank you for the convincing performance," she blurted when she could find her voice again. "It got me out of a difficult predicament."

"A word of warning," Gino said in a masterful tone. "Don't ever come to a place like this alone. I want your promise."

"You have it."

"Sitting back here by yourself is an open invitation."

"I know. I simply wasn't thinking." She swallowed hard. "How did you know I was here?"

"When I got home, Bianca told me you'd gone out in the truck. So I asked Paolo to drive me around until I spotted it in front of the theater. You're a fan of this film?"

"Yes."

"So am I. Let's enjoy the rest of the film, shall we?"

It was so exciting to be sitting here with him like this, she could only nod.

"How about some of that chocolate? Your mouth tasted so delicious, I've got to have more."

She thought he wanted some of her candy, but he leaned over and started kissing her again.

"No, Gino." She pushed at his shoulder with her free hand. "There's no one around me now."

"I hadn't noticed," he murmured, giving her another thorough kiss before letting her go.

Without asking her permission, he popped a piece of chocolate into his mouth.

Then he clasped her hand possessively, and sat back to enjoy the movie.

She knew what he was doing. No other man in

the theater would dare approach her now. She had her own personal bodyguard to protect her.

She never watched the rest of the film. She was much too conscious of the gorgeous man sitting too close to her. He kept caressing her palm with his thumb, filling her body with desire.

Every touch made it impossible to concentrate on anything else.

At the end of the movie, the lights went on. Gino slid his hand up her back to her neck and walked her out of the theater to the truck. He asked for the keys.

She fumbled in her purse for them. "Here."

After helping her in the passenger side, he went around to the driver's seat and started the engine.

"Do you often conduct business into the evening?"

Once they merged with the traffic, he darted her a piercing glance. "Only if I want to get everything out of the way so I have all of tomorrow off to spend with my family."

Ally bowed her head, relieved he hadn't been with Merlina for any reason.

"Sofia will be delighted."

"What about you? How does another picnic by the river sound? This time we'll take Leonora with us so the girls can get acquainted."

"I think it's an excellent idea. Sofia needs more interaction with girls her own age."

"Agreed. If you'll give her a morning violin lesson, we can leave afterward and enjoy the rest of the day."

His fingers played with the curls near her nape. His touch sent a yielding feeling of delight through her body. She was still trembling from the kisses they'd shared in the theater.

Terrified Gino would think this widow was falling in far too easily with his plans, especially after the kisses they'd just shared she decided to bring up the subject she'd been putting off.

"Gino—— I wonder if you would do me a favor."

"Of course."

"I've been waiting for you to give my husband's laptop back to me."

She heard his sharp intake of breath. "If you were hoping to see the pictures, they've been deleted."

She recrossed her legs. "You had no right to do that."

"You didn't want to see them. Trust me."

Ally swallowed hard. "Were they all of Donata?"

"Yes, if that's any consolation."

"It isn't."

A sound broke from his throat. "I swear I didn't look at anything else. While you were in jail, I was so determined you were up to no good, I didn't take the time to look at the e-mails or anything else your husband might have stored in there."

"I believe you." She'd found out for herself that Gino was a man of uncommon integrity.

After a pregnant pause he said, "If you didn't know what was in the laptop, why did you bring it to Europe?"

"It's a long story…" her voice trailed.

"I'd like to hear it. We've got all night."

Since he knew her most painful secret anyway, what did it matter if she satisfied his curiosity.

"On my way out the door of my condo to drive to the airport, I listened to one of my phone messages. It was a man asking to talk to Jim." After she explained everything to Gino she said, "Since I needed to get to the airport, and Troy had just been cleaning out lockers, I couldn't very well ask him to keep the laptop until I returned. So I put it in my suitcase.

"I would have taken a look after I reached St. Moritz, but realized I didn't have an adaptor."

Gino made a strange sound in his throat. "When we get back home, feel free to use my study."

"Thank you," she whispered shakily.

"You might not thank me later if you find anything that could be hurtful."

"I'm past being shocked, Gino."

"Until I saw those photos, I thought I was, too."

CHAPTER SIX

BEFORE long they pulled into the courtyard of the farmhouse and went inside. Without preamble he guided her into his study off the foyer. It was a cozy room with print curtains, leather chairs and couches, books and paintings.

"Sit down at my desk."

While she did his bidding, he opened the closet and pulled the laptop from the shelf.

After placing it in front of her, he opened a drawer and reached for an adaptor, then plugged the cord into the wall.

"I'll leave you to it while I say good night to my family."

His handsome features were marred by lines that made him look older. He left the room, shutting the door behind him.

Haunted by the change in his demeanor, since she'd mentioned the laptop, Ally was almost afraid to open it. Though she'd insisted that nothing could bother her now, it was obvious Gino wasn't convinced. Neither was she...

After a minute she found the courage to turn the computer on. Evidently Jim hadn't bothered with a password or Gino wouldn't have been able to see those photographs.

She booted up the system. Soon the home page Jim had created flashed on the screen.

Ally's eyes darted to the favorite pictures icon. Gino had said he'd deleted them. There was one way to find out, but something held her back and she clicked on the e-mail account.

Ally wasn't at all surprised to discover it full of messages from the same person.

She opened the top one he'd received in January before leaving for Switzerland.

I feel the same way, *amore mia*. Everything is now done.
I'll be waiting for you in our usual place with a car my husband can't trace. Once we reach the port, the family yacht will be waiting for us. We'll sail directly to Sicily where we'll be home free. Did I say that right?
Hurry!

Ally felt as if she'd just been slugged in the stomach.

She scrolled below to an earlier message he'd sent Donata.

That's how I felt the first day we met. Luckily for me Ally isn't the suspicious type. She's too into her music and has no idea I'm leaving her for good. I don't know what she'd do if she ever found out. Probably turn into a bitter woman like her mother.

It'll be much better if I disappear. She'll never know you and I are together. I live to be with you, Donata. You know that don't you? You're the fulfillment of my every fantasy.

The depth of Jim's deception left Ally speechless. Her eyes held a faraway look because she knew it was the real Jim talking.

No doubt Donata had been a true beauty, but more importantly, she'd had the right credentials Ally's husband required.

To think Ally had spent four months sobbing for her loss when Jim had been making plans to run away forever.

Compelled to read on, she opened the e-mail further down.

I've told you my husband changed into a very suspicious and calculating man. He would never allow a divorce. If he knew what I was planning, he would have me committed for insanity because he has that kind of power. That's why I've asked you to be patient until

I've made all the financial arrangements so nothing goes wrong.
Now that you've come into my life, I want only you.

Sickened by what she was reading, Ally buried her face in her hands. Though Jim and Donata might have been full grown adults, they talked like two naughty children who didn't have the emotional capacity to feel anyone else's pain.

Jim's poor parents who lived in Eugene—the knowledge of what their son had done would be so damaging, she didn't know if she could ever bring herself to tell them the truth.

Or her mother—especially not her mother who'd never trusted men since Ally's father had walked out on them when she was two.

Ally mulled over the revelations Jim never thought she'd see.

He'd met his match in Donata. If anyone was cal-culating, it was Sofia's mother. No wonder Gino was desperate to protect his niece from any more pain.

If Troy hadn't been super conscientious about his job, Ally would be clueless about the extent of their betrayal.

But since these e-mails *did* exist, and Ally was in possession of them, then Gino had every right to read them, too. She was heartsick to think he and

Sofia had been forced to wait *four* months to hear any news about Donata.

When he read these and found out what exactly Donata and Jim had been planning, he'd be beyond angry.

So was Ally. Enraged was more like it! Enraged over the injury they'd done to their families on both sides of the Atlantic without counting the cost.

She was appalled at their utter selfishness and cruelty.

It was one thing to have an affair. But to run away together and let their loved ones wonder what had happened? Ally couldn't comprehend it. As far as she was concerned, she and Gino's family were the victims here.

If Jim had told Ally he'd met someone else, she would have suffered, but in the end she would have agreed to a divorce. Could anything be worse than trying to hold on to a man who didn't know the meaning of love?

It had taken Jim with his blond tennis star looks, and his hunger for a woman of Donata's class and money, to charm her into disappearing with him. As long as she brought her inheritance with her, of course.

The whole thing was absurd. Outrageous!

Ally flung herself out of the chair and raced over to the door to find Gino.

She was in such a hurry, she didn't see him until they practically collided in the hallway. He put out his hands to steady her.

She tried not to be affected by his nearness, but it was impossible. The feel of his hands on her arms sent tingles of sensation through her body.

His jet-black eyes assessed her relentlessly. "I knew I shouldn't have left you alone."

"It's horrible in a way I would never have anticipated, Gino." She tiptoed so she could whisper in his ear. "Sofia must never find out."

He relinquished his hold and rushed into the study ahead of her.

She closed the door behind her. "I made the mistake of reading the top e-mail first. If you start at the bottom, it will read in chronological order," she explained unnecessarily.

Since she already knew what was in the e-mails, there was no point in reliving something she wanted wiped from her memory, so she stood in front of the desk and waited.

An electric silence filled the room before Gino exploded with a string of expletives. Suddenly he shot to his feet. One glimpse of the wild fury in his eyes caused her to tremble.

"I knew she was capable of a lot of things," he muttered in a lethal tone, "but to forget she'd ever given birth—"

Ally rubbed her arms to try to stop the shivering.

"I know," she whispered. "There's no mention of Sofia, no mention of your brother's illness. Yet she had Jim believing her husband was a cruel, calculating man."

Gino stared at her through eyes that had become black slits. "She was describing *me*, not Marcello. *I* wasn't the one blind to her faults from the beginning. She hated me for that."

His fingers made furrows through his vibrant black hair. "Ever since I repelled Donata's advances, and refused to give her money, she's been telling stories out of school about me to the tabloids."

Stunned by his words Ally said, "What kind of stories?"

His features looked like chiseled stone. "The one where I was in love with her first, but she preferred my brother. In my jealousy, I would do anything to have her for myself…"

Ally groaned.

"It's true I met her before he did. A mutual friend of our family gave a party. Marcello had the flu and couldn't go, but I did. The host introduced me to Donata who'd come from Rome. She *was* exceptionally beautiful," Gino admitted, "but let's just say she didn't appeal to me. I left the party never expecting to see her again.

"A few months later I found out Marcello had met her at another party. He fell hard for her.

"The last thing I expected was that she would end

up my sister-in-law. It was the only time I remember my brother having made a bad choice about something, or someone. Of course I wouldn't have let him know it. I loved him and wished for his happiness above all else."

She folded her arms tightly against her waist. Gino carried an even heavier burden than she'd realized.

"For what it's worth, Gino, if Donata had told my husband the truth about her family situation, Jim wouldn't have cared. He wanted Donata because she was the personification of everything he desired. After we were married I learned that he felt entitled to live a life he hadn't been born to. I'm convinced that's why he worked in Europe, so he could prey on women like your sister-in-law. As you said, she was beautiful," her voice trailed.

"She couldn't hold a candle to you."

"Spare me the platitudes, Gino."

He flashed her a rapier glance. "If you don't think I meant it, take the advice you gave Sofia and look in the mirror. It will remove any doubts."

She shook her head in denial. "This isn't about me."

He moved closer to her. "Did you know your marriage was in trouble before he was found with Donata?"

She rubbed her temples where she could feel another headache coming on.

Finally she turned to him.

"When my husband didn't get off the plane in Portland four months ago, I hired a detective to look for him.

"It took two months before I was told Jim and another woman were found dead together. It validated my suspicions that he'd been unfaithful for some time."

"How long were you married?"

"Two and a half years, but it was during the latter half that he spent longer times in Switzerland, always phoning with an excuse of some kind for not coming home sooner. Somewhere, deep down, I knew he was lying, but I wouldn't admit it to myself."

She heard a savage sound come out of her host. It made her shiver all over again.

"Donata did the same thing. She'd be gone for long periods, then call and say she'd been detained. It killed Sofia every damn time that happened."

Ally's eyes filled with liquid. "The poor darling. I'm just thankful it's over so she's not still waiting for the phone to ring, or for her mother to walk in the house."

Gino nodded, but he looked so drawn it alarmed Ally.

"Six days ago, the detective who'd worked on my husband's disappearance called me into his office.

He told me about Donata. At that point I felt driven to fly to Europe to see if I could get a few more answers. How ironic to think they were hiding in Jim's computer all this time. Now that I've read the e-mails, everything is crystal clear."

She took a deep breath. "I'll leave it up to you to destroy the laptop and everything in it. Now if you'll excuse me, I'm tired and want to go to bed."

She left the room and hurried upstairs, more wounded for Sofia than anything else. Donata had planned to abandon her own daughter! Ally was so deeply hurt for that precious girl, Jim's rejection of Ally hardly made a dent.

She tried to imagine Gino going off with some woman never to be seen again, but she couldn't because he was a different breed of human being. Decent, honorable. Willing to give his all for everyone's happiness without having anyone to support him.

Marcello had been Gino's best friend. To be denied it now because of his illness while trying to be both mother and father to Sofia would place an enormous strain on Gino. Ally was glad that for a little while she could be here to ease his burden in some small way.

Before washing her face, she happened to glance in the mirror. There was a speck of chocolate on her cheek, but it appeared Gino had kissed away her lipstick. Despite the new revelations in the e-mails, just remembering the sensation of his male mouth devouring hers left her breathless and pushed everything else to the back of her mind, even after she'd turned out the light and had climbed under the covers.

Her heart did a little kick when she realized he was taking all of them to the river again tomorrow. She found herself counting the hours.

After a few minutes she turned on her side and reached for the vase of lavender, needing to breathe in its fragrance one more time. She'd never been given flowers for no reason before.

When Gino had handed them to her with that glint in his black eyes, she felt like she'd just been handed the world.

It was after two in the morning when Gino shut off the computer and went up to bed. He'd read through dozens of back pages of e-mails. There were dozens more but he didn't have the stomach for it.

He couldn't get his mind off Ally who didn't seem to know how truly wonderful she was. It explained her vulnerability, put there by a man who hadn't known how to love anyone but himself.

Unfortunately even if the fire had gone out of her marriage, Gino knew love wasn't always that cut and dried. Marcello had said as much when he'd admitted that he and Donata weren't going to make it. "I wish I were a faucet, Gino, so I could turn off certain feelings."

In Marcello's case the illness had done it for him.

Where Ally was concerned, Gino feared that deep down in her psyche, she still had some feelings for her husband in spite of what he'd done to her.

Gino couldn't fathom the other man not cherishing her, not wanting to come home to their bed every night.

He paused on the second floor, fighting the overwhelming impulse to knock on her door and ask if he could come in. He wanted to tell her how beautiful she was—show her.

Before Marcello's illness, when Gino had been playing the field with no intention of settling down, Marcello had warned him that one day there'd be a woman who would bring him to his knees. Gino had laughed at his brother, but he wasn't laughing now.

His limbs felt heavy as he climbed to the third floor. Tonight he would pray for sleep to come quickly.

When his phone roused him from oblivion at six in the morning, he realized he'd gotten his wish and cursed the person who dared to call him this early. On a groan, he reached for his cell.

It was Carlo. That brought him awake in a hurry.

"What's going on, Carlo?"

"I'm afraid you could be in trouble, Gino. I've arranged for us to meet in Rome with Alberto

Toscano at nine this morning. That gives you three hours to arrange your affairs."

Gino levered himself off the bed. Toscano was one of Italy's top criminal defense attorneys.

"Don't tell me that insane story about the tampered brakes has grown legs—"

"I've just seen the forensics report on the car. There was definitely foul play involved."

Gino's eyes closed tightly as his mind grappled with the stunning news.

"It gets worse, Gino. The prosecutor has discovered that Signora Parker was in St. Moritz. He's trying to link the dots that prove she collaborated with you to carry out this crime."

A groan came out of Gino.

"I'll fill you in later. *Ciao.*"

The line went dead.

In the middle of the violin lesson, Bianca came in the living room. "Forgive me for interrupting but Leonora's papa just dropped her off and Gino's not here to make the introductions."

"No problem, Bianca. Bring her in here."

Ally sensed Sofia's disappointment, but it really was better for her to start making new friends.

"Hello," Ally said as the housekeeper ushered Leonora in the room. "I'm Ally, and this is Sofia. We're so glad you've come over."

"Thank you. I wanted to come before, but Mama said my fever had to go away first."

"Do you feel better now?" Sofia asked.

"Yes." The girl was shorter than Sofia with dark blond hair. "You're so lucky to be learning the violin."

"I think so, too. Do you want to hear Ally play?"

"I'd love it!"

The girl was so warm and natural, Ally was charmed by her.

"All right. One small piece. How about something from Peter and the Wolf?"

"What's that?" both girls asked at the same time.

"You haven't heard of it before?"

They shook their heads.

"Well, it tells a story, and each instrument represents one of the characters. The music you're going to hear is Peter's theme song."

Ally had always loved it. When she finished playing, Leonora acted as enraptured as Sofia.

"I wish I could play."

Ally looked at Sofia. "Why don't I give my violin to Leonora, and you can show her what you've learned."

Leonora's dark eyes sparkled. "You would let me?"

"Of course. Have fun you two."

Ally ducked out of the living room, delighted to realize the violins were a perfect ice breaker.

With time on her hands waiting for Gino, she walked to the kitchen to get a piece of fruit from the bowl on the table.

Bianca met her at the doorway. "I didn't want to say anything in front of Sofia, but Gino had to go to Rome on unexpected business for his brother this morning. He's not sure when he'll be back."

Ally's spirits plummeted, but she didn't dare let the housekeeper know how the news had affected her.

"That's fine. If Paolo is willing, I'll take the girls to the river as planned and have another picnic."

Bianca looked relieved. "That's good for Sofia. I'll get everything ready."

"Let me help. I don't have anything else to do."

"*Bene.*"

They worked in harmony while sounds of a violin lesson being given drifted through the house to the kitchen.

Bianca smiled. "Sofia is very happy since you came."

"She's a lovely girl."

"Gino is happier, too. Everyone is glad you are going to stay."

Only until July, Bianca…

Ten minutes later Sofia and Leonora came running into the kitchen.

"Ally? Have you seen Rudolfo? Leonora wants to watch my cat do tricks."

"Have you checked the terrace? He likes to sun himself on the swing this time of day."

"That's right! Come on, Leonora."

They dashed out again.

The two women exchanged an amused glance.

"I'm going upstairs to change into my swimming suit."

"While you do that, I'll call Paolo and have him bring the car around."

"Thank you for making me feel so welcome, Bianca."

"It's my pleasure, *signora*."

As she left the kitchen, she turned to Bianca. "Please call me Ally." Bianca nodded and waved her off.

The trip to the river turned out to be an all day affair. Toward evening Ally asked Paolo to drive them into Remo where they enjoyed a pasta dinner al fresco before driving Leonora home.

By the time they returned to the farmhouse, Sofia looked pleasantly tired. They'd all picked up some sun.

Sofia gave Ally a hug. "Thank you for a wonderful day. Now I'd better go see how Papa is doing."

"I'm sure he's missed you."

Despite the fact that Gino hadn't been able to join them, it *had* been a wonderful day.

After reaching for the picnic basket, she started for the kitchen door. That's when she heard the sounds of a car coming into the courtyard. When she looked around she saw an unfamiliar sports car pull into the detached garage. It was Gino!

He looked impossibly attractive in a light gray suit and tie. Her heart skipped a dozen beats.

He walked toward her with his gaze narrowed on her face.

"I'm sorry about today, Ally. It couldn't be helped."

"You don't have to explain to me. It's fine."

"I called the house just now. Bianca said Sofia and Leonora had a fabulous time with you at the river."

"We did."

"Even before the violin lessons started, my niece felt a bond with you. After today her attachment to you is much stronger."

"Then it's good I'm leaving at the end of the month. I can't let her become too emotionally dependent on me."

"She already is." His voice sounded like it had come from a deep, underground cavern.

"I wish you hadn't said that. It worries me how vulnerable she is right now."

"I'm glad you recognize it because the end of June will be here before we know it. She'll be crushed if you talk about leaving."

Ally sucked in her breath. "But that was our arrangement, Gino. If I were to stay longer, it will only hurt her more when I have to go."

"That was Donata's pattern. Come and go at will, regardless of Sofia's pain."

Heat swamped her cheeks. "How dare you compare me to Donata! I'm not Sofia's mother, but if I were," her voice trembled, "I'd love that child and do everything in my power to help her feel safe and happy for the rest of her life!"

He took a step closer. "I believe you really mean that."

"Of course I do. I already love her," Ally admitted before she realized she'd said too much. "Who wouldn't?" she cried out to cover her mistake.

"Her own mother, for one," Gino responded with bitter irony. "Her own father for another, although through no fault of his own. That leaves me, her uncle, who might not be able to protect her much longer."

Ally stared at him mystified. "Bianca said you had to leave on some urgent business for Marcello."

"I lied."

Her hands curled into fists. "If you're trying to scare me, you're doing a good job of it." He still didn't say anything.

"Gino—" she exploded. "I'm starting to get really frightened."

"That makes two of us. Give me an hour to shower and say good night to my family, then meet me on the terrace. We have to talk."

In a few swift strides he was gone.

CHAPTER SEVEN

TREMBLING with anxiety, Ally followed at a slower pace. After putting the basket on the kitchen counter, she went upstairs to shower, too. A day in the hot sun had made her messy and sticky. But Gino had upset her so much, she went through the motions of washing her hair and getting dressed without conscious thought.

He said he needed an hour. She gave him another fifteen minutes before going down to the living room.

The French doors to the terrace were ajar. With her heart pounding so hard she felt slightly sick, she stepped outside. The first thing she saw beyond the patio furniture was Gino's tall, masculine silhouette standing there in the darkness. The only light came from a slip of a moon that had just appeared above the horizon. Once again she was reminded of the way he'd looked to her the night he'd taken her to jail—like the fierce, proud falcon of his namesake.

He made an intimidating presence standing there with his legs slightly apart, his arms folded. He eyed her with frightening solemnity. She put a nervous hand to her throat.

"It's obvious something terrible has happened. Tell me what it is."

His mouth had become a tight thin line.

"So far Sofia knows her mother died in a car accident. Period. That's all I want her to know."

"I realize that. Let's hope and pray she never learns the true circumstances. At least not until she's a lot older."

"That's the idea," he bit out, "but something's come up beyond my ability to control, let alone stop."

The blood in Ally's veins started to chill. "What is it?"

"A few days ago the first stories about the accident came out in the paper with the usual sensational lies attached. This time they took the tack that foul play was involved."

She frowned. "Foul play? It was an accident! One of the Swiss authorities drove me to the bridge and explained what happened. He told me the blow to both their skulls had been caused by the bridge's beams when the car plunged into the river."

"Ally—" he said in a tortured whisper. "This is going to be hard for you to hear. The forensics report on the car came back a few days ago. It proved that the brakes had been tampered with."

She reeled. *"What?"*

"I'm afraid it means someone wanted your husband and Donata out of the way permanently."

She shook her head in disbelief. "Who?"

He drew in a deep breath. "In the words of the police, a jealous husband or wife who caught the two of them together and committed a crime of passion at the height of their pain."

"But that's preposterous! Marcello is incapacitated, and I was home in Portland when the accident happened."

"That's true," he muttered.

It took a minute for his words to sink in. When they did, her head flew back.

"They're not trying to say *you* did it?"

His face became an inscrutable mask. "Based on past lies generated by Donata herself, the prosecutor is convinced I'm guilty. He's already building his argument to present to the judge. It's a process not unlike your grand juries in the States. If the judge feels the prosecutor has a strong case, it'll go to trial. If I'm convicted by a jury, I could go to prison for life."

She couldn't credit what he'd just told her.

"On what evidence?"

"For one thing, I went on several overnight searches in January looking for Donata. I can't prove that I wasn't in Switzerland at the time the accident occurred."

"But that's not proof of anything!"

This couldn't be happening...

As her thoughts darted ahead to the possibility that he might be arrested, she clung to the side of the patio swing for support.

"If that happened, who could possibly take care of your family? It would kill Sofia!"

Silence followed her outburst. Her gaze flew to his once more.

He stared at her for a long moment.

"If anything happens to me, I only know one person beyond all else I could trust to do the right thing for both of them."

"W-who is it?" She didn't think it could be a distant relative or he would have mentioned it sooner.

"A woman I'm planning to marry in a few days."

Marry?

Ally wasn't able to hide the gasp that escaped her throat.

If she'd been shot, the pain inflicted couldn't possibly have hurt her the way this shocking piece of news did. She still hadn't recovered from being in his arms when he'd kissed her senseless in the movie theater.

For a moment she'd thought—

Oh, what a fool she'd been to think they'd meant anything to him beyond getting rid of the other man who'd been annoying her.

"I see." She struggled to keep her voice steady. "Does she know you're suspected of a crime that could put you in prison?"

"Yes."

Suddenly Ally had difficulty forming words. She swallowed a low moan.

"Does Sofia know her?"

"Yes."

It had to be one of his girlfriends. "Does Sofia like her?"

"Yes."

Ally refused to face him. "Then why haven't you married her before now?"

Her question rang in the night air. She hoped no one in the house heard her.

"The time wasn't right."

"But now it is? Just at the moment when you could be arrested and taken away?"

"Yes. There's no other way."

She forgot her promise not to look at him and swung around in his direction.

"Don't you think that's unfair to this woman?"

"Totally."

"Stop being so glib, Gino. I'm trying to have a conversation with you."

One of his black brows lifted. "I thought we were having one."

Red stained her skin. "You know what I meant. But all you do is answer in monosyllables."

Again there was no response.

"Does Sofia know what you're planning?"

"Not yet. I thought we'd tell her together in the morning."

"You mean the woman you're going to marry will be here so the two of you can talk it over with Sofia?"

"Yes. I hope that puts your mind at ease. Now you won't have to worry about my niece clinging to you."

"I was worried about it for *her* sake, not mine," she defended quietly, hurt to the quick by his comment.

"I'm well aware of that fact, Ally. So let's agree you'll go on giving her lessons until the wedding."

"But if that's only in a few days, then I'll leave at the same time, and—"

"No. You won't be going anywhere. I'm planning to take Sofia on our short honeymoon. After we get back, she'll resume her lessons."

The mention of a honeymoon tore Ally up inside.

"I—I'm sure Sofia will love being with both of you, but when you return, your wife won't want another woman in the house. I'm sure if you talk to the owner at the music store in Remo, he'll supply you with names of several violin instructors who would love to teach your niece."

He shifted his weight. "I'm afraid it's too soon to be switching teachers on her. You've become her heroine. No one else will do."

Afraid to hear anymore she said, "If that's all, then I'll say good night."

"Not yet," he muttered. "There's something important we still haven't touched on."

"What?" She needed to be alone where she could give in to this fresh new pain.

"The matter of an attorney for you."

The shocks just kept coming. "I don't understand."

"My friend Carlo informed me the prosecutor hasn't ruled you out as a coconspirator."

She blinked. "On what grounds?"

"That you conspired with me to get revenge on your husband and Donata. Maybe you didn't do the actual deed, but you'd be held equally to blame under the law. The insurance policy your husband took out on you before he left for Switzerland in January could have provided an additional motive for you to join forces with me."

She shook her head in utter bewilderment. "How did he know about the insurance?"

"Yesterday the prosecutor's office talked to the detective in Oregon who's been working with you on your husband's disappearance. The case against you isn't nearly as strong, but I'm afraid you're going to need legal counsel, too."

Ally had gone numb inside. "When I get home, I'll retain one."

"How will you do that on your salary? You won't be able to afford the kind you need."

She lifted anguished eyes to his. "What else haven't you told me about the case?"

She heard him draw in a deep breath. "My attorney, Signore Toscano, said that your appearance in Switzerland the other day would lead the prosecutor to think you'd flown over to visit the scene of the crime you and I planned. It's not unusual for a criminal to do that.

"He suggested that since you're already here in Italy, and haven't yet contacted a criminal lawyer, he believes it will be to our advantage if he represents both of us."

"But, Gino— That's impossible! Besides the fact that I could never afford him, it would be a conflict of interest. In order for him to represent both of us, I'd have to be your wife."

"Exactly."

"But you're getting married soon."

"That's right. If you'd asked me, I would have told you the name of my bride-to-be. She's an American named Allyson Cummings Parker from Portland, Oregon."

The shock of his words propelled her into the swing. She sat down with such force, it rocked back and forth.

He came to stand in front of her and stopped the motion with his hand. When their legs brushed against each other, he made no move to allow her breathing room.

"I know your heart, Ally. When you discovered what your husband had done, you felt compassion for Marcello and didn't hesitate to fly here to talk to him.

"Even at the height of your own pain, even at the risk of getting into trouble by defying me, you put Marcello's welfare ahead of your own.

"I've never known a man or woman with your kind of selflessness and courage.

"No matter how I treated you in the jail, you wouldn't break down because you didn't want to repeat anything to the wrong ears. I owe you everything for your discretion."

"No, Gino. Any woman in my position would have done the same thing."

His eyes glimmered with a strange light. "No. You're one in a million. Now I have a way to repay you.

"If we're married, then we can't be forced to testify against each other. My money will ensure the toughest defense attorney there is. Best of all, if anything happens to me, you'll be there to raise Sofia and watch over Marcello.

"Once you take my name, you'll inherit all that I possess, and you'll be given power of attorney to run my brother's affairs until Sofia turns eighteen and takes over her birthright."

He leaned closer, bringing his face within inches of hers.

"Before you come up with a dozen reasons why you can't marry me, tell me exactly what there is for you to go home to. Certainly not a husband who was unworthy of you.

"If it's a matter of leaving the orchestra, we have excellent orchestras here. Any conductor hearing you would hire you on the spot.

"Sofia told me about your mother. If you'd like her and your aunt with you, we have a whole palazzo for them to stay in.

"Sofia also told me you wanted a family, but your husband died before that could happen. I've seen the way you interact with my niece. She'll fill your heart the way she fills mine.

"If you and I have to stand trial, I'll testify that you had nothing to do with the accident, which will only be the truth. If I have to go to prison, and it's still a big if at this point, it will help me to survive knowing my brother and niece will be in your care. You'll be a wealthy woman who can do with the money as you see fit.

"Should the real culprit be apprehended and brought to justice, then we'll reassess our situation and go from there.

"Don't dismiss this out of hand, Ally. I love my family more than my own life." His voice shook. "You're the one person I trust to watch over them and see to their needs like you would your own family. There's a goodness and purity in your character that sets you apart from the other women I've known. Sofia could never go wrong under your guidance.

"As for Marcello, your gentleness to him the second you realized his condition was a revelation. Both Bianca and Marcello's nurses have remarked on it.

"They like you very much already. All the staff will be faithful to you should I have to go away.

"Think about it tonight, Ally, and we'll talk in the morning before breakfast."

He brushed her lips with his own, then left the terrace.

Ally sat stationary in the swing, unable to make a sound. She'd never heard anyone pour out their soul to her the way he'd just done.

Though Gino needed her to say yes to his marriage proposal, what he was really asking was that she enter into a sacred trust with him.

He wasn't offering his love. How could he? He hadn't known her long enough for that miracle to happen—if it could at all.

But should the unspeakable occur and he had to go to prison, she could understand how desperate he was to get his affairs in order first.

In return for becoming his wife, she would be getting something entirely different: financial security, his name and protection, a home and the chance to be a mother to a girl who needed one, the opportunity to be a caregiver to a cherished brother.

Should she marry him and he was arrested, she would have the kind of money Jim once dreamed about.

With it she could hire the manpower necessary to find the real killer and free Gino.

She sat there for a long time deep in thought.

It was well after midnight when she finally left the terrace and went up to her room.

After preparing for bed, she got under the covers, tossing and turning as her thoughts drifted back to Jim and the way they'd met.

When she'd literally run into him while they were both skiing at Mount Hood, there'd been an attraction that had led to serious dating and marriage. But after the first few months following their honeymoon, the passion didn't seem as intense. He started doing more ski shows in other parts of the country like Tahoe and Vail. The shows coincided with her concerts so they were spending more time apart. But it was the show in Las Vegas that brought about a major change in their marriage.

Jim met a Swiss promoter who offered to let him sell Slippery Slopes skiwear in St. Moritz on a trial basis. It meant being out of the country for big blocks of time.

Of course Ally had wanted him to be successful so he could realize his dream to be the owner of the company one day. But as she'd learned on her honeymoon, he'd had bigger dreams than that. Ones in which her input didn't matter to him. She'd only been a stepping stone on his way to bigger and better things.

How different in every way it was from her experience with Gino who knew his place in life and was steady as the sun coming up every morning. A man who put everyone's comfort ahead of his own and found joy being with the family he loved.

There was nothing shallow or selfish about him. Dear God how she loved him!

No one at home, not her family or friends would understand if she married Gino only four months after burying her husband.

What they didn't realize was that she'd been out of love with Jim longer than she'd been in love. But it had taken a remarkable man like Gino to remove the blinkers so she could see how empty her life had been with Jim, how barren.

Just being with Gino filled all those desolate places inside her. He was like a hot fire she rushed to embrace after coming in out of the freezing cold.

She knew that neither she nor any woman would have been his choice if the circumstances had been different.

The fact that he wasn't married yet proved it. But the precarious situation in which he found himself forced him to reach out to her because he knew he could trust her.

After her experience with Jim, she realized trust was the key element in a solid marriage if it was going to work…trust and the incredible passion she already felt for Gino.

Only time would tell if he could ever come to love her, let alone with that same intensity. But how could she compete when there'd been real beauties in his life like Merlina?

Still—Gino had turned to Ally in his darkest hour. Though he hadn't mentioned them having a child of their own, it was something she wanted with every fiber of her being. If he wanted a child, too, that would be a sign that he expected to sleep with her and make her his wife in every way.

Just thinking about lying in his arms made her breathless. She wanted to give him his answer now, but it was only four in the morning.

He expected to talk to her before breakfast. Since Bianca served it at seven-thirty, that wasn't too far off. She set her watch alarm for seven before catching a few hours sleep.

When she heard the little tinkle of the bell three hours later, she slid out of bed to shower. Normally she would be exhausted, but with Gino waiting for her, her adrenaline was working overtime.

Once dressed, with her curls brushed and fresh makeup, she hurried downstairs. The housekeeper was already up and busy in the kitchen.

"Good morning, Bianca. Have you seen Gino yet?"

"*Si*. He's outside changing a tire on the truck."

"Thank you."

Ally left the kitchen through the side door to find him. Her heart was skipping all over the place.

* * *

A flash of pink caught Gino's attention. The sight of Ally moving toward him in a T-shirt and jeans her body filled out to perfection caused him to pause in his task of tightening the lug nuts.

If he didn't miss his guess, she hadn't been able to sleep, either. She walked with purpose, a sign that he feared didn't bode well for the desired outcome. But he was prepared for any hurdle she was determined to put in his way.

"*Buon giorno*, Ally."

"Good morning. I didn't realize we'd driven home on a flat tire the other night."

"It felt low, so I decided to change it, just to be on the safe side."

He put the wrench back in his toolbox, then dusted off his hands.

The sun had just come up over the lavender fields. Standing there in the early morning rays that gilded her hair and brought out the startling green of her eyes staring through to his soul, she looked like a piece of chocolate he would give anything to devour. But it wasn't the right time or place. Not yet…

If she was hoping he would help her find an opening, then she would have a long wait.

"After learning that someone caused that accident, I'm afraid I got very little sleep last night. I don't care how much circumstantial evidence the prosecutor says he has, I can't believe the case against either of us will go to trial. But on the outside chance that I'm wrong, I—I'll marry you provided we stay married until Sofia's eighteen."

Gino fought not to reveal his elation. He'd feared she would turn him down flat for several reasons he could think of, like the fact that she wasn't in love with him.

As for her ultimatum, there were ways around it. He'd worry about that later. All that mattered right now was her capitulation. "If some monstrous miscarriage of justice puts you in prison, Sofia will need constancy from at least one parent."

"Agreed," he murmured, still holding his breath.

"However if the person who caused that accident is caught, it would be criminal for us to suddenly dissolve the marriage, and for me to go back to the States. Sofia would grieve all over again for another loss."

Gino could scarcely control his joy. "I couldn't have said it better myself."

By the way her chest rose and fell, she still had more to say. He waited eagerly for the rest.

"To this point in time you've avoided marriage."

"I wouldn't have if the right woman had come along. I've been waiting…"

"Yes, well I thought the right man *had* come along, but it turned out I was wrong. After the fiasco of my first marriage, I'm nervous about entering into another one."

"Then we'll both be nervous together."

"Don't tease about this, Gino. This is much too serious for that."

He took a step closer. What he wanted to do was crush her in his arms, but at this early stage it might frighten her off.

"I didn't know I was doing that. I'm only trying to say that since I've never been a husband before, I want to do it right."

"So do I," she whispered. "I want your happiness more than anything."

"You think I don't want the same for you?" he challenged.

"What you've offered me has already made me very happy," her voice throbbed. "I always wanted a family of my own. My father left when I was two. I grew up in a home without him, or siblings or cousins.

"It was hard because my mother was too immersed in her own pain to realize how lonely I felt. Don't get me wrong. She's a wonderful person in every way, but she had a warped vision of men that was hard for me to throw off. My grandparents were the bright spot in my life, but they died early.

"Mom warned me not to marry Jim. She said he was too good-looking just like my father, that he'd never stay faithful.

"I refused to listen to her. I thought—well, it doesn't matter what I thought. The truth is, I married a selfish man, so my dream of a happy home with babies didn't come to fruition.

"I'm almost twenty-nine, Gino. When I found out he'd died, I felt like I was beyond that part of life where anything and everything is possible. Mother kept saying, 'You have your music, honey. It's enough.'

"But when I met Sofia, I knew it *wasn't* enough. I saw myself in her. Because of you, I can have that family I always wanted. Sofia is a joy."

"She is that," he concurred. "As long as we're sharing let me say that any hope I had of finding the right woman and settling down pretty much died when Marcello married Donata and I saw the grief she brought to his life. Her amoral behavior was a huge turnoff. Once Marcello was afflicted with Alzheimer's, I gave up the idea of asking someone to be my wife and take on my niece and her father. It wouldn't be fair to a woman with expectations of starting out the marriage with no responsibilities except to each other.

"As you and I have discovered to our horror, your husband and Donata tried to hide their liaison from everyone, but they came to a surprise ending that caused their secrets to become public knowledge. For that reason, I have no intention of marrying anyone unless it's you. Sofia needs to believe in me, in *us*, Ally. She needs to know that what we have is real and worth imitating when she's old enough to be married. Her parents were never friends. That's what she'll see with us. Therefore there'll be no divorce when she turns eighteen. That's *my* condition."

She lowered her head, not saying anything.

"Ally?" he prodded. "Did you even have friendship with Jim?"

It took a long time before she said, "No."

He could always count on her honesty.

"Then we have more going for us than either of us has had up to now because my relationships with women to this point haven't had the depth needed to survive over a lifetime."

Slowly she raised her head. "What reason will we give Sofia why we're sleeping in separate bedrooms?"

He'd wondered how long it would take her to get around to that question. There was a nerve throbbing frantically in her throat. It intrigued him no end. Obviously she wasn't quite ready for the big step of going to bed with him yet. He'd give her a little more time to get used to the idea.

"We won't have to tell her anything. By day we'll interact like a happily married couple. At night there's an anteroom off my bedroom. What goes on behind closed doors is our business, no one else's."

There were all kinds of side roads leading home. If necessary Gino would travel down every one of them to reach it.

"Gino?" she whispered tentatively.

"What is it?"

"I'm afraid."

"That makes two of us. But having seen the courageous Ally Parker in action, I'm willing to leap into the fire with you."

He could see her swallowing hard. "I—I'm terrified you might really have to go to prison for something you didn't do."

Deeply moved by her concern he said, "If I have my way, neither of us will be found guilty. In the meantime we have the power to make one special girl happy."

Her green eyes glistened. "If you're sure…"

His chest tightened. "I suppose everything in life is a gamble, but this time I like the odds. Shall we go inside and tell Sofia?"

She bit her lip, drawing his attention to the succulent mouth he'd wanted to taste over and over again the other night. Once he'd coaxed her lips apart, some divine chemistry had been responsible for the rest. Her passionate response had almost caused him to lose control. In a movie theater no less. It had to be a first for him.

Right now it looked like she needed a little help in the confidence department.

He reached for her left hand which was trembling. He stared pointedly at her bare ring finger.

"Where's the wedding ring you once wore?"

"Buried with my husband."

Her stunning answer pleased him in ways he didn't have the time to examine right now.

He felt in his pocket for a certain item. If she didn't fight him on this, then there'd be no going back.

"My mother gave me this before she died. It was her engagement ring. It's unpretentious, just the way she was. The way *you* are.

"She knew I loved nature and encouraged me to be a farmer if that was my choice."

One thing he did know beyond everything else. Ally Parker didn't have an avaricious bone in her gorgeous body, either.

He trapped her gaze with his. "I need you to be very sure before I slide it home on your finger. Is there anything else you want to ask me?"

She moistened her lips nervously. "I can think of a thousand things."

"But?" he prodded.

"But every time I think of what would happen to your family if you were arrested, I get so sick, I *can't* think."

"Then you agree to become a farmer's wife under the worst of circumstances? I can't promise the 'for better' part yet."

A little smile came and went as he slid the gold circle home on her finger. It happened so fast he almost missed it before she looked into his eyes with a haunted expression.

"Surely you once had dreams."

He nodded. "You've made them come true by filling this old farmhouse with heavenly music. The kind the Montefalco family has always loved. Every husband should be so lucky."

As they walked in the house, Gino had no idea Ally's heart was breaking. She'd been waiting to hear him say he wanted to fill his house with children. *Their* children.

But those words hadn't left his lips.

To her chagrin their entrance in the kitchen coincided with the rest of the family's arrival, forcing her to put on a pleasant face when she was dying inside.

While Luigi helped Marcello, Sofia ran around to hug Ally, then Gino.

He swept her up in his arms with an exultant laugh.

Sofia's intelligent eyes studied him. "You look different this morning, Uncle Gino."

"That's because I feel different."

"Why?"

"I'm happy, sweetheart."

Ally's heart plummeted to see what a brilliant performance he was putting on in front of his niece. By now everyone had settled at the table. Gino took his place across from Ally. Once Bianca served them, Gino said, "I have an announcement to make."

Ally felt close to fainting. "Is it that surprise you told me about a few days ago?" Sofia asked.

"As a matter of fact it is. I'm taking the family on a trip."

Her eyes brightened. "Where?"

"To the island of Ischia."

"I've never been there."

"You'll love it."

"How soon are we going to go?"

"On Monday."

"Why not today?"

"Because I need the next few days to get ready."

Sofia eyed Ally who was already squirming in her chair, then she looked at her uncle again. "What about my violin lessons?"

"After we get back, you can resume them."

Sofia sent Ally another troubled glance. "What will you do while we're gone?"

"Why don't you ask Ally to come with us," Gino suggested suavely.

"Would you come with us, Ally? Please say yes," she begged.

Ally wasn't immune to the pleading in her voice.

"I'd love to."

In the next instant Sofia's face lit up like a roomful of sunshine. "Have you ever been to Ischia?"

"No, but just the idea that it's an island intrigues me."

"Me, too."

"I have something else very important to tell all of you," Gino broke in. "This includes Luigi, Roberto, Bianca and Paolo."

He shot Ally a piercing black glance that defied her to say or do anything to upset Sofia now.

"On second thought," he added in a silky tone, "maybe I should let Ally be the one to explain since she's equally involved in this decision."

"What is it, Ally?" Sofia asked softly.

Ally's heart palpitated wildly because she realized he'd just thrown her in at the deep end. She had no choice but to swim.

"Y-your uncle Gino has asked me to marry him," she stammered. "How do you feel about that?"

Ally didn't have to wait long to find out. His niece bolted from her chair and came around to hug Ally's neck.

"Last night I told Papa that I hoped Uncle Gino would marry you. Papa always said Uncle Gino was waiting for the perfect woman to come along."

Gino nodded. "My brother always understood me better than anyone else."

Ally avoided looking at Gino right then. "You actually told your father that?"

"I swear it." Sofia crossed herself. "You told Uncle Gino yes, didn't you?"

Ally was in over her head now. She held out her hand for Sofia to see the gold band.

"Grandma's ring!"

"Yes," Ally whispered, but everyone in the room heard her.

Bianca clapped her hands and offered her sincere congratulations. Luigi made a little speech welcoming her to the family. If the staff was surprised by the announcement, they hid it beautifully.

"We're going to be married on Sunday at the church in Remo by Father Angelini," Gino informed them. "After the service we'll drive to Ischia and stay until we feel like coming home again."

Unless the police summoned Gino to Rome, Ally's heart cried.

Sofia kept her arm around Ally's shoulders. "Is your mama going to come for the wedding?"

"She would like to," Ally lied, "but my aunt can't travel that far with her new hip. I'm sure they'll fly over later in the year when she's better."

No way could Ally tell her mother about this yet. That would have to come later. Much later…

If or when her mother did come, she would find Ally in a vastly different situation from the one she'd been in with Jim.

"My mama won't be able to come, either, but *I'll* be there," Sofia assured Ally.

"That's all I could ask for, darling. How would you like to be my bridesmaid?"

"That's an excellent idea." Gino's black eyes gleamed. "Maybe Anna and Leonora would like to be bridesmaids, too. Ally will take you shopping for dresses when she picks out her wedding dress."

Suddenly Sofia pushed herself away from the table. "Excuse me for a minute. I have to call Anna and tell her what's happened!"

After she disappeared from the kitchen, Gino reached across the table to cover Ally's hand. He squeezed her ring finger especially hard.

"You've just seen a miracle before your very eyes. Asking her to be a bridesmaid was inspirational, but then you have all the right instincts."

Ally hoped that was true because she'd just agreed to take on a lifetime responsibility and didn't want to fail.

"I hear someone out in the courtyard," Gino said before removing his hand. "It must be Dizo. I asked him to bring Leonora over again today. Come with me, Ally. I want him to meet my future wife."

Just hearing Gino say it sent a shiver of delight through her body.

She followed him out the door to the driveway where she saw Leonora and her father get out of a truck.

The two men greeted each other warmly. Then Gino turned to Ally and put his arm around her shoulders. The gesture seemed to come so naturally to him, she could hardly credit it. "Ally? This is my friend and manager, Dizo Rossini. You've already met Leonora."

"How do you, *signore*." Ally shook his hand.

His daughter hung on to Gino's arm. "Is she your new girlfriend, Gino?"

"No." He ruffled her dark blond hair. "Ally Parker is my fiancée. We're getting married on Sunday."

The other man whooped in surprise. "You are a sly fox, Gino. Where have you been keeping this beautiful woman all this time?"

"Why don't you tell him, *bellissima*," Gino said to Ally before giving her a quick kiss on the mouth.

Gino didn't play fair, so she'd better get used to it.

"He kidnapped me off a train headed for Rome. I'm afraid one thing led to another," she said poker-faced.

"Ah, Gino. Love has hit you at last. I can see it in your eyes when you look at her."

Dizo winked at her. "He has had many women chase after him. All kinds," he chatted like the old friend he was. "Finally he found a woman *he* had to chase. That is very good."

Gino grinned. "She didn't make it easy for me."

The other man threw back his dark head and laughed. After he sobered, he waved an index finger in front of Gino. "It makes me glad this crazy business about Donata hasn't stopped you from living your life. It's your turn to have all those bambinos you've wanted to help you run the farm.

To think they might all be musicians!" He nudged Gino's arm.

Ally kept the smile pasted on her face.

She turned to Leonora. "You can go in the house if you want. Sofia should be off the phone by now."

"Okay."

As she headed for the house, Sofia ran outside with a joyous smile. The difference in that face from the one Ally had seen for the first time a few nights ago almost made Gino's niece unrecognizable.

Ally was doing the right thing for Sofia. But nothing could take away the pain in her heart that Gino wasn't in love with her. It had been too much to ask, and now it was too late to change things. All Ally had to do was look into Sofia's eyes to realize there could be no going back.

Ally followed them in the house so the two men could be alone.

Sofia was full of excitement about the coming wedding and asked Leonora if she wanted to be a bridesmaid, too. While the three of them were in deep conversation in the living room, Gino entered. His dark eyes sent Ally a private message that he wanted to speak to her alone.

"Excuse me, girls. I'll be back later."

"Okay," Sofia said, but her whole attention was focused on what kind of dresses they would wear.

Gino guided Ally into the study and shut the door. She could hear his mind working.

"Tomorrow we have to meet in my attorney's office. It will take a good part of the day, so we're going to have to get a lot accomplished today."

Before he could say anything else there was a knock on the study door.

"That'll be Father Angelini," Gino explained. "Yesterday I phoned and asked him to drop by. Now that you've agreed to marry me, he needs to talk to us about the ceremony.

"After he leaves, we'll drive into Remo for the marriage license. Once that's done, we can concentrate on shopping and our preparations for the trip to Ischia."

Ally could hardly keep up with him. One minute she was a widow. The next minute she was engaged to be married to this dynamic man who could move mountains with a snap of his fingers.

The way he was acting, there was no murder case pending that could rip her newfound happiness to shreds. Little did Gino know that his mention of an anteroom where one of them could sleep after they were married had plunged her into despair of a whole new kind. But she would hide it from him if it killed her.

CHAPTER EIGHT

"WE'RE almost through, Signora Parker. This is the last document. Sign beneath Gino's signature, please."

Ally eyed Mr. Toscano. "What does this one say?"

During the lengthy process, he'd patiently translated everything from Italian to English for her.

This morning she'd thought Gino had brought her to his attorney's office to talk about the case.

Instead they'd both signed forms giving her power of attorney, not only to act in Gino's name, but to be Marcello's and Sofia's guardian if Gino were absent.

However the greater portion of the time she sat listening to a detailed explanation of the vast assets and holdings of the entire Montefalco family.

"This document will go into effect the minute you become Gino's wife. It says, 'In the event of the untimely deaths or mental incapacities of both Gino and Sofia, *you* will automatically become the Duchess of Montefalco.'"

Ally's gasp permeated the elegant law office. Her fingers shook so hard she couldn't hold the pen.

Beneath the conference table she felt Gino's hand slide to her thigh. It sent shock waves through her system. He squeezed gently.

"It's just a formality," he whispered.

She jerked her head around. "Is there something you haven't told me?" she cried. "Marcello's condition isn't hereditary is it?"

She couldn't stop the tremor in her voice.

Gino's surprised expression should have told her the answer to that question. But the thought of anything being wrong with him had upset her so much, she wasn't thinking rationally.

"I swear to you there's not a thing wrong with me or Sofia," came his solemn declaration.

Though she believed him, she couldn't prevent the shiver that ran through her body.

"Sign it, Ally, then this part will be over and I'll finally have peace of mind."

Knowing how vital it was for him to get his affairs in order at such a precarious time in their lives, she managed to write her name on the dotted line one more time.

When she laid down the pen, a haunting sigh escaped his lips, reminding her this was no game but a life and death situation.

Gino handed the document back to his attorney, then turned to Ally.

"With that out of the way we can enjoy our trip to Ischia."

"Ischia?" Mr. Toscano questioned.

"That's where I'm taking the family after the ceremony."

The older man shook his head.

"I'm afraid it's out of the question now, Gino. You could be arraigned at your farmhouse as early as this afternoon."

Ally let out a cry. "Surely not this soon—"

"Anything's possible, *signora*. If they have to track you to Naples and beyond, it could be ugly for Sofia."

"I don't want my niece hurt in any way," Gino muttered grimly.

"Neither do I," the attorney said. "But if the prosecutor decides you pose too much of a threat, he can order you brought in anytime he likes."

"How long will they keep him?" Ally tried without success to keep the alarm out of her voice.

"It could be anywhere from one to three days. Depending on the judge's findings, a trial date could be set. After that Gino will be released on his own recognizance, but he'll be under house arrest. That means both of you stay on the farm."

Ally rubbed her temples where they'd started to ache. "I had no idea it could happen this fast."

Mr. Toscano eyed her with compassion. "It may not happen today or tomorrow. It might not happen for another week. But I know how this prosecutor works. He's ambitious and hungry.

"It's crucial to this case that you two keep your

marriage under wraps before he makes his first official move against either of you.

"Since you took out a special license yesterday, I'd advise you to get married right now."

"You're reading my mind," Gino murmured, pulling out his cell phone.

Her adrenaline gushed. "But how can we do that?"

The attorney spread his hands in an expansive gesture.

"Very easily, *signora*. The Montefalco name opens doors. You're welcome to use this conference room. Judge Mancini is just across the courtyard. There shouldn't be a problem of his stepping over here long enough to officiate. Shall I get him on the phone, Gino?"

Gino simply nodded because he was already talking to someone.

While both men were thus occupied, Ally's thoughts reeled.

The second Gino ended his call, she grasped his arm.

"What about Sofia? She's going to be devastated if we do this without her."

"Maybe not." His black eyes flashed her a searching glance.

"Barring another emergency, Father Angelini has agreed to be available at any time. If I'm not officially served this afternoon, he'll perform the ceremony at the church this evening."

"He would do that?"

"Of course. Either way it's the only plan to stay ahead of the prosecutor."

"Y-you're right," she whispered, but he was already making another call and probably didn't hear her response.

She tried to school her feelings. Tonight would be their wedding night…

Even if they wouldn't be sleeping together, Ally's heart pounded furiously.

After a few minutes of conversation, he hung up and looked at her.

"Provided nothing goes wrong, it's all arranged with Bianca and the staff for seven o'clock. Sofia and the girls can still wear the new dresses you picked out yesterday," Gino assured her. "The few people we've asked to attend will come just the same."

"What will you tell everyone is the reason for the change?"

"That I might have to go out of town on business at a moment's notice, and didn't want to wait any longer to make you mine. Our guests will understand."

He leaned over and kissed her warmly on the mouth.

She wished he hadn't done that. The world might not know the real reason they were getting married, but Mr. Toscano did.

Bemused by the way Gino made her feel every

time his hands or mouth touched her, she got to her feet.

"If you'll excuse me, I'd like to use the powder room."

The attorney nodded. "It's down the hall to your right."

"Thank you."

Without looking at Gino she left the conference room, but he caught up to her and put a detaining hand on her upper arm. Warmth seeped through the material of her cream suit jacket to her skin.

"What's wrong, Ally?"

"I'm worried about Sofia's reaction when we tell her we'll have to postpone the trip."

That wasn't all Ally was thinking about, but her other thoughts were too private to share with him. "She was looking forward to going snorkeling."

"She understands when business calls. There'll be other times, Ally. I promise you that."

If it were humanly possible, Gino would always keep his word. But because someone had intentionally caused Jim and Donata's accident, the situation was out of their control.

And what if there'd been no accident?

Ally would have lived her whole life not knowing what happened to Jim.

I would never have met Gino...

She couldn't imagine not knowing him now. Such a possibility was beyond her comprehension.

The very thought of his going to prison when she loved him so desperately— It seemed happiness was going to elude her again.

Gino eyed her with concern, obviously unconvinced she'd told him everything. But she kept on walking, not daring to tell him the truth.

Twenty minutes later the young judge who appeared to be on friendly terms with Mr. Toscano pronounced them man and wife. It was a very brief to the point ceremony because he was in a hurry.

The obligatory kiss Gino gave her was brief but thorough.

"Congratulations, Signora Di Montefalco. It was an honor to officiate for you and the Duc."

The judge appeared duly impressed by Gino's title. She supposed Gino *was* the Duc until Sofia came of age. Incredible.

"May you both be very happy in your new life.

"If you and your beautiful bride will put your signatures across from mine on the wedding certificate, my clerk will file it today."

Ally didn't think there was a wedding ceremony on record done with such dispatch.

It took family connections in high places that only someone of Gino's name and stature could arrange on a moment's notice.

When she'd signed her name, Gino put his arm around her shoulders and hugged her to him.

"Thank God for you," he whispered into her silken gold curls. "I swear on my parents' grave to do everything in my power to make certain you never regret this decision."

She lifted tremulous eyes to his. "I promise you the same thing, Gino."

"Let's go home," he murmured.

Home...

He kept his arm around her as they left the building and hurried to the parking area where Paolo was waiting.

He wasn't alone.

Ally pulled back. "What are those two men doing at your car?"

She heard Gino curse, even though he'd said it in Italian.

"Alberto must have been psychic. They've come to escort me to the magistrate's office for questioning. Poor Bianca must have been forced to tell them where I was."

No matter how much Ally wanted to scream at this injustice, she couldn't fall apart now. Gino needed her to be strong for him.

"We knew it was just a matter of time, Gino. I'm glad it happened here instead of the farmhouse."

"So am I."

"I'll take care of everything. We'll have that church service for Sofia after you return."

Gino squeezed her hand with so much force she

wanted to cry out, but she didn't because she knew he wasn't aware of his own strength. Not when he'd just been plunged into hell.

"Ally—" His dark eyes stared straight through to her soul. She knew what he was trying to say.

"Don't worry about anything. Go with them. The sooner you comply, the sooner you'll be back."

"Signore Di Montefalco?" They flashed their identity cards.

"Get in the car now," he whispered to Ally.

She rushed to do his bidding. The moment she closed the door, Paolo sped away.

She turned to look out the back window. To her horror she saw some paparazzi gathered on the pavement.

Flashes went off as the man who was bigger than life to her climbed into the back of an unmarked car with both men flanking him.

"Quickly, Paolo. I need to talk to Bianca on the phone."

"*Si, signora.*"

He rang the farmhouse, then passed the cell phone to her.

"Bianca?" she cried when the housekeeper answered. "It's Ally. Listen very carefully."

She explained about them getting married in the attorney's office.

"It didn't happen any too soon. Gino has been arraigned."

The older woman's cry echoed her own.

"Whatever you do, don't tell Sofia anything. I'll talk to her myself the second I get home."

"I will say nothing, Ally. She and Anna are playing outside on the terrace with Rudolfo."

"Good. Keep them there. Thank you for everything. Paolo and I will be home shortly. Then you and I can make the necessary phone calls to Father Angelini and Gino's friends."

"*Bene.* May I say congratulations again, *signora*. I'm very happy for you and Gino. With you in the house, he won't be so worried about everything while he's gone."

"That's what I'm hoping. Bless you, Bianca."

After hanging up, she said, "Paolo? I've got lots of ideas to keep Sofia busy, but I'm going to need your help with some of them."

"I'm at your service."

"Is there a place in the garage where Sofia and I could separate some lavender into bundles to make small gifts?"

"I'll clear a place for you."

"That would be wonderful. On our way home, we need to stop at a store in Remo that sells cellophane paper and ribbon."

He gave another nod. "I know just the place where Gino has an account."

"Perfect. We also need to stop at a paint store."

"Anything you want."

Maybe it was too much to hope that she could keep Sofia in the dark while Gino was gone.

But with security in place around the farm, and help from the staff, Ally was determined that if at all possible, her new stepniece would be spared any more pain to do with Donata.

To Ally's relief, Sofia didn't see her arrive at the farmhouse when they drove in an hour later.

Bianca informed her Anna's father had come to get his daughter. For the time being Sofia was on a walk with her father and Roberto.

It gave Ally time to help Bianca make phone calls explaining that the wedding ceremony had to be postponed until Gino could get back from an important business trip.

With that done, Ally swallowed a late lunch. Before long Sofia returned with her father.

When the girl saw Ally, she put the cat down and ran over to hug her. "I'm glad you and Uncle Gino are back, Anna, and I can't wait until tomorrow."

"I know exactly how you feel." She took a fortifying breath. "Would you believe some important business of your father's came up? Gino has to deal with it, so we're going to be married in a couple of days when he gets back."

Sofia's eyes filled on cue. "But everyone is planning on it tomorrow!"

"Your uncle called Anna's parents, and the Rossinis. It's all set for a few days from now. Father Angelini is standing by."

Sofia was doing her best not to break down. "When, exactly?"

"Maybe three days at the most. In the meantime, I thought you and I would get busy on several projects I have in mind to surprise Gino."

She wiped her eyes. Partially mollified, she asked, "What projects?"

"Well for one, I need you to teach me Italian. I want to be able to say some things to Gino in his language on our wedding day. I would like to speak with such an authentic accent, he'll be shocked. It'll be our secret of course."

The girl's brown eyes suddenly sparkled. "You mean like 'I love you'?"

"Exactly. Like, 'I can't live without you.' Like, 'you're the most wonderful man I've ever known. Like, 'you're my heart and soul. Like 'I love your niece like my own daughter.'"

Sofia went perfectly quiet. "I love you, too, Ally. More than anything!"

"Then we're the luckiest people in the world."

"Gino?"

The second Gino heard Alberto's voice, he sprang from the hotel room bed where he'd spent the night going mad without a phone. His family's power may not have prevented him being investigated but did give him certain privileges.

Two security guards took turns bringing him meals, but there was no communication.

Today would be his second day before the chief judge while he made statements and listened to the prosecutor's charges against him.

The judge would decide if there was enough evidence to call for a trial.

So far it sounded even worse than Gino had first supposed.

Mercifully Alberto had come. He was the only person allowed in to talk to Gino.

Speaking in hushed tones his attorney said, "I've talked to your wife. All is well with her and Sofia for the moment."

Gino swallowed hard. "That's the kind of news I needed to hear."

"I only have a few minutes. Thanks to the e-mails that placed Donata and her lover in the one location no one thought to look, those P.I.'s you hired to nose around Palermo, Sicily, have unearthed interesting news. It seems Donata had a great-aunt on the Castiglione side who's still alive and holds the purse strings to their family fortune."

Gino shot to his feet. "I don't think even Marcello knew about that, otherwise he would have told me."

Alberto eyed him shrewdly. "She probably kept that a secret from him like she did a lot of things.

This aunt was the one who let Donata stay with her, and allowed her to use the family yacht.

"Apparently James Parker was a guest there and on the yacht several times. One of the crew let it out that the yacht picked them up in Portofino, Italy, but some members of the family weren't happy about it, particularly the great-aunt's oldest son named Vassily.

"He's next in line to inherit the money, and wouldn't stand for sharing it with a long lost family member from Rome like Donata who suddenly decided to ingratiate herself and her lover."

Gino's heart pounded like a jackhammer. His thoughts leaped ahead.

"This Vassily could have pretended to be Donata's friend by helping her procure that getaway car. All he had to do was pay off a couple of thugs to fix the brakes."

Alberto nodded. "Give the P.I.'s a little more time to investigate Vassily's activities, Gino. If everything adds up, we might well have our culprit."

Gino clapped his attorney on the shoulder. "Get all the extra help you need. I don't care how much it costs."

The other man nodded. "I'll tell your wife you're doing fine and should be home in another day or two."

"*Grazie*, Alberto."

"See you in chambers in a little while."

* * *

Ally stood in the alcove to Gino's bedroom with her hands on her hips. After dinner she and Sofia had come back with vases of fresh flowers to provide the finishing touch.

She and Sofia had spent most of yesterday painting the walls in both rooms a tan color with white trim. It covered the off-white paint which had probably been on the aged walls since the farmhouse was built.

"What do you think, Sofia?

"Uncle Gino's going to love it!"

"I hope so. That daybed and table from the storage room are a good fit."

Sofia nodded. "It looks a lot better than an empty nook. I guess Uncle Gino didn't know what to do with it."

"If he gave up his old room for you and your father, then it makes sense he hasn't had time to worry about this suite of rooms. That's what wives are for," Ally quipped.

Sofia flashed her a mysterious smile.

"What's that look all about?"

"If you and Uncle Gino have a baby, this would make a sweet nursery."

"You're right," Ally said, trying to sound matter-of-fact.

"There's room for a crib," Sofia observed.

"Signora Rossini has a new baby. Leonora tends it all the time. She says it's so much fun."

"What's so much fun?"

They both turned at the same time.

"Uncle Gino!" Sofia flew into his arms.

Ally's urge to do the same thing was so intense, she was in pain holding herself back.

He'd been gone three endless days. She'd given up hope he'd be home tonight.

He was still wearing the pale blue suit he'd been arraigned in, which meant he'd just been released and needed his suite to shower and change.

Ally thought he looked tired and leaner, yet all the more attractive for it.

"I was just telling Ally I hope you have a baby soon."

"What kind would you like? I'll see what I can do," he teased.

Heat swamped Ally's face.

"I don't care if it's a boy or a girl. Do you?"

"As long as the baby's healthy, I'll take whatever comes and be grateful."

"Me, too." She hugged Gino again.

"Do you like your surprise? Ally and I did all the painting ourselves. It's your welcome home present."

Ally saw his gaze take in the alcove's furnishings, but his eyes were hooded making it impossible to read their expression.

"I feel like I've just wandered into one of Rome's most fashionable furniture galleries."

Sofia laughed. "It was Ally's idea. Do you like the new matching bedspreads?"

They were a café-au-lait with white swirls.

He tousled his niece's hair. "I love them. They're classically modern. Did you pick them out?"

"We both thought this was the prettiest pattern. Ally said the daybed was perfect if you ever want Papa to be close to you during the night."

Gino's eyes swerved to Ally's. She noticed a strange flickering in their black depths. New sensations fired her blood.

"Ally is always concerned with everyone else's needs. That's why I'm marrying her first thing in the morning."

Sofia did a close approximation of squealing in delight.

"I made all the arrangements on the drive home from Rome. The ceremony will be at ten o'clock."

Ally rubbed her hands against her jean-clad hips, all the time aware of Gino's scrutiny.

"In that case I'll say good night to the two of you, Gino. It's already late, and I need my sleep for the big day ahead."

She sensed Gino had a lot to tell her, but now wasn't the time. She didn't want anything to alarm Sofia this close to the wedding.

Sofia ran over to her and gave her a big hug.

"Good night, Ally. I can't wait for morning to come."

Neither could Ally.

"I feel the same way." She kissed the girl's cheek, then hurried out of the bedroom.

His suite was located at one end of the third floor.

She went down the stairs to her room on the second. Sofia's and her father's suite lay at the other end of the hall.

Before Gino had been forced to move his family here, he'd had the farmhouse for himself. By virtue of taking on a wife, he'd now been invaded.

She hoped he didn't mind what she'd done upstairs. They already had an understanding that they'd be sleeping apart. She just didn't want him to think she planned to turn his whole household upside down.

When she could talk to him alone, she would explain that she felt this had been a good way to keep Sofia's spirits up, and accomplish what needed to be done without anyone questioning her real motives.

But once under the covers of her own bed, her mind wouldn't shut off.

What a difference it made knowing Gino was home. His mere presence gave her an overwhelming feeling of contentment.

Growing up in an all woman household, Ally had never known such luxury.

Something about Gino engendered this marvelous feeling of well-being and security. She knew he would slay dragons for them.

How odd that Jim hadn't had this same effect on her. Physically he'd been a strong, capable man. But she must have recognized instinctively he would always put himself first. In the end, he did it to his own demise.

Gino was a different breed of man altogether. No one else measured up.

She couldn't believe she was his wife. Even if it was in name only, she vowed to be his equal in all the ways that counted.

After the ceremony tomorrow, she would call her mother on Gino's cell phone and tell her she was married.

Much as she would have liked her mother's blessing, she hadn't needed it to function.

It was all because of Gino.

As for Jim's parents, depending on many factors, she would phone to inform them she had remarried. But for the time being it would be bett—

"Ally?" Gino whispered in the darkness, jarring her out of her thoughts.

Surprised to hear his voice, she raised up on one elbow. "I didn't hear you knock."

In the next breath she felt her side of the mattress dip to take his weight.

"I hope you don't mind."

Her heart was pounding in her ears. "No. Of course not."

He was sitting so close, she could smell the soap he'd used in the shower. She started to move to give him room, but he stopped her by placing both hands on either side of her pillow, forcing her to lie back.

He was wearing a robe, and as far as she could tell, little else.

"You ran from my bedroom so fast, we didn't have a chance to talk."

Her breathing had grown shallow. "Sofia needed you."

He traced the curve of her jaw with his finger. "But my wife didn't?"

"That isn't what I meant," she whispered.

"Then what did you mean?" His fingers had trailed to her earlobe, turning her bones to liquid.

"I—I've been sick with worry waiting for you to come home and tell me everything. But I didn't want to let on in front of Sofia."

"You've done a magnificent job of keeping her occupied. I've never seen her this happy before. Now it's my turn."

"I don't understand."

"I've spent two hellish nights away from my wife. I'm not prepared to be alone tonight.

"Let me lie here. It's all I ask. I need my best friend."

She heard a strange nuance in his voice. An impending sense of dread took over.

"Something's wrong—" she cried in alarm. "What is it? Don't tell me it's nothing because I wouldn't believe you. Hasn't the investigation uncovered anything that will help our side?"

"They have several promising leads."

"But?"

His fingers tugged on one of her curls. "There's been a new twist in the case."

Moving with the stealth of a panther, he reached the end of the bed. Before she knew it, he'd come to lie on top of the comforter next to her. She felt him cover his forehead with his arm.

Making love to her had to be the furthest thing from his mind. She felt so stupid for even imagining that's what he'd had on his mind when he'd first come into her room unannounced.

They were two people intrinsically linked to a murder, fighting for survival. Gino had no one but her to turn to for the kind of mental comfort he craved. She was the only person who understood what he was going through.

Three days ago she'd vowed to comfort him for better or worse. This was definitely the worst time of their lives.

She turned so she was facing him. "Tell me what's happened," she urged softly.

In the intimacy of the darkness he began talking.

"There's going to be a trial. It has been set for a month from now."

Even though Ally knew it might come to this, the news was shattering.

"I just found out Merlina of all people is a witness for the prosecution."

Ally quivered inwardly, but she was determined to stay on an even keel for him.

"Did you meet her through Donata?"

"No. Merlina's father is a wholesale florist from Gubbio. I met her almost a year ago while she was helping her father.

"We went out several times, but I lost interest and told her it was over, By that time Donata's long vacations were starting to take their toll on Sofia. Comforting her was all I had on my mind."

"But Merlina didn't want to stop seeing you," Ally said out loud.

"No. She started coming to Remo once a month. She would show up at the flower stand waiting for me. I told her my life was complicated, and we could only be friends. I hoped she would give up without my having to spell it out to her."

Listen to what he's saying, Ally. Just listen, and learn.

"Without my knowledge, it seems she got in contact with Donata."

"Sofia told me she came to see her mother."

Gino groaned. "During those conversations Donata

told lies about me. She made me out to be a dangerous man capable of committing bodily harm."

Ally was horrified. "Like what specifically?"

"According to the prosecutor, she told Merlina I used to come to her room at the palazzo and force myself on her because Marcello could no longer protect her."

"That's sick," Ally cried.

His breathing had become labored. "Donata showed Merlina the bruises to prove it."

Ally sat straight up in the bed. "Gino—if Merlina had believed Donata's lies, she would never have shown up here in the last few days. What reason did she use for coming to the farmhouse after all this time?"

"She wanted to know why I'd really stopped seeing her. I told her what I'd said before. That it was over, and it wouldn't be fair to go on seeing her.

"But she refused to accept it. And then of course she saw you, Ally. She knew you were a guest in the house."

Ally moaned in disgust. "So she put two and two together, and in her jealous rage she decided to pay you back by running to the prosecutor with more lies."

"As Alberto keeps reminding me, her story won't be believed. Her credibility will be ruined when he gets her on the witness stand and it's learned she came to see me after Donata had warned her off.

Nevertheless I have to admit I didn't see that one coming."

"Of course not. It's awful. I'd say it's a miracle you trust anyone." Her voice shook.

"You're it, Ally."

Her heart went out to him.

"You sound exhausted. Go to sleep."

After a few minutes she could tell he'd passed out from fatigue.

For the rest of the night she guarded him. When it grew cooler in the room, she stole out of bed to get an extra blanket from the cupboard. She put it over him.

Without conscious thought she smoothed the hair from his brow where his forearm had disheveled it.

Even the man she'd likened to Apollo needed respite from his burdens.

Toward morning she fell asleep and knew nothing until Sofia knocked on her door.

Ally's first thought was Gino. She opened her eyes to discover he'd left her bed already. She hadn't even noticed. Some guard she'd make.

"Come in, Sofia."

Her brunette head peeked around the door. "Uncle Gino says to hurry and get up. It's eight-thirty. Almost time to leave for the church."

"I slept that late?"

"After all the work you've been doing, he said you deserved to sleep in. He says he's so excited to get married, he can't eat."

After what he'd revealed to Ally in the darkness of the night, she wasn't surprised he'd lost his appetite. "Have you eaten already?"

"Yes. With Papa. Now I'm going to get dressed."

"Okay. I'll hurry. Meet you downstairs in twenty minutes."

She threw off the covers and padded into the bathroom for a quick shower and shampoo.

After putting on new underwear, she went over to the closet.

For the wedding she'd picked out a two-piece suit in pale pink with a lace overlay on the short sleeved jacket.

The knee length chiffon skirt floated around her legs.

She fastened the tiny pearl buttons, before slipping into matching pale pink high heels. A pink frost on her lips, plus a poof of floral spray, and she was ready.

Gino stood waiting at the bottom of the stairs in a black tuxedo.

Once again an image flashed before her eyes of the fierce bodyguard who'd stepped from the wall into her life one dark night.

Who would have guessed the gorgeous, enigmatic stranger wearing a security guard's uniform would turn out to be her husband dressed in impeccable groom's attire?

Ally grew weak at the sight of so much male beauty.

As she reached the bottom step, he drew close. She heard him murmur something under his breath in Italian. She would have given anything to know what he said.

"A certain young, upcoming violinist told me these would match your suit."

From behind his back he produced a corsage of pink roses he pinned to her jacket.

Her heart thumped so hard, it caused the petals to rustle with each beat.

"If you hadn't been there for me last night, I swear I don't know what I would have done."

"I didn't do anything, Gino," she whispered shakily.

He kissed her forehead. "You believed in me from the beginning. Knowing that, I can get through this."

His trust in her was absolute. He didn't need anything else. Unfortunately she wanted and needed much more from him. But to behave like Donata and Merlina, neither of whom could take Gino's rejection, would be the kiss of death.

After tonight she was more convinced than ever she'd done the right thing by having a certain inscription engraved on the gold wedding band she'd bought him.

He'd wanted a best friend for a wife. That's what he was getting. She would have to find a way to live with the pain.

CHAPTER NINE

FATHER ANGELINI smiled at both of them. "And now I pronounce you Rudolfo Giannino Fioretto Di Montefalco, and you Allyson Cummings Parker, husband and wife. May you live long and be fruitful. In the name of the Father, the Son and the Holy Ghost, Amen."

Gino didn't hesitate to give her another thorough kiss in front of the small assembly of friends. They were now officially married in the eyes of the church.

In the periphery, Ally caught sight of Sofia's shining face. She and the girls looked adorable in white lace dresses with garlands of pink roses in their hair.

Marcello might have been in a wheelchair, but he looked every inch the aristocrat in his formal attire. He wore the crest of the Montefalco family on the scarlet band stretching from his right shoulder to his left hip.

Before Ally had started down the aisle of the church

on Dizo Rossini's arm, his wife Maria had handed her a sheaf of long stemmed pink roses to carry.

"Do you know how many of my country women could claw your eyes out for getting Gino to marry you not once, but twice?" she teased.

Ally chuckled, but little did Maria know her bittersweet remark made Ally want to laugh and cry at the same time.

When the wedding party congregated on the steps of the church, one of Gino's friends took pictures for them.

Everything seemed so normal and happy, but Ally knew they were living on borrowed time. Like a bomb ticking away, their lives could be shattered by an explosion if Gino didn't win his case.

"Stop worrying," he whispered against her neck after they'd climbed in the back seat of the car.

"I'm not."

"Yes you are," came the no nonsense rejoinder. "I can tell by your eyes. They're a dark green. When you're happy, they turn a lighter shade and shimmer. Today is ours to enjoy."

She bowed her head. "I want to enjoy it, but I keep remembering those men waiting for you outside Mr. Toscano's office. If that were to happen in front of Sofia and all your friends—"

"No one's going to snatch me away again. That part is over."

Unless he was found guilty at the trial and taken away in handcuffs.

At the mere thought of it, Ally shuddered in horror.

"Where's my Joan of Arc who stood calmly before her enemies at the jail without as much as the quiver of an eyelash."

His question gave her a needed jolt. She'd better start acting the part she'd committed to play for life.

She raised her blond head. "I'm right here."

He grasped her hand. "I haven't told you how exquisite you look yet."

"Thank you."

"I'm the envy of all my friends."

"I have a few friends who would think the same about you."

When he kissed her fingers, she wanted to pull her hand away. How could she possibly remain friends with him if he kept doing things to remind her he was irresistible yet untouchable flesh and blood husband?

"I'm sorry your friends and family couldn't be here, Ally. One day our home will be open to everyone, and we'll be able to travel to Oregon."

"Sofia keeps asking me how soon you'll take us to see Mount Hood, Gino. She's fascinated by volcanoes."

"Aren't we all."

He slid his arm behind her shoulders. "I'm

anxious to meet your mother and tell her what an exceptional daughter she has."

"You're going to come as a tremendous surprise to her."

"Is that good or bad," he mocked in a playful tone.

"I'm not going to bother answering that question. Suffice it to say that with my father's defection, my mother has lost her trust in men. But when she gets to really know you, her whole attitude will change."

"Trust is everything," he said in an emotion filled voice.

Ally already knew that. She stirred in place. "I agree."

Though she wanted to rest her head against his shoulder, she didn't dare for fear she'd give herself away.

"Before we left the church, Sofia told me to examine my ring carefully. I think I'll do it now."

He removed his arm in order to pull off his own ring.

Ally held her breath while she waited for his reaction.

"My kingdom for a friend," he read the words aloud.

After a breathless moment of quiet, he touched the ring to his lips, then slid it back on his finger.

By now they'd reached the courtyard of the farmhouse. Most of the guests had already arrived. More pictures were being taken.

Gino got out of the car and came around to help her. His black eyes resembled smoldering embers.

"In case you didn't know it, you've made me the happiest man alive."

Before she could take another breath, his mouth descended on hers. Like the effect of slow moving magma, it caught every particle of her body on fire.

Not until one of his friends shouted for Gino to keep on kissing her for the camera did Ally realize how carried away she'd gotten. Her husband couldn't have helped but be aware of her hungry response. She could only hope that since he was playing to the crowd, he assumed she was doing the same thing.

He pretended to be the amorous lover to such perfection, no one could have guessed the real reason for their marriage.

Everyone clapped. There were a few wolf whistles that brought a grin to Gino's handsome face. He ushered her inside the farmhouse where Bianca and some local helpers had arranged food and champagne in the dining room.

The guests filled their plates and wandered out to the back terrace where a group played music.

Without hesitation Gino pulled her into his arms and started dancing with her.

Soon others joined in. Eventually his friends broke in to dance with her, depriving her of the joy of being that close to him.

But she needn't have worried who Gino's next partners would be.

He gave each flower girl a turn around the patio before spending the rest of his time with Sofia.

Ally finally excused herself to spell off Luigi and Roberto, both of whom were there to help with Gino's brother and celebrate.

"I'll watch Marcello while you get something to eat," she told them.

When they got up, she grasped Marcello's hand in case he decided to start walking around the terrace.

Maybe it was the music, or the presence of so many people, but his thumb kept pressing the top of her hand.

She hoped it meant that in some obscure way he was enjoying himself.

The cruelty of his affliction made it hard on everyone who loved him. He and Gino had been exceptionally close.

Today should have been a time for the two brothers to rejoice.

But of course it would have been a happy time because Gino would have married someone else. A pain seared her heart to imagine missing out on marrying him.

"Ally?" Her husband appeared out of nowhere and put his hand on her arm. "What's made you go pale?"

"Did I? Maybe it's because I was wishing I'd known Marcello before he became ill."

His dark eyes flickered. "He would have been crazy about you even before he heard you play the Tchaikovsky."

"Do you know he's been pressing his thumb against my hand?"

He slanted her a mysterious glance that caused her pulse to race.

"He senses your kindness. Would you be as kind to me if I asked you to play something for our guests? I want to show you off, and I can't think of a present I'd like more on my wedding day."

"Gino—"

"Is that a yes, a no, or a maybe."

His charm made it impossible for her to refuse him anything.

When she thought of all he'd given her, it was so little to ask in return. But he had no idea how full her emotions were. They threatened to overpower her.

"Well, perhaps one piece."

"I'll ask my niece to bring out your violin."

He disappeared just as Luigi and Roberto came back on the terrace.

Soon a smiling Sofia walked over to her with her case.

The background music ended and Gino asked for everyone's attention.

"Ally and I want to thank you for sharing the most important day of our lives with us.

"Few of you know she's a gifted musician. I've

asked her to play something for you as a special
favor to me and my brother.

"Our parents instilled the love of music in us.
Now we have Ally to fill the house with it again."

His touching words made Ally want to burst
into tears.

To fight them off, she opened her case and tuned
her violin until she felt she was in control once
more.

"I'll play something from the Brahm's First Symphony."

Brahms was her favorite composer, whether it be
piano or orchestral music.

This was the piece she'd been practicing when
the migraine had hit her so hard during rehearsal in
Portland. Little had she known what awaited her
when she'd gone out in the hall to call the doctor
and discovered there was another message waiting.

In a matter of weeks that voice mail from Troy
had literally transformed her life.

Here she was in the heart of the Italian countryside,
playing at her own wedding for her brand-new
husband. The man she loved beyond comprehension.

For a little while she simply immersed herself in
the beauty of the piece, wanting it to please Gino.

When she finished playing, there was an unnat-
ural quiet.

Perhaps the greatest tribute to any artist was the
hushed silence that followed a performance.

She looked across the patio and met Gino's gaze. Even from the distance separating them, his eyes seemed to be aflame.

Suddenly he began to applaud. Soon the others followed his lead.

"Grazie," he mouthed the words to her before she was besieged by their guests.

Sofia clung to her hand and announced she was taking lessons. That brought on requests from several parents for Ally to teach their children.

Everyone asked for an encore but to her relief Gino came to the rescue.

"I don't want my bride worn-out before the wedding day is over."

His remarks incited the men to make their little jokes. Ally didn't need a translator to know they were talking about the pleasures of the wedding night to come.

She laughed along with them because they were among friends here and Gino needed a moment like this to get him through the dark days of the trial coming up.

While she was putting her violin back in the case, she felt a pair of strong arms slide around her waist.

"Leave the violin on the chair and dance with me again."

Ally's heart leaped in response. It was frightening how much she wanted to be in Gino's arms. But this couldn't go on much longer or he would know he'd married a woman who wanted to be much more than friends.

Avoiding his eyes, she followed his lead. He seemed determined to show his friends that he was in love with his wife. Ally had to withstand his wrapping both arms around her with his hands splayed across her back, his face pressed into her curls.

Unlike the other couples, he more or less moved them in place. You really couldn't call it dancing. She could feel every hard line and sinew of his body.

Desire like she'd never known in her life engulfed her. She felt the telltale weakness in her limbs. Her palms ached with pain only he could assuage.

She couldn't do this any longer.

Placing her hands against his chest, she pushed away a little, but not so anyone else would notice.

Still not looking at him she said, "I'm sorry, Gino, but I need to be excused for a minute."

"Of course. Hurry back." He gave her mouth a lingering kiss before letting her go.

The mere contact set off a conflagration inside her.

In a daze, she made her way through the crowded house to the hallway. As she started up the stairs she saw Bianca welcome another guest into the foyer. Ally didn't recognize the middle-aged man. He hadn't been at the church to witness the ceremony.

If the housekeeper hadn't greeted him like an old friend, Ally would have been terrified it was someone from the prosecutor's office.

She continued up the stairs to her room to freshen up in the bathroom. In truth she'd needed to get away from Gino.

Ally soaked a washcloth in cold water and pressed it to her hot face, surprised she didn't hear it sizzle.

Her biggest mistake had been to dance with him. When she went downstairs again, she would make certain it didn't happen again. That way she might just be able to make it through her wedding day without the whole world knowing how she felt about Gino.

A few minutes later she felt settled down enough to leave her room and rejoin their guests.

To her surprise she almost collided with a white-faced Sofia who'd been running from the direction of her own bedroom further down the hall.

"Sofia—what is it? Has something happened to your father?"

"No." In the next breath the girl's expression closed up. She started for the stairs, but Ally pulled her back and held on to her.

"Was someone mean to you?"

"No."

"Then what's wrong, darling? Don't you know you can tell me or your uncle anything?"

"I don't like Uncle Gino anymore," came her muffled cry against Ally's lace jacket.

Sick to the pit of her stomach, Ally drew Sofia into the bedroom and shut the door.

She walked her over to the bed and helped her to sit down next to her.

Though they had a house full of guests downstairs, this was a problem that needed to be taken care of right now.

"Why do you feel that way about Gino? He loves you so much."

"I know."

The girl was talking in riddles.

"What's upset you? Please tell me. You can trust me."

"I'm afraid to tell you." She burst into tears. "It would hurt you too much."

"Hurt me? How?"

"Because you love him. But he—" She couldn't go on.

"He what?" Ally prodded.

"It'll make you cry."

"Then we'll cry together. Tell me."

"I found out he wishes—he wishes—" She couldn't say it. Breaking into half sobs, she clung blindly to Ally who by this time feared this had something to do with Donata. Ally couldn't let this go.

"Please, Sofia. You can't keep this to yourself or it will make you ill."

Sofia finally raised her head. "He said he wished he hadn't married you, but it was the only thing he could do at the time."

It was one thing for Ally to know the truth in her own heart, but to hear Gino's niece say it was like undergoing a second death.

Fighting to remain calm Ally said, "Is that what he told you?"

"No." She kept wiping her eyes. "I heard him talking to Signore Santi."

"When?"

"Just now."

"You mean they're in your father's room?" It had to have been the man who'd come late to the reception.

"Yes. When I saw them leave the party and you weren't downstairs, I came up to see what was going on. That's when I heard Signore Santi tell Uncle Gino it was too bad he married you when it wasn't necessary."

Not necessary— Did that mean there'd been a break in the case?

"Then U-Uncle Gino said—well you know what he said. I—I couldn't believe he said that."

Sofia's shoulders shook with silent sobs. "I thought he loved you."

Poor Sofia had been caught up in the romance, but cruel reality had intruded.

"Did you hear anything else?"

"No. I didn't want Uncle Gino to know I was listening."

Thank heaven for that!

Ally's arms closed around her. "Your secret is safe with me."

The girl lifted her tearstained face. "I shouldn't have told you. Now you'll go away and I'll never see you again." Her voice throbbed.

"That's not true, Sofia. I'm going to live right here with you forever.

"The fact that he doesn't love me doesn't change my love for him or you."

"How can you say that?"

"Listen to me, darling. When your uncle proposed, I knew he didn't love me. We're friends you see? So you mustn't stop loving him. He can't help how he feels. But I know he'll always be kind to me. He wants us to be a happy family. So do I."

Sofia studied her for a long time. "I love you, Ally. Do you think someday I could call you Mama?"

The question melted Ally's heart.

She winked at her. "As long as I can refer to you as my daughter, you can start calling me that anytime you like. Now wash your face and we'll go downstairs before everyone starts to wonder what has happened to the wedding party."

Alone for a moment, Ally squared her shoulders. Where Gino's feelings were concerned, she hadn't learned anything from Sofia that she didn't already know. The difference was, realizing Sofia knew it, too, would make things much easier around here.

When Sofia emerged from the bathroom, Ally grasped her hand.

"After we leave this room, we'll pretend we never had this conversation, agreed?"

"Yes," she answered in a sober tone.

But it was easier said than done. When they joined their guests, Gino still hadn't come downstairs. That as much as anything let her know something of tremendous import had happened, otherwise Gino wouldn't absent himself from the festivities this long.

For Gino's sake she hoped Signore Santi's arrival meant that Gino was no longer under suspicion.

How would they go on protecting Sofia if there were a trial and he had to leave the farm every day to be in court?

She was an intelligent girl and no one's fool. Ally feared it was going to be sooner than later that she learned the whole ugly truth about her mother. Then it would come out that Ally's first husband had died with Donata.

Ally dreaded the day Sofia knew everything.

After urging Sofia to be with her friends, Ally mingled with the guests who were all enjoying themselves.

Ally caught up with Maria and talked to her about the possibility of Ally and Sofia helping out part-time at the flower stand for the rest of the summer.

Maria couldn't have been more enthused over the idea. They agreed to talk about it in a few days.

"Provided Gino is willing to share you by then."

To Ally's surprise Gino reappeared. He slid his arm around her waist.

"I saw your heads together. What plot are you two hatching behind my back?"

Ally wanted to ask him the same question about his conversation with Signore Santi who was nowhere in sight.

"Your wife and Sofia are going to come to work at the stand this summer."

"Provided you agree," Ally said to him.

She felt his probing glance.

"You'd really like to sell flowers?"

"I'd love it. So would Sofia. She'll help me with my Italian."

"Leonora will be overjoyed," Maria assured her.

His arm hugged her a little tighter. "My wife lights her own fires. She's out of my sight for five minutes, and already we're a farming family."

"It's what you always wanted, Gino. I couldn't be happier for both of you."

"Thank you, Maria." He kissed her cheek. "Now if you don't mind, I'm going to whisk my bride away to a secret place."

He guided Ally toward the hallway.

"We'll slip out the side door of the kitchen," he murmured against her ear.

She swallowed hard. "What about Sofia?"

"Anna's parents are keeping her with them tonight."

"Does Sofia know that?"

"I told her before I came to find you."

"W-was she all right with it?"

"Of course. She's old enough to know a wedding couple needs time to themselves."

He swept her out the door to the courtyard where Paolo was waiting with the car.

"Where are we going?"

"The palazzo."

"I thought we couldn't leave the farm."

"Legally we're not supposed to. But Carlo Santi came to the reception with news that necessitates a visit there. Since it's our wedding night, he's taking the responsibility of vouching for us while we break the rules."

Now everything made sense. This was a charade for Gino's friends in order to perpetuate the pretense of the happily married couple going off on their honeymoon.

By the time they started to pull away from the courtyard, their guests had assembled to see them off.

Ally exchanged a soulful glance with Sofia who ran out in front of everyone who were taking pictures to wave. She was on the verge of tears.

"Gino—we can't leave Sofia behind. Look at her face."

"I've seen it, but she's better off with friends until we return."

Ally knew he was right, but it hurt to leave her when Ally knew his niece was suffering since overhearing Gino's talk with Carlo.

"We'll be in Montefalco shortly. When we start the climb up the road to the west gate, we'll lower our heads to avoid the paparazzi camped nearby. I'm phoning ahead to tell the guards to have the gate open for us. That way Paolo won't have to stop."

Ally waited until he'd used his cell phone before asking, "How long are you going to keep me in suspense about the case?"

He reached for her hand. His eyes flashed her a fiery glance. In the next few minutes he told her about the information uncovered by the P.I.'s in Sicily.

"One of the crew of the yacht has claimed that the great-aunt's grandson, Tomaso, has villas in Prague and Portofino. It seems he became friendly with Donata and your husband.

"It's possible he knows something about the accident, or even caused it. But without some sort of proof, it's the crewman's word against a wealthy member of the Castiglione family.

"In four months the authorities investigating this case haven't ever found evidence linking Donata and your husband. But you and I know the laptop exists. Which means Donata had to use some sort of computer on her end. "The fact that the authorities don't know of the correspondence between them plays to our advantage.

"Both Carlo and Alberto think she must have kept one at the palazzo, but it was hidden so well, the police never came across it.

"Naturally they went over Marcello's computer as part of the initial investigation, but nothing turned up.

"That's why I originally had my P.I.'s looking in all the coffee houses with computers in and around St. Mortiz, hoping to discover she'd used one of them. Unfortunately they never found anything."

Ally sucked in her breath. "Then let's tear the palazzo apart."

"That's the idea," Gino muttered. "Maybe we'll find it. If she had someone like Tomaso helping her, that information has to be somewhere. She couldn't have carried out everything without help from someone she thought she could trust.

"It's the kind of proof needed to take to the chief judge. It will force him to consider other suspects."

"We'll spend all night if we have to," she declared.

Not only could it mean Gino's freedom, but she'd be spared having to go to his room with him in order to fool the staff that the newlyweds couldn't wait to be alone.

She stared out the passenger window. They were

near the town now. She checked her watch. It was only five in the afternoon. The sun wouldn't be setting for hours yet.

"Wouldn't it have been better to arrive in one of the estate cars with the smoked glass?"

Gino shook his head. "That's a dead giveaway. The paparazzi won't be expecting a car I use at the farm. It will buy us the time we need to make it inside the grounds."

A few minutes later Paolo muttered that they'd better get down.

Gino reached for Ally and pulled her over so the top portion of her body lay against his hard thighs.

When she was settled, he leaned over her where she could feel his heart pounding against her back.

"Am I crushing you, Ally?"

"No. I'm fine."

"I knew my beautiful bride would say that," he whispered. "Hold on. The car's picking up speed. You won't have to suffer much longer."

That depended on the kind of suffering he was referring to. She had a lifetime of it ahead of her, but it would remain a secret between her and Sofia.

Suddenly the car came to a stop. Paolo gave the all clear.

Gino kissed Ally's brow as she raised up. "By now you have to know I'd rather be with you than anyone else in a situation like this."

She knew…

He came around to her side and opened the door. "Let's go in and get busy."

The palazzo was an eighteenth century palace so fabulous in its architectural beauty as well as its furnishings, Ally followed Gino around in awe.

He introduced her to the staff who congratulated them on their marriage. She could tell they held Gino in the greatest affection.

"We'll go to my apartment first and change."

"I don't have any of my clothes with me."

"You can wear something of mine."

He led her up marble stairs and through marble hallways to his apartment on the second floor. It was a fabulous home within a home where he could be totally self-contained.

Ally had thought his farmhouse was out of this world. But this kind of splendor left her speechless.

He pulled a pair of clean navy sweats from one of the drawers and handed them to her.

"Go ahead and use the bathroom while I change in here. Then we'll get started in Donata's dayroom where she spent a lot of time."

Once inside the large, modernized bathroom, Ally took off her wedding outfit and hung it on the door hook.

After removing her high heels, she put on Gino's clothes. They pretty well drowned her, but it was all right because she rolled up the sleeves. The elastic at the bottom of the legs kept her from tripping.

She padded back in the suite in her nylons.

He'd put on a pair of gray sweats. When he saw her he grinned.

"We look like a pair of athletes ready for a run."

Her mouth curved in a half smile. "I'm glad we'll be doing it inside here, or my poor feet couldn't take it."

His gaze traveled down her curvaceous body. "New shoes are the price of looking gorgeous on your wedding day."

"It was a wonderful day, Gino. Thank you for everything. Now let's see what we can find."

A half hour later they'd searched every square inch of the elegant dayroom on the main floor without success. Lines darkened his features. She hated to see him like that.

"I've been thinking. If I were Donata and wanted to hide something, I think I would have put it in Sofia's room."

His jaw hardened. "The police searched it thoroughly."

"But they weren't necessarily looking for a computer of some kind."

"You're right."

"Of course there's always the possibility she didn't own one, but had access through a friend."

"We'll take one last look anyway," Gino murmured. Sofia's bedroom was across the hall from Marcello and Donata's apartment at the other end of the second floor.

"If Donata wanted to send messages, it would have been easy enough for her to slip across the hall when Sofia was at a friend's house or at school,' he said before ushering her inside his niece's room.

Ally felt like she'd entered the domain of a princess.

Her glance fell on the floor to ceiling bookcase with all kinds of books, puzzles and games.

"A laptop isn't so easily disguised, Gino. My guess is, if Donata had one, she camouflaged it in some way."

Gino shot her a piercing regard. "You're a woman with amazing instincts. Where would *you* hide it, Ally?"

She examined everything in sight.

"What's in that chest at the foot of Sofia's bed?"

"It has a lot of her toys in it. When Donata wanted to get rid of them, Marcello insisted on keeping them in case they ever had another baby."

She walked over to it. "The police probably did a cursory search, but toy boxes are notorious for holding treasures you never expect to find."

Ally opened the lid. It was a deep rectangular piece of furniture.

Gino got down on his haunches next to her and they began sifting through the jumble of items. When her hands came in contact with something about the right size, Ally let out a little cry of excitement.

But she soon groaned at the sight of a play type-writer in a plastic case.

"I was so sure—"

Gino went back to searching. She dug in at the other end and found a doctor's kit. Gino produced a makeup kit.

Starting to lose hope, she felt around the bottom. Her fingers came in contact with what she presumed was a radio in a leather case. Out of curiosity, she opened it.

A gasp came out of her. "Gino—this looks like a palm pilot! Do you think it's real?"

He took it from her and pressed the on button.

"It's real all right," his voice grated. "State-of-the-art four gig drive. Ally—" He crushed her against him. "You found it!"

She pulled away from him, unable to take much more of their physical contact.

"Get inside it quick!" she cried.

He helped her up from the floor. By tacit agreement they sat down on the side of Sofia's canopy bed.

The next five minutes felt like five hours as Gino started retrieving messages. Suddenly his tall, powerful body sprang from the bed.

"This says it all, Ally. Tomaso was the one to arrange for the car from a garage in St. Moritz. It names the place and the mechanic who let Donata buy the used car off him. Everything's there. The plan for them to drive to Portofino and board the yacht on January 25.

"Ally—" His eyes blazed with light. "Come on."

He grasped her hand. "We'll go to Marcello's study and phone our attorney."

Ally's gaze swerved to his. "If Signore Toscano needs an affidavit from Troy, I know he'll cooperate. It will prove the connection beyond any doubt."

Gino nodded. "You cracked the case wide-open, Ally. What would I have done if you hadn't come to Italy with your husband's laptop?"

Ally was euphoric to realize the horrible nightmare would soon be over. Whoever had tampered with those brakes, it wasn't Gino!

But because Ally had flown to Italy, Gino was now a married man, tied for life to a woman he would always consider his best friend.

But she couldn't imagine a virile man like him remaining celibate for that long. There was only one thing to do. She would talk to him about it after they'd returned to the farmhouse.

CHAPTER TEN

GINO got out of the car and hurried into the farm-house.

"Ally?"

Bianca came rushing into the foyer. "She's doing errands in the truck."

He frowned. "Is Sofia with her?"

"No. She got home a little while ago and is upstairs with her father."

Gino could scarcely contain his disappointment. Not with the news he had to tell her. He'd asked Ally to be here when he got home.

Last night Alberto had told Gino to come to Rome and they'd work all night to present their case before the chief judge. Carlo had gone with him.

It was decided Paolo would drive Ally back to the farmhouse. Gino had assured her they'd celebrate today. He'd been living for it and couldn't imagine where she'd gone. But Sofia would know.

He took the steps three at a time and hurried toward Marcello's suite.

The last thing he expected to find was his niece sobbing her heart out on her father's lap.

"Sofia?" he called to her.

She lifted her head. "Hello, Uncle Gino."

Normally she came running to him.

"What's wrong, sweetheart?"

"Nothing," she answered in a dull voice.

Gino's eyes met Luigi's. The nurse shrugged his shoulders, indicating he didn't know the reason for her tears.

"Let's go in your room and have a talk."

"I'd rather not."

He felt like someone had just kicked him in the gut.

"If something happened at Anna's house, I need to know about it."

"This isn't about Anna."

"Are you upset with me for asking you to spend the night at her house?"

"No." She wiped her eyes.

"Did you and Ally have words?" He couldn't fathom it, but he had to know the truth.

"No. I love her. She said I could call her Mama."

Though those words thrilled him, he still didn't have his answer.

"Then there's something I've done to hurt you. If I did, you know I didn't mean to."

"I know."

"Then I *have* hurt you. If you don't tell me what I've done, then I don't know how to fix it."

"You can't fix it." She sounded like a woman three times her age.

He'd never seen Sofia behave like this before. His body broke out in a cold sweat.

"Why do you say that?"

"Because it's true."

"Then I've failed you, Sofia, and that devastates me."

He left the room and went upstairs. How could the joy of this day be trumped by the pain he was feeling now?

The fact that Ally wasn't here caused him to wonder if she'd left on purpose so he and Sofia could be alone to sort things out.

Was it possible his niece had learned the truth about her mother, and believed Gino was guilty of driving Donata away? The very thought made him so ill, he staggered over to his bed, wondering how in the hell to help Sofia if he was right.

He could provide the proof that he wasn't the culprit. But he couldn't do anything about Sofia's deep seated sorrow where her mother was concerned. If she knew it was Ally's husband who'd died with her, Sofia would feel so betrayed, she'd never get over it.

Ally—where are you?

In his agony, he heard a rap on the door and raced across the room to fling it open and embrace his wife.

It was his niece.

"Sofia—"

"Can I come in?"

"What do you think?"

He could thank God she was at least speaking to him.

"Ally told me not to blame you because you couldn't help it."

"Blame me for what, sweetheart?"

She stared at him for the longest time. "I heard you talking to Signore Santi in Papa's room during the reception."

Gino replayed their conversation in his mind.

"What exactly did you hear?"

"He said something about you not having to get married after all. And you said—you said you wished you hadn't gotten married, but it was the only thing you could do at the time."

Gino had been holding his breath. "And from that you deduced that I don't love Ally. Is that it?"

She nodded slowly.

"Did you tell Ally what you overheard?"

"I had to. She caught me in the hall and wanted to know what was wrong."

He closed his eyes. With those words he'd gone from joy to a new depth of despair in a matter of seconds.

"Are you angry at me?"

"No, sweetheart. But just so you know, I fell in love with Ally the moment I met her. In fact I loved her so much that when I heard she was only going to stay in Italy for one more day, I had to do something to keep her here."

"You mean like asking her to be my violin teacher?"

Gino smiled at her. "Exactly. In my fear of losing her at the end of the month, I'm afraid I rushed her into marriage before she was ready. As you know, she lost her husband a while ago and it would be understandable if she still had feelings for him. But I didn't want to wait for her to be my wife.

"I know I should have given her more time, but when you love someone as much as I love her, you're not thinking clearly.

"That's what I was telling Carlo when you happened to overhear us talking. He didn't know how I felt about Ally. All he knew was that I'd asked her to marry me because he thought I wanted you to have a mother.

"Sofia—do you know where she is?"

His niece studied him with those intelligent brown eyes of hers. "No, but you've got to find her, Uncle Gino!"

"Don't worry. I won't come back without her."

He flew out the door and down the hall to the stairs.

He almost had a heart attack when he discovered Ally coming up the stairs from the foyer.

She was composed as he'd ever seen her. Too composed.

"I was hoping you'd be here when I got back from Remo," she spoke before he could. "Tell me what I need to hear."

He knew what she was asking, but he wanted her to mean something else entirely different.

"All charges have been dropped against me. We're free, Ally."

"Thank heaven," she cried with her heart in her throat.

"It's all because of you. Now we can leave on our trip to Ischia."

"Sofia will be overjoyed."

He took another step towards her. "What about you?"

"You know I've been looking forward to it, but before we do anything, I need to talk to you."

His heart skipped several beats. "Then let's go to your room. It's closest."

He sensed her hesitation before she nodded.

Ally entered the room first and waited for him to shut the door.

"I hoped, but didn't dare to dream you'd be freed from suspicion this fast." He could tell she was breathing hard. "With this news, we can now discuss something that has been on my mind for a while."

Adrenaline riddled his body. "If it's about our marriage, you're my wife now and that's the way things are going to stay."

She eyed him with a calm that unnerved him.

"I want to stay married to you, too, Gino, but I just wanted you to know that you're free to live the way you did before we were married."

"I'm not sure I understand. I'm afraid you're going to have to spell that out for me."

She heaved a sigh. "If there's a woman you want to be with from time to time, I'll understand."

"You're talking about an open marriage?"

She averted her eyes. "Yes."

"Does that go for you, too?"

She paled. "Of course not. I plan to stay true to my wedding vows."

"But it's all right if I break mine, is that it?"

"As long as you're discreet, the eyes of the world will continue to view us as a married couple."

"So we are…"

She lifted a tremulous gaze to him once more. "I want your happiness, Gino."

"We went over all this before we got married. We agreed to stay married no matter what."

"But a lifetime is too long for a man like you who can finally stop worrying about everyone else's needs and concentrate on your own for a change.

"I have no doubts there's a remarkable, marvelous woman out there somewhere waiting to meet a man like you. If and when that time comes, you can tell her the truth about us. If you decide to act on that love, you can do it knowing we had this conversation. You're an honorable man, Gino, but you'll be carrying it too far if you have to deny yourself a full life. I can't let our marriage stand in the way of your true happiness."

His hands formed fists. "Did you make this decision before you left the palazzo? Or after Sofia admitted eavesdropping on my conversation with Carlo?"

She didn't break eye contact with him. "Before."

She was lying, just the way she'd lied to him at the jail when she'd made that ridiculous confession in order to be set free. The fact was, she didn't have a dishonest bone in her body.

"What if I told you I want you in my bed."

"That doesn't surprise me."

Her answer stunned him.

"A man can sleep with his wife and the woman he really loves without much problem."

"Your husband did a lot of damage, but don't judge every man by his behavior."

"I'm not talking about Jim."

"I think you are," he challenged her. "That's what I've been afraid of since I made up my mind I was going to marry you whether you were ready or not."

"Ready?"

He shifted his weight. "I know the kind of woman you are, Ally. You would never have married Jim if you hadn't been in love with him.

"You think I don't know that what he did has

scarred you? But I was willing to take the chance that I could get you to love me like that one day.

"The only trouble is, in forcing marriage, I may have acted too soon. That's what I was telling Carlo, that I should have given you more time to get used to me.

"Unfortunately Sofia only heard the first part. If she'd stayed to hear the rest, she would know I fell hopelessly in love with you the night we met. I couldn't imagine life without you, so despite the risks, I got you to marry me first, and planned to spend the rest of my life finding ways to make you fall in love with me.

"When I repeated my vows before God, I meant every word of them, Ally. I love you more than my own life. If I can't get you to love me back, then I'd still rather live with you than anyone else. Do you understand what I'm saying?"

Her lovely body quivered in response. It defeated him more than any words she might have spoken.

"I've been a fool to hope for a miracle," his voice grated. He started for the door, needing to get out of there.

"Don't leave, darling," she called to him. But she said it in Italian, not English.

In the next minute he was treated to words in his native tongue he never expected to hear pour from her lips and heart. When he turned in her direction, she came running toward him.

"I love you, Gino Di Montefalco." She threw her arms around his neck. "I love you more than I thought it was possible to love a man."

She covered his face and hair with kisses. "When I met Jim, I fell in love, but it didn't take long to realize he didn't have the substance I'd endowed him with. Somewhere along the way my love died. Maybe he sensed it before he ever met Donata. I'll never know the answer to that, but I do know that the night I met you changed my entire life."

She cupped his face in her hands, staring up at him with adoring green eyes.

"Do you honestly think I would have agreed to marry you if I hadn't wanted it with all my heart and soul?

"Oh, Gino— Love me, darling. It seems like a century that I've been waiting for you."

Ally waited impatiently for her husband to wake up.

The sun had risen above the horizon. The birds were singing. The marvelous scent of lavender filtered through the open window of her room.

She lay facing him with their legs entwined.

They'd never made it up the stairs to his suite. In their desperate desire to love each other, they'd never come out of her room.

She knew he needed sleep. After being up all night while he'd been in Rome, only to spend all of last night making love to her, he deserved his rest.

But she was so on fire for him, it was impossible not to touch him.

He had silky black lashes she loved to feel against her cheek. Even in sleep his mouth had a sensuous curve that turned her blood molten.

He held her possessively. If she tried to move, she would waken him. Part of her was tempted. Maybe just one little kiss wouldn't hurt.

The second she pressed her mouth to his, he responded with breathtaking urgency. Then his eyes opened and she saw the flame of desire burning in their black depths.

"Buon giorno, bellissima," he said deep in his throat.

"Buon giorno, Apollo mio."

"Apollo?" he questioned, pulling her on top of him.

When she explained what she meant, he laughed triumphantly. When he did that, she thought she'd die with love for him.

He sobered for a moment. "I wish I'd met you when you were eighteen."

"Why eighteen?" she teased, tracing the line of his male mouth with her fingertip.

"You would have been old enough for me to carry you off without fear of the law coming after me."

She buried her face in his neck. "I know how you feel. So many years have already gone by. How is it you never married? You've never really told me."

He wrapped her closer in his arms. "I was waiting for you."

"Be serious, my love."

"I'm deadly serious," he came back with that hint of steel in his voice.

"In my teens and early twenties, I enjoyed women as much as the next man and didn't feel the need to settle down yet.

"After Marcello married Donata and I saw the way it was going, I thanked providence I was still a free man. That is until I met you.

"Your physical beauty attracted me immediately. Couple that with your defiance and your loyalty to my brother, a man you'd never even met, and I knew I'd met my soul mate. The trick was to get you to feel the same way about me."

She kissed him with passion, no longer afraid to express her love.

When he finally let her up for air she said, "No trick was needed. The moment I emerged from the door of the *pensione* and saw you standing there like some proud, fierce Italian prince, I felt my whole soul quake."

He chuckled before giving her a long, hard kiss she felt to her toenails. "I like the way you talk, Signora Di Montefalco. The sun god and an Italian prince. What about just plain old Gino the farmer?"

She searched his eyes. "You're so many things,

there aren't enough adjectives in the world to describe you."

So saying, she switched to Italian and told him she loved him.

She heard his sharp intake of breath. "Who taught you so well, you don't sound like a foreigner."

She kissed his eyelids. "My new daughter."

"Sofia's a little monkey. She held that bit of information back from me."

"I asked her to keep it a secret."

Gino suddenly moved so she was lying on her back. He stared down at her with fire in his eyes.

"Speaking of our niece, I think it's time we concentrated on producing a male heir just to keep the balance."

Ally smiled up at him. "If it's a girl we'll call her Gina and just keep trying until we get our own little Marcello."

Gino's eyes went suspiciously bright before his mouth fell on hers. She responded with the hunger of a woman who loved her husband beyond all else.

EPILOGUE

"CAN we swim a little longer, Mama?"

Ally checked her watch. "Ten more minutes. Then I need to get back to the house to feed the baby."

Two months had gone by since their precious Marcello had entered the world. Now Ally was determined to get her figure back. At this point she was within five pounds of her goal, but it was hard with Bianca's cooking always tempting her to eat more.

Gino had offered to come home at lunch to tend the baby. Father and son needed some playtime together.

If ever a man was made for fatherhood, it was her husband.

Little Marcello, who looked like his namesake, had already twisted his father around his baby finger.

The farmhouse was such a happy place, Ally felt like she was living in paradise.

When Gino had put it to a vote, no one wanted to live at the palazzo.

It would remain in the family until Sofia decided what to do with it.

The weather was already warm for the first of June. It was hard to believe that a year ago this month she'd come to Montefalco where Gino and a new thrilling life awaited her.

With Tomaso Castiglione behind bars for his crime, the horrific trauma of the past was over. Best of all, Sofia had been spared the details.

Feeling alive and glowing, Ally got out of the river and threw on a lightweight robe over her bikini.

Sofia's naturally curly hair was cut short these days. It only needed a brisk toweling to look perfect.

In the last year she'd grown into a young teen who was starting to resemble Donata more and more.

Sofia kept pictures of her mother in her room. Donata had been a beauty all right, and her daughter was following in her footsteps.

The two of them got in the truck and headed for home. With Sofia being such an excellent tutor, they talked mainly in Italian.

It made a huge difference when Ally helped out at the flower stand. Of course it would take years to talk and sound like Gino, but that was her goal.

She loved the language and the country. She loved his family. She adored *him*.

Hoping he would be able to stay while she nursed the baby, she drove faster than usual.

"Look, Mama—there's a taxi driving away from the house."

"You're right!"

Ally couldn't imagine who'd dropped by. She slowed to a stop and parked the truck around the side, hoping their visitor wouldn't be able to see her looking like this.

They hurried into the kitchen, then stopped. Ally's mother sat at the table next to Gino, feeding the baby his bottle. Her husband trapped Ally's gaze with a silent message before she cried, "Mom—"

Her mother's dark blond head lifted. She wore a smile that transformed her.

"Oh, honey— I shouldn't have waited so long to come. My little grandson's adorable."

Though Ally had invited her mother to come many times, she'd never taken her up on it. But with a new baby in the house…

Ally's eyes filled. "He and Sofia are the light of our lives. Mom? I'd like you to meet my daughter, Sofia."

"Come around here, honey," her mother said to Gino's niece. "I need to get to know both my grandchildren."

"Just a minute, Grandma. I've got to get something for you."

"For me?"

"Yes. I made it last summer and have been saving it for you. I'll be right back."

Ally had an idea where she was going. Taking advantage of the time, she hurried around the table and hugged her mom and the baby.

Her mother studied her. "You look wonderful, honey. Obviously marriage to this man agrees with you."

With those words her mother had let her know she'd put the past behind her and was ready to move on.

"He's the most wonderful thing that ever happened to me." Her voice shook with emotion.

Gino pulled her onto his lap.

"Careful, darling, I'm wet after just getting out of the river."

"I like you exactly like this," he whispered, kissing the side of her neck.

Sofia came back in the kitchen and walked around to Ally's mother. She carried a sheaf of dried flowers wrapped in cellophane and tied with ribbon.

"Lavender—" she cried. "Just the way my mother used to preserve it for gifts."

Tears welled in her gray eyes.

Ally took the baby so her mother could hug Sofia. "Thank you, honey. This is a priceless gift."

"Mama taught me how to do it. I have my own little sticker on it. See?"

Ally's mother looked closer. "Sofia's Scents. That's brilliant." She kissed her cheeks.

"Oh, Ally—" She turned to her. "I begged Edna to fly over with me, but she said I should come alone the first time."

"There'll be other times, Mom."

Gino hugged her tighter around the waist, baby and all. At least he could reach around her now. The thought gave Ally no end of satisfaction.

"We're hoping you'll move here permanently," Gino said to her mother. "You and your sister can have the run of the palazzo if you'd like."

"I'd love it if you and Aunt Edna lived here, Mom. I've missed you so much. You're the children's only grandparents. You'd be so proud of Sofia."

She turned to Sofia. "Darling? Go get your instrument and play something for Grandma."

"Okay." She ran out of the kitchen.

"My wife's been teaching her the violin. I understand I have you to thank for Ally blessing this house with music."

Her mother was genuinely overcome. "What a beautiful thing to say."

Soon Sofia returned and played several pieces that showed she was no beginner.

When she'd finished, Ally's mother got out of the chair to hug her. "If you keep this up, you're going to be able to play like Ally."

"I hope so."

"Is there a piano in the house?"

Sofia nodded. "In the living room."

"Then let's take a look at your music and I'll accompany you."

Ally got to her feet. "While you do that, I'll put the baby back to bed and get changed."

Gino kept his arm around her shoulders as they climbed the stairs.

By the time she'd put the baby in his crib, the strains of Mendelssohn reached the third floor.

Gino had the shower ready and waiting for her.

She stepped under the spray, waiting for him to shut the door, but he kept it open and simply watched her.

No matter how intimate they'd been, she still blushed.

"You're more gorgeous than ever. I never want to go to work."

"I never want you to go."

"I'm glad your mother finally came."

"So am I."

"This house feels normal, the way my parents' once did."

"Mine never felt quite normal because Mom was so unhappy." She reached for the towel he kept just out of reach.

"Gino—" she begged.

He finally relented and wrapped it around her.

"I didn't see any shadows in her eyes just now."

"Neither did I."

"The two of them are going strong downstairs, and our son is asleep."

"The answer is yes," Ally cried, so out of breath with longing, it was embarrassing.

He picked her up in his arms and carried her to the bed.

"This is what heaven is all about," he whispered against her lips moments later. "When Marcello was diagnosed, I didn't think I'd ever be happy again."

His fingers tightened in her damp curls. "You came into my life when I least expected it."

"You'll never know how happy I was when you showed up on the train and whisked me away to the farmhouse."

"Carlo had ordered me to make you go back to the States, but I couldn't allow you to do that." He devoured her mouth once more. "I couldn't stay away from you, *bellissima*."

"I hoped that was the reason," she whispered shakily.

"Now no more talk or your mother will think we're inconsiderate hosts."

"She knows what we're doing, Gino darling. I'm pretty sure she wants to make up for lost time, so let's give her her wish. Maybe I can grant you your wish at the same time."

"I have everything I want," he asserted.

She smiled at him. "Not everything. I was thinking we could work on another bambino to keep Marcello company and help you on the farm."

His eyes gleamed. "I believe in that kind of work. I'll give you fair warning. I'm prepared to work day and night, plus overtime."

"I think I'll put that in writing," she teased.

"You won't have to, Ally. I'll always come running home to you. Don't you know that yet?"

Oh, yes. She knew. And for the rest of their lives, she'd be waiting…

* * * * *

PRINCESS AUSTRALIA

BY
NICOLA MARSH

Nicola Marsh has always had a passion for writing and reading. As a youngster, she devoured books when she should have been sleeping, and later kept a diary, which could be an epic in itself! These days, when she's not enjoying life with her husband and son in her home city of Melbourne, she's at her computer doing her dream job creating the romances she loves. Visit Nicola's website at www.nicolamarsh.com for the latest news of her books.

For the real princesses in my life.
Thanks for your warmth, your friendship
and the many laughs we share.

CHAPTER ONE

'I WANT a crate of soda, a monster bowl of hot chips and a triple layered choc-fudge banana-split sundae. Got that? And make it snappy!'

Natasha Telford glared at the back of Australia's youngest pop star as he strutted towards the lift after snapping his order at her. She surreptitiously squeezed a stress ball under the concierge's desk while wishing she could rip a few more slashes into the upstart's trendy torn T-shirt.

How old Harvey did this job on a daily basis she'd never know.

As a kid growing up in Telford Towers, she'd thought the concierge had the most glamorous job in the world. Until this week, when she'd had to fill in while Harvey had his hip replacement. Giving polite tourists directions to Melbourne's famous sites she could handle. It was the sulky, rude, demanding famous—especially young punks barely out of school—she could politely strangle.

Speaking of famous, the Prince of Calida was due any second, and she cast a quick, assessing look around the lobby, ensuring everything was in place. The demanding little snot of a pop star could wait for his sundae. She had a bigger guy to impress, namely Dante Andretti, soon to be crowned monarch of a tiny principality off Italy's west coast, if the info she'd gleaned off the Net was accurate.

The lobby looked perfect, from its polished marble floor to gleaming brass-trimmed check-in desk, its plush chocolate-brown sofas and muted antique lamps with the stunning floral bouquets ordered on a daily basis arranged strategically throughout.

Natasha smiled, infused with the same pride she experienced every day she entered the Towers. She loved this place. Every last square inch of it. And she'd do anything to make sure it stayed in the family. Anything.

'So when's His Uptightness due?'

Natasha's smile broadened as she whirled around and came face to face with Ella Worchester, her best friend.

'Don't call him that. He's probably a really nice guy,' she said, rearranging a pile of maps, a box of theatre tickets and a credenza of tourist flyers for the umpteenth time. Her nerves were working overtime, and if the prince didn't arrive soon she'd go into serious meltdown.

Ella rolled her eyes and stuck her ink-stained hands in the pockets of her low-slung denim hipsters. 'Yeah, I bet he's a real prince.'

Natasha ignored Ella's cynicism as she usually did. Right now, a prince was exactly what she needed—or, more accurately, what the Towers needed.

'Do you know much about him?'

Not enough. And that was what had her worried.

Usually, she knew everything about the VIPs staying at the hotel. It was her job. In this case, even more vital than usual. Telford Towers needed the prince's presence, like, yesterday.

Natasha shrugged. 'Only what I've gleaned off the Net, which isn't much. There was a whole heap of geographical stuff about Calida, a tiny bit about the royal family and that's about it.'

'Is he cute?' Ella stuck out a slender hip in a provocative pose, and Natasha laughed.

'Couldn't tell much from the pic on the website. Too small.'

'You wouldn't be holding out on me by any chance?' Ella's teasing tone elicited more laughter and Natasha held up her hands in surrender.

'Give me a break. From what I could see, the guy was trussed up like a turkey in some fancy-schmancy uniform, had his hair slicked back in army fashion and looked like he couldn't crack a smile if his life depended on it. There, satisfied?'

Though there was one thing that had stood out in the prince's picture.

His eyes.

Beautiful, clear blue eyes that had leapt off her computer screen and imprinted on her brain.

She'd always had a thing for guys' eyes, believing in the whole 'windows to the soul' thing. Pity she hadn't read the real motivation behind Clay's eyes. It would've saved her a lot of heartache, and would've avoided putting her family in the invidious position of losing the one thing that meant everything, courtesy of her greedy ex.

'Well, don't let him boss you around, okay? You're only filling in for Harvey; doesn't mean you have to take anything from anyone, prince or not.'

Natasha squeezed Ella's hand. 'The prince is important for business, and I'll treat him like I treat the rest of the customers. With respect, care and—'

'Yeah, yeah. Save the spiel for someone who hasn't heard it a million times before.' Ella held up her hand, though her fond grin underlined the lack of malice in her words. 'Now, if you don't mind, I have a gardening column to write and a few more botanical drawings to do before lunch.'

'Coffee at Trevi's, usual time?' By then, she'd definitely need a caffeine hit.

'Sounds great. See you at five.'

Ella gave her a cheeky wave and sauntered away, a slim, tall figure in head-to-toe denim with her short, shaggy auburn bob swinging in sync with her steps.

Her best friend was stunning, enjoyed life and had energy to burn, while Natasha felt like a worn facecloth wrung dry. Stress did that to a person, the type of stress that dogged her every waking moment, and unfortunately most of her sleeping ones too. Little wonder she looked so pale next to her vibrant friend.

Glancing at her gold and silver link watch—the one her dad had given her for her twenty-first, years before money had become a problem for them—she wondered why the prince was late. Most of the VIPs she usually dealt with had their itineraries scheduled to the last second and she assumed royalty would be more pedantic than most.

Especially a prince who looked like he couldn't crack a smile, if that tiny pic on the Net had been any indication.

At that moment, a gleaming black Harley roared to a stop outside the front door, and Natasha nibbled nervously on her bottom lip, hoping Alan the doorman would get the noisy thing valet-parked as soon as possible. First impressions counted, and she desperately needed to make this one count with the prince.

After another nervous glance at her watch, and more subtle rearranging of the tourist brochures stacked on the concierge desk, she glanced up in time to see the Harley's rider stride through the glass doors.

And her mouth went dry.

The guy looked like a walking advertisement for Bad Boys Inc: tall, over six feet, with broad shoulders hugged in soft grey cotton, long lean legs encased in faded denim, black wavy hair mussed by a helmet and a gusty southerly Melbourne wind, and a bone structure that could've been chiselled by one of the Italian masters.

Natasha took a deep breath, closed her eyes and tried to refocus. What on earth was she doing? So the guy looked like every woman's fantasy come to life—since when did she have time to ogle guys, let alone lose her concentration on the job?

Especially at a time like this!

Mentally slapping herself for letting her long-dormant hormones get the better of her in that one, glorious moment when he strode into the foyer, she exhaled and opened her eyes, ready to march out onto the street and haul the prince into her hotel the minute his limo pulled up.

Being antsy was getting the better of her and making her think all sorts of crazy things, like how much she'd like to walk up to the sexy bad boy and ask in her best, sultriest voice, 'Can I help you?'

He saved her the trouble.

'I need your help.'

Natasha quickly smoothed her cuff over her watch—she really had to stop glancing at it every five seconds—and fixed her professional welcoming smile in place. However, her smile froze when she looked up and locked gazes with the bad boy.

Clear blue eyes.

Almost aquamarine, the mesmerising colour of the Great Barrier Reef on a sunny day.

A colour imprinted in her memory banks, considering it was the only stand-out feature she could remember from the prince's fuzzy picture.

'Miss Telford, is it?'

The bad boy glanced at her name tag before returning his gaze to her face. A face flushed with heat at the realisation that she really must be losing the plot if she thought for one second that this scruffy, wind-tossed guy could be the Prince of Calida.

She really needed a day off to unwind. Badly.

'Yes, that's right. What can I do for you?'

Apart from bustle you out of here and get ready for the most important meeting of my life.

'Plenty, hopefully.'

He rested his forearms on the desk, and she tried not to stare at the way his biceps bunched at the simple action.

Oh boy, maybe she needed to change her whole non-dating policy. It had been eighteen months since the Clayton disaster, and she hadn't been out with a guy since, preferring to concentrate on fixing the mess Clay had lumbered her family with.

Resisting the urge to take a peek over his shoulder towards the door in case the prince snuck in without her seeing, she said, 'Do you have a reservation, sir? If not, perhaps I can arrange it with someone at Check-in and we can discuss your needs later?'

'No, I need this sorted now, and you're just the woman I want.'

His low, gravelly voice sent an unexpected shiver

down her spine, and her smile faltered as he fixed her with a penetrating stare.

Those eyes…that colour…no way!

It couldn't be.

His voice dropped lower as he leaned across the desk barely inches from her face, enveloping her in a heady scent that reminded her of hot cross buns: warm and sweet and cinnamon. *Yum.*

'I think you've been expecting me. I'm Dante Andretti.'

Natasha gripped the desk to steady her wobbly legs.

This couldn't be happening.

No way could this guy be the prince.

'The Prince of Calida,' he added as an afterthought, the corners of his mouth lifting in a small, sexy smile which did strange things to Natasha's insides, things she'd never felt before, things she had no right to experience now.

He was the prince.

This…this…*rebel* was the man she'd pinned all her hopes on for saving her father's business?

Lord help her.

'Is there a problem, Miss Telford?'

Swallowing her first response of 'you bet your sweet butt there is', she said, 'Not at all, Your Highness.'

'Ssh!' He shook his head vigorously and put an index finger to his lips, like some second-rate spy. 'Someone might hear you.'

'And that might be a problem because…?' Her voice held a slight tinge of hysteria, and she took a few steadying breaths.

This was crazy. It had to be one of those stupid *Candid Camera* stunts where her dad and Ella would leap out at any moment and say 'Gotcha!'

She'd expected the prince to arrive in a stretch limo; this guy had revved in on a motorbike.

She'd expected the prince to have an entourage of bodyguards; this guy was solo.

She'd expected a stiff upper lip, hair-slicked-back pompous ass, and this guy was laid back, ruffled and very, very sexy.

Way too sexy.

'In case you hadn't noticed, I'm not advertising my identity and I'd like to keep it that way.'

Natasha sighed, wishing for one ounce of the kind of saint-like patience that Ella demonstrated when she sat for hours in front of a plant to sketch it. 'I'm not following this. You're booked in under your real name but you don't want anyone to know you're here?'

He snapped his fingers under her nose, his smile broadening. 'Exactly.'

No, no, no!

Natasha wanted to stamp her feet like one of her rock-star guests having a tantrum.

This wouldn't do. She needed to broadcast the prince's presence in her hotel to the world, and he wanted to keep it a secret? Was the guy out of his mind?

'Is there a security problem? Something I should know about?' *Like why you've turned up here looking like a jeans model and spouting a whole lot of nonsense?*

'No problem. But I would like a chance to talk further. Like I said, I need your help while I'm here. Let me check in, and perhaps we can meet when you've finished your shift, yes?'

'No!'

Natasha lowered her voice, deriving some satisfaction from the surprised glint in those too-blue eyes. Good. Let him see how it felt to be on the receiving end of a few surprises for once. She'd had her quota for the day.

'No?'

Schooling her face into what she hoped was a professional mask, she said, 'What I meant was I'm busy here for the next few hours. It will be a while before I finish up.'

'No matter.' He waved his hand as if her answer meant little, and she suddenly realised that though this guy didn't look like a prince he had the commanding mannerisms down pat. 'I will wait. I'm booked in as Dan Anders.'

Her mouth twitched, the first time she'd felt like smiling since this crazy, prince-impersonating-a-bad-boy had strode into her hotel.

'Nice pseudonym.'

He shrugged, and she stared at those muscles again, the way they bunched and shifted beneath the cotton T-shirt, and she wondered if they felt as firm as they looked.

'Dante Andretti, Dan Anders. I chose something similar not to confuse myself.'

His self-deprecating grin displayed a row of even white teeth, made more startling by his sensational tan.

She knew pictures often didn't do their subjects justice. In the prince's case, he should have the royal photographer shot.

The guy was gorgeous, impressively so. And for a girl who had sworn off guys after Clay that was saying something.

So she wasn't blind. She could look, couldn't she? Like window shopping; you didn't have to touch—oops, she meant buy—the merchandise!

'Why don't we meet in the Lobby Bar for a coffee around four-thirty? I have plans at five.'

There was no way she'd be popping into this guy's room for a rendezvous, prince or not. She had a reputation to uphold in this place, not to mention the fact he unnerved her with that steady, blue-eyed stare.

He shrugged. 'Fine. I'm not surprised a beautiful woman like you would have plans.'

Okay, so she could add charm to his list of impressive attributes.

'Right,' she said, suddenly flustered when he didn't look away, her hands fiddling with the stress ball behind the desk. 'We'll talk about this more then, but let me tell you, I'm not happy about this situation. I don't like lies, I don't like subterfuge, and having you stay at our hotel is important for business.'

On and on she babbled, hating the way his mouth curved deliciously at the corners, the way his eyes glinted with amusement, and the way she kept noticing inconsequential details like that.

She was making a fool of herself, sounding like an uptight schoolmarm scolding a recalcitrant kid. She always did that when she was nervous, getting all defensive and huffy. Ella teased her about it. Sadly, she spent too much time these days on the defensive.

'We'll talk about this business later, then, Miss Telford.'

'Call me Natasha,' she said, a blush heating her cheeks for some inexplicable reason. Gee, it wasn't like she was telling him to call her for a date or anything!

'Dante.'

His polite nod reaffirmed what she'd thought earlier: you could take the bad boy out of the prince but you couldn't take the prince out of the bad boy.

'See you at four-thirty.'

She managed a tight smile, the type of smile that

made her teeth ache with the effort. This cloak and dagger business with Dante reeked of trouble.

Big trouble.

And she'd had enough of that lately to last a lifetime.

CHAPTER TWO

DANTE cast subtle glances Natasha's way while an efficient young woman checked him in.

She intrigued him.

He was used to subservience, deference and awe when people learned his identity, but the stunning brunette hadn't batted an eyelid. In fact, she'd grown more prickly, tension radiating off her in palpable waves.

She didn't like him.

That much was obvious, and he wanted to know why. Maybe she had a hang-up about wealth? Or maybe his title?

No matter. The minute he'd set foot in the hotel, he'd known he would need the concierge onside if he was to perpetrate his plan. The fact the concierge was a gorgeous woman with caramel eyes, long legs and a fabulous body behind that frumpy dark green uniform just made his task all the easier.

Not that he could rely on charming the woman to his way of thinking. If anything, she'd give him a hard time, he just knew it. Her little holier-than-thou speech had been a dead giveaway that Miss Natasha Telford wouldn't stand for any hanky-panky. Not that he had any in mind. Not really…

'Here's your welcome pack, Mr Anders. The card for your room is inside. Enjoy your stay at Telford Towers.'

He smiled his thanks at the young woman behind the check-in desk, grabbed his key and headed for the lifts.

Of course, it wasn't his fault he had to pass directly in front of the concierge's desk again, and it definitely wasn't his fault that the sexy concierge chose that exact moment to look up.

He gave her his best smile, the one his mother said could rule Calida alone, and a half salute, enjoying the faint blush staining her cheeks.

So, she wasn't immune to a little charm after all?

He'd have to remember that.

His plan to remain anonymous on the first leg of his trip might depend on it.

Natasha rifled through her wardrobe, flicking past formal dresses, sundresses, skirts and casual trousers before coming to rest on her favourite pair of jeans. At times like this, being super-organised—or obsessively tidy, as Ella liked to tease—was a definite plus. She'd dithered long enough.

Sliding the worn denim off the hanger, she wriggled into them, noting with irony the only good thing Clay had left her with was a slimmer figure. Stressing out over what he'd cost her and her family had shed pounds by the bucketful, and she'd never been so thin.

After slipping a fitted pink singlet top over her head, pulling her hair back in a low ponytail, fixing silver hoops in her ears and sliding her feet into black wedges, she stood back and stared in the floor-length mirror behind the door.

Her favourite outfit, the type of outfit that made her feel good, that gave her confidence.

Then why did she want to rip it off and pull a serious black dress over her head?

You're a fraud, that's why.

She poked her tongue out at her reflection, hating when her subconscious was right. No matter how casual she tried to dress, or how confident her clothes were supposed to make her feel, she was a mess.

Dealing with Dante Andretti would've been hard enough without the runaway prince playing some weird rebel game where he wanted to hide his identity. The same identity she needed to shout from the rooftops to boost the hotel's profile and, ultimately, save it.

'Damn it,' she muttered, dashing a slick of gloss across her lips and waving a mascara wand over her lashes, knowing it would take a heck of a lot more than a bit of make-up to give her a much needed boost.

She needed the prince's help.

Apparently, he needed hers.

Then why the awful, sinking feeling their needs were poles apart? Or, worse, she'd be coerced into putting his first…and all because of a charming smile and a pair of blue eyes that had haunted her memory since the first time she'd seen them in grainy print on a computer screen.

Why couldn't he be a boring, fuddy-duddy prince hell-bent on performing normal royal duties—like getting his face on every media outlet?

Why was he masquerading as some sexy bad boy? Okay, so he couldn't help the sexy part but, honestly, wasn't he taking the whole rebel image a tad far? How did a guy like that own a pair of worn jeans anyway? Wouldn't he wear perfectly pleated formal trousers all the time?

And why did he specifically need *her* help to perpetrate whatever game he was playing?

Determined to get answers to the questions swirling in her mind, Natasha picked up her keys and purse and headed for a rendezvous with a prince.

Dante glanced around the cosy bar, surprised by the homey feel. He'd travelled the world, stayed in the best hotels and sampled the finest luxuries money could buy, yet something about this place tugged at him.

The rich, mahogany coffee-tables and bar covering an entire back wall, the deep comfy armchairs in burgundy, the muted light from brass lamps and the scattering of antiques were nothing out of the ordinary. Yet together they created an ambience which beckoned like the privacy of his own room at the palace at the end of a long day.

Suddenly it hit him—the privacy aspect of the room, the same comforting feeling he'd expect from a private lounge, not some hotel lobby bar. That was it. This room beckoned like his sitting room back home.

Someone had gone to a lot of trouble to create this effect, to offer travellers a home away from home. Someone with taste, good business sense and a keen sense of what it felt like to belong.

At that moment, Natasha walked into the room, and his desire to admire the decor went up in smoke.

He smiled and waved her over, mesmerised by the sway of her slim hips in poured-on denim, the way the lamplight highlighted the toffee tints in her hair, and how her overall outfit combined sassy casual with an innate elegance. Though he guessed that had more to do with the woman inside the clothes than the garments themselves.

Natasha Telford, quite simply, took his breath away.

Now he only hoped she had an open mind to go along with his plan.

'Glad you could make it,' he said, rising to his feet and pulling out a chair.

'No problems.' She inclined her head in thanks and sat down, gesturing to a waiter behind the bar. 'What would you like?'

'Espresso, please.' *And a healthy dollop of your co-operation.*

'Make that two,' she said, smiling at the waiter in a way that made Dante's pulse roar.

Why couldn't she give him one of those smiles? Was the young guy a flame?

He studied her carefully, watching for a flushing of cheeks, a coy expression, a change in body language, but he came up blank. In fact, while he'd been making a few irrational leaps of thought it looked like she'd been studying him just as intently. By the slight frown marring her smooth forehead, he'd come up lacking.

'So what did you want to discuss?'

She sat ramrod-straight, her hands clasped firmly in her lap, a determined look on her face, and Dante had a sneaking suspicion his plan was about to hit a major snag in the form of one beautiful wet blanket.

'I need your help.'

'So you said earlier.'

Her caustic tone didn't inspire much confidence and he ploughed on, choosing his words carefully.

'My visit to your country is multi-faceted. Official duties, fostering foreign relations and a family visit. Everyone knows the prince will be staying at your hotel and for how long. What they don't know is that

I've arrived on schedule, assumed a different identity and will have my secretary ring to say I've been delayed by a week. So during that week I wish to remain anonymous.'

'Why didn't you let me know your need for anonymity when you booked?'

Good question; he just couldn't give her an honest answer. How could he explain to a woman he barely knew that the spur of the moment decision had as much to do with a desperate need to escape as his desire to spend time with a nephew he'd hardly seen?

'My extra week here is impromptu and I need some time out from my duties.'

She raised an eyebrow, a delicate gesture that made him smile. Somehow, he knew there was nothing delicate about Natasha Telford. She came across as a vision of feminine loveliness...with a backbone of steel beneath.

'I see.'

By the tiny frown creasing her brow, he seriously doubted that.

'For family reasons?'

'Uh-huh.'

Natasha sat back in the armchair and fixed the prince with a suspicious glare, wondering if he thought she were completely stupid.

Guys like him didn't flit around countries trying to hide their identity for 'family reasons'. They did the whole cloak and dagger thing for floozies, mistresses or whatever the name was for their hidden love interests.

The prince must have a secret lover, someone he didn't want the press to get wind of, and that had to be the real reason behind this elaborate farce.

So what? It wasn't any of her business. As long as

he came out of the closet—so to speak—at the end of the week, she'd still get the much-needed publicity boost for the Towers. And, after playing along with His Sneaky Highness, she had every intention of milking his royal presence for every cent he was worth.

'You don't look too impressed.'

Silently cursing her expressive face, Natasha said, 'What you do in the next week is no concern of mine.'

'That's where you're wrong.'

The arrival of their espressos put paid to the questions raging through her brain, and she waited till they were alone again to continue.

'I don't follow.'

'You are the only person who knows my real identity and I want it to stay that way. It is imperative. Do I make myself clear?'

She stared at him in open-mouthed shock. Who did he think he was, talking down to her like that?

Then again, he was a prince, and obviously used to ordering people around. Not to mention the guy who would get her family's business out of crisis.

She'd bite her tongue. For now.

'Perfectly clear,' she said, taking a sip of her coffee, enjoying the caffeine rush and trying not to notice the way his long, tanned fingers wrapped around the tall glass mug with ease, as if they were made to hold things…caress things…

'Good.'

He stared at her over the rim of his mug, those blue eyes capturing her attention and making it impossible to look away no matter how much she wanted to.

'How long have you been a concierge?'

His question came out of left field though she should

have been grateful. With his probing stare, she'd half expected something more personal.

'Less than a week.'

He lowered his mug, surprise etched across his handsome face. 'By your surname, I assumed you were part of the Telford family and in the job for a long time. Maybe I've entrusted my secret to the wrong person?'

'Relax,' she said, enjoying her first genuine smile of their meeting.

No matter how laid back His Highness seemed, this whole secrecy thing was getting to him. She could see it in his suddenly tense shoulders, his rigid neck, his clenched fingers. His floozy must be some woman for him to go to these lengths to protect her identity.

'My father runs Telford Towers and I've worked here since I could walk. Our concierge is away for the next twelve weeks on sick leave, so I'm filling in for seven days till his temporary replacement starts next week. Does that allay your fears?'

He nodded and visibly relaxed, placing his mug on the table between them and leaning back in his chair. 'So, what do you usually do here?'

'Everything.'

From ensuring things ran smoothly, to mediating staff disputes, to pampering VIPs, she did it all. It was what she loved about this place, had always loved about it. Being a part of Telford Towers came as naturally to her as breathing and she couldn't let it slip away.

Especially when this entire mess with Clay was her fault.

'Such as?'

She should've been flattered by Dante's interest, but she wasn't a fool. Now that he had her here, he wanted to know every last thing about the only person who knew his little secret. He probably still didn't trust her.

'I'm my father's right-hand woman. After I graduated with an MBA, I joined him in the everyday running of the Towers. Whatever needs to be done, I do it.'

His eyes widened, the admiration in the steady blue gaze warming her from the inside out. 'Is it only the two of you?'

'Uh-huh.'

And the painful fact ripped through her, reopening old wounds. Would her mum have survived the heart attack without the added stress Clay had brought upon them? Would Natasha have to spend the rest of her life harbouring the unspeakable guilt that she had contributed to her mum's death as well as potentially ruining the family?

'You should be proud. Your father and you have done a marvellous job. This hotel is wonderful. This is wonderful.'

He threw his arms wide in a dramatic gesture characteristic of his Italian heritage, and she managed a tiny smile when in fact she felt like bolting to the sanctity of her room and bawling her eyes out. Memories of her mum always made her feel like crying.

'Did you hire a designer to create this room?'

Natasha shook her head, a burst of pride making her sit up straighter, and she quelled the urge to sniffle. 'I did it.'

'Really?'

If his eyebrows shot any higher, they would've reached the elaborate cornices lining the patterned ceiling.

'That's right. I wanted to create a home away from home for weary travellers. It's the type of room I'd like to spend time in if I was stuck in a hotel miles away from everything familiar.'

Her voice rose as she spoke, filled with excitement, and she marvelled at the sudden change. It had been a long time since she'd felt anything bar intense, draining responsibility. She'd made a major mess of things and she had to clean it up.

Where every day used to bring joy and a thrill as she flitted from task to task, the last year had brought nothing but guilt, recrimination and a weary determination to do a job she used to love wholeheartedly.

But that was all about to change. Starting with the prince-playing-hooky sitting in front of her, if he agreed to help.

'You've captured the exact feeling I had when I first sat down,' he said, glancing around the room with a sparkle in his eyes before his gaze came to rest on her. 'You're a very talented woman.'

'Thank you.'

She blushed, an annoying surge of heat that probably made her look like a sideshow clown. Somehow, his simple compliment meant more to her than all the accolades she'd received in the hotel business.

She really was in a soppy mood. Time to escape before she did something silly like beg him to head up the Towers' next ad campaign or, better yet, grovel in the hope he would book out the Presidential Suite for the next decade. Both would be financial boons and either option would get them out of trouble.

Making an obvious show of glancing at her watch, she said, 'If our meeting here is over, I really must go.'

The cheeky glint in his eyes faded. 'Ah, yes, your secret assignation.'

That's your game, bucko, not mine.

Thankfully, she bit back that retort. 'Nothing too

secret about meeting my best friend for our daily catch-up at our favourite trattoria.'

She could've sworn she saw relief in his eyes before his super-sexy smile drew her attention. 'You meet your friend every day?'

She nodded, knowing she would never have survived the last few years without brash, exuberant Ella, the sweetest, most loyal friend a girl could ever wish for. The two of them had met through Telford Towers when Ella had moved into one of the apartments five years ago.

The dastardly duo, her mum had called them.

Natasha preferred 'dynamic duo' because that's how great Ella made her feel. Her best friend was reliable and loads of fun. And it seemed like so long since she'd had any.

'Yeah, keeps us sane. Nothing better than unwinding over a latte at the end of a hard day.'

'You are lucky.'

He shrugged, a simple, eloquent gesture that spoke volumes when combined with the wistful tone in his voice.

At that precise moment, Natasha could've sworn the prince sounded lonely. Very lonely.

'I know. Now, I'm sorry, but I really must dash.'

She stood quickly, eager to put distance between them before she leaned over and gave him a comforting hug. He looked like he needed one.

Though maybe that had more to do with her crazy hormones coming to life after a few glimpses of his muscled chest beneath cotton?

Either way, she wasn't sticking around.

'Thank you for agreeing to meet with me. And for agreeing to assist with that other matter.' He stood and gave a strange, little formal bow which made her want to giggle, considering his bad-boy outfit.

Guys with day-old stubble, unruly hair and faded denim didn't bow. They rode motorbikes and broke hearts maybe, but bowing? *Uh-uh.*

'If you need anything, don't hesitate to contact me,' she said out of habit as she grabbed her purse and stood.

Not that His Sneaky Highness would need anything more of her. She bet he had his whole week planned out, starting with a rendezvous with the royal floozy.

'How do you propose I do that?'

She halted, surprised by the hint of urgency in his voice. 'Uh…through Reception.'

He sent her a sceptical look as if knowing she was giving him the brush-off.

Okay, so it wouldn't be too smart to get her walking, talking promo-dream offside this early. She needed to appear a tad friendlier, more approachable.

Unsure if what she was about to do was the right thing or a huge mistake, she rifled through her purse and handed him a business card. 'Or, here's my mobile. You can contact me on that number if you need anything.'

As long as it wasn't a triple choc-fudge sundae in the middle of the night!

'Thank you. I appreciate it.'

Natasha returned his smile, knowing he was only being polite but unable to shake the deep-seated niggle that there was more to this prince's charade than met the eye—and she'd just handed him an easy way to involve her in it!

CHAPTER THREE

'YOU'RE late.'

Ella tapped her watch and sent a mock glower Natasha's way as her friend rushed into Trevi's and fell into her usual seat.

'Sorry,' Natasha said, unable to stop a smile spreading across her face.

She'd never been any good at keeping gossip involving guys from her best friend and, considering the afternoon she'd had, starting with meeting Dante and ending in agreeing to assist his clandestine plans, she knew this would be another one of those times where she couldn't help but share. Every last juicy detail…

'No, you're not.' Ella grinned and gestured for Luigi, their favourite waiter, to bring them the usual. 'You've got that look that says you've been up to no good. And enjoying it way too much.'

Natasha laughed and threw her hands up in surrender. 'Give me a chance to catch my breath! And remind me to never try and hide anything from you. What are you anyway—the secret police?'

Ella pounced as soon as the words left her mouth. 'Ah! So you do have a secret! Come on, tell all.'

'Can't I at least wait till my mocha-cappuccino arrives?'

'No!' Ella shouted, and Luigi's head snapped up from the coffee machine, an indulgent smile on his face as he winked at his two favourite customers. Though Natasha suspected he said that to all the girls.

Natasha usually enjoyed toying with Ella, feeding her tiny titbits of gossip gleaned from her varied and unusual jobs in the hotel. However, by the avaricious gleam in Ella's eyes, she knew now wasn't one of those times to tease. Besides, she had the strangest urge to blurt the whole truth out and get her friend's point of view.

'Okay. Though what I'm about to say must adhere strictly to our lips-zipped policy, right?'

'Absolutely,' Ella said, miming a quick-lock zip over her lips and throwing away the key. 'It's nothing serious, is it?'

'No, everything's fine.'

She'd make sure of it.

There was no way she'd ever burden her friend with her financial troubles or the fact she could lose her home if the Towers went under.

Ella snapped her fingers. 'I know! It has something to do with the prince. How did it go? Has he swept you off your feet? Does he want to take you back to his castle and make you his love slave? Should I buy you some of those funky princess slippers?'

Natasha laughed, more than a little disturbed that Ella's preposterous questions elicited a thrill of excitement. What would it be like to be swept off her feet by a prince and spirited away to his castle to live happily ever after like the fairytales promised?

Something you'll never know about, her voice of

reason screeched, and even the small romantic part of her that had survived Clay's treachery, the part that still harboured dreams of finding the elusive 'one' despite what she'd been through, had to agree.

'You can hold off on the slippers,' Natasha said, watching Ella lean forward with an avid look on her face. 'I don't think I'm the prince's type.'

'But you're gorgeous! You could have any man you want.' Ella's indignant quick-fire response brought an unexpected lump to Natasha's throat.

Ella had stuck by her through dating disasters, the Clay fiasco and her mum's death. She was loyal, fierce and beautiful inside and out.

'Thanks, but I think the prince has other fish to fry, so to speak. He's going incognito for a week and has asked me to keep his identity a secret. He's checked in under a false name, is parading around like an unshaven lout, and is determined to keep his true identity under wraps.'

'Wow.' Ella's eyes widened, digesting the interesting news before her razor-sharp mind predictably focussed elsewhere. 'Unshaven lout? I thought you said he looked pretty uptight.'

'I was wrong.'

Very wrong.

An instant image of dazzling blue eyes, day-old stubble, tousled dark curls and a sexy smile flashed across her mind.

'Uptight' didn't begin to describe what she thought of Dante.

Unfortunately, some of what she was thinking must've shown on her face for Ella leaned closer and patted her forearm. 'Okay, spill it. You've given me the official lips-zipped version. Now, tell me more about this prince. Is he hot?'

Natasha smiled at Ella, who was an expert at picking up on nuances especially when they had anything to do with the male species.

She could've avoided the question, danced around it or made up a whole heap of boring platitudes. Instead, Natasha sat back and fanned her face with a red-and-white checked serviette.

'He's hot.'

Ella's eyebrows shot up in a familiar sassy look that demanded the whole truth and nothing but the truth. 'How hot?'

Natasha stopped fanning her face, threw the serviette on the table and tapped her lips as if deep in thought when, in reality, she didn't need time to ascertain how hot Dante was.

She'd known the minute he'd strutted into the lobby, all six-feet-plus of testosterone-filled male with the body of a Greek god and the face of a model.

'Tash, you're killing me here,' Ella said, her tone implicit with warning that, if Natasha didn't spill soon, she'd drag it out of her.

'Hang onto your latte, I'm trying to get my adjectives right. After all, how many ways can you say bad-boy babe with a smile that can make your knees wobble at twenty paces, and eyes that could melt a maiden aunt?'

'He's that good?'

Natasha nodded, heat seeping into her cheeks at the memory of Dante's eyes staring at her over their espressos, an unfathomable expression in the true-blue depths. 'Better.'

Ella squealed and clapped her hands. 'This is fabulous.'

'What's fabulous?'

'This is the first time I've heard you notice a guy in months, let alone sing his praises,' Ella said, a genuinely pleased smile on her face. 'You usually pretend guys don't exist, or criticise my dates to hell and back, which is usually totally accurate by the way. Men can be scum. But this is fabulous. You're into this guy. Who cares if he's a prince? Time for you to have a little fun.'

Natasha frowned, dread creeping through her. If she was negative about guys, she had reason to be. Clay had used her, hurt her and left a lasting legacy which still threatened those she loved the most. She couldn't help the protective barriers she'd erected around her heart, but was she as bad as Ella made her sound?

Usually she would've laughed it off, but maybe her friend had a point. Perhaps she'd sounded like a shrew the last few years? As for Ella's other observation, that she was 'into' Dante, nothing could be further from the truth.

'I'm not planning on having fun with the prince,' Natasha said, ignoring her dormant devilish side which insisted it would be a blast to try. 'He has asked me for a favour, that's it. Once this week is over, I'm going to ask him for one and milk his presence in the hotel for all it's worth.'

Ella grinned. 'You don't think you're protesting just a tad too hard?'

'No!'

Okay, so that had come out a bit too defensive. Natasha forced a smile and said, 'Give it a break, will you? I've given you your gossip fix for the day, so lay off. Can't a girl enjoy her mocha-cappa in peace?'

As if on cue, Luigi bore down on their table bearing a tray filled with steaming mugs.

'*Ciao, bambinas.* How are my favourite girls today?'

He grinned broadly and placed the usual skinny latte in front of Ella and Natasha's mocha-cappuccino directly into her outstretched hands. She needed the creamy blend of chocolate and coffee desperately. The earlier espresso with Dante had barely touched the sides; besides, she'd been too engrossed in listening to His Royal Sneakiness.

Ella batted her eyelashes in the usual semi-flirtation she carried on with most men. 'We're fine, Luigi. And you?'

The Italian, old enough to be her father, kissed his fingertips and threw his hand into the air. 'All the better for seeing you, *bella.* Now, would you girls like anything else? Maybe some of my best tiramisu? Or better yet, you stay for dinner?'

'We're right for now, thanks,' Ella said, her bold smile sending the old guy into another fit of finger-kissing, hand-throwing and wistful grinning.

After Luigi had left, Natasha shook her head. 'I swear you must've come out flirting with the doctors when you were born.'

Ella shrugged, a self-satisfied smirk playing about her glossed mouth. 'Hey, if you've got it, flaunt it. Besides, the old guy loves it. And what better way to ensure we keep getting the best coffees this side of Carlton, huh?'

Natasha chuckled and took another mouth-watering sip of her mocha-coffee blend. 'You're a menace.'

'And you are changing the subject. Is there anything else about this prince I should know?' Ella took a healthy slurp of her latte and sighed with pleasure.

'No.'

Though, try as hard as she could, Natasha couldn't dispel the memory of Dante's intense gaze as she'd handed over her card and he'd locked stares with her, his holding more than a hint of challenge. 'The prince will go about his business, I'll go about mine.'

'We talking about funny business, here?' Ella winked, and Natasha rolled her eyes before burying her twitching smile behind her giant mug.

'No, I'm not interested, and besides he's a prince,' Natasha said, amused by Ella's shenanigans despite herself.

'And?'

'And nothing.'

Natasha's response had a hollow ring to it and she knew it. However she wanted to explain it away, however she wanted to dress it up, the bizarre exchange with Dante hadn't been 'nothing'.

Dante was something.

Way too much something for her peace of mind.

'I'll let you finish your mocha,' Ella said, smiling at Natasha like a co-conspirator before spoiling the effect with, 'I'm sure you'll keep me posted about your stud-muffin prince.'

'He's not my prince!'

However, as the words left Natasha's mouth, she wondered what the stab of disappointment was about.

Natasha had just stepped out of the shower and slipped into a fluffy purple bathrobe when her mobile rang. She considered ignoring it, as she had a date with a thriller DVD and a super-size bowl of her favourite choc-fudge ice-cream.

However, it could be her dad calling from Perth.

Or it could be the prince.

She wavered for a few seconds, hoping for the

former, knowing a quick glance at call display would put her out of her misery. The phone continued to shrill its funky tune, and she finally gave up, crossing the room and grabbing it out of her bag.

She didn't know the number.

Punching the answer button, she put on her best phone voice, the one Ella said could scare an army into battle.

'Natasha Telford speaking.'

'Natasha, Dante here. I need your help. Urgently.'

She swallowed, surprised by the quick thrill of pleasure at the sound of his deep voice, annoyed that the movie and ice-cream would have to wait.

'What's up?'

'I'm being followed. Can you meet me out the front of the hotel in two minutes?'

Okay, so this was slightly crazy. What did he expect her to do—pull some bad-cop routine on his stalker, who was probably some lovesick girl anyway?

Shaking her head, she said, 'I'll be there.'

'Thanks, hurry,' he said, hanging up and leaving her staring at the phone.

'Drama prince!' she muttered, pulling on underwear, sweatpants and a hoodie in record time, slipping her feet into flip-flops and keys into her pocket.

She pulled her hair into a dripping ponytail as she rode the lift down to Ground, making it out the front of the hotel with thirty seconds to spare, and in time to see Dante strolling around the corner as if he didn't have a care in the world.

'So where's the fire?' she said, before he strode straight up to her, enfolded her into his arms and planted his lips on hers.

Nuts.

Insane.

Crazy.

However, as his warm, firm lips plied her with a skill she'd expect from a guy like him, her initial reaction that he'd lost his mind was quickly replaced by heat.

Burning, scorching, intense heat which raced through her body and promised to consume her from the inside out, the kind of heat that could make a girl lose her mind and do something completely out of character, like kiss him back.

Before she could react, he broke the kiss and murmured, 'Sorry, go with me for now.'

He didn't leave her much choice as he resumed kissing her, his arms sliding around her waist and feeling way too good, his chest pressed up against hers as one of his hands strummed her back like a virtuoso.

Natasha prided herself on her logic. She was a thinker, weighing up options carefully, always doing the right thing.

Then what on earth was she doing responding to the prince's passion, the heat crackling between them turning to bone-melting sizzle, enjoying this kiss more than she could've dreamed possible?

Someone moaned—to her endless embarrassment, she had a sneaking suspicion it was her—and she clung to him, belatedly realising that his rock-hard chest felt as good beneath her splayed palms as it looked.

Her senses reeled as he deepened the kiss to the point where she could've forgotten who she was, where she was and all the reasons she shouldn't be doing this, if it wasn't for one small intrusion.

'Natasha?'

Her head snapped back and her shocked gaze swung

between Dante, the prince who'd just lost his mind and kissed her senseless, and Clay, the man she'd once loved and now despised.

CHAPTER FOUR

'WHAT are you doing here?'

Natasha glared at Clay, hating the perfection of his smooth blond hair gelled within an inch of its life, the supercilious sneer, the cocky squared shoulders ready for battle.

She loathed him.

She despised him.

Yet she'd once loved him with all her heart.

Thank goodness she'd had a wake-up call before she'd made the biggest mistake of her life. Being engaged to the pompous ass had ruined her family as it was. She shuddered to think what would've happened if she'd gone all the way.

But then, she already knew.

The scumbag had told her in great detail when she'd broken off their engagement after learning the truth about why a suave entrepreneur was really interested in marrying a hotel jill of all trades.

'Guess there's no need to ask you,' Clay said, sending her a look that could kill. 'It's pretty obvious you've taken up sport since we parted. Tonsil hockey.'

'Leave the lady alone,' Dante said, his voice low with

menace, a protective arm still wrapped around her waist, and Natasha instinctively snuggled deeper before realising what she was doing. By then, she didn't want to move. Having his arm holding her, supporting her, felt way too good in the face of Clay's derision.

Clay's withering gaze turned on Dante. 'And I must've been mistaken about you. I thought you were the Prince of Calida back there, but guess I was wrong.'

'You got that right,' Dante said, his hand tightening on her waist.

Natasha stiffened, knowing how much Dante's privacy meant, and what a louse like Clay would do with the information if he found out. Guys like Clay did everything for a reason, which usually involved getting ahead in the world and looking out for number one.

'Instead, you're Natasha's new boyfriend. How sweet.'

There was nothing remotely sweet about the false saccharine dripping from Clay's every word or the nasty leer he turned on her. 'I should've known. There's no way a prince would be remotely interested in someone like you.'

Natasha flinched despite the shield she'd built around her ego after ending the relationship with Clay.

Damn him, for still having the power to hurt her.

Damn him, for being here and potentially ruining her plan to use the prince to salvage something from the mess he'd lumbered her family with.

'Apologise to the lady. Now.'

Dante's arm slipped from her waist as he took a step forward and, crazily, she missed its solid warmth.

Clay's sneer turned sinister, the same expression she'd seen eighteen months ago when she'd told him what he could do with his two-carat baguette diamond.

'And who are you to give me orders?' Clay matched Dante's step forward till the two were almost toe to toe.

Natasha laid a steadying hand on Dante's arm, shocked that she noticed how hot his bare skin felt under her palm and how much she liked it.

'He's someone you'll never be,' she said, wishing she'd had the guts to inject this much scorn into her voice the last time they'd spoken, when he'd threatened her family yet again. 'Now get lost.'

Clay's eyes narrowed to slits, reminding her of a snake she'd once seen at Australia's biggest reptile park: dangerous, slimy, lethal.

'You'll be sorry,' he said, so softly she could've imagined it.

However, Dante's bunched forearm muscles under her hand told her she hadn't. He was wound tighter than a spring, and looked ready to defend her honour whether she needed it or not.

As much as she liked his chivalry, she didn't need an international incident on her hotel's doorstep. Besides, Clay wasn't worth it. He wasn't worth anything as far as she was concerned.

Not any more.

'First you don't apologise, now you're threatening the lady? Who the hell do you think you are?'

Dante had shrugged off her restraining hand and now stood in Clay's face, while Natasha struggled between leaping on Dante's back to distract him and slugging Clay herself.

'I was the fool who was going to marry her,' Clay said, casting one last malevolent glare her way before turning on his heel and walking off.

Clay's cowardice shouldn't have surprised her.

Nothing about him surprised her, considering what he'd put her through, what he'd put her whole family through.

Dante turned to face her, incredulity lending his handsome face a comical look. 'You were engaged to that slime?'

'Don't remind me.'

She held up her hand as if trying to ward off any further talk of Clay. Needless to say, a smart guy like Dante didn't buy it for a second.

'You can do so much better than him.'

Dante spoke softly, his blue eyes warm, a tentative smile flirting around his mouth as he reached out and captured both her hands.

Natasha had expected him to interrogate her, to question her lousy judgement, to do any number of things apart from what he was doing now—holding her hands with a gentle tenderness that brought a lump to her throat.

She stared at their linked hands, enjoying the solid warmth they provided, a comfort which she'd never got from the few times Clay would deign to be touched in public.

Reality check—the guy is a prince. A prince you need to save your business. A prince who needs his identity protected, yet here you are getting all mushy with him out the front of your hotel.

Disengaging her hands from his, she folded her arms over her chest. 'So what was the urgent business?' *And what on earth was all that amazing kissing about?*

Though she wisely kept that question to herself for now. She needed to reassemble her wits before she tackled him over his lip-lock, considering her resistance was at an all-time low following his whole knight-in-shining-armour impersonation.

'That idiot was following me. He called out "prince" several times but I ignored him. I wanted you to meet me out the front so you could pretend to be my girlfriend and throw him off the track.'

He had the grace to look sheepish. 'I didn't know he was your ex. I'm sorry about that.'

Okay, so that explained his over-zealous welcome when he'd first seen her outside the hotel. But darn it, his kisses had seemed so real…

Giving herself a mental shake, Natasha tilted her chin up and glared at Dante. 'Pretty stupid plan.'

He shrugged, looking more adorable than guilty or apologetic with that sexy smile tugging at the corners of his mouth. 'It was all I could think of on the spur of the moment. I can't let anyone know who I am. You know that, it's too important to me.'

Natasha stifled a snort. Too important to his floozy, more like.

'When I gave you my number for emergencies, I didn't expect…' She trailed off, not wanting to bring up the sizzling kisses, knowing it couldn't be ignored. 'This,' she finished lamely, waving a hand between the two of them.

'You mean the way I kissed you?'

With a glint in his eyes, his gaze dropped to her lips, which tingled at the memory of his wonderful technique, how he'd made her forget every worry she had.

'Yes, that.'

Heat seeped into her cheeks, scorching with embarrassment. It wasn't so much the fact he'd kissed her but how she'd responded, like a woman who enjoyed it. Way too much. And she had an awful suspicion he knew that.

'Like I said, a spur of the moment thing, an impulse,'

he said, a hint of laughter in his voice. 'I apologise if it wasn't right.'

'Oh, no, it was fine,' she blurted, before clamping her lips shut in horror.

He'd meant it wasn't the right thing to do; she'd responded about his technique. Could the ground just open up and swallow her now—please?

Thankfully, he didn't call her on her monstrous gaff. He just stood there, looking way too sexy with his smile, his tousled hair and those gorgeous blue eyes sparkling with humour.

'Thank you for rescuing me,' he said, giving her another of those quaint little bows that must have been standard for royalty in Calida. 'Shall we retire?'

Natasha nodded and managed a sedate 'Uh-huh,' before she made a total ass of herself and took his question as an invitation to go up to his room and tuck his royal pain-in-the-butt in.

As they entered the elaborate lobby, and she caught site of herself in the huge ornate mirrors lining the pillars, Natasha stifled a groan. Grey sweatpants, a pale blue hoodie and navy beaded flip-flops did little to accentuate her make-upless face and wet ponytail.

She looked like a bedraggled waif next to a tanned god, and for a split second chastised herself for wishing things were different, annoyed that she cared.

Forgetting his royal status, she wondered what would it be like to stroll into a hotel with a guy like Dante by her side? A guy who protected his woman, a guy who looked like every woman's walking talking fantasy, a guy who could kiss like the prince in a fairy tale?

'In your dreams!' she muttered, grateful when the lifts came into sight.

'Pardon?'

She forced a tight smile. 'Goodnight.'

'Sleep well,' Dante murmured, planting a quick kiss on her cheek before she could move. 'And thank you once again.'

Natasha whirled on her heel and entered the lift for the apartments, her cheek tingling, her emotions in turmoil. She waited till she heard the zing of the lift for the hotel before turning around, hitting the button for her own floor and sinking against the side wall, grateful for the support.

She needed it. With her head spinning from encountering Clay, kissing Dante and the pathetic way she'd tied herself up in knots, she was a mess.

Definitely time for that choc-fudge ice-cream. Though, after the last half hour she'd had, nothing less than the tub would do now.

CHAPTER FIVE

DANTE shrugged out of his leather jacket, tossed it on the bed and headed for the bathroom. He needed a shower, a cold punishing shower, considering what he'd just done.

You didn't play fair, he muttered to his unshaven reflection in the huge mirror above an equally large marble basin as he braced himself against it.

Then again, who'd said anything about playing?

Adjusting the mixer, he splashed icy water on his face and dabbed it with a baby-soft towel which smelt like freshly squeezed lemons. Only the best for Telford Towers. And that extended to its stunning stand-in concierge who took her job to extremes.

He shouldn't have kissed Natasha.

He knew that.

She knew that.

But he'd gone ahead and done it anyway, giving her some lousy excuse about using her as his girlfriend to put that crazy jerk who'd been following him off the track.

He'd had it all worked out: get her to meet him out the front of the hotel, slip a casual arm around her shoulders, give her a quick peck on the cheek and stroll to the nearest café like they'd intended on meeting all along.

Instead, the minute he'd caught sight of her, all fresh faced and righteously indignant, his plans for a quick peck had taken on a life of their own and he'd swept her into his arms before he could think twice.

At least the ruse had worked.

But at what cost?

He'd sensed a connection between Natasha and her ex, some unfinished business. Unresolved feelings, perhaps?

If he'd jeopardised something for her, he should feel bad. Instead, the thought of that supercilious creep anywhere near the petite brunette made him want to order a royal head-lopping—if they still went in for that sort of thing in the twenty-first century.

The jerk had been rude, arrogant and condescending, and he couldn't see a feisty woman like Natasha putting up with him. Then again, what did he know about women? His sister Gina was driving him mad, and his mother would have him married off the second he stepped back on Calida.

Speaking of Gina, the way Natasha had handled the situation earlier could make her the perfect candidate for what he had in mind. After today, Dante couldn't handle Gina and her idiosyncrasies alone, that much was clear.

He needed the help of a woman, a very astute woman.

Thankfully, he had a good feeling that Natasha could be just what he was looking for.

Natasha sipped at her mocha-cappuccino and strode towards Telford Towers, unable to hide a proud smile behind her styrofoam mug. With the early morning sun tipping the sandstone turrets in pale gold, the cloudless blue sky framing the impressive façade and the gleaming windows, the place looked incredible.

It looked like home.

The only home she'd ever known.

Yeah, for how much longer?

Her smile vanished and she took another gulp of coffee, knowing the bitter aftertaste had nothing to do with caffeine and everything to do with Clay and his treachery.

The guy was pure evil and, the sooner she made the final two payments and got him out of their lives for good, the sooner she could rest easy.

Seeing him yesterday had resurrected too many painful memories: of how gullible and stupid she'd been to fall for his smooth lines and good looks. But it had been more than that.

Having Dante look at her with confusion that she could've been associated with a creep like Clay had affected her more than lousy memories. She didn't like looking a fool. She wanted him to see her as cool, collected and capable. After all, why else would he want to be associated with her hotel?

She'd cursed fate when she'd learned the truth about Clay and their engagement, and it looked like fate still liked to grab hold of her leg and yank hard. Only problem was, she wasn't laughing.

And she hoped Dante wouldn't think her a complete moron for ever looking twice at a guy like Clay.

Finishing off the last of the coffee, she tossed the mug in a bin and headed for the front of the hotel. She had five minutes before her shift started, and she wanted to have a quick chat with the night concierge before handover.

However, like most of her intentions these days, it wasn't meant to be.

'Can I have a word?'

Dante stepped from the shadows of an ornate column

near the hotel's entrance, and she had no option but to stop. Either that or fob off her big chance to save the hotel once and for all.

'Sure, but I don't have long,' she said, fixing a polite smile on her face, hoping her surprise didn't show.

For royalty, this guy had the whole casual thing down pat. Dark denim, khaki T-shirt, boat shoes. Throw in the mussed hair and designer stubble, and he looked like he'd just strolled in from a dawn sail on the bay—wind-ruffled, tousled and sexy. Very, very sexy.

'This won't take long.'

He laid a hand in the small of her back and propelled her to a quiet spot behind a towering flower pot.

'If this is about last night, don't worry about it. I'm not.'

Yeah, right. That's why she'd guzzled a half-carton of ice-cream, missed most of the best thriller released this year and spent half the night tossing and turning over the way he'd kissed her.

'Actually, this has got something to do with last night.'

He rubbed a hand over his face, a strangely weary gesture for a guy who had it all.

'I was very impressed with how you handled the situation, and I was wondering if you'd consider being my temporary PA for the next week?'

'What?'

Okay, so the whole jaw-dropping thing wouldn't look too good, but for a minute there she could've sworn His Royal Scruffiness had asked her to be his PA?

'I know it sounds crazy, but the family business I need to take care of is a lot more complicated than I first thought. I need help and that's where you come in. If you'll agree, that is.'

He smiled, a beguiling, seductive grin that could've

coerced an ice-cream addict to part with her last scoop. Totally unfair.

'So, you do have family business?'

Oops; her first thought slipped out before she could stop it and she hoped he'd gloss over it. *As if.*

'Of course. That's what I told you before.'

A tiny frown marred the almost too-perfect rugged face before a spark of enlightenment flashed in his eyes.

'You didn't believe me.'

'No…yes…of course I did,' she blustered on like a moron, a growing blush adding to her embarrassment.

What was it about this guy that tied her up in knots? She'd handled VIPs her whole life and had never been this flustered, this out of control.

Okay, so most of those guys had looked like the back end of a Melbourne tram, but that didn't mean anything. It wasn't Dante's sexy looks that had her flustered—well, not much anyway—but more to do with the way he made her feel: valued, important, someone he could depend on.

'No, you didn't. What did you think I was doing here a week earlier than my official business?'

Natasha took a steadying breath. Ella often accused her of being brutally frank but now wasn't a time to be honest.

'Well, I thought you might've had other friends to visit, apart from family, that is.'

Hmm…not a bad save.

'You thought I had some secret mistress hidden away somewhere, didn't you?'

Not a bad save…a terrible one! He hadn't bought her fluffed explanation for a second. So the guy wasn't just a pretty face. Couldn't he have some flaws?

When in doubt, Natasha reverted to type and went on the offensive.

'Mistress? You sound like you've stepped out of the seventeenth century. I didn't think you royal types would use terminology like that any more.'

She sent an obvious glance at her watch, implying she had more important things to do, like start work, rather than stand here and feel like a fool.

For that's exactly what she was, a big fool, making assumptions about a guy she didn't know and solely based on his royal status and incredible looks.

'You don't think much of me, do you?'

His clear blue eyes narrowed, watching her, assessing her, probably judging her, just as she'd judged him.

She stiffened, hating that her plan to smooth things over after last night's fiasco was going horribly awry.

'I don't know you.'

He paused, his face inscrutable, before the corners of his mouth twitched. 'Well, we'll just have to remedy that, won't we? And what better way than have you help me out as my PA for the next week?'

'You're crazy. I have a job, remember? And speaking of which...' She tapped her watch face and sent a pointed glance over his shoulder. 'The concierge will be late if you don't let me go.'

'I'd only need a few hours of your time each day. Maybe after your shift? I promise it won't be difficult. I just need someone with local knowledge of Melbourne, and I think you'd be perfect. From what I've seen, you can handle anything.'

His lips curved into a knowing smile, the type of smile that implied he knew exactly how he'd affected her last night with those scintillating kisses, whether they'd been part of a mock charade or not.

'You will be handsomely reimbursed.'

Natasha refrained from snorting. *Handsomely reimbursed.* Despite his scruffy appearance, he really did sound like a pompous…pompous…*prince* at times!

'I don't need your money.'

However, as soon as the words flew out of her mouth, she knew it was a lie. The hotel did need the money. Though Dante couldn't offer her anywhere near the kind of money that would come close to clearing her debts.

Suddenly, inspiration struck. She needed what his reputation could bring to the hotel—the prestige, the raised profile, the fame would send bookings through the roof—and she'd intended on approaching him for help at the end of this week.

But what about right now? The way she saw it, a perfect exchange: her help with his mysterious 'family business' in exchange for his princely profile once he came out of the royal closet at the end of the week.

She couldn't lose.

'I won't take your money, but I think we could come to some other sort of arrangement,' she said, hoping he'd go for her idea.

Rather than looking surprised, his eyes glittered with intrigue as he leaned towards her, enveloping her in a sensual cloud of fresh air, the citrus soap the hotel favoured and pure Dante. Intoxicating, heady and totally addictive…if she lost her mind!

'What sort of arrangement did you have in mind?' His low, husky voice rippled over her, making her feel more woman than she ever had in all the clinches with Clay.

'Not that sort!'

She stepped back and held her hands up, as if trying to ward him off. This guy was seriously dangerous to her peace of mind. She should be telling him what to do with his PA offer and running a hundred miles in the opposite direction.

However, she didn't have an option. She'd plain run out of options around the time she'd landed her family in this mess in the first place.

Dante was the answer to her problems. All she had to do was get her overactive imagination under control and she'd be fine. Telford Towers would be fine. Her family wouldn't lose the business that meant everything to them, and her friends and employees wouldn't be homeless and jobless.

She could do this.

She had to.

'The hotel needs to raise its profile, and I was hoping after your week of going incognito is over you wouldn't mind me advertising the fact of your presence here. Perhaps take part in some promotions?'

The sensual glitter vanished in a second, his eyes turning a cold, hard, arctic blue. 'Fine.'

Though he didn't look fine. In fact, he looked like she'd just insulted him.

'Look, if you're not comfortable—'

'I said it's fine. Your help in exchange for mine. Now, what time do you finish?'

'Three.'

'I'll meet you in the lobby at three-thirty.' He sent her a brief, dismissive nod, and she knew exactly how his army of servants must feel back in his homeland.

'Okey dokey,' she muttered, casting a confused glance his way before heading inside.

However, she'd barely made it past him when he stopped her with a hand on her arm. She stared at his hand: the long, elegant fingers, the clean, blunt fingernails, and the smooth tanned skin. The type of hand that had never done a day's manual labour in its life, the type of hand used to the best manicures and people fawning over it—the type of hand she should scorn but couldn't, when its barest touch sent her pulse tripping.

'Thank you,' he said, so softly she had to lean forward to hear it, giving her another whopping dose of his heady scent.

'No worries.'

She managed a tight smile before slipping out of his grasp and heading into the hotel.

No worries indeed…

CHAPTER SIX

AFTER slipping into black denim hipsters, a funky red top and pulling her hair free of its constricting chignon she usually wore for work, Natasha barely had time to run a brush through her kinky hair and slick gloss over her lips before rushing out to meet Dante.

'Hey, where's the fire? Or, more to the point, where's the fireman?' Ella wolf whistled as the lift doors slid open and Natasha all but tumbled in.

'I've got a meeting,' Natasha said, avoiding Ella's inquisitive stare as she smoothed her hair in the mirror over the lift buttons.

'With anyone I know?'

Ella's silky tone told Natasha her best friend knew exactly where she was going and who she was meeting.

'Dante and I have some business to discuss.'

'I just bet you do.'

Ella made childish puckering noises and Natasha rolled her eyes.

'So, how's it going with the bad boy formerly known as prince?'

Natasha chuckled at her friend's joke. 'Not bad. He's actually an okay sort of guy.'

'I know, I know.' Ella made mock fanning motions in front of her face. 'I saw him in the lobby today. And, let me tell you, okay doesn't begin to describe that guy!'

'He is pretty hot, isn't he?'

Okay, so she was only human. She could admit the obvious without letting the fact turn her head.

'Hot?' Ella's voice shot up five octaves. 'The guy is drop-dead gorgeous! Pity about the royal stuff, because he'd be perfect for you.'

'What makes you say that?'

Ella knew she'd been through hell with Clay, though she didn't know the half of it or why Natasha so desperately needed Dante's co-operation. Ella knew she rarely dated and how she'd totally lost trust in guys. So what made her think some prince she barely knew would be perfect for her?

'Oh…just something he said.'

Ella studied her chipped fingernails at arm's length, trying to stifle a cheeky grin and losing.

'What did you do?'

Natasha's heart sank to the soles of her high-heeled black boots. Though she loved Ella dearly, subtlety wasn't one of her friend's strong suits. And if she'd said something to Dante…*help*!

'Nothing.' Ella widened her blue eyes, aiming for a guileless look and failing miserably.

'Ella!'

'Okay, okay. All I did was ask him if he'd seen the concierge because I needed to ask you something, and he got this goofy look on his face when he glanced over at your desk. That's it, I swear.'

'You sure?'

'Positive.'

'Stay out of this, El,' Natasha said, as the lift slid to a smooth stop and the steel doors opened. 'I mean it,' she added as Ella opened her mouth to respond.

'Spoilsport,' Ella muttered as she brushed past her, twirling to a stop when they exited the lift, waiting for the doors to close on a large group of Japanese tourists. 'Enjoy your *meeting*.'

Natasha resisted the urge to poke her tongue out at Ella's retreating back. She didn't expect a bit of imaginary matchmaking from Ella, who was usually totally pragmatic, even if she did flirt with every guy lucky enough to enter her sphere.

The only goofy look Ella must've seen on Dante's face was the same look Natasha had got this morning when she'd proposed he help her with promoting the hotel. Now that suggestion had gone down a treat—not.

His frigid expression had been pure royal, a cold reaction used to snub people who didn't please him, and entirely at odds with his casual appearance. He might try to play down his royal blood for the week with laid-back clothes and ruffled hair, but she knew better. Guys like him were used to being obeyed, used to things going their way, and he probably hadn't liked being trumped by an upstart like her.

What did he think, she'd help him purely out of the goodness of her heart?

Yeah, right. She'd tried that once before and look where it had landed her: neck-deep in financial trouble.

She'd been gullible, trusting and sweet at one time. Not any more.

Dante had something she wanted and vice versa.

She just hoped she wouldn't confuse exactly what it was she wanted from him.

* * *

'You want my help with *what*?'

Natasha stared at Dante like he'd just asked her to strip naked and dance down Bourke Street.

He shrugged, a sheepish expression on his way-too-handsome face, managing to look needy and gorgeous at the same time. 'You live in Melbourne. You'd know where all the best toy stores are and who I can hire to organise the best party.'

'For a two-year-old?'

She shook her head and blew her fringe out of her eyes. She should've stuck with the chignon. That way, she could've taken out the pin holding it up and stabbed him with it.

'It's hard work. I spent the whole day traipsing around your city yesterday and came up with nothing. I have a few days to get this party organized, and I don't know where to start.'

'Then why did you take it on?'

His eyes glittered with emotion and she swallowed her next sarcastic question about what an Italian prince would know about kiddie parties.

'My sister is a scatterbrain. She isn't the most organised person in the world, and by what I've seen so far planning stuff like birthday parties isn't her forte. I want Paolo to have a special day.'

A day he probably wouldn't remember when he was older, but Natasha kept that gem to herself too.

So the guy had a good heart. She couldn't fault him for caring about his nephew. But a kid's party? She knew as much about organising that as she did abseiling. Absolutely nothing.

'Think you can do it?'

She met his challenging gaze head-on, knowing

she'd make this work if she had to don a clown costume and take a crash course in juggling herself.

This was too important.

Getting Dante's reciprocal help at the end of the week was vital.

Tilting her head up, she said, 'You bet. Let's get started.'

'I knew I could count on you.'

He smiled, just another of his regular run-of-the-mill smiles which made her feel like she was the only woman in the world. Obviously a part of his Prince Charming act, something he used to coerce people to bend to his will on a daily basis, but boy did those curving lips pack a power punch!

'First up, we'll need to surf the Net, come up with a concise list. It'll save us loads of time. Then I'll narrow down the choices with your help and check out our options.'

'Very efficient.'

'Okay, then. I'll get to it.'

He arched an eyebrow, the imperious prince questioning a serf's insubordination, and she stifled a smile at the analogy.

'I thought we'd be working on this together?'

Oh no. He'd thought wrong. Spending one-on-one time with the gorgeous prince, work or not, wouldn't be good. He awakened feelings in her she'd rather suppress. Feelings of being appreciated and, worse, feeling like he saw her as a woman, an attractive woman, and she wouldn't go there. She couldn't. She'd done it before with a smooth, handsome charmer and her battered self-esteem was still recovering.

'I don't need you.'

Ouch! That came out a lot harsher than she'd

intended and she bit her lip, wishing he didn't make her feel so gauche, so out of her depth.

'You sure about that?'

A teasing glint lighting his eyes, he leaned forward a centimetre. It felt much closer, like he'd infused her personal space with too much manly presence, and she was grateful that they hadn't left the lobby yet.

'Positive.'

Her less than emphatic nod did little to convince him, given his lips curved upwards in a knowing smile.

'Look, I want your help, but I need to be involved in this too. That's the whole point of me coming out here a week earlier and going through this ruse. I wanted to make this special for Paolo, to get to know my nephew, and I can't do that if I delegate all the work to you. I'd hoped we'd work as a team, you coming up with the information I need, me having enough input to feel like I'm not a totally useless uncle breezing through on a fly-by-night official visit.'

The anti-men shield surrounding Natasha's heart cracked just a fraction at his declaration. Who couldn't like a guy for wanting the best for his little nephew?

If only Dante could be more uppity, more demanding, more…princely! That way, she could despise him for his airs and keep him at arm's length. As it was she found him too attractive, and now with this softer side she had a sinking feeling he could undermine her carefully erected defences all too easily.

She didn't like trusting men.

She didn't like opening herself up to feeling like a fool.

And she sure didn't like her self-esteem taking another swan dive when she admitted that the only reason a guy like Dante paid any attention to her was because of what she could do for him.

'Okay. I'll get my laptop and meet you back here. We can grab a coffee at one of the nearby trattorias while we work.'

'Perfect,' he said, pinning her with an intense stare that made her wish for a host of crazy things: that his husky 'perfect' referred to her, that her not-so-perfect persona was willing to take a chance on having a little fun, and that maybe, just maybe, she could shrug off the weight of familial responsibility weighing down her shoulders and live a little today without thinking about tomorrow.

'Back in a sec.'

She turned and managed to walk to the lift with all the finesse of a runway model, minus the hip swivels those girls had down pat. However, she couldn't shake the feeling Dante watched her every step, and when she risked a quick glance over her shoulder before stepping into the lift, which thankfully appeared sooner rather than later, he raised his hand in a brief wave.

She stumbled into the lift and hit the button for her floor, leaning on the cool steel wall for support.

So much for poise.

It wasn't his wave that had undermined her cool act as much as the sexy grin which said he'd watched her fake strut to the lift and had enjoyed every minute of it.

Prince or not, saving her hotel or not, the guy was trouble.

And it looked like she'd just landed in a whole heap of it.

Dante dealt with people from all walks of life, from diplomats to prime ministers, kings to blue-collar workers.

His mum said he had a gift for reading people, for knowing the right thing to say and when.

Somehow, the way the woman sitting next to him reacted every time he opened his mouth, he felt his 'gift' needed some serious re-wrapping.

'Come up with anything yet?'

She held up her hand, a tiny frown creasing her brow, giving her an utterly adorable studious look.

'Give me another minute then I'll show you what I've got.'

'Good,' he said, sitting back to finish his espresso and free to study her.

He couldn't figure her out.

She had this uptight business persona that she wore with pride, even in her out of work hours. And though she dressed like any other fashion-loving woman in her twenties—he'd had a difficult time tearing his eyes away from the way her cute butt had filled out the black denim earlier and how that racy red top accentuated every luscious curve—she didn't act her age.

He found spontaneous, fun-loving and flirty women irresistible. Yet, Natasha didn't appear to have an impulsive bone in her sensational body. She was serious, fastidious and solemn. What would it take to get her to loosen up a little?

Why do you care?

He sipped his espresso, studying the way her shiny brown hair hung in a sleek curtain around her face, a deep, rich brown, the colour of Swiss chocolate, and a perfect frame for her expressive face. He wouldn't call her beautiful in the classical sense but there was something about her that was striking...the full lips, the slightly elongated nose, the large hazel eyes... Her face was memorable, and he could easily spend the next few hours staring at it.

By the serious frown she fixed him with when her gaze swung up to meet his, he guessed that wouldn't be happening.

'Okay, here's what I've come up with so far.'

She grabbed a pen and started ticking off the extensive list she'd made as she'd surfed the Net. 'We've got pony parties, Clarice the Clown, roaming reptiles, magicians, ventriloquists, go-karts, mobile animal farms, painting parties, fire engines and the old standard bouncy castles.'

She looked at him expectantly, not waiting for a response, before snapping her fingers. 'Or, if Paolo is a new-age sort of guy, there are fairies, discos and belly dancers.'

Dante shook his head. For a guy who'd hosted world summits and mastered complex budgets, he had no idea when it came to this sort of stuff. 'You discovered all that in ten minutes?'

'Uh-huh.'

Her sceptical look said it all. She obviously wondered why he hadn't jumped on a computer and done the same, and he'd be damned if he clued her in to the fact he had other people do this type of research work for him all the time.

She already seemed to have little regard for his background; there was no use emphasising the yawning gap between them.

'Well done. How about we narrow it down to about three and screen them tomorrow?'

Her eyebrows shot up. 'You want me to interview some clown?'

'No. I need you to make sure the reptiles are docile enough.'

'As if.'

She joined in his laughter, and it took every ounce of his willpower not to take advantage of the shared camaraderie of the moment and ask her what was bothering her, why the reticence.

'I want Paolo's party to be perfect, and I have full confidence you'll ensure that.'

He barely caught her muttered 'I'm glad someone has confidence in me,' as he leaned forward to get a better look at her list, rather pleased it brought him closer to her.

She wore a subtle fragrance, a light floral, which intrigued him. The smell had lingered after she'd joined in the girlfriend charade, his senses filled with the taste of her lips, the feel of her in his arms and the unique scent which enticed him to come back for more.

'Personally, for a two-year-old, I'd go with the animals or the bouncy castle. All kids like animals and have energy to burn.'

She rapped the pen against the list, studying it with great attention to detail and avoiding looking at him.

'Let's consider both possibilities tomorrow.'

He reached out and stilled her hand with his, her head snapping up as she shot him a startled look. However, she didn't pull away, and in that first loaded second when her gaze met his, he saw something which surprised him.

Pure, honest interest. A spark of something more, something bordering on desire?

It couldn't be.

He was projecting his own attraction to the sexy brunette onto her, wishing for something that wasn't there. Not that he would act on his impulse if there was.

He didn't do dalliances, especially when visiting foreign countries. He'd made that mistake once before, and the ensuing publicity had dogged him for months.

'Can I borrow this? I want to make a list of possible gifts before I forget.'

He plucked the pen out of her fingers, wondering if she bought his smooth cover-up for the momentary gaff.

Touching her wasn't a good idea when looking was difficult enough.

'Sure.'

She reached for her lukewarm latte, avoiding his eyes.

Damn. So much for that camaraderie he'd imagined a few moments ago.

'I'm thinking about buying a racing-car set, an electric train-set, a few computer games, something along those lines.'

She rolled her eyes, just as he'd expected her to at his ludicrous suggestions, but at least he'd achieved what he'd set out to do. She was looking at him again.

'You have no idea about kids, do you?'

'Not much.'

A fact which saddened him. For a carefree bachelor who knew his single days were numbered—Calida needed heirs, and it was only a matter of time before he succumbed to his mother's meddling—he wasn't so scared of losing his freedom any more, and kids were a part of that.

Not that he'd ever been free in the true sense of the word. He'd had responsibilities from the time of his birth, and with the early death of his father and his mum threatening to abdicate and hand over the reign to him any day now, he'd never been free.

'Okay. Here's what we'll do. Tomorrow after work, we'll check out the animals and the castle then we'll hit Toys R Us for some serious gift hunting. Sound like a plan?'

He nodded, enjoying her take-charge attitude. It got tiring making all the decisions all the time.

'Are you always this organised and thorough?'

She blushed and fiddled with the list, folding the paper edges into tiny creases. 'I try to be,' she said, her tone defensive.

'Relax. It was a compliment.'

'Thanks.'

She didn't look grateful. In fact, she looked downright uncomfortable, and Dante knew he had to quit while he was behind. Yet another conversation heading south with the woman he couldn't read.

And it was frustrating the hell out of him.

'Would you like to have dinner before we go back?'

He asked out of politeness, but a small part of him wished she'd accept. He never had a chance to eat like this: casually, anonymously, without a horde of people waiting for him to finish his soup or take a sip of wine before touching their own.

'Thanks, but it's been a long day.'

She gathered her papers, laptop and pens and stuffed them all into a large black bag which looked like it could carry a year's worth of hotel bathroom supplies.

'Maybe tomorrow?'

A half-hearted nod in his direction didn't inspire him with confidence, and he knew without a doubt the minute they concluded their business tomorrow night he'd get the same response.

He couldn't figure her out.

It was driving him insane.

CHAPTER SEVEN

'SO YOU won't eat with me but you'll let me buy you a drink?'

Natasha cradled her glass, swirled the full-bodied shiraz and stared into its ruby depths. Nope, no answers to her confusion there, considering she'd been wondering the same thing since they'd entered the Lobby Bar a few minutes ago.

'I usually have a nightcap before I go to bed,' she said, knowing her steaming mug of hot chocolate complete with two pink marshmallows didn't really compare to sharing a smooth red with a sexy prince.

'Really?'

He quirked an eyebrow, no doubt at the thought of her quaffing wine by herself before bed. Hmm…not the type of image she wanted to portray.

'I'm a cocoa addict,' she admitted, joining in his laughter and ruining her sophisticated act totally. 'But this is great,' she quickly added, lifting her glass in his direction, feeling gauche and unworldly compared with his polish.

'You didn't really answer my question,' he said, fixing her with the type of stare she imagined he used on wayward inferiors.

'Maybe I didn't want to bruise your ego totally, so softened the blow of refusing dinner by sharing a wine with you?'

His startled expression had her hiding a grin behind her wine glass. She doubted His Royal Highness received many knock-backs let alone had his ego bruised too often.

In reality, she'd refused his dinner invitation because it had seemed too intimate. She was attracted enough to him without sitting across a cosy table for two for hours, giving him the opportunity to captivate her with his natural charm.

Dante made her feel like a woman and then some, the monstrous cultural gap between them disappearing when he stared at her like every word she uttered was a riveting soliloquy. Worse, he made her forget every logical reason why she was with him—to work—and that scared her beyond belief.

He shook his head, smiling. 'You're still not answering me.'

Uh-oh; it looked like she couldn't put him off. She could try flirting, which she was hopeless at, or she could fluff around and look more of a fool in the process. Or she could take the only way out she knew and be upfront.

'Honestly? I feel out of my depth around you.'

His smile disappeared in a flash, replaced by an instant frown. 'How so?'

Natasha sighed, hating her bluntness at times. How could she articulate how Dante made her feel when she barely knew herself?

'I'm not sure. I guess it's been a while since I've socialised outside of work, and I'm not so good at it any more.'

'Have I made you feel inferior in some way? Is that the problem?'

'No!'

'Would you like some time to think about that?'

Natasha chuckled. 'You're not like that. In fact, apart from the odd pompous word or two, you're nothing like what I imagined royalty to be.'

He didn't have an Italian accent, but she guessed that's because he'd gone to school in England and spent most of his schooling life there, or so his Net profile said, but he didn't speak with a plum in his mouth either. Also, his laid-back attitude surprised her, and he didn't use power like she'd assumed he would.

Unlike Clay, who'd thought nothing of belittling waiters or valets when it suited.

'Then what's the problem? It was only dinner.'

Exactly. It wasn't like he'd asked her to spend the night or anything.

Oh-oh. She didn't want to think about what spending the night with a guy like Dante would be like. If being around him had her flustered, imagining those sorts of scenarios would be enough to push her over the edge.

'Dinner seems more…casual. So far, every time we've met, it's for business and I want to keep it that way.'

'Understandable, but dinner can be businesslike.'

Given the glint in his too-blue eyes and the sexy smile playing about his mouth, the last thing she would be concentrating on over dinner was business.

Natasha twirled a strand of hair around her finger, wishing she'd never opened her big mouth and gone down this track in the first place. 'Can we change the subject, please?'

He hesitated before nodding. 'I've never met a woman so honest before. It's refreshing.'

It's suicidal, she thought, knowing she must look like

a backward hick to a refined man of the world like him. For goodness' sake, it had been only a simple dinner invitation and she was acting like an uptight prude.

She wished she was the type of girl to flirt, have fun and then wave *bon voyage* to Dante at the end of his stay. But she wasn't. She'd never been frivolous, and her bitter experience with Clay had ruined her take-a-chance side.

Sure, Dante was gorgeous and nice and nothing like she'd expected, but she couldn't do the whole casual thing. It just wasn't her.

'You don't appreciate me talking so openly?'

'Like you, I find it refreshing. I'm not used to it.'

Clay had been a duplicitous creep, and she hated her foolishness in believing every word his lying mouth had uttered.

'You have been hurt.'

He pronounced it like a royal decree, and she wavered for a second, torn between unburdening herself and running screaming from the room.

She really shouldn't drink wine on an empty stomach; it gave her crazy ideas.

Perhaps she could move on one day and learn to trust again. Though trust a prince with the looks of a model and the glib lines of a playboy? She'd do better trusting a snake.

'Not hurt so much as had my eyes opened. The business world is tough, and Telford Towers means a lot to me. I've invested my life in the place.'

Nice save.

She'd brushed aside his personal take on her ramblings and turned it into a business one. Now maybe she could take her foot out of her mouth and turn the next few minutes into a pleasurable exchange of light-hearted conversation rather than baring her soul and sending the prince running.

She'd never done the normal dating thing other girls did, just never had the time, and it showed. Here she was, sharing a perfect shiraz with a gorgeous prince, and she was one step away from making a prize ass of herself. She really needed to get out more.

'The business world is a cut-throat one. And I can see why this hotel means so much to you.'

He raised his glass in the general direction of the mahogany woodwork and brass sconces, and she sighed in relief. He'd bought her brush-off.

'You have done a marvellous job here. I'm not surprised you agreed to my outlandish proposal if I can help you let the world know about this.'

She almost choked on her wine, clearing her throat with a few discreet coughs. If he only knew her actual motivation…

'Being your PA for a week isn't so unusual.'

'But checking out animals and bouncy castles is,' he said, his smile crinkling the laugh lines around his eyes and adding to his charm. 'I'm not sure quite what to expect.'

She relaxed, the wine warming her from the inside out while the easy-going camaraderie they shared surrounded her in a comforting cocoon. 'In this business, I'm used to handling anything, so stick with me and you'll be fine.'

'Does that mean you'll protect me from rabid raccoons and scary clowns?'

Crooking her finger at him, she leaned forward. 'I'll let you in on a secret. We don't have raccoons in Melbourne, let alone rabid ones. As for the clowns, they're just make-believe. But, rest assured, if Your Highness is in any danger from cute furry animals or kids' entertainers, I'll protect you.'

He joined in her laughter and she leaned back, the sting of tears taking her completely by surprise.

Tears? What was happening to her? She never cried. Not any more. She'd shed enough to fill the Pacific Ocean when she'd discovered the truth behind Clay's impulsive proposal and later over her mum's death. Tears were wasteful, futile and draining.

She had more important things to worry about these days, like the Towers surviving.

If a glass of wine and some light-hearted conversation made her this maudlin, she'd never make a dating diva. Her impulsive decision to share a drink with him would definitely be her last, if this was how she carried on!

Forcing a hearty laugh, she ignored the real reason behind her sudden self-pity. She liked the warmth, the shared conversation, the time with Dante, and the thought she would soon lose it saddened her more than she expected.

You don't have to think beyond tomorrow or next week. Just enjoy his company, maybe a dinner here or there, and that's it. Your confidence is low, what better way to build it up than with a guy who looks like Dante paying you compliments?

Mistaking her sudden downturn in mood, he said, 'Forgive my lame attempts at humour. I'll be fine with the animals, even imaginary raccoons, I promise.'

Natasha drained her glass, and placed it on a coaster on the side table.

'Your humour is fine; it's this marvellous wine that

has me rather tired and drifting off. I'm sorry for being such poor company.'

As if sensing her need for solitude, he placed his half-empty glass on the table and stood, extending a hand to help her up.

'I'm being insensitive. You've worked hard all day in the hotel and then I've made you work even harder with my business. Thank you for sharing the wine and your company, but it is time to say goodnight.'

She accepted his hand, her knees wobbling slightly as she stood, though that had nothing to do with the fine wine and everything to do with the finer prince's welcoming touch.

'Thank you,' she said, matching his formality, her heart sinking at the yawning gap between them. He may try to look the part of a bad-boy, but when he spoke like that he drew her attention to their differences and put her fanciful imagination firmly back in its place. 'I'll see you tomorrow.'

'Until then.'

Their gazes locked, and for one, insane second she thought he would raise her hand to his lips and kiss it. Instead, he gave it a gentle squeeze and released it. Acute disappointment effectively doused the alcohol in her system.

She managed a tremulous smile as they parted in the foyer, her stomach doing funny flip-flops as she watched him enter the lift.

Crazy.

She was one-hundred-percent crazy for turning what could've been a pleasant evening into a tense mess.

She'd been so busy mulling over Dante's intentions lately, wondering if he was toying with her, if there was more behind needing her help with his family business, that she'd stopped being able to consider the situation rationally.

So, her confidence was at an all-time low. She didn't have to impress the guy, just lighten up a little and enjoy his company. No big deal.

Natasha straightened and headed for her office, silently vowing to loosen up around Dante, starting tomorrow.

'Not a raccoon in sight.'

'Lucky for you,' Natasha said, her gaze riveted to Dante's denim-clad butt as he bent over to pick up a rabbit. So, there was no harm in looking. She could appreciate a fine tail—rabbit, of course!—like the next girl.

'We don't have places like this in Calida. I'm impressed.'

Dante cuddled the white furry rabbit he'd picked up close against his broad chest. Natasha quickly looked away before she decided to take the rabbit's place.

The guy was gorgeous, rich, genuinely nice and loved animals?

There had to be a catch.

Maybe he hid a pointy tail beneath those faded denims and kept his pitchfork in the closet?

'The animals are pretty cute,' she said, picking up a Dalmatian puppy and laughing as it licked under her chin. 'Make that seriously cute.'

'You said it,' he said, his gaze unerringly locked on her and not on the wriggling puppy in her arms.

Oh boy.

Heat crept into her cheeks as she bent down and placed the puppy next to its siblings, giving it a final pat with reluctance. One of the drawbacks of spending her life growing up in a hotel was the 'no pets' policy. She'd petted other kids' guinea pigs and kittens at school, but it wasn't till recently that she really craved the company and unconditional love of a pet.

Dogs didn't usually turn on their buddies—unlike smarmy fiancés.

Standing up and dusting off her turquoise jacket, she said, 'Okay. I take it the animals are a hit. I'll organise the booking. Day after tomorrow? Eleven a.m.?'

'Sounds good,' Dante said, smiling at her like she'd worked some kind of miracle rather than found suitable entertainment for his nephew's party.

'Okay then.'

But Natasha didn't move. She wanted to, but her feet wouldn't co-operate. Instead, her attention stayed riveted to Dante's hands and the gentle way they stroked the previously quivering rabbit, which had stilled and seemed quite content to burrow into his arms.

She couldn't blame the animal for that. It looked like a mighty comfortable place to be.

Stroke…stroke…soft, rhythmic strokes, with those strong yet elegant hands, a gently lulling motion which she could've watched for ever. She suddenly wished for a pair of long ears and a fluffy tail!

'Bouncy castles next?'

Her gaze snapped up to his, curiosity lighting the blue depths of his eyes, and she mentally slapped herself for being so out of touch with guys that the mere sight of one patting a rabbit had her hypnotised.

'You bet. Meet me at the front desk. We'll finalise the deposit then it's onto something you'll be great at testing out.'

His forehead crinkled in confusion and she laughed.

'Castles? You being royalty and all? Or has this anonymity for a week gone to your head?'

He chuckled, a forced sound with no genuine amusement in it.

'Do you live in a castle?'

They hadn't talked about his sovereignty much. In fact, they hadn't talked much at all, unless it involved perpetrating his subterfuge, organising his nephew's party or her lack of social skills. What better way to loosen up a little and learn something about the guy in the process?

'Yes. It has been in my family for generations,' he said, placing the rabbit back in its pen and dusting off his hands.

Okay, so he didn't want to elaborate. Maybe if she lightened the mood he'd be more forthcoming.

'Complete with drawbridge, moat and dungeons?'

His mouth twitched. 'No, but it does have a fire-breathing dragon. Its name is Elena.'

'Sounds harmless enough.'

He rolled his eyes. 'You haven't met my mother!'

Natasha laughed, enjoying Dante's reversion to being teasing and funny. She didn't like the serious expression she'd glimpsed earlier, like he shouldered the weight of his country on his shoulders.

'Is your mum that bad?'

'She's been trying to marry me off for years. Looks like my stalling tactics won't work much longer.'

'Oh?'

He grimaced. 'Mother wants to hand over the throne to me as soon as possible. I need a wife for the country to take me seriously, for the people to see me as a genuine monarch and not some playboy prince. She's pushing and, quite frankly, I'm sick of running from the responsibility.'

'That's some responsibility,' she said, her heart

sinking that this vibrant, fun-loving guy would be forced into a marriage he didn't want.

Or, if she were completely honest, was she more upset at the thought of Dante married?

Not that it affected her one way or another. He'd be out of her life once his business in Australia was concluded and she'd never hear from him again.

Which is exactly why this whole 'lightening up' thing wasn't such a great idea. It led to all sorts of fantasies, like seeing herself living in a fairy tale castle beside her Prince Charming, just like she'd always imagined as a little girl growing up.

But life wasn't a fantasy. At least, not for her.

She had harsh realities to face up to, and a fair few responsibilities of her own. She could definitely empathise with him there.

'Let's not talk about that now. I'd prefer to concentrate on my time here in Melbourne,' he said, laying a guiding hand in the small of her back and propelling her towards the barn door. 'If my carefree days end when I get back to Calida, I intend to make the most of my stay in your beautiful city.'

'Good idea,' she said.

And it was. It made perfect sense.

Then why the awful feeling that she was just another attraction of Melbourne he intended on having a little fun with before he ascended to the throne?

Isn't that what you want? To have some fun, flirt, relax with a guy who won't pressure you?

Of course she wanted that. She'd decided as much last night after her chat with Ella.

Then why the hollow, empty feeling that there was more to life than fun?

For a girl who hadn't had any light-hearted fun in a long time, she shouldn't even be thinking long term. That was what had got her into trouble with Clay in the first place: limited romantic history, falling totally for the first guy to pay more than two seconds' attention to her, envisaging the whole 'white wedding' thing way too early.

Here was her golden opportunity to ease back into the dating stakes with a little harmless flirtation, and what was she doing? Worrying about whether he was dabbling with her or not.

She really needed to get a life.

'Is something wrong?'

Realising she hadn't moved past the doorway, she shook her head and sent him a confident smile. 'No. Just thinking about how much fun I'm going to have watching you test run the bouncy castles.'

'Is that right?'

His answering smile warmed her from the inside out, like the richest, sweetest hot chocolate.

'That's right. So come on, Your Highness. Let's see what you're made of.'

As they left behind the smells of warm, clean animals and dry hay, Natasha knew that whatever happened she intended on making the most of her limited brush with royalty.

'You call that jumping?'

Dante glared at Natasha, who was the smarter of the two of them, standing with both her feet firmly planted on the ground while he bounced around a huge piece of colourful blown-up plastic like a lunatic.

'If you're so clever, Miss Telford, why don't you show me how it's done?'

He folded his arms, which didn't improve his situation. He wobbled and would've fallen flat on his face if he hadn't stepped wider and braced himself.

'You're on,' she said, clambering up into the giant mock castle, complete with turrets and windows. 'Now, move over and you'll see what jumping's all about.'

However, he didn't move. He just stood there like a star-struck kid and watched a stunning woman bounce around him like a madwoman. A very beautiful madwoman, with her dark, shimmering hair streaming out behind her like a chocolate ripple, her hazel eyes glittering gold in the soft light filtering through the castle windows, and a smile on her face he'd never seen before.

He'd seen her forced smile, her polite smile, her business smile, but he'd never seen her like this. She looked genuinely happy, like she was having a good time, and he was glad.

Make that ecstatic.

He'd been completely honest with her earlier, as much as it had pained him to discuss the situation back home. Time enough to face his responsibilities. For now, he wanted to enjoy himself and, if it so happened to be in the company of a lovely woman like Natasha, all the better for him.

'Come on. Let's see who can jump the highest.' Her grin widened as she placed her thumb on her nose and wiggled her fingers at him. 'Unless His Highness is too chicken, that is?'

With a mock growl, Dante crouched and pushed up with all his strength, propelling himself high into the air. Natasha clapped her hands and laughed loudly. Until he came back down.

With the force of his jump, his landing wasn't so soft,

and the rubbery floor moved in a wave beneath his feet, tossing Natasha into the air like a featherweight. She landed in an undignified heap in the far corner of the castle, and Dante was torn between helping to her feet and keeping his distance in case he couldn't let her go once he helped her up.

'Good one. Lucky jump,' she said, leaping to her feet and bouncing towards him like a man walking on the moon.

'Are you all right?'

'Never better.'

He had to agree. Her eyes hadn't lost their sparkle and her cheeks glowed with vitality. And that mouth... With a jolt, Dante realised he wanted to kiss her. Badly.

When he'd kissed her outside the hotel as part of his pathetic ruse, it had been an impulse. Yes, he'd enjoyed it, and yes he'd been fantasising about more. Hell, he was a red-blooded male, and who wouldn't want the luscious woman before him in their arms?

But this was different.

His gaze strayed to her lips, stayed there, riveted by their fullness, their gloss, their delicious shape.

He wanted her with a ferocity that stunned him, and there weren't too many things in this world that surprised him any more. He'd seen a lot and done a lot in his time.

However, nothing in his past had prepared him for this unfamiliar helpless feeling, wanting something but with no idea how to go about getting it.

Or what he'd do with it if he got it.

'Okay. You asked for it.'

Natasha jumped, breaking his concentration, and in

a second he was jumping alongside her as they laughed and jostled and fell about like a couple of kids.

'You like?'

'I most certainly do,' he said, falling in an undignified heap next to her as they ricocheted off each other and collapsed to the rubber floor.

However, he wasn't talking about the castle, and by the gleam in her incredible eyes she knew it.

He expected her to look away as she'd done repeatedly before when he'd half flirted with her but she surprised him. She rolled onto her side, propped her head on her hand and stared right back.

'You know we're lying where thousands of grubby kids have jumped before?'

'So?'

'We'll probably get kid cooties.'

'Cooties?'

She smiled, a soft upward tilting of her lips that had him aching to reach out and trace their shape.

'You really are a prince, aren't you?'

'Did you doubt it before?'

Her smile widened, her teeth gleaming white in the filtered light. 'You don't exactly look the part.'

'And how do I look?'

'Like the type of guy my mum would've warned me to stay away from.'

'Ouch!'

He clutched his heart in mock pain, wishing she hadn't lost her smile when she'd mentioned her mother.

For some bizarre reason, lying here with her in the semi-darkness on an old piece of rubber invited questions, confidences, and he didn't want to lose the tentative connection he'd established with her. He thought he'd made a start on building bridges last night when she'd accepted his invitation to have a drink with him, but it hadn't happened and they'd parted on uncomfortably formal terms.

For some reason, he sensed she didn't trust him and, though he liked her honesty, she harboured secrets, bearing an undercurrent of emotion tinged with sadness. Perhaps if he drew her out, got her talking about herself, she'd learn to look at him like he wasn't the ruthless king out to trample on his serfs.

'You haven't mentioned your parents much before,' he said, expecting the shutters to come down, and pleasantly surprised when they didn't.

'My dad's in Perth on business for a month. He'll be back soon.' She paused, sadness flickering across her face like a shadow. 'Mum died a while ago. Heart attack.'

'I'm sorry,' he said, placing a comforting hand on her arm before thinking better of it.

Touching her so soon on the heels of his earlier impulse wouldn't be a good thing. No telling what he might do in the muted evening light in a mock castle with the most beautiful woman he'd ever seen.

Sadness fell across her face like a dark cloak. 'Thanks. It was tough. We were really close.'

'And there I was complaining about my own mother. You must think I'm heartless.'

And an unfeeling clod for blundering into territory he wished he'd never entered. Inviting confidences was one thing; making her sad after the evening they'd had was downright stupid.

'Everyone has their own demons to battle.'

She softened her words with a tentative smile, but not before he'd glimpsed the darkness in her eyes again, a darkness bordering on fear, the same fleeting expression he'd seen several times as if she had some awful secret weighing her down.

'I think all that jumping around has rattled our brains and made us morbid. How about we have a coffee?'

He wanted to say a meal, but thought better of it. She'd refused his dinner invitation last night; he wouldn't push his luck. He'd made inroads tonight, establishing more of a friendly interaction in how they related, and he didn't want to ruin it.

Besides, he had another favour to ask her and he had a feeling she'd draw the line at this one.

'Sounds great.'

She jumped up and dusted off her butt, sending a sizzle of heat shooting through him. She had a great body, and knew how to accentuate it. Tonight, she wore a soft, turquoise cashmere jacket, a clingy beige top underneath and camel hipsters with matching high-heeled boots. The outfit highlighted her light tan and chocolate-brown hair to perfection, and he'd been staring at her all night.

For a guy who'd socialised with the most beautiful women in the world, from supermodels, actresses and princesses, he'd never been as drawn to anyone as he was to her. Ironic, considering he couldn't do anything about it no matter how much he wanted to. There was a price to pay for his birthright, and at times like this it really hit home.

Sliding to the ground, he held out his arms to help guide her down. She hesitated a fraction and he wondered why. Surely he hadn't scared her off that much?

'Promise I won't drop you,' he said, lifting his arms higher.

'That's not what I'm afraid of,' she muttered under her breath, and as she leaned forward he placed his hands around her waist and gently lifted her to the ground.

If he were prone to theatrics, he could've sworn time stood still as she stood toe to toe with him, her hands braced lightly against his chest while his rested on her trim waist, their gazes locked while tension stretched between them like a taut elastic band.

Her floral fragrance enveloped him, teasing him to do what he'd wanted to do earlier—pull her close and kiss her senseless. To savour her warmth, banish her demons, do whatever it took to assuage the burning need he had for her.

'Thanks,' she said, breaking the loaded silence, snapping him back to reality.

He couldn't do it to her. Natasha was a woman with problems, and he didn't want to add to them by having a quick fling with her before heading home. She didn't deserve that. No matter how much he wanted her.

'At your service.' He released her and did a mock bow, relieved when she laughed. 'If m'lady is tired of playing in her castle, we can retire to the nearest café?'

'Lead the way,' she said, and as she tucked her hand into his proffered elbow he wished it didn't feel so damn right.

CHAPTER EIGHT

'I'LL take the lot.'

Natasha rolled her eyes at Dante, who looked like a little boy in a toy shop. An apt analogy, considering he was a big boy in a toy shop, and not just any toy shop. The king of toy shops, a toy super-megastore, a place she'd never had reason to visit but couldn't blame him for liking. She'd been pretty smitten herself from the second she'd set foot inside the massive front doors.

'You can't buy everything,' she said, belatedly realising that actually he could. 'I think you should choose between the toddler train-set, the building blocks, the farmhouse or the tunnel and tent.'

He stared at the toys, his brow furrowed as if she'd asked him to make a choice between which heads of government received access to trade talks with Calida.

'The decision is a difficult one. I can't choose.'

Okay, if Dante was behaving like a little boy, she'd use the same reverse psychology on him as she would with any kid.

Shrugging her shoulders, she said, 'Fine. If you want Paolo to be a spoiled rich kid, take the lot. It'll be good for him to know that when he breaks one toy, he'll have a whole heap of others from his uncle to choose from.'

Dante's frown deepened. 'I don't want him to be a spoiled brat.'

He hesitated for only a second before pointing to the train set, a colourful conglomeration of multiple trains made from big stacking blocks, perfect for little hands, wide wooden tracks and enough extra blocks for the odd station or two. It should keep Paolo occupied for the next few months.

'I'll take the train set.'

'Good choice,' she said, hiding her triumphant grin behind a smothered cough when he glanced her way. 'And if that offer for coffee still stands I vote we grab one ASAP. I'm all shopped out.'

And drained, more than she'd ever thought possible. Yeah, she'd had a fun evening, but that was just it— having fun with Dante was exhausting. Trying not to preen under his appreciative stare, trying not to melt in a heap at his feet every time he sent her one of his trade-mark sexy smiles, had been hard work.

It wasn't fair. The guy shouldn't have so much natural sex appeal.

As for the loaded moment back at the jumping castle, she wished it had never happened. Being held in his arms like that, having him stare at her like he desired her, had almost been too much to bear.

She'd barely stopped herself from swaying forward and kissing him. It had been touch and go. He'd touched her, she hadn't wanted to move, but the longer he'd stared at her, and the longer she'd enjoyed it, the more frightened she'd become.

Having fun with Dante was one thing, falling for

him another, and she had no intention of going down a one-way street to heartache again.

'Thanks for your help tonight. I couldn't have done any of this without you.'

He gave her arm a gentle squeeze, a friendly, impersonal touch which meant nothing, yet her skin tingled, her pulse raced and she knew that this fun stuff was dangerous. Very dangerous.

'No problems.'

She wished.

From where she stood, Dante Andretti was one big problem. To her overactive imagination, that was.

'I'll pay for the purchase, get them to deliver and we'll have that long-awaited coffee. Does that suit?'

She nodded, hating the way her heart lurched at his fancy words uttered in that deliciously deep voice.

This fun business was playing havoc with her long-dormant hormones. Once Dante left the country, maybe it would be time to try the odd date or two. If this was how she reacted to a guy simply talking to her, she really needed to get out more.

Then again, she'd never gone in for the whole dating thing anyway. Making the Towers flourish had been her main priority for as long as she could remember, and she loved her job.

But what if she lost it?

What if the one thing that had kept her focussed through losing her mum, discovering Clay's scam and coping with the aftermath of both was taken from her? From her dad?

It would probably kill them both, and she'd be responsible for it.

Yeah, so much for her dating plan.

She'd be better off getting rid of Clay once and for all and trying to save the Towers in the process. Easy—not.

'Everything is organised. Are you ready?'

Dante appeared before her, rubbing his hands together like he'd just successfully conducted state business rather than negotiated a simple toy purchase.

'Uh-huh.'

She smiled, enjoying his enthusiasm, marvelling at how easy it was to be in his company.

No pressure, no expectations, just a laid-back feeling she'd never experienced with a guy before. Her time with Clay had been fraught with tension once the initial star-struck stage had worn off; he'd seemed so polished, she'd always been afraid of making a faux pas. She'd aimed to please; he'd always find fault no matter how small or insignificant.

Yet with Dante she felt more relaxed than she had in ages. Strange, considering her problems hadn't eased. If anything, with every day that passed, the screws on the Towers tightened.

Determined not to ruin the evening they'd had, Natasha banished her morbid thoughts and turned to Dante. 'You hungry? Perhaps we could grab dinner along with that coffee?'

He grinned, his face lighting up. 'I didn't want to push my luck.'

'Push away,' she said.

'Dinner it is.'

They fell into step and made it two doors from the toy shop before finding a quaint little trattoria complete with old wooden tables, red-and-white checked tablecloths and candles stuck into empty Chianti bottles.

'You do like Italian food?'

She managed to keep a straight face at his surprised look.

'Of course. I'm Ital—' He broke off at her laughter and shook his head. 'You are teasing me? Or, as I've heard people here say, "pulling my leg"? My sister has also gained this same strange sense of Australian humour. It confuses me.'

'No worries, mate.'

Natasha's exaggerated ocker drawl seemed to confuse Dante further if the tiny frown on his brow was any indication, so she led the way into the restaurant and chose a table near the front window, determinedly ignoring the cosier romantic options tucked away at the back.

'What's your sister like? You haven't said much about her.' She slid into the chair Dante held out for her, silently thrilled by his old-fashioned manners. 'Must admit, I'm surprised she's giving you total control over her son's birthday party. And even more surprised you're staying at a hotel for your week of anonymity instead of with her.'

Dante's frown deepened. 'Our relationship is complicated.'

Intrigued, Natasha leaned forward. 'Okay, now you have to tell me all about her.'

'Gina is lovely, but a little self-absorbed. She loves to be spoiled and expects it from everyone around her, including her brother, who's been aware of her games since childhood.'

So that's why he'd been so struck by her barb back at the toy shop about spoiling Paolo.

'She's had my mother twisted around her little finger since birth, but being a female she hasn't had the responsibilities of Calida that I have. Once Gina came of age, no one could hold her. I think Mother was almost relieved to have her meet an Australian cattle baron and get married so quickly.'

Mmm…a rebel princess. Looked like that particular trait ran in the family.

'And she's lived here ever since?'

Dante nodded, an intense, brooding expression darkening his eyes to midnight. She'd never seen him so serious, and she bet there was more to this story than he was letting on.

'Gina is a single mother now. I don't blame her husband for leaving. Not many men could live with someone as pushy and opinionated as her. Hence my choice of hotel. I love my sister, but living with her even for a week after all this time would drive me mad.'

Natasha chuckled, trying to lighten the mood. 'Is she that bad, or do you have a case of sibling rivalry going on? You know—the poor prince gets saddled with all the tough stuff while little sis gets to run wild?'

His look could've frozen Hades.

'I don't blame her for wanting freedom but I do blame her for bringing a helpless child into this world and making him suffer for his mother's mistakes. We all have choices to make, and when thoughtless people make stupid choices that affect their family it's unforgivable.'

Icy tentacles of dread seeped through her veins. What would Dante think of her choices—the stupid choices she'd made, and how they'd adversely affected her family? He'd probably look at her with the scarcely disguised contempt he felt for his sister's decisions and she'd hate that.

She didn't want him to see her as some pathetic loser

who'd fallen for a slick charmer determined to get what he wanted right from the start.

In fact, she didn't want him to see her as anything other than the woman he'd looked at with ill-concealed desire a scarce hour ago.

Thankfully, he would never know about her past. And, with a little bit of luck, he'd play a major role in shaping her future. The publicity from his stay at the hotel would be a boon. It had to be.

'If you'd rather not talk about this, I understand. Sorry for bringing it up.'

He waved away her apology. 'Don't be. You were simply curious about my family. I should be the one apologizing to you for airing my family's dirty sheets.'

The corners of her mouth twitched. 'Dirty laundry, you mean?'

He snapped his fingers and finally smiled. 'That's it! My English sometimes lapses.'

'Your English is perfect. In fact, I was surprised you didn't have an Italian accent when we first met, but assumed spending the bulk of your education in the UK took care of that.'

A thoughtful gleam glowed in his eyes. 'You studied up on me?'

'Part of my job is to know about the VIPs who stay at the hotel.'

It sounded plausible. Now, if she could only control the heat seeping into her cheeks, perhaps she could stay seated and not slink under the table in embarrassment.

'Attention to detail. Very important,' he said, his steady gaze flicking over her hair, her face and settling on her lips, sending her blush out of control.

Thankfully, the long overdue appearance of a waiter

saved her from answering, and while they made hasty choices from the menu and placed their order she deliberately avoided looking at him.

However, once the menus were gone, the pasta ordered and the wine glasses filled, she had no option but to stare at the man who was slowly but surely driving her crazy.

'You have done a superb job with everything I have asked. I am eternally grateful.'

He raised a glass of Chianti her way, something in his tone alerting her to the fact he wanted to say more but wasn't sure how far to push.

'And?'

He took a sip of wine, placed the glass on the table and smiled. 'And I have one more favour to ask, though after our earlier conversation I won't be surprised if you say no.'

'Try me.'

For a second, his blue eyes flashed danger, desire and a host of other possibilities, and she quickly rephrased, petrified by the glimpse of 'what if' in those aquamarine depths.

'I can't respond if you don't ask.'

He clasped his hands, placed them on the table and leaned forward. She imagined he would look like this when handing down some princely verdict on an indecipherable problem of the world.

'I would like you to be at Paolo's party. You have made the arrangements seem effortless, and I know having your presence there will ensure that nothing goes wrong.'

Oh no.

No, no, no!

Doing a bit of easy legwork was one thing; fronting

up to a pushy princess and fending off a dozen two-year-olds?

No way.

'Please? I know it's a lot to ask, but you're remarkable. You have to know that.'

Remarkable? What did he mean by that?

This was getting more complicated by the minute.

'Please say yes.'

Natasha opened her mouth to say no. Her lips formed the word, her tongue rolled around it, but somehow when a word actually came out it sounded suspiciously like a half-muttered yes.

'Yes?'

Sighing in resignation, she nodded. 'Why not? But let me warn you, your publicity duties next week are going to be hell.'

He laughed, a rich, warm sound that rolled over her like the sun's rays on a perfect summer's day. 'As they say in your country, bring it on.'

'You asked for it,' she said, joining in his laughter, her heart quaking.

This felt too good.

The rich garlic and oregano aromas wafting from the kitchen, the cosy ambience, the muted candlelight all served to highlight the fact she was seated opposite one of the nicest, sexiest men she'd ever met.

And she liked him, genuinely liked him. The kind of like that could quite easily turn into something more if she was prone to craziness.

But thankfully she wasn't that kind of girl.

She'd always been sensible, responsible, dedicated.

Then why the niggling feeling that it was time to take a chance on crazy?

* * *

'Who is this woman you are bringing to Paolo's party?'

Gina whirled on Dante, her mop of dark curls swinging across her shoulders in riotous abandon, the same way she'd worn her hair since her teens, the same pouting bottom lip, the same self-indulgent-princess expression on her face.

Dante plucked a stuffed olive off the antipasto platter, popped it in his mouth and chewed slowly. He'd never given in to his sister's bossy ways and he sure wasn't about to start now.

'Well?'

Gina planted one hand on a curvy hip and glared, her dark eyes flashing.

'Natasha Telford is a friend. That's all you need to know.'

And was all he was going to tell her.

The more Gina knew, the more she'd dig and probe and interrogate—and make Natasha's life a living hell at the party. He had no intention of putting her through that. She didn't deserve it after all she'd done for him. In fact, no one deserved to be on the receiving end of Gina on a roll.

Gina pouted for another second before shrugging her shoulders and turning away. 'You have many *friends* around the world. What's another one?'

'Natasha's not like that.'

He jumped in too quickly and Gina quirked an eyebrow his way.

'No? Then what's she like?'

Muttering a soft curse, he said, 'She's a nice young woman, and I don't want you giving her a hard time. Got it?'

'Sure.' Gina's smug grin did little to assuage his concerns. If anything, they intensified.

Maybe he'd been wrong to invite Natasha to the party? It had seemed like a great idea at the time. He wanted to get closer to her, to spend as much time as he could with her, and she'd been a real trouper in going along with everything he'd asked of her.

He'd hoped that in spending time with his family she'd see another side to him, a side that wasn't caught up in his heritage and who he was and where he'd have to be in a few weeks' time: back in Calida, in the job he'd been born to, probably engaged to a woman he didn't love.

Somehow, having Natasha see him in a good light had become important to him. He liked her, beyond her beauty and sassy mouth, and a small part of him wanted more. A lot more. But what could that be?

He didn't want to indulge in a tawdry fling with her; she was too special for that.

He didn't have time to explore anything deeper.

The way he saw it, he didn't have many options and, for a smart guy used to making economic decisions for a country and running world-affairs meetings, he didn't like the strange fog pervading his brain when it came to Natasha.

He needed clarity of thought, some idea of what to do about his growing attraction to a woman who sparked him like no other ever had. But he couldn't think beyond how great it felt to spend time with her, and how her caramel eyes glowed with vitality.

'Uh-oh.'

'What?'

Gina waggled a finger at him. 'You've got a funny look on your face, big brother.'

'Probably indigestion from that awful gnocchi you fed me earlier.'

'More like an awful case of wanting to have your cake and eat it too.'

He should've ignored Gina, but Paolo hadn't returned with the nanny yet and he had no option but to face the firing squad. Besides, he did love his sister no matter how painful she could be and they rarely got to see each other these days.

'Okay, I'll bite. What's that supposed to mean?'

'We both know Mother will have you betrothed as soon as you step off the plane in Calida. She won't hand over the crown without you being engaged, so this thing with your *friend* Natasha is your way of having what you want before getting what you don't.'

Gina smiled, but Dante sensed a tinge of sadness behind it rather than smug satisfaction or her usual gloating. 'I don't envy you, that's for sure. Must be tough having your life mapped out.'

You don't know the half of it, Dante thought.

'It's my duty.'

'But is it what you want?'

Dante cast a quizzical look Gina's way. He'd never seen her like this: serious, interested in him rather than the latest fashion trend.

'It's irrelevant what I want.'

He'd learned that from an early age.

When the village kids had skipped down to the water's edge and jump off the cliffs into the crystal clear azure sea, he'd been flanked by surly bodyguards warning him of the dangers.

When his few teenage friends had wanted to ride beat-up old scooters around the island, he'd had to stay behind to entertain the neighbouring island's king's son.

And when he finally reached a legal age when he could've done anything he wanted like other guys his age, he'd been busy taking diplomacy lessons and learning to speak eight languages.

No, it didn't matter what he wanted. It never had.

To his surprise, Gina crossed the short space separating them and gave him a quick hug. 'You're one of the good guys. And, believe it or not, I'm on your side.'

'Thanks,' he said, thankful he'd made this trip to Australia. Gina was doing okay, Paolo was adorable and he'd seal a few trade deals next week.

As for Natasha, he still had no idea where they went from here.

And it was killing him.

CHAPTER NINE

'LET me get this straight. He's taking you to a kid's party?'

Ella shook her head, tore the top off a sugar sachet and tipped the contents into her black coffee. 'For a prince, the guy has no idea how to impress a woman.'

'He's not trying to impress me,' Natasha said, sipping her mocha-cappuccino and sighing with pleasure.

He didn't have to. Dante already impressed her just by being him.

Last night had sealed it.

Not only was he one of the sexiest men to walk the planet, he didn't seem to have many faults from where she stood. He was polite, cultured, approachable and, oh… Did she mention sexy?

Then he had to go and pull out the big guns, showing her his soft side for animals and toys. It wasn't fair. If she hadn't liked him before, she would've fallen at his feet the minute he'd picked up that adorable rabbit and cuddled it close.

'I think it's sweet he's taking me to his nephew's party,' she said, spooning the last of a chocolate-cream cannoli into her mouth and smiling like she'd just gone to heaven. She'd tasted every sweet in Luigi's range, and every calorie-laden morsel was to die for.

Ella's eyes narrowed. 'Whoa! Hold on a sec. You didn't tell me it was his nephew's party! That puts an entirely different slant on proceedings.'

'You make it sound like a law case,' Natasha said, not minding her friend's interrogation one bit.

It was a gorgeous Melbourne day, the type of crisp spring day with a hint of chill in the air but the glorious sun to warm you. Throw in the fact she'd just finished her third-to-last shift as stand-in concierge, organised another payment to Clay, and the end of the week was looming bringing her one step closer to saving the Towers with Dante's help, and life couldn't be better.

Well, it could be, if the Towers was safe and Dante wasn't a prince destined to ride off into the sunset in the not too distance future but, hey, no use wishing for the impossible.

She'd learned that a long time ago.

'What's your take on the party?' Natasha lay down her fork and pushed away her plate, patting her stomach with a groan.

'Simple,' Ella said, snapping her fingers like a magician conjuring up doves out of a hat. 'He wants to introduce you to the family. Serious stuff.'

Natasha rolled her eyes. 'It's only his sister. And he's only asking me along to make sure nothing goes wrong with the animals or the bouncy castle.'

'He can pay any old body to do that,' Ella said, stirring her coffee before taking a sip. 'Want to know what I think?'

'I'm sure you'll tell me anyway.'

'He wants to get the royal stamp of approval. You know, like having you vetted before taking any big steps.'

'You're out of your mind,' Natasha muttered, hating

the tiny, irrational surge of hope deep in her soul that her friend could be right.

She'd never been any good at playing the 'what if' game, but since she'd met Dante she'd found herself doing it all the time.

What if the attraction between them meant something?

What if it grew into something more?

What if fairy tales did come true and she finally got the happily ever after she'd only ever dreamed about?

But 'what ifs' could be painful. They led to silly dreams and big let-downs. If anyone should know, she should. The way she looked at it, the only big steps Dante would be taking around her involved him heading in the direction of the airport and all the way back to Calida.

Ella shrugged. 'Hey, it's just my opinion.'

'And I don't need that sort of pressure. I'm just enjoying spending time with the guy, remember?'

'Uh-huh. Besides, you don't need anyone's stamp of approval. You're fine just the way you are.'

'Thanks for the vote of confidence.' Natasha grinned at Ella's quick backtrack. 'Being with Dante is fun, and it's been a long time since I've had any. So lighten up, will you?'

Looking suitably chastised for all of two seconds, Ella took a few gulps of coffee before chirping up again. 'Big steps. You'll see.'

Ella ducked under a barrage of scrunched up serviettes and empty sugar sachets while Natasha decided she needed to improve her aim.

Big steps…big steps…

Uh-uh—she wouldn't go there.

She wouldn't even contemplate what it could mean if Ella was right.

For now, she was safer sticking with her original theory. Big steps only led to big trampling, and she had no intention of getting caught underfoot of any guy ever again.

'So this is why you wanted the gift delivered?'

Natasha cast a dubious look over the gleaming Harley waiting at the kerb, its chrome shining and in perfect contrast to the highly polished black paint.

Dante smiled and held out a helmet to her. 'It's the only way to travel,' he said, while she silently begged to differ. 'Ever been on a bike before?'

She shook her head, not quite convinced she ever would. Though the bike was big, it still appeared too flimsy lined up against the cars, trucks and SUVs on Melbourne's busy roads.

'It's easy. Just hold on tight and you'll be fine.'

Okay, so he'd convinced her.

She might be afraid of big mechanical things she couldn't control, but the thought of being plastered against Dante's back with her arms wrapped tight around his waist held a certain appeal.

Besides, what had happened to her 'let's just have fun for now' motto?

'Okay.'

She slipped the helmet over her head, fiddling with the chin strap for a second before Dante reached over and cinched it. Her breath hitched as his fingers brushed the skin under her chin, the barest and lightest of touches, enough to send heat ripping through her body.

Her eyes closed involuntarily as she savoured the unusual sensation, the purely visceral reaction of a strong, uncontrollable attraction. She'd never experienced anything like it and it was heady stuff.

'You sure you're going to be okay? We can always take a cab.'

Natasha opened her eyes, her gaze connecting with Dante's concerned one.

'I'll be fine. I haven't had much to eat today, just felt a bit woozy for a second.'

She tried not to cringe at how pathetic she sounded but, thankfully, he bought it.

'Gina has catered enough food to feed the entire population of Calida, so we'll get you something when we arrive. Is that soon enough, or would you prefer a quick snack before we go?'

'I'm fine, really,' she said, feeling increasingly guilty and finding it difficult not to laugh.

She'd told him she was hungry. Unfortunately, it wasn't for food, and she wondered what he'd think if he knew he was the tastiest dish on her menu right now.

'Sure?'

She nodded and clambered on before she changed her mind. 'Sure.'

Dante didn't move, grinning at her like a loon. She guessed the sight of her perched on the back of a bike didn't look as cool as she hoped. Thankfully, she'd worn black hipsters and a matching polo but perhaps the buckled up salmon-pink trench coat was a bit much?

Then again, it wasn't her fault. She'd been expecting a civilised mode of transport, not to play out some biker chick role.

'You going to ride this thing, or just look at it?'

Ignoring her brisk tone, his smile broadened as he climbed aboard, and that's when the fun really started.

Before starting the engine, Dante ensured her arms were clasped firmly around his waist, and as she dug her fingers into the buttery soft leather of his black jacket a thrill of pure anticipation shot through her.

Now, this was exciting!

As he revved the engine and carefully pulled into traffic, Natasha closed her eyes and sent a silent prayer heavenward.

Please let me be safe…

The bike shot forward, turned several corners and hit the beach road curving along Port Phillip Bay. Adrenalin coursed through her body and she'd never felt better but she continued her prayer.

Let me be safe from falling for a guy like Dante. Please.

Sadly, as the short ride between the hotel and his sister's beachside mansion ended, she had a sinking feeling it was too late.

'Do I have helmet hair?'

Dante took the helmet Natasha held out to him and stared at her like she'd just spoken Martian.

'Helmet hair?'

She chuckled. He was adorably, royally stuffy at times and didn't have a clue.

'Is my hair messy from wearing the helmet?'

Realisation made his blue eyes sparkle, and before she could move he reached out and tucked a strand of hair behind her ear.

'Your hair looks fine.'

His fingers brushed her earlobe as he withdrew his hand, sending a delicious shiver through her body.

Maybe it was the last ten minutes being plastered against his body, maybe it was the heat radiating off his body and warming her better than the sun's rays, but whatever it was her body seemed super-sensitised to him.

For goodness' sake, all he'd done was touch her hair and

brush her ear and her body was in orbit. Time to douse her fever with a little reality check; an hour in the company of twenty toddlers and his sister should do the trick.

'You look beautiful,' he said, sending her one of his sexy trademark smiles that made her *feel* beautiful. 'Now, if you're ready, time to face the firing squad.'

'Firing squad?'

She didn't have time to ask anything else as a woman wearing a blinding-white designer suit and a monstrous matching wide-brimmed hat strode up to them.

'You must be Natasha.'

'That's right.'

Natasha took the proffered hand of the stunning woman and smiled.

'I'm Gina. Welcome.'

Though Gina's smile seemed genuine enough, Natasha saw the cool, calculating gleam in her eyes and suddenly she wished she hadn't come.

This was ludicrous. Helping Dante and spending a casual evening over dinner was one thing, getting sized up by his family another.

'Now that you two lovely ladies have met, shall we join the party in the rear garden? I can hear the kids squealing from here.'

Dante's light touch in the small of her back soothed Natasha's slightly frayed nerves and she straightened, determined to enjoy the party.

Gina extended an arm towards her endless cobbled driveway. 'Please come through.'

Her voice sounded formal and somewhat stilted, and Natasha marvelled at the difference between brother and sister. Where Dante's eyes were piercing blue, Gina's were almost coal black. While Dante spoke with a casual lilt, Gina's upper class accent screamed status, wealth and power.

'Paolo hasn't stopped asking for you since the castle and animals arrived an hour ago. He's very impressed. And so am I.'

Gina's praise almost sounded begrudging, and Natasha pondered the strange undercurrent which passed between brother and sister when Dante glared at her.

'I couldn't have done it without Natasha,' he said, his smile warming her from the inside out.

'Mmm.'

Gina's guarded response and sideways stare almost sent Natasha scuttling back to the motorbike, but at that second a small boy ran around the corner of the sandstone mansion, screamed and lunged towards Dante.

'Hey, Paolo, my little man. Happy birthday,' Dante said, squatting down to hug the little boy close before picking him up and swinging him high in the air, eliciting more ear-splitting shrieks.

Natasha's breath caught in her throat as she watched Dante and Paolo pull apart, their foreheads touching as they rubbed noses in an Eskimo kiss.

The emotion on their faces, the joy of a special shared moment, made her heart clench.

She wanted that.

She wanted a special connection, the type of heart-wrenching elation that came with being with the right person, with sharing a family with that person.

And right then, right there, standing in the waning afternoon sunlight on a clear Melbourne day, it hit her.

She wanted that special connection with Dante.

A tremor shuddered through her body and she stiffened, reluctant to acknowledge the startling revelation, determined to ignore it.

It must've been the excitement of that darn motorbike ride. The stupid speed machine had rattled her brain. But the longer she tried to deny it, the more her gaze was drawn to the cosy picture of uncle and nephew cuddling, and how much Dante affected her.

'Dante's smitten with my son.'

Natasha managed a polite smile for Gina and nodded. 'He sure is. Not that I blame him. Your son's adorable.'

'Spoken like a woman who doesn't have children.' Gina's cynical laugh raised the hairs on the back of Natasha's neck, and she racked her brain for something to say.

'You have a lovely home. Do you enjoy living in Melbourne?'

'Melbourne is convenient. We're settled here now, and it's far enough away from Calida to keep me sane.'

The bitterness in Gina's voice surprised Natasha and before she could say anything else, or make frantic eye signals in Dante's direction for him to save her from his scary sister, Gina stepped closer and dropped her tone to barely whisper pitch.

'Dante's not like me, though. He's a born and bred Calidian. It's his destiny.'

'I'm sure it is,' Natasha said, wishing she'd opted for a quiet afternoon in her room rather than this.

'You know this thing with you can't be serious, don't you? When he returns, he'll be taking a bride and ascending to the throne, so don't grow too attached. My brother has a duty to our homeland and won't give that up even for…what you can offer. After the trouble you've gone through for my son's party, I feel it only fair I warn you.'

Icy dread trickled through Natasha's veins. Nothing Gina said surprised her. She'd known Dante had responsibilities back home; he'd said as much. As for what she could offer, it didn't take a genius to figure out what the woman was implying.

But it still hurt.

The cold, harsh reality that Dante could only be toying with her, hoping for a final fling before settling down, hurt. A lot.

Fixing a brittle smile in place, she nodded at Gina. 'Thanks for your concern, but Dante and I are just friends.'

With that, Natasha forced her feet to move and walked over to Dante and Paolo, where the little curly-haired cherub took one look at her and ducked his head into the crook of his uncle's shoulder.

'Paolo, meet my friend Natasha. She helped me bring the animals and bouncy castle here. And, later, you'll see what she helped me choose for your present. Say hello.'

Dante winked at her and tickled Paolo, who lifted his head and peeked at her with wonder in his dark eyes.

'Tasha? My birfday?'

Natasha's heart melted as she stepped forward and gently ruffled the little boy's hair. 'Yes, sweetheart, happy birthday. Are you having fun?'

Paolo nodded, a hint of a grin tugging at his mouth. 'Fun, fun!'

'Can I see the animals? Will you show me?'

'Yeah!'

Paolo wriggled in Dante's arms, and they laughed as he placed the strapping boy down on his feet, where he promptly shot off towards the back yard, stopping for a brief second to see if they were following.

'You coming, Gina?' Dante called over his shoulder while Natasha wondered if she could bolt after Paolo and thus escape spending any more time with Gina.

'I've got some things to take care of inside. You go ahead.'

Natasha's sigh of relief must've been audible as Dante fell into step beside her. 'Did Gina say something to upset you?'

'No, why?'

The little white lie popped out easily. She had no intention of letting him know how rattled she was, first by the stunning realisation of how much he meant to her, closely followed by how little she must mean to him.

'My sister has a habit of saying the wrong things, and you had a strange look on your face when you walked up to Paolo.'

'Gina didn't tell me anything I didn't already know,' she said, managing to keep the sadness out of her voice with difficulty.

She'd never been one for crying. Sure, she'd cried buckets when her mum had died, and even when Clay had shown his true colours, but she'd grown stronger since then. She'd had to.

Then why the sudden, dreadful urge to sink onto the nearest stone bench in the shade of a huge maple and bawl her eyes out?

'What did she say?'

Dante laid a hand on her arm but she didn't stop.

Instead, she shrugged him off and fixed the best smile she could muster in place.

'Nothing important. Now, we've got a party to go to.'
Even if celebrating was the last thing she wanted to do.

CHAPTER TEN

NATASHA would've liked nothing better than to go to her room, sink into a warm bath and listen to a relaxation CD. If playing the happy party person had shredded her nerves, riding up close and personal with Dante on the way home had undone her completely.

However, the minute she caught sight of Clay waiting for her in the Lobby Bar, she knew her wish for solitude would have to wait.

She had business to conduct and, in the mood she was in, Lord help her ex if he put a foot wrong.

'Thanks for accompanying me to Paolo's party.'

If Dante had bowed to go along with his formal little speech she wouldn't have been surprised. Somehow, he'd picked up on her reticent vibes and was reacting accordingly.

Good. Only two more days, and at the end of the week his visit here would become public knowledge and, soon after, he could return to his *responsibilities*. None the wiser to the fool she'd almost made of herself.

'No problems. Thanks for asking me.'

He didn't move, his steady gaze searching her face, as if looking for clues to her sudden turnaround in behaviour. Well, he could keep looking. She'd mastered the art of the poker face a long time ago, around the first time Clay had demanded payment, and she'd been forced to go along with it for the sake of her family.

'Would you like a nightcap? A cocoa, perhaps?'

'No,' she blurted quickly, realising how rude it sounded a second too late. 'Thanks, but I'd rather not. Good night, Dante.'

She couldn't bear to see the bewildered, almost hurt look in his eyes so she turned away quickly and walked towards the front office.

'Good night, Tasha,' he said, his low voice not affecting her as much as his use of the pet name Paolo had given her.

Something about the way he said it—soft, personal, intimate, as if he'd never called her anything else—made tears spring to her eyes, and she blinked rapidly to dispel them.

She couldn't show weakness in front of Clay. He thrived on that sort of thing, something she'd learned far too late.

Natasha ducked into the front office, waited till Dante took the express lift, before stepping out and crossing the marble foyer to the Lobby Bar. Taking a deep breath, she patted her back pocket, felt the reassuring rustle of paper and headed for the man who had torn her world apart and that of her family.

'You're late,' Clay said, not looking up from his double Scotch on the rocks.

'And you're only welcome here because you're a paying customer.'

She noted the slight flush beneath his collar, deriving petty satisfaction from her barb. It was stupid, and she shouldn't stoop to his level, but he brought out the worst in her these days and, in her current frame of mind, he'd be lucky if she let him walk out of here alive.

Draining his drink in one, long gulp, he swivelled on the bar stool to stare at her with cold avarice in his emotionless eyes. 'You have something for me?'

Meeting his stare, she reached into her back pocket and handed him the folded piece of paper. 'Here.'

She expected him to grab the cheque, scan it like he usually did, slip it into his pocket and give her one of his signature sleazy smiles before strutting out the door. They'd been through this scenario three times previously and, thankfully, there would only be one more.

One more month and she'd be free, her family would be free.

If they didn't lose the Towers in the meantime.

However, this time Clay surprised her. Rather than taking the cheque, he captured her hand and, taking advantage of her shock, used his superior strength to pull her close.

'So, how are things with lover boy? If it doesn't work out, you know I'm more than man enough for you.'

Natasha almost retched as his Scotch-laden breath hit her in the face, but rather than struggle—he would've liked it too much—she went slack against him.

'You're not a man, you're a sub-human with the intelligence of a gnat, with the rest of you in proportion too,' she said, lingering long enough to insult him before pushing off his chest so hard he would've fallen backwards if the bar hadn't propped him up.

'And one more thing. If you ever touch me again, you won't get another cent out of me. I don't care how many threats you throw my way, and I'll let the world know exactly what you are.'

She ignored his string of muttered expletives—she'd heard them all before when she'd exposed him for the creep he was first time around—and walked out the door, head high.

Her heart thumped, her head ached and she wanted to hide away for a week. Instead, she didn't look left or right. She couldn't. She needed the sanctity of her room in the next few minutes before she fell apart.

There was only so much she could take and, after the day she'd had, she'd well and truly reached her limit.

Dante slammed into his room, headed for the mini bar, screwed the top off a sparkling mineral water in record time and drank deeply. He needed to erase the bitter taste in his mouth at what he'd just seen, even if he knew nothing could erase the awful image.

Gripping the half-empty bottle in his fist, he was surprised he didn't crush the glass to sand.

The woman he'd come to like, to respect, and to want more with every passing minute, had been too tired to have a nightcap with him. However, she hadn't been too tired to cosy up to her ex.

He dashed a hand across his eyes, knowing it would do little to erase the memory of the two of them: the creep holding her hand against his chest, her body up close and personal with his, their faces inches apart.

Anger burned deep in his gut. Not at Natasha, who he'd sensed had secrets and wasn't over her ex from the one time he'd seen them together, but at himself for being such a fool.

For letting his guard down, for letting a woman

affect him as much as Natasha did. Worst of all, for letting himself believe in the possibility that he didn't have to control everything, that some things were bigger than responsibilities and arranged marriages and duty.

He drained the rest of his drink, threw the bottle in the bin and sank down into a comfy armchair, staring out at the glittering Melbourne skyline.

The city had enchanted him.

Not as much as Natasha.

Cursing his inner voice, he allowed his anger to fester, knowing it would be the only emotion to keep him detached enough to not barge back down to the bar and wrench her from her ex's arms.

However, the longer he nursed his anger, the more it grew and morphed into something nastier, swerving direction away from him and pointing straight at the woman who had got to him.

He could've sworn she'd returned his interest: the sparkle he'd glimpsed over dinner, the almost-kiss in the bouncy castle, her tiny, satisfied sigh when she'd first wrapped her arms around him on the bike earlier today.

She'd probably thought he hadn't heard it, but he had and it had shot straight to his heart. That's why he'd asked her for a nightcap, to perhaps explore their mutual attraction, maybe see where things could lead given half a chance.

The crazy thing was, when he was with her he forgot about Calida and his impending duty. In fact, he forgot everything but the way she looked, the way she smelled and how incredible she made him feel. Being with her was a heady rush and he wanted more. Hell, he wanted it all.

He couldn't escape the responsibilities of his birth,

but what if he had a woman like Natasha by his side rather than a bride hand-picked by his mother?

The thought had insinuated its way into his head on the way home tonight and he'd wanted time to ponder it, develop it and, most of all, see if the woman in question had the slightest interest in being more for him than a PA or a friend.

Well, he certainly had his answer.

Yes, he'd definitely been a fool.

His mother was right. When the heart ruled the head, it could only end in disaster.

And, like an awful train wreck, he knew he'd have a hard time turning away from Natasha and the havoc she'd wrought.

The throb behind Natasha's eyes intensified, and her fingers shook as she stabbed at the calculator buttons one more time, hoping that by some miracle the numbers would change the more times she entered them.

They didn't.

She'd tried every permutation, every combination, shaving a profit margin here, skimping on a goods purchase there, but the answer was still the same.

She didn't have the money she needed for Clay's last payment.

And she needed the money. Now.

After what she'd just endured downstairs, she couldn't wait another day let alone another month to get rid of him once and for all.

It had taken every ounce of self-control she possessed not to punch him when he'd groped her in the bar. It would've felt so good, but then what sort of example would that set for her staff? Not to mention the stray paying customer that could've strolled in.

Besides, she had more class than that. In fact, for a guy who'd attended the best private schools, and was hung up on appearances and his standing in Melbourne society, Clay had the class of a slug.

Pushing the uncooperative calculator away, she sat back in her chair and rubbed her temples, knowing being free of Clay would soothe her better than any massage or paracetamol.

But how?

Having Dante help with publicity would raise the hotel's profile and bring in much-needed money over the next month, but she needed that money now.

Thoughts swirled around her head: banks, lending societies, business associates, contacts. Around and around, the same avenues she'd exhausted when all this had started, when she'd been foolish enough to agree to Clay's demands in the first place.

But, then, what option had she back then?

Lose the family business at the hands of a bitter and twisted man who had only wanted one thing from their relationship? And it sure hadn't been her!

No way.

She'd got her family into this mess with Clay, she'd get them out of it. Though it had to be now. She couldn't have him threatening her or the Towers any longer. Tonight had been the final time he'd laud anything over her, or touch her for that matter.

There had to be a way out…something she hadn't thought of…

The harder she concentrated, the more her head

ached, but in the midst of random thoughts and wishful thinking a glimmer of an idea took shape.

No, she couldn't.

Sure, she'd established a friendship with Dante, but that didn't mean she could take advantage of his position or status. Besides, she'd always fought her own battles.

Having a prince slay the dragon might hold a certain appeal but she couldn't involve him. She had her pride, and having a virtual stranger witness her folly—a stranger she'd been stupid enough to fall for despite all her self-talk—would be tantamount to running down Bourke Street buck naked.

And hadn't she embarrassed herself enough?

Falling for a prince might be stupid, but harbouring dreams that he felt the same way went way beyond that. Try moronic, self-defeating and crazy.

Gina had done her a favour in setting the record straight and, no matter how much she'd like to pretend otherwise, Dante had been toying with her.

A line from an old Eddie Murphy comedy sprung to mind, something about a prince travelling to the opposite side of the world to sow his royal oats, and unfortunately it looked like Dante had been doing the same.

She should be mortified. In fact, she should be downright affronted at the thought. But she wasn't, and a small part of her knew why.

Something wasn't right.

The scenario Gina had painted might have fitted a lesser man but Dante didn't seem the type. If the guy wanted a fling, why hadn't he pushed her? Hassled her? Flirted outrageously with her, sweet-talked her, tried to sweep her off her feet?

Dante hadn't done any of those things. Sure, he'd

flattered her, flirted a little, but his behaviour had been irreproachable.

Surely a guy with less than a fortnight in a foreign country would go for it? Would pull out all stops to get a girl into bed if that was his intention?

Uh-uh, something definitely didn't sit right.

Either Gina was wrong—which begged the question, why would she lie?—or Dante was playing another type of game.

And, if so, what was it?

CHAPTER ELEVEN

NATASHA didn't believe in coincidences.

So when she walked into Trevi's, and spotted Dante at a quiet table in the back corner, she wondered if sneaky Ella had played a trick on her.

Not in the mood to face His Royal Sexiness, or ponder the question of his oats, she made for the long, polished teak counter, head down, determined to grab a mocha-cappuccino to go.

'*Ciao*, Natasha! Why is my favourite girl in such a hurry today? You no want to sit?'

Natasha fought a blush as Luigi's bass voice boomed across the café and Dante's head snapped up from the newspaper he'd been buried in.

'Actually, I have lots to do today—'

'Nonsense! You know that nice young man, *si*? The one pushing a chair out for you?'

Luigi pointed straight at Dante and she had to agree it did appear as if Dante was inviting her to sit down. 'Now, you go and chat while I bring your coffee. And tiramisu?'

Natasha shook her head, the thought of forcing a morsel of food down her throat making her nauseous.

She hadn't been able to eat a thing this morning, her mind in a muddle from last night.

Her main problem should be Clay and clearing her debt, but somehow Gina's words kept popping into her head and she'd find herself pondering Dante's motivations, her own, and the complete mess she'd made of her life without trying.

'Just the coffee, thanks, Luigi. And I will take it over there.'

Luigi beamed and she headed to Dante's table, basking in the appreciative once-over he gave her favourite summer dress, annoyed that she cared, and surprised when he blanked his gaze as she drew nearer.

'You don't mind if I join you?'

'Please sit.'

He stood and pulled out her chair further, and as she slid into it she couldn't help but inhale, savouring his citrus scent mingling with the rich aroma of coffee beans and vanilla in the air.

She would miss this. Miss him. His scent, his smile, his company, the works.

She would miss it all when he left and, no matter how hard she tried to sugar-coat it, she knew it would leave her more devastated than she'd thought possible.

'Is something wrong?'

She searched his face, looking for the telltale crinkle of laugh lines around his eyes, the ever-present sparkle in their clear blue depths, the cheeky smile quick to appear at the slightest provocation.

Nothing.

If he'd effectively blanked his stare when she'd reached the table, he'd done a similar job on his face.

Expressionless, devoid of emotion, he stared at her with a forced, polite interest.

'I am leaving today,' he said, his tone dead.

A shiver of apprehension shot through her as she concentrated on his lips, sure she'd just heard him form some words about leaving.

'Leaving?'

Her voice came out a tiny squeak and she cleared her throat, hating the desperation she heard in the one word she'd uttered.

'Yes. I've done what I set out to do.'

'Oh.'

Her mind refused to compute what he'd just said. Sure, he'd taken care of family business as he'd said at the start of the week, but what about the rest? What happened to his official duties?

Suddenly, it hit her like a bolt of electricity, leaving her shocked and breathless and in need of resuscitation. If he didn't stick around for official business, where did that leave her? Or, more precisely, the hotel's publicity she'd been depending on?

'What about our agreement? You said you'd help with the hotel publicity. I've upheld my end of the bargain, what about yours?'

Not a flicker of expression crossed his face. It was like talking to an automaton, and she had an impulse to jump up and down, wave her arms in front of his face and yell, do anything to elicit some emotion, some recognition that she was the woman he'd spent the last week with, chatting, making her laugh, making her feel special.

'You will be suitably compensated,' he said, his cold, flat tone matching the cold, lifeless aquamarine depths she'd seen glitter with fire. 'This should cover it.'

He reached into his pocket and slid a folded piece of paper across the table, his long, elegant fingers lingering over it while she stared at it in disbelief.

He was paying her off.

The small, folded bit of paper had to be a cheque, but she wouldn't give him the satisfaction of looking at it.

'It's that easy for you, isn't it?'

She swallowed, hating the way her voice shook, wishing her heart didn't ache at the thought of him walking out of this café without a backward glance.

She could've fooled herself and attributed the vice-like pain squeezing her heart to the thought of losing the hotel's one-way ticket out of trouble. But she was through lying to herself. What was the point?

She'd suffered through the indignity of Clay's demands and she'd battled on, but losing Dante sent an arrow of pain shooting through the organ she'd learned to protect more than life itself.

Fool.

The cap fit; she'd be the first to admit it. What she hated to acknowledge was, no matter how much self-talk she'd indulged in, she'd still gone ahead and fallen for the wrong guy. Again.

'Easy? You mean my leaving?'

Dante frowned as if he hadn't understood her question. 'Of course. What else could I mean?'

Easy for you to walk away without a backward glance?

Easy for you to flirt a little to get your own way?

Easy for you to make someone like me fall for someone like you?

At least her sarcastic response elicited a reaction out of him, if she could call the slight compressing of his lips a reaction.

Those same lips she'd experienced crushing hers in an all too brief, fake encounter. And, as stupid as she felt at that moment for falling for him, a small part of her couldn't help but wonder what it would've been like to have those lips caress her with serious passion, with intent.

'I thank you for your assistance this week. It has been invaluable, but it is time for me to move on.'

If he'd executed a snappy royal bow to go along with his polite nod and stilted speech, she wouldn't have been surprised.

As for 'it' and not 'you' being invaluable, she could quite easily tip a sachet of arsenic in place of sugar into his coffee for that little gem.

'Guess I shouldn't be surprised at the turnaround.'

'I beg your pardon?'

She could've held her tongue and let him walk away. But, then, since when had she let a guy get away with anything?

She'd called Clay's bluff and, though she'd had to eat humble pie for the sake of her family, Dante couldn't do a thing to hurt her that Clay hadn't already done.

She leaned forward, fixing him with a glare, trying to soothe her bruised ego without losing control of her fragile temper.

'Your turnaround. The whole about-face. You were the laid back, rebel prince one minute, schmoozing up to a pleb to get what you wanted done, and now that's finished you're reverting to type. Using money or power or whatever you have to get the job done. Nice.'

She should've stopped there. In fact, his frigid stare would probably have made the sassiest big mouth shut up, but unfortunately she was on a roll.

She needed to do this, to have her say.

She needed closure, and she knew without a doubt that, by the time she'd finished here, the Dante and Natasha interlude would be well and truly over.

'Are you quite finished?'

'Actually, no. Bear with me for a sec while I tell you a story and then you can walk away.'

She didn't expect him to stay. In fact, she expected him to push his chair back and stroll out of the café and out of her life without a care.

Instead, he sat back, his glacial expression not warming. Then again, after what she'd just said to him, he would've been within his rights to ignore her completely.

'I've met many people in my line of work over the years. Rock stars, film stars, VIPs, families, businessmen, people from every walk of life. Working as a concierge this last week, I've had a bunch of interesting requests, from a guy requesting three hundred and sixty five red roses to be delivered by porters for his wedding anniversary, a media mogul requesting I buy a Porsche for his girlfriend and insisting it had a fuchsia ribbon around it, and a guy who asked me to organise a gondola ride down the Yarra for his girlfriend and a footpath artist to write "will you marry me?" surrounded by love hearts for when they docked.'

She'd actually been a little green at that one. Why couldn't she find a guy who'd go all out to make her feel that special?

Thankfully, Dante hadn't bolted at her long-winded speech and she continued before he did. 'All unique requests, things I managed to deliver without batting an eyelid, and then in walks this rebel prince. Nothing what I expected, mind you. In fact, the antithesis of every preconceived royal idea I had in my head. Of course, he had an unusual request, to preserve his anonymity for a week. Being the good little concierge, I agreed, but you know the part I don't get?'

She'd sparked his interest, glimpsing a flicker of fire in those incredible eyes.

'What's that?'

'The part where the prince masquerading as a pauper went a step further and established a friendship with me. He was fun to be with and he made me feel like I was a part of his life, even for a brief moment.'

He made me fall for him, to feel things I've never felt before.

He made me trust again.

He made me wish for a future, no matter how far-fetched or unobtainable.

He made me want the fairy tale happy ending.

Blinking back the sudden sting of tears, she said, 'Then he goes cold on me. Says he's leaving. Just like that. If you ask me, that's stranger than any of those other things I've had to deal with all week.'

Natasha sighed and leaned back, all out of puff. What had started out as an accusatory monologue had petered out to a pathetic cry for answers.

She scanned his face, knowing every plane and angle as if she'd studied it her entire life. She saw the slight widening of his eyes, the tense jaw, and the flash of something akin to anguish cross his face.

That couldn't be right. What did she expect, that he felt pain at walking away after the meaningless week they'd shared?

As if.

'I don't owe you any explanations,' he said, his stony

expression unchanging, sending any faint hope she might get closure plummeting.

'No, I guess you don't.'

She glanced away, shame flooding her. What had possessed her to rave on like that? The guy was a prince, for goodness' sake. He wasn't used to answering to anybody. What made her think she was so special that he'd actually give her an explanation for his strange behaviour?

'Goodbye, Natasha.'

Dante pushed away from the table and inclined his head in her direction. She nodded back, aiming for the same polite little action, and knowing she probably ended up looking like Noddy on fast-forward.

He hesitated for a fraction and their gazes locked, hers enquiring and hopeful, his dark and unreadable, before he turned and walked out of her life.

Dante forced himself to walk out of the café and not look back, despite every instinct urging him to run back in there, sweep Natasha into his arms and never let go.

He hadn't expected to see her again. He'd planned on leaving a terse note along with the cheque for her to collect at the hotel once he'd gone.

After stewing all night, he'd finally managed to get his frustration under control and knew the best thing would be to change hotels. He'd had six days of blessed anonymity, and now he couldn't stay at Telford Towers for the next week, seeing her, running into her, having to pretend that everything was fine between them, when every time he closed his eyes the image of her in the arms of her ex flashed before him like some awful clip of a natural disaster.

It had been a simple plan, one that would've been

executed to perfection if he hadn't had a hankering for one last cup of espresso, and hadn't chosen the same café Natasha obviously frequented.

She must be a regular, judging by the old man's reaction when she'd walked in, but Dante couldn't fathom his own response. He'd invited her to sit down when it was the last thing he wanted, yet the minute he'd seen her he'd wanted to talk to her, to give her a chance to explain.

But he couldn't do it.

He couldn't ask her.

Maybe he was a proud man, maybe he was stubborn like his mother always said, but when she'd sat opposite him, looking cool and fresh in a strapless summer dress the colour of ripe watermelon, he'd lost it.

He'd wanted to demand answers, to discover why she still loved her ex despite telling him otherwise, why she didn't feel more for him, why she didn't feel the connection.

He'd wanted to touch her, to taste her full lips that matched her dress in colour perfectly, to run his fingers through her silky hair and savour her light floral fragrance.

He'd wanted her.

He'd wanted it all.

Instead, he'd sat there consumed by a cold, hard rage, that a man who could have anything he wanted in this world couldn't have her.

He'd done the only thing possible: shut down emotionally, maintained a frosty façade, while anger at the futility of it all had bubbled hot and searing beneath the surface.

She could've said anything, done anything, and he wouldn't have reacted. He couldn't. He'd learned a long time ago the only way to deal with hardship, with disappointment, was to shut down.

This defence mechanism had served him well before and would now.

It was his way, the royal way.

Natasha sat in frozen silence, her fingers clasped so tight together she didn't register the pain of her fingernails digging into her flesh till Luigi placed a steaming mocha-cappuccino in front of her.

'Your young man left? What a pity,' he said, the old man's black eyes twinkling in his podgy face.

Luigi loved gossip almost as much as Ella, but right now she had no intention of becoming fodder for the rumour mill.

'He had to go. Thanks for the coffee; smells fabulous as usual.'

Luigi was also a sucker for flattery and, predictably, he preened like a proud peacock before bestowing a huge smile and strutting away.

Leaving her exactly where she'd been a few seconds ago: alone, bereft and shattered.

She didn't understand Dante's behaviour, any of it. From the time he'd strolled into the hotel and enlisted her help, none of it had made sense.

Though it was useless to ponder that now. She was more interested in his current abrupt turnaround—from welcoming her into his family one night to walking out on her the next morning without as much as a 'this is the reason why'.

Uh-uh, no sense at all.

He sure hadn't acted as if he'd been expecting her, either—the whole lack of warmth thing had been a dead giveaway! So, if she hadn't craved a mocha-cappa and dropped in at Trevi's, would he have even said goodbye?

If his icy demeanour had been any indication, she seriously doubted it.

Shaking her head, Natasha took a soothing sip of her cappuccino, savouring the creamy coffee sliding down her throat, enjoying the kick of caffeine.

Nothing made sense, least of all the empty sadness clawing at her soul, the devastation that indicated she felt a lot more for Dante than she'd let herself believe.

After another soothing sip, she spied the folded piece of paper on the table. Reaching across, she picked up the small rectangle and unfolded it, knowing it was a cheque. However, what did surprise her, what in fact shocked her, was the amount.

Enough money to clear her debt with Clay, to set her free, to set her family free.

Stifling the insane urge to giggle, she refolded the cheque and slipped it into her handbag. She could tear it up, but couldn't afford to let pride get in the way of common sense.

She'd wished for a miracle last night, had even considered approaching Dante for help, and ironically it looked like she'd got exactly what she'd hoped for.

Then why did it feel like the price she'd paid to gain her miracle was heartbreakingly high?

CHAPTER TWELVE

'SEEING you twice in less than twenty-four hours—you sure you still haven't got a thing for me?'

Natasha heard the click of the door behind her and wondered if it was too late to make a bolt after Clay's secretary.

If his smarminess had made her skin crawl last night, seeing him again so soon made her want to retch.

Ignoring his pathetic greeting, she said, 'Thanks for seeing me. I have something for you.'

She kept her tone brisk, businesslike. She had to, otherwise she'd scream at him.

'This sounds promising.'

He didn't stand. Instead, he leaned back in his gigantic director's chair, hands clasped behind head, smug smile firmly in place, surrounded by a plush office backed by a million-dollar view.

She'd once been impressed by this: his status in the business world, his confidence, his suave looks. But now she saw it for what it was, a set of fake props for a con man. The type of man who would set out to make an innocent woman fall in love with him all in an attempt to get his hands on one of Melbourne's premier hotels.

Clay could've gone for any other hotel—he already owned a number of them—but he'd had to have the best, the crowning glory, the hotel which had been in a family for generations. So he'd set out to get his grubby hands on Telford Towers the only way he knew how.

By deception.

'I've got the final payment for you and the contract for you to sign off.'

'You're kidding?'

His cocky grin slipped, only to be replaced by a cruel twist of his thin lips.

'I'm not in the mood for jokes.' *Especially considering I'm looking at one.* 'Here. Sign next to the cross.'

'The hotel's floundering. How did you get the money so quickly?'

Forcing a sickly sweet smile, knowing it would infuriate him further, she said, 'That's none of your business. Now, sign along the dotted line like we agreed and let's put this all behind us.'

Clay's eyes narrowed to nasty slits as he suddenly bolted upright, his hands slamming on the monstrous mahogany desk.

'You weren't supposed to make the final payment. You were supposed to lose the lot, to me!'

Revulsion rose like acid bile in her throat, and she swallowed with effort. She'd suspected someone had been undercutting their supplies and interfering behind the scenes with the running of the Towers and, as much as she'd seen Clay's hand in it, hearing the man she'd once been engaged to admit his treachery made her physically ill.

'It was always about the Towers, wasn't it?'

The sneer on his face was more eloquent than any words. 'If you'd married me like you were supposed to, none of this would've happened. I'd be the current owner of your pathetic little family hovel, you'd still be running around like an errand girl, we'd have been happy. You wouldn't have had to pay back the money I gave you, I wouldn't have threatened to run a smear campaign on the hotel. Instead, you had to make a big song and dance about discovering my girlfriend, I told you a few home truths, and look where we ended up. Squabbling like a couple of kids.'

She knew the exact moment he'd give it one last go, the sly gleam of cunning lending his opaque eyes a demonic edge. A desperate man tried desperate means, and she knew what was coming before the slime ball opened his mouth.

'Come on, babe. We can give it one last try. Let's put all this behind us and start afresh. You know we'd be a dynamite team in the hotelier field, the best in the business. What do you say?'

Drop dead?

Bite me?

A whole host of less polite responses sprung to mind, but Natasha swallowed them all.

While her feet itched to turn around and make a run for the door, she stood still and tapped the contract in front of him.

'As you can see, this is a legally binding document. It states that my debt to you is paid off, that there will be no further business between us. Is that clear?'

He stood up so quickly she took a step back, hating the glitter of triumph in his cold eyes at a sign of her weakness.

'What if I don't sign? What if I instigate that smear

campaign just as I threatened before, and drag your precious family through the mud?'

It took every ounce of self control for Natasha not to pick up the nearest paperweight and throw it at him.

'You will sign, and you can keep your empty threats. You want to play dirty? Go ahead and try me.'

His sneer solidified her resolve to rid herself of this slime once and for all. 'What are you going to do?'

Clenching her hands into fists, she said, 'Fight back. The only reason I let you get away with any of this is because of my mother. You knew about her heart condition, you knew she was a worrier who'd been advised to avoid stress, but what do you do? You ram the fact you loaned us money down our throats and that you wanted it paid back in blood.'

Her voice choked with raw emotion, the devastation of losing her mum bubbling to the surface, the cold, hard rage that he'd been the cause of it all.

Taking a step forward, she jabbed a finger in his direction. 'You killed her. With your pathetic ruse to get your grubby hands on the hotel through me and your outrageous demands for payback with interest. You rubbed our noses in it, rubbed her nose in it, and you killed her, you bastard.'

His jaw dropped, and if she wasn't so furious she would've laughed at his shock. 'Well, guess what? The damage is done. I've lost my mother, so any smear campaign you run now can't hurt her. I gave into your demands for her sake, to avoid further scandal ruining her health. But that's a moot point now. Go ahead, do your worst. The Telford name can hold its own, but can the same be said for your precious ego? You want me to tell the whole of Melbourne how you really do business and ruin your reputation? Go ahead and try me.'

'No one will believe you.'

She towered over him, wishing she could take a swing, knowing she'd never give him the satisfaction.

'You really take me for a fool, don't you? I have documents stating the original loan amount and the cashed cheque details made out to you. Everyone will know you're a shark, a greedy, manipulative user. So just keep my little proof in mind if you feel the urge to open that big mouth of yours and slander my hotel.'

As Clay's cheeks turned puce with rage, she tapped the contract. 'Sign here. I don't have all day.'

She knew she had him.

His threats might have frightened her at the start, when she would've done anything to save her family the pain of living through the mess she'd made, but not any more. She'd lost her mum, she'd lost her pride and she'd almost lost the hotel courtesy of trusting the wrong man.

But she'd repaid her debt, every last cent, she'd once seen as a generous handout from a caring fiancé who had strutted into her life with pledges of love and endless devotion. Of course, the scheming lowlife had demanded full payment plus interest when she'd ended their engagement, and she'd agreed to his terms for the sake of her family.

Now, Clay wouldn't bother her again. He had an enormous ego and valued appearances beyond any-thing; he would never risk his society cronies or his business associates finding out what he'd done to her. Making her repay a debt was one thing, charging her interest to stop him ruining her family via slander in the hotel business another.

Finally, she'd repaid every penny of his exorbitant interest charges, and as he picked up a silver pen, signed the contract and turned his back on her, she was free.

Folding the contract and tucking it into her purse, she headed for the door and didn't look back.

In fact, she held her head high and practically floated from the Collins Street skyscraper, intent on putting as much distance between Clay and her past as possible.

However, her elation lasted all of two seconds as she boarded a tram, took a seat and glanced out the window at the stunning Sofitel hotel, one of her major competitors, and spotted a familiar figure standing beside a gleaming silver stretch-limo.

Dante hadn't left.

She had to assume he'd merely changed hotels, given that the valet was opening the door for him and doffing his hat.

If he hadn't left the country as she'd thought, he'd changed hotels because he couldn't stand to be near her. It was the only explanation that made any sense.

Tears flooded her eyes and she blinked them away. She must've made a mistake. It wasn't Dante.

But as she watched a broad-shouldered guy in a designer suit, his too-long hair now trimmed to within an inch of its life, his too-blue eyes fixed on a thick pile of documents in his hands, she had her answer.

Dante had resumed his princely duties. He'd returned to normality, to his usual life which didn't include her. Seeing him dressed to the nines, clean shaven and short haired, merely reinforced that the guy she'd known didn't exist.

He never had.

He'd been trying to escape his life for whatever

reasons and she'd got caught in the crossfire. Stupidly, irrevocably, caught in the crossfire which had wounded her heart along the way.

Watching the limo pull away, she swiped at her eyes and sank back into her seat.

Dante had left.

He'd left her.

And, for a woman who'd learned to cope with whatever traumas life threw her way, it hurt more than she could've imagined.

'He's left? What do you mean he's left?'

Natasha took a deep breath, not in the mood to placate Gina who bristled like an angry porcupine, her dark curly hair spiking in all directions as she leaned over the concierge's desk.

'But he told me he was staying here! Why would he change hotels?'

Natasha had pondered that very fact on the interminable tram ride home, grateful when she'd arrived back at the hotel to find she had to fill in for a shift. Anything to dull the pain of realising Gina must've been right. Dante had only been after one thing and, when she'd been too slow in producing the goods, he'd decided to cut his losses and run. Who knew, maybe he was over at the Sofitel right now buttering up some other gullible female with his sexy smile and piercing eyes.

'I have no idea,' she said, sending Gina a glare which said 'don't push me, lady, I'm not in the mood'.

Right now, she was beyond reason. She should've been doing cartwheels through the hotel foyer after finally getting rid of Clay. Instead, she wanted to rant and rave and scream at the injustice of losing the man she'd fallen for. She didn't need to face up to his sister when Gina was the last person she wanted to see.

'But you're his friend. Surely he would've given you some idea why he changed hotels?'

Gritting her teeth in frustration, Natasha said, 'I'm not your brother's keeper. I provided a service for him while he stayed here, that was all. If you need to speak to him, try ringing him.'

Though she wouldn't get the location of his new hotel from Natasha. She'd gone through enough trouble for the royal heartbreaker and being sued because she leaked information was more than she was willing to do.

'This is all very strange.' Gina fixed her with a suspicious glare, as if she didn't believe a word Natasha was saying. 'Dante doesn't do anything impulsively. His official hotel residence was scheduled here months ago. I can't understand why he'd up and leave, especially without telling me.'

Natasha refrained from rolling her eyes, just. If Gina didn't understand the workings of Dante's mind, what hope did she have? Trying to figure out how he might think was a total waste of time.

'If you want answers, the only way to get them is to ask Dante.' *And leave me alone!* 'I'm sorry I can't be of more assistance.'

'Perhaps I should be saying the same to you.'

Gina's dark eyes took on a speculative gleam and Natasha backed away, not liking where this was going.

'I don't know what you mean.'

Gina waved a bejewelled hand in front of her face. 'I'm not blind or stupid, despite what my brother might think of me. I may have made some silly decisions with my own life, but that doesn't mean I can't see what's going on with his.'

She leaned closer and dropped her voice to a dramatic whisper. 'Dante likes you. He would never have brought you to my home otherwise. And, by the look of your long face, I'd say you're just as confused as me by his departure.'

Natasha stiffened, despising herself for the surge of hope Gina's words elicited. Dante liked her? Yeah, right, that was why he'd high-tailed it out of there without an explanation, leaving so fast her head still spun.

Keeping her voice steady with effort, Natasha said, 'Dante's departure has nothing to do with me. Now, if you don't mind, I have work to do—'

'Dante is a proud man, a stubborn man. Don't let his casual attire this last week fool you. He is regal to the bone, and if you want answers you'll have to go straight to the source.'

'I'm not going to see Dante!'

Damn it, the words popped out of her mouth before she could stop them, and Gina's gaze glittered with triumph. 'I can see his interest isn't one-sided. You have feelings for him too.'

Natasha shook her head, wishing her brain hadn't gone into overdrive at Gina's suggestion.

What if the woman was right? She could waste hours, days, longer, wondering why Dante left and why he lied about it. She was a worrier just like her mum; it was an integral part of her personality and she couldn't shut it off.

She'd worried about what her family would think of her hasty engagement to Clay.

She'd worried about taking money from her fiancé when the hotel hit a really tight spot.

She'd worried about losing the family business being her fault.

And now this.

In the grand scheme of things, her interlude with Dante should mean nothing. She should be able to move on, forget about him, chalk up her foolish crush to a woman whose self-esteem had taken a battering and who'd fallen for the next nice guy to smile her way.

However, what she'd shared with Dante hadn't been nothing. It had been something. A big something that kept her awake at night dreaming the impossible dream.

'You know I'm right,' Gina said, her tone surprisingly gentle. 'Go see him.'

She needed answers.

She needed closure.

She needed some sort of reassurance that what they'd shared hadn't been entirely in her imagination. If her self-esteem had been butchered by Clay, it would be nothing on the realisation that she'd conjured up some imaginary bond with Dante to soothe her weary soul.

How pathetic could a girl get?

Suddenly, Gina flung her hands in the air with typical Italian flamboyance. 'You're in love with him!'

Natasha stared at Gina in open-mouthed shock. 'What?'

'You heard me.'

Yeah, she'd heard her, and apart from being stunned by the words themselves she couldn't believe a woman she barely knew, a woman who had warned her off falling for her brother, had uttered them.

'You don't know anything about me,' she said, covering her discomfort with a fake chuckle. 'And I must say, coming hot on the heels of you warning me off Dante, it sounds rather hilarious, not to mention presumptuous.'

Gina reached out as if to grab her hand and Natasha scuttled back, wondering if her day—her week—could get any crazier. 'I'm sorry for what I said to you at Paolo's party. I love my brother and I'm protective of him. He has a hard life and I didn't want it to get harder if he fell for the wrong woman.' She shook her head. 'I can see I'm too late.'

'There is nothing between Dante and me.' She kept her voice steady with extreme effort, trying to project enough force without knocking the other woman down. Besides, what had she meant 'the wrong woman'?

This had to stop. She didn't have to stand here and listen to this.

'I think you should go.'

Her harsh tone should've convinced Gina to leave her alone but it didn't work. She merely stood there with a sorrowful expression on her expertly made-up face. Damn it, the woman had a hide like a rhinoceros.

'Deny it all you like. I know my brother and I can see it in your eyes. You cannot hide it.'

Great, now Gina subscribed to her 'eyes the window to the soul' motto too. 'Well? Are you in love with him?'

She couldn't love Dante.

She may be many things but she wasn't a complete fool. Falling in love with a bad boy would be crazy, falling in love with a rebel prince from the other side of the planet insane. He had a country to run, a suitable bride already chosen and waiting for him back home. She couldn't interfere with that even if she did love him.

Suddenly, an image flashed across her mind of her Dante with his too-long hair, dark stubble and sexy smile, trussed up like she'd seen him in his Internet photo and standing next to a princess. Another Dante altogether, a fake Dante, a Dante who wasn't hers.

Spots swam before her eyes and she gulped for air, hating the constricting band tightening around her chest, leaving her breathless and woozy.

And that's when it hit her.

She wanted *her* Dante, the guy she knew, the guy she'd fallen for, and she wanted him all for herself.

She did love him.

Heart and soul.

The kind of love that lingered long after the person had left your life, the kind of love you remembered for ever, that lasted for ever, no matter how much you tried to forget.

Natasha blinked several times, somewhat surprised to find Gina staring at her with concern, a concierge desk between them in a room where she'd sought refuge so many times over the last few years.

Her hotel's foyer, with its familiar ochre and red swirly rugs, its chocolate-brown suede couches and a hand-carved wooden chest her mum had given her for her twenty-first taking pride of place at the entrance to her office.

Other mums would've called it a glory box and hinted at a future of wedded bliss for their daughters, but not her mum. Her chest had been stuffed with her favourite things: a hand-made quilt, one of her mum's best patterns, with red Chinese silk alternating with gold, five boxes of her favourite caramels, the entire collection of Robbie Williams CDs, and a jade Buddha for good luck.

Her mum had been the best and she missed her terribly. Every time she snuggled up in the quilt she felt secure, as if her mum was right there, wrapping her arms around her along with the silky comforter.

What would her mum think of Dante?

She'd always had a thing for royalty, and Natasha remembered staring through the banisters of the hotel as a little girl, mesmerised by a visiting Asian king and queen that her mum had spun fantastic tales about.

Yeah, her mum would probably have liked Dante, but would she recommend her only child taking a chance on love knowing it could only lead to heartache?

'You don't have to say a word. Your face says it all.' Gina reached over the desk and patted her on the shoulder. 'Go and see him. It's the only way.'

The fool's way.

The dreamer's way.

Right now, she was a combination of both. She'd spent her life living up to responsibility, taking control of what needed to be done.

Well, she was tired of all that. Maybe it was foolish, maybe dreams were for suckers, but facing up to the truth after hearing it from a woman she barely knew had been the wake-up call she needed.

'I guess I should be thanking you, but I'm too busy blaming you.'

'What did I do?' Gina's tentative grin took years off her face, and Natasha could see a glimpse of the princess Dante had described, the type of woman who'd fallen for a foreign guy and had left her home to follow her dream.

If only she had the courage to do something like that…if only she had the opportunity…

'If you weren't so terrible at organising kids' parties, Dante wouldn't have needed my help and none of this would've happened.'

Gina shrugged, not at all insulted by her bluntness. 'I am a princess, what can I say?'

Natasha joined in her laughter, though it petered out quickly. No matter how she felt or whether she was willing to acknowledge it—let alone suss out how Dante felt—this couldn't end well.

There would be no happy endings here.

Dante had a country to run, she had a hotel to run.

They lived oceans apart.

And even if by some miracle he felt something for her, what did she think? That he'd ask her to be his princess? Fat chance.

However, she needed to do this for herself, and confronting Dante would be the first step in getting over him.

You wish.

'I'm going to see him right now,' she said, frantically signalling at a front-desk employee to act as stand-in concierge before she changed her mind.

'Good.' Gina's smug grin annoyed her, and she fixed her with a glare.

'Why are you doing this?'

'Because I love Dante.' Well, that made two of them. 'I care about what happens to him.'

Though Natasha didn't have a sibling, she understood where Gina was coming from. If anyone ever messed with Ella, she would interfere too.

'If there's anything else I can do—'

'Please don't take this the wrong way, Gina, but I've listened to your crazy theories about me loving your brother.' *Well, not so crazy as it turned out.* 'And I've considered what you've said when I hardly know you, but I think I can take it from here.'

Could she say 'butt out' any more politely?

'I think that will change very soon—the part about you not knowing me,' Gina said, not fazed in the slightest by her outburst. 'Now, I must go. Tell the runaway his sister is looking for him and get him to call me? *Ciao.*'

Gina blew her a kiss and strolled across the lobby, looking every inch a princess in head-to-toe designer black.

She must be crazy to listen to his sister, a woman who the day before had been warning her to stay away.

She must be totally insane to consider confronting Dante after he'd made it perfectly clear he wanted nothing more to do with her.

Well, luckily for her, she was in a loco type of mood, and after the fastest handover in history she sprinted for her room.

'I'm not trying to impress him,' Natasha muttered, yanking her favourite black cargos and apple-green halter out of the wardrobe as she shimmied out of the boring navy suit she'd worn to her meeting with Clay. 'But I don't want to scare him off either.'

Besides, perhaps a change of outfit would give her a much needed boost in confidence.

Okay, now she was taking fashion advice from her inner voice, which just so happened to be making itself heard. Could she get any more pathetic?

Annoyed at her interior monologue, she dressed, slipped her feet into strappy high-heeled sandals and fastened small silver hoops in her ears, running a quick slick of gloss over her lips.

Go get him, princess.

While Natasha frowned at her frightened reflection, she couldn't help but like how the title sounded.

CHAPTER THIRTEEN

TAKING a deep breath, Natasha knocked on the door of room 1718 before she lost her nerve.

Her sharp rapping at the door shattered the peace of the plush corridor with its soft lighting and thick carpet.

Maybe Dante wasn't in. She'd been so fired up to confront him and get this ordeal over and done with that she hadn't considered that scenario. Besides, her mind had been too busy devising a way to discover his room number when Lady Luck had smiled down on her. Running into Fay, the Sofitel's day manager and her one-time room-mate at an hotelier's conference, had been a major bonus.

She hadn't felt so great having to tell a little white lie to get the information she needed out of Fay. But, hey, the whole 'a client left something rather delicate behind at the Towers and I thought I'd bring it over and deliver it personally' story had been the most plausible thing she'd been able to come up with on the spur of the moment.

Thankfully, it had worked like a charm and Fay had given her Dante's room number—after ear-bashing her for ten minutes on how utterly dreamy the prince was. As if she hadn't noticed!

Glaring at the wooden door and wishing it would open, Natasha almost stumbled back when it did.

'What are you doing here?'

Okay, not the most pleasant of greetings, and Dante sure didn't look happy to see her if that massive frown and lack of a smile was any indication. Well, too bad. She hadn't come all this way to turn tail and run now.

'Can I come in?'

Calm, collected, straight to the point. If only she could keep it up, if he ever let her in the door.

'Fine, but I have a lot of work to do, so make it quick.'

He stepped aside and, ignoring his rudeness, she entered the room, her keen eye doing a quick scan of the competition. Larger than the Towers' average room, the Tiffany lamps, the comfy armchairs, the antiques and the fresh flowers all faded into oblivion when her gaze lit on the bed, a huge king-size monstrosity covered in the richest cream damask fabric. It appeared larger than life, and seemed to beckon with its plump cushions and thick quilt.

When the door shut, she quickly averted her gaze and swung around to face Dante, desperately trying to erase the vivid image she'd just had of the two of them together on that inviting bed.

'Would you like something to drink?'

'No thanks.'

'Why are you here, Natasha?'

Well, that took care of the formalities, but in a way she was glad he cut to the chase. She hadn't come here to rehash old news, she wanted answers, closure, anything to ease the tension winding her tighter than a spring.

'You said you were leaving. You're still here.'

A wary expression flickered in his eyes, the clear aquamarine highlighted by his pale blue business shirt, the faintest gold pinstripes catching the light. On anyone else, the shirt would've looked wrong. On him, it accentuated his status and screamed royalty.

By the rest of his outfit, it seemed he'd stepped back into prince mode well and truly: designer trousers with a perfect crease, the fancy shirt and a royal-blue tie bearing what looked like a small crest. Probably the Andretti coat of arms. He appeared all business, and then some, and she didn't like it.

Natasha had thought he might still be casual. The Dante she knew…and loved. However, there wasn't a peep of denim or stubble in sight, and she missed it, missed the warmth they'd once shared if for an all too brief moment.

Dante in his fancy outfit looked every inch the untouchable prince, and served to reinforce the huge gap between them. What hope did she have?

'But why are *you* here?'

She hated when people didn't give her direct answers or, worse, answered a question with a question. Her parents had raised her to be upfront and honest at all costs.

Then why don't you go ahead and tell him why you're really here?

Hmm…maybe her whole 'honesty is the best policy' motto could wait just a tad longer.

Trying not to shuffle under his steady stare, she thrust her hands in her pockets and squared her shoulders. 'Gina is looking for you.'

He raised an eyebrow, obviously not expecting that response. 'I'll get in touch with her. Now, if there's nothing else—'

'Actually, I wanted to clear the air between us,' she rushed on, hating his stilted formality, wanting to recapture the closeness they'd had.

His frown deepened. 'We have nothing to discuss that I'm aware of.'

'Then we agree to differ. The way I see it, we were getting along just fine and then yesterday, out of the blue, you up and leave. Only you didn't leave Melbourne as you led me to believe, you changed hotels, which begs the question—why?'

'I don't owe you any explanations,' he said, staring over her shoulder at the stunning view of the Melbourne city skyline she'd glimpsed when she'd first entered the room.

'You're right, you don't owe me anything. But you're a decent guy and I thought we had a connection. The time we spent together seemed special, and perhaps there was something more than just friendship between us. Maybe I was wrong?'

There, she'd said it.

So the words had tumbled out in a confused jumble, and she'd spoiled the ending by her voice rising, but she'd made the first overture, had told the semi-truth—*'connection' could be a euphemism for love, right*? Now she waited, breath held, for some kind of response from the man who set her pulse pounding just by being in the same room.

He didn't flinch, he didn't move, he didn't speak, and for an endless, embarrassing moment Natasha thought she'd have to walk out the door with her pride as well as her heart in tatters.

Finally, something shifted in his eyes, cold wariness replaced by a flicker of warmth, and he gestured to the armchairs. 'Please be seated.'

Not exactly the answer she'd been hoping for, but it was a start. At least she was still here and, by his softening posture, she might get the answers she'd hoped for yet.

After folding his tall frame into the chair opposite, he sat back and regarded her with a suspicious stare.

'I didn't say I was leaving Melbourne. You chose to interpret it that way.'

'But why would you leave Telford Towers? I thought you liked it there from what you said, and after the time we spent together…' She trailed off, surprised by the sudden flash of fire in his eyes.

'That was a business arrangement.'

The fire she'd glimpsed quickly dimmed to glacial coldness, matching his icy, clipped tone.

'Which you reneged on!'

Wrong answer. He froze, his posture screaming 'back off'.

'Was the cheque not suitable?'

'The cheque was fine. In fact, it was very generous, but that's not what I meant and you know it.'

'I have other business to attend to this week and taking part in your hotel's publicity would not have fit in. I made a business decision, nothing personal.'

Right then, it hit her, and Natasha sagged against the plump cushions.

Nothing personal…

Unfortunately, that was the problem here. She'd obviously built a ludicrous fairy tale in her head about mutual attraction and friendship and camaraderie when in fact, from Dante's point of view, there had been nothing personal in any of it.

Nothing personal, indeed.

'I'm sorry to take up your time.' She rose, aiming for a dignified exit.

She'd come here for answers and she'd got what she wanted. Unfortunately, her heart refused to comprehend what her head had computed a long time ago: she wasn't cut out for relationships or whatever it was she thought she'd shared with Dante.

She didn't like pain, particularly the dull ache residing around her heart which would take a lifetime to shift. It wasn't an entirely new sensation. She'd felt something similar when she'd learned of Clay's betrayal, and later when her mum died, but the pain had been different. More acute, less pervasive.

Nothing like the building pressure, the constant ache, which centred around her heart now and spread its tentacles outwards, squeezing the very breath out of her.

She had to get out. Now.

Crossing the room took an eternity as she concentrated on forcing her feet to move, and she sighed in relief as her hand hit the cold door-handle.

'You lied too.'

Natasha stopped, her hand poised in mid-turn, not sure if she'd heard correctly.

'There couldn't have been any connection between us because you're still involved with your ex.'

Without thinking, she whirled to face him, her desperate escape plan thwarted by the urge to throw something at him.

'You're crazy. I loathe him. You saw how he was when you pulled your little stunt out the front of the Towers. Why would you think I'd still be involved with him?'

He folded his arms and glared, the epitome of a guy not used to being crossed.

'I saw you in the Lobby Bar. All over him.'

She shook her head, wishing she could take hold of his and knock it against the wall to bang some sense into him.

'That wasn't how it looked.'

Suddenly, Dante moved towards her in a blur, his hands gripping her upper arms so tight she almost cried out.

'You want to know how it looked? It looked like you were a cosy couple, that you were enjoying it, that you were the type of woman to flirt with one man and wrap him around your little finger for a week, while still involved with another.'

He spat the words out, his voice laced with contempt, his arms rigid, and as she stared into the furious face of the man she loved Natasha knew she finally had her closure.

'You saw what you wanted to see,' she said, breaking his hold and opening the door in record speed, hating the sobs which bubbled out of her throat, and tore free, dashing the tears from her eyes.

She may have fallen in love with a prince but Dante had just proved himself a lesser man than she'd thought.

'Tasha, I'm sorry—'

She didn't wait to hear the rest as the door slammed shut and her feet flew down the long corridor.

She'd heard enough.

'What is troubling you?'

Dante turned from the parapet, not in the mood to have this conversation with his mother. Then again, he wasn't in the mood for much these days.

'Nothing,' he said, knowing she wouldn't leave it alone.

Elena Andretti, Queen of Calida, didn't disappoint.

'Ever since you returned from Melbourne yesterday, you look like the sky is going to fall in. Or, worse, that I'm going to announce your betrothal in your first week home.'

She crossed the ancient stone flag way and took hold

of his hand, her grip as strong as ever. 'Please, give your old mother some credit. I'm going to wait till next week at least!'

He usually laughed at his mother's feeble jokes. Today, he couldn't even muster a half-hearted chuckle.

'What happened? Was it a woman?'

'It was nothing.' He shook his head, hating how insignificant that sounded.

Nothing…what a lie.

Natasha had been the woman with the potential to rock his world, and in many ways she had, yet no matter which way he looked at it the whole thing with her had been a sham. He'd seen the proof with his own eyes.

'If you don't tell me, Gina will.'

His mother dropped his hand and turned away, leaning on the parapet and taking in the view he'd just been staring at without seeing.

'I never tire of this view. The unique colour of the ocean, the fishing boats, the whitewashed houses, the mountains. We're blessed, Dante, to rule such beauty. It is a gift from God, and we can never take it for granted. You know that, don't you?'

Dante propped himself next to her, knowing this was yet another variation on her usual 'you are a man with responsibilities' speech, the same speech he'd heard in a thousand different ways since he'd been able to walk and talk.

'I don't need a lecture, Mother.'

She turned to face him with a surprising turn of speed for a woman who used an ornate cane to get anywhere these days, her gait usually a slow, regal shuffle.

'You need something to snap you out of this lethargy. It won't do for people to see you like this.'

'It's jetlag, that's all.'

Though he knew that excuse would soon wear thin. Somehow, he knew his lack of sleep on the long flight home and since his arrival had nothing to do with a haywire body clock and everything to do with a stunning brunette he couldn't get out of his mind.

'Well, see that you get enough rest. We're entertaining several prominent families over the next few evenings, starting tomorrow. You need to be at your best.'

Dante stifled a grimace, deciphering his mother's code easily. 'Entertaining prominent families' meant she'd chosen a selection of prospective brides and he'd be expected to make a decision before the week was out.

An appalling old tradition at the best of times, but now, with his head still spinning with memories of Natasha and his heart doing goodness knew what, he couldn't summon enthusiasm to get out of bed let alone entertain his future wife.

'It is your duty, Dante.'

With those ominous words ringing in his ears, he watched his mother walk away, an old lady in tailored finery but an old lady nonetheless.

He knew about duty.

He'd been born to it, raised to it.

He didn't have a choice.

But what if there was more to life?

He'd never questioned his birthright and, even while envying Gina her freedom to marry whomever she chose and live wherever took her fancy, he'd always known where his duty lay.

Meeting Natasha had changed all that.

For the first time in his life, he'd known what it felt like to belong, and it had nothing to do with location or possessions or home. Instead, it had everything to do with being with the right person, the type of person who made you laugh and smile and want to be a better man.

Unfortunately for him, he'd felt all that and more in less than a week of knowing her, a woman who belonged to another.

However, one thing still niggled: her visit to his hotel and the motivation behind her passionate outburst. He'd analysed it, considered it from every angle, and it didn't make sense.

She'd had no reason to visit him and accuse him of lying about leaving, even less reason to discuss the connection they'd shared. Her bluntness had surprised him, taken him off guard, but he'd quickly dismissed the whole thing as a desperate attempt on her part to get him involved in her hotel's publicity again.

However, she hadn't mentioned any of that. And when he'd lost his cool at the end about seeing her with her ex, the look of devastation in her eyes had nearly killed him. He's glimpsed raw, savage pain before she'd run away, her sobs tearing at his soul.

He'd almost run after her before his damned pride had kicked in.

She'd made her choice, who was he to interfere in her life? If anyone knew what that was like, he did.

His whole life had been open to scrutiny, available for anybody and everybody to interfere with. He'd accepted it a long time ago but that didn't mean he had to like it. He respected Natasha's freedom of choice, almost envied it, even if the thought of her with her ex made him want to jump off the castle.

Why the visit?

It all came back to the same question, reverberating

around his head till he could quite happily thump it against the ancient stone parapet just to clear it.

She hadn't acted like a woman trying to stay close to him for the sake of business. In fact, the longer he pondered her motivation, the harder it was to shake off the conviction that she'd acted like a woman who cared. About him.

Ridiculous.

Wishful thinking?

Whatever, he needed to forget her.

He had a life of responsibility ahead of him, a life as a husband, a life as a king.

Starting tomorrow, he'd take the first step in doing the right thing, the honourable thing, the type of sacrifice expected of a ruler. He would choose a suitable bride and make the most of it, just like leaders of Calida had done for centuries before him.

Starting tomorrow...

For today, he would purge his mind of Natasha's memory as best he could.

And pray to God his future bride sparked as much passion, as much interest in him, as she had.

CHAPTER FOURTEEN

'How's my favourite girl?'

Natasha looked up from the ledger she'd been poring over, smiling for the first time in a week.

'Welcome home, Dad.'

She flung herself into his arms as she had as a little girl, fast and furious, needing a comforting hug more now than she ever had back then.

'I take it you missed me?'

Roger Telford stepped out of her embrace, holding her at arm's length. 'If that's the type of welcome home I get, remind your dear old dad to go away more often.'

Natasha chuckled. 'You make it sound like I take you for granted when you're here.'

'Just kidding, princess.' He tapped her on the nose and sank into the nearest chair, patting the arm while her heart somersaulted.

She'd had a whole week to put the Dante fiasco behind her, seven long days to concentrate on business, throw herself into making the hotel flourish now it was properly theirs again. One hundred and sixty eight endless hours to fill with girlie chats with Ella, work and sleep, anything to stop her thinking of Dante and how wrong she'd been about him.

And all it took was her dad to call her by an ancient pet name and it all flooded back, every embarrassing detail of how she'd virtually thrown herself at Dante and how he'd rebuked her.

'Is everything all right?'

Mustering a smile with effort, she said, 'Fine. And you will be too when I tell you my news.'

She needed to distract her dad, and quickly. Since the Clay debacle, he'd been extra protective and if he got a whiff there was something wrong—or worse, that it had to do with a man—he'd never drop it.

'What news?'

His jovial smile vanished, the wrinkles around his eyes deepening as he fixed her with a worried stare.

'It's good, Dad, and I didn't tell you while you were in Perth because I knew you'd probably fly straight back here.'

'This doesn't sound good. Now, sit down before I get a crick in my neck.'

Natasha perched on the chair's arm, remembering the many times she'd done the same thing growing up. Her parents had always had an open-door policy and, with Natasha being an only child, they'd been an incredibly close family.

She'd come to them when Debbie MacCraw had bullied her the first day of school, she'd come to them when Samuel Grace hadn't asked her to the graduation dance, and she'd come to them when she'd discovered Clay's true colours—lily-livered stripes.

However, no matter how understanding her dad would be, she'd save the Dante disaster for another day.

He'd only just arrived home, and she'd make sure the news was all good.

'Relax, Dad. You're going to love this, I promise.' She patted his shoulder, surprised to feel the bony prominences under the thin cotton shirt.

Her dad had always been larger than life for her, as healthy as a horse, but when her mum had died she'd noticed a certain frailty about him and it looked like he hadn't been eating well while away.

'The Towers is ours again. One hundred percent debt free.'

'You paid that scumbag off? How?'

Rather than alleviating the lines around her dad's eyes, his frown increased them tenfold.

'The Prince of Calida helped. I did some PA work for him while he was here; he paid me well. It was a win-win situation for everyone.'

Then why did she feel like the biggest loser in the world?

'That is good news. I can't believe it.'

Her dad sat back, his frown disappearing, replaced by a stunned expression which took years off him. 'We're seriously debt free again?'

'Seriously.'

Natasha smiled, squeezed her dad's shoulder and stood up. Now that she'd delivered the good news, time for her to escape while her dad was still absorbing it. Otherwise, he'd turn his eagle eye back on her, and she couldn't stand the scrutiny right now. Who knew what she might blab under duress?

'Guess we owe the prince one.'

Her smile faltered but she recovered quickly. 'I

thanked him. He was very impressed with our hotel. I'm sure he'll recommend us.'

As if.

He'd been so impressed he'd vacated quicker than she could say 'please come again,' and crossed town to the opposition.

'Have I told you lately what an asset you are to the hotel? And how lucky I am to have you as a daughter?'

His eyes misted over, and Natasha knew she'd have to make a run for it before she started blubbering.

'You don't have to tell me. I know. Now, you relax and I'll organise supper to be brought up to you.'

Her dad smiled. 'I am a bit tired. See you in the morning?'

'You bet.'

Blowing him a kiss, Natasha left the room where she'd spent her happiest years with her family. However, come morning, she wondered if the happy times would be a thing of the past once she dropped the next bomb-shell on her dad.

Natasha had just finished the new concierge's orienta-tion when Gina walked into the hotel foyer, her search-ing gaze zoning in on Natasha before she could duck behind the front desk.

Great, just what she needed, a blast from the not-so-distant, not-so-pleasant past.

'Not you again!' She was *so* not in the mood for whatever the princess had to say.

Ignoring her blatant rudeness, Gina smiled. 'Just the woman I wanted to see. Do you have a minute?'

Natasha made a big show of checking her watch

when she knew the only pressing engagement she had
was with her dad to tell him her decision.

'One minute.'

Natasha indicated the comfy couches in a secluded
corner of the lobby, and Gina nodded.

She looked amazing in a fitted burgundy coat-dress
with matching designer handbag and shoes, her make-up
immaculate, her curls in perfect smooth ringlets. Natasha
felt like Orphan Annie in hand-me-downs next to her.

'If you've come here to talk about Dante again, forget
it.' Natasha hated how rude she sounded, but she didn't
care. She was over the Andretti family, well and truly.

Gina sighed and shook her head. 'Did Dante tell you
about our mother?'

Natasha wondered if she'd entered the twilight zone.
Every time Gina showed up and opened her mouth, her
confusion meter went up a notch.

'A bit.'

'Mother is pushy, opinionated and always right.'

'Hmm…' Natasha mumbled, stifling a grin as she
recalled Dante saying something along similar lines
about Gina.

'Dante's life has been mapped out since birth,
whereas I had the fortune to be born a girl, and second,
so I could escape. My brother hasn't had the privilege.'

Everything was still clear as mud, so Natasha opted
for her usual honest policy.

'I'm not sure why you're telling me all this.'

With a swift change in mood that left Natasha
reeling, Gina's dark eyes pinned hers with an accusatory glare. 'Dante didn't say goodbye to me, he simply
vanished back home. He isn't taking my calls either.
Normally I wouldn't interfere any more than I already

have, but this is getting out of control. Apparently, he's behaving like a love-struck fool in Calida. My mother is at her wits' end and she's pestering me every day to find out what happened when Dante was in Melbourne. I had to see you and find out how your last visit went with Dante before my mother drives me mad. Or worse, visits me.'

Gina paused to take a breath while Natasha tried to ignore the fact of Dante in love with some lucky woman.

Love-struck…love-struck…

The phrase made her head ache, and froze her heart in a veneer of icy misery.

It shouldn't hurt this much.

She should be over him.

She'd tried everything, from distracting visualisation techniques—somehow, a calm beach scene morphed into her and Dante frolicking in the waves together—to rainforest CDs—the soothing bird chirps reminded her of animals, which reminded her of Dante and their visit to the animal farm.

On and on it went: the memories of the loaded stares and that scintillating kiss, fake or not. She couldn't get him out of her head, and now Gina had to show up to rub her nose in it. What was with this family?

Natasha stood and towered over Gina, trying to make a point with her intimidating stance. 'Look, I'm happy for Dante, but I have no idea why your mother is hounding you or why in turn you're hounding me. You don't even know me!'

Gina's perfectly shaped eyebrows shot up. 'You're happy he's pining over you? Aren't you going to do something about it?'

Natasha sat down as quickly as she'd stood up. 'You can't possibly mean—'

'Come on, you don't need to play games with me any more. We both know he's totally in love with you but for some reason you're here while he's there. I'd hoped maybe you'd sorted out something. Maybe you're going to join him shortly?'

Natasha wanted to strangle the woman. However, if she did that, she'd never get to the bottom of this whole mix-up. For some bizarre, twisted reason, Gina thought Dante was in love with her.

She wished.

Knowing it would take the blunt truth to get rid of Gina, Natasha said, 'Dante and I didn't part on the best of terms after *you* prompted me to go see him. And I can categorically say I'm the last person he'd be in love with. So there's been a mistake, and I'm sorry, but you'll have to sort it out yourselves.'

Gina shook her head, her slick curls tumbling around her heart-shaped face. 'No mistake. Dante loves you.'

Natasha sat back in an undignified slump, despising herself for the surge of hope Gina's words fuelled.

Dante loved her? No way.

They'd definitely had a spark, but he'd even denied that when she'd confronted him, when she'd put her heart on the line and he'd trampled it without a thought.

She'd harboured a faint hope he might've cared more than he was letting on when he'd been jealous about seeing her with Clay, but that hope had soon faded into oblivion around the time he'd let her walk out of his life without giving her a chance to explain, or putting up a fight.

Uh-uh, he couldn't love her.

He didn't love her.

But what if he did?

Gina snapped her fingers like a conjurer creating magic. 'You should go visit him in Calida. Sort everything out. Stay there. Get married. Whatever. Just be gentle. Dante's a good man and he deserves to be happy.'

Natasha stared at Gina as if she'd lost her mind. 'I can't. I put myself on the line with your brother once, he didn't want me. End of story.'

'That's what you think,' Gina said, leaping up from the chair as if she'd sat on an ant hill. 'I was wrong about you. You weren't a last fling for my brother, you're the only woman he wants.'

Natasha shook her head, formulating another argument to convince Gina she'd lost her mind. However, she never had a chance as Gina bent to give her a quick hug, muttered 'I'll be in touch' and stormed away before she could say another word.

This can't be happening, Natasha thought, while a glimmer of an idea flickered in the far recesses of her brain. The news she had to tell her dad involved a break. A much needed break from the hotel, a little R and R, a chance to regroup her thoughts, heal her heart.

She'd planned on taking a mini holiday. Somewhere warm, remote, secluded, with little interference from the outside world. A small island, perhaps?

No, no, no!

Gina had messed with her head. She had no intention of visiting Calida, now or ever.

If her self-esteem had taken a battering with Clay, it had fractured for ever with Dante. She didn't need him reinforcing how he didn't find her appealing, how much she'd got the whole situation skewed. She may be many things, but a masochist wasn't one of them.

Her plan was simple.

Now that her dad was back, she could take a well-earned break and figure out where her life was heading. She'd invested most of her life in the hotel, and suddenly its dazzle had worn off. Whether the lure of the unobtainable fairy tale or meeting a go-get-'em guy like Dante had tainted her view, she knew it was time to take stock.

And banish thoughts of a blue-eyed sexy prince from her mind for ever.

'You've been avoiding me.'

Dante sat behind his desk, used to facing pushy dignitaries and world leaders via the wonders of tele-conferencing, but never had he faced an irate Gina.

His sister looked mad enough to jump on a plane and return to Calida, and that was saying something.

'I haven't been avoiding you. I just didn't have time to say goodbye in Melbourne and I've been very busy since I returned home.'

'Liar,' she said, her black eyes flashing with disgust clearly visible even on a grainy screen. 'You were never any good at telling lies.'

'A good thing, I would suggest.' He sat back and folded his arms, wishing he wasn't so defensive around her all the time.

He'd always been like this with his younger sister: vacillating between condescending and superior, firm and in charge. He couldn't help it. Once his father had died, he'd become the man of the family, his mother had seen to that.

In a way, he felt like he'd failed Gina in not protecting her better from her disastrous marriage, in not making her understand the beauties of home. Maybe if he'd done a better job looking after his sister, she wouldn't have done absolutely anything—including marrying the wrong man—to escape.

'Cut the smug act, big brother. I need to discuss something important with you.'

He sat forward, concerned. 'Are you all right? Is Paolo all right?'

He was so wrapped up in his misery that perhaps he'd missed something.

'We're fine, though we're both hurting from you running out on us without saying goodbye.'

Dante flinched as if she'd reached through the screen and struck him. He hated how he'd left without talking to his family, especially when he'd specifically travelled to Melbourne earlier to rebuild bridges with his sister.

But he couldn't face her after the debacle with Natasha, couldn't face her inevitable probing, her bossy brand of curiosity, so he'd taken the easy way out and had withdrawn into official duties. For Gina to talk about emotions, he must've hurt her beyond belief. His super-confident sister never thought of anyone's feelings let alone her own.

'I'm sorry. I had a lot on my mind.'

'I know. I visited her. Twice.'

He sat up and peered at the screen. 'I beg your pardon?'

Gina smiled, the same cheeky smile she'd given him a thousand times growing up, when she'd put snails in his bed, snatched the last sweet cannoli off his plate, and fed his algebra to a goat.

'Natasha. Your *friend*. I've seen her, twice.'

His heart flipped at hearing her name, his mind blurring with images of her and the special time they'd spent together in a city far away.

'Why would you do something like that? You don't even know her.'

'So she keeps telling me.' Gina rolled her eyes. 'She's as stubborn as you, that one. You're a match made in heaven.'

'You didn't answer my question,' he said, ignoring the stab of pain lancing his soul. Perhaps they could've been a good match if only Natasha had been more honest with him and he was a different man.

'I'm doing this because I want you to be happy,' she said, her voice dropping unexpectedly. 'Because I don't want you making the same mistakes I did.'

Damn it, they should've been having this talk face to face, not via nebulous technological means. He'd screwed up with his sister—again.

'Are you sure you want to talk about this?'

Gina nodded, her dark curls bouncing around her face. 'Don't you think we've avoided it for too long?'

She was right, but was this the time or place? His mind was in a muddle over Natasha and his emotions swinging all over the place.

After a long moment, he finally nodded. 'You know I love you, right?'

Her bittersweet smile spoke volumes. 'Yes, but you also resent me. You always have.'

An instant rebuttal sprung to his lips and he swallowed it. As much as it pained him to admit it, she was right, and he'd fostered this latent animosity long enough.

'I've envied your freedom, your ability to take charge of your own destiny,' he said, hating how petty he sounded but feeling like a weight had slipped off his shoulders for admitting it.

'Even when I made a mess of things?'

'At least it was your choice to make. I may have come across as the disapproving brother, but that's only because of my own inadequacies at not protecting you better. Besides, you're happy now?'

Gina's genuine smile warmed his heart better than any confession. 'I love Melbourne. Don't tell Mother, but I'm proud to be Calidian and I even miss home at times. Though I wouldn't trade my current life for the world…or a crown,' she added, a pointed glance his way, which lost some of its impact through the screen.

'Don't get carried away. I may envy you your freedom, but my duty is important to me. It's what I've grown up with, it's what I know, and I'd never let my country down.'

'But what about yourself?'

Her almost whisper slammed into his conscience, resurrecting similar questions he'd asked himself but successfully buried when he'd put his interlude with Natasha behind him.

'I am content,' he said, hating how hollow his forced statement sounded.

His sister finally sounded at peace and they'd broached their feelings; the last thing he wanted to do was laden her down with his problems.

'Content is not happy. Content does not recognise love. Content does not keep you warm at night or stand by your side while you rule.'

'Leave it alone, Gina.'

He had, leaving his brief taste of true happiness behind when he closed his heart to the one woman who made him dream about possibilities and future.

Gina smiled and waggled her finger at him. 'Now, what sort of a caring sister would I be if I left you to your own devices? What I wanted to say before we got all sentimental was that Natasha is in love with you, so whatever is keeping you apart get over it and make yourself happy for once. Calida will always be there, the crown will always be there, but your one shot at true love may not be, so don't screw it up.'

She didn't have to add 'like I did'. He could see regret written all over her face.

Not wanting to hurt his sister after she'd gone to a lot of trouble to finally pin him down and open up, he said, 'I appreciate all of this.'

Non-committal, honest and brief, his usual way of handling news which made him uncomfortable. And right now the thought of Natasha truly loving him and the fact he'd thrown it away didn't only make him uncomfortable, it made him downright sick to his stomach.

'Good luck, big brother.'

Gina blew him a kiss and he returned the action, feeling exceedingly stupid sending kisses to a screen.

Not half as stupid as he'd feel if he'd managed to ruin any chance of a future with the woman he loved.

CHAPTER FIFTEEN

'YOU sure you want to do this?'

Natasha zipped her case, plopped onto the bed next to her dad and slipped an arm around his waist. 'I'm sure, though I'm going to miss you.'

'Bet you won't even give us a second thought.'

Ella leaned in the bedroom doorway, a mutinous frown on her expressive face, the same kind of look Natasha had seen a million times when Ella was trying to contain her emotions. No way would her feisty friend ever let anyone see her cry.

'I'm taking a break, not leaving for ever. Come on, guys, be happy for me.'

Her dad hugged her. 'We are, sweetheart. It just won't be the same around here without you. But take as long as you like. We'll be fine.'

'Yeah,' Ella said, swiping a hand over her eyes at the same time she did. 'Jinx!'

For Natasha's sake, she could do without any jinxes. She needed a change of luck, starting today.

'Right. Time to go.'

She hated goodbyes for the simple fact she'd never had to face many. A homebody all her life, she'd loved the Towers too much to leave, loved her family too much to be away for longer than school camp. Familiarity bred security, and right at that moment, surrounded by her dad and her best friend, she'd never felt so secure.

But she was a big girl now.

Time to shake her life up a little, step out of her comfort zone and give her self-esteem a much-needed boost—starting with a month-long sojourn on one of Australia's northernmost beaches.

'Love you, Dad,' she said, succumbing to her dad's bear hug and blinking back tears.

'Love you too, princess,' he said, ruffling her hair like he had when she was four, and making her want to bawl more than ever.

Pulling away, she turned towards Ella with arms outstretched. 'Hug me if you think I'm cool.'

Ella snorted and, as she hugged her tight, she knew she couldn't have survived the last few years without her, and hoped her extended break wouldn't change things between them. They were more than best friends; Ella had become her surrogate sister, and she needed her as much as her dad.

'Enough of the mushy stuff,' Ella said, breaking the hug as both of them made surreptitious sweeps at their eyes.

A loud knock at the door startled Natasha and she glanced at her watch. 'Must be the bell boy. Okay, load up the bags. Looks like I'm on my way.'

Ella opened the door while she bustled around the room, making sure she hadn't left anything behind.

'Anyone seen my Palm Pilot?'

An eerie silence greeted her and she swung around, wondering if the others had ducked out on her rather than face any more goodbyes.

However, Ella and her dad hadn't left. Instead, they surrounded the open doorway like a welcoming committee while a guy wearing a uniform—not one of the hotel's—slowly turned around.

Natasha's heart stopped and she held her breath, her head reeling from lack of oxygen or shock, or a combination of both, as she stared in open-mouthed amazement at the last man she'd ever expected to see.

'We'll leave you alone,' Ella said, herding her confused dad out the door and closing it behind them in record time.

'Hello, Tasha.'

'What are you doing here?'

To her surprise, she managed to work her mouth and brain in sync, though now her heart had kick-started again the roaring of her pulse in her ears almost deafened her.

'I'm here on official business.'

Dante hadn't moved far into the room, giving her plenty of opportunity to study him. She'd never seen him like this: navy uniform, myriad medals pinned over his left breast pocket, hair slicked back without a curl in sight. However, what threw her the most was his expression: uncertainty warred with hope, warmth battled with—dare she say it?—desire.

'Official business, huh?'

He nodded, a stilted action which fitted perfectly with his formal attire, a regal action befitting a prince.

'Yes. I've come to apologise for my atrocious behaviour when we last met. And to convince the woman I love to take a chance on me. A very important task I couldn't entrust to anybody else, so here I am.'

Natasha gaped, knowing he couldn't possibly mean

what he'd just said, knowing he couldn't possibly be referring to her.

'Well?'

Suddenly, her brain kicked into gear and she snapped out of the befuddled fog that had pervaded the room the minute he'd stepped into it.

'Well what? You expect me to believe that? Come on, I'm not that gullible.'

She folded her arms and propped on the hall table, wishing her pulse would slow down, wishing he didn't look so darn appealing even trussed up like a rigid soldier.

'I'm sorry you've come all this way, but Gina's playing some warped trick on the both of us, sticking her nose where it isn't wanted when we both know you're duty bound to marry your perfect little chosen bride and live happily ever after.'

'But I love you,' he said, his steady, blue-eyed stare compelling, hypnotising.

Suddenly, the penny dropped. Not just one, but a whole bagful of screeching metal, crashing down on her conscious and making her see red.

'Let me guess, you want the dutiful wife at home and a Melbourne mistress on the side. Feed me a few pathetic lines of love, hope I'll wait around for you whenever you're in town, is that the general idea?'

She paused for a second, wishing the film of crimson mist in front of her eyes would clear so she could give him a proper staring down.

'Well, I've got news for you, Your Royal Delusional Highness. You can't just waltz back into my life and say you love me and think that makes everything okay. It just doesn't work that way. Besides, after what you've just implied, I wouldn't go near you if you were the last man on earth!'

So there.

Dante didn't move, he didn't flinch, but the blazing expression in his eyes made her want to take a step back.

'Maybe I can convince you otherwise?' he said, his voice soft, low, menacing.

'Forget it.'

She let her guard drop for a second, pleased with her unwavering front when inside she quaked like jelly, and before she knew it Dante had crossed the room, hauled her into his arms and locked his lips on hers.

'No—ooo…'

Her protest died on a moan as his lips gentled, coaxed, and finally triumphed when she opened her mouth beneath his, desperate for the first thrust of his tongue, meeting him, challenging him, wanting this kiss to last for ever.

Heat streaked through her body, waking her dormant libido with a jolt, making her want him with a desperate hunger.

She needed him. All of him.

Body to body, skin to skin, joined in an intimacy she'd never craved till this man had entered her life and turned her world upside down.

Her hands splayed against his chest, caught in the act of pushing him away, helpless to resist the pull of heat radiating from him. She basked in it, warming quickly, reaching burning point within seconds. Burning for him, only him, the only man she'd ever really loved.

The man who is toying with you, again.

She broke the kiss, annoyed, reluctant, breathless, her gaze drawn to his lips merely inches from hers.

'Tasha, look at me.'

He placed a finger under her chin and tilted her head up, gently, without force, giving her time to pull away if she wanted.

She didn't.

If she'd thought his body radiated heat, it had nothing on his eyes, the aquamarine depths a bubbling pool of molten blue heat, the hottest part of a flame, the most hypnotic, and the most seductive.

'I love you. Every stubborn, self-reliant, capable inch of you. You captured my heart from the first minute I saw you, and I didn't stand a chance. Maybe my approach needs some work but, forgive me, I have been trying to phrase my declaration exactly right. I want you to marry me, to trust in me enough to make a new beginning in a new country. This isn't a game or a ploy or some scenario playing out. This is about you and me, and the rest of our lives. If you want it to be.'

He wanted to *marry* her? Hope sparked deep in her soul, but her self-esteem had taken a beating once too often for her to jump up and down with joy just yet.

She'd heard smooth words before, practised words designed to deceive, to obtain an end goal.

She needed more.

She needed proof.

'If you love me, why did you leave? Why did you let me walk away when I'd laid my heart on the line?'

Dante didn't look away, his steady gaze unwavering and filled with a clear-eyed honesty which took her breath away.

'I was a fool. A man who's never been in love before doesn't know the symptoms, can't recognise the cure even when it's staring him in the face. I knew we were attracted to each other, I valued our friendship and I wanted more, but when I saw you with your ex something short-circuited in my brain.'

'You were jealous,' she said, trying to absorb the impact of his words without letting her topsy-turvy emotions get in the way.

'And stupid. In all honesty, I was probably looking for a way out, a way to explain away the feelings I didn't understand, and I took it. You made it easy to love you, but you also made it easy for me by giving me an excuse to walk away because I wanted to.'

He closed his eyes for a second, a pained expression crossing his face before opening them again.

'I didn't know what love was till I reached Calida. When I couldn't think, couldn't function, couldn't breathe without going mad for thinking about you.'

He cupped her cheeks, caressing her with his fingertips, sending shivers down her spine. 'Thinking about how beautiful you are, how your eyes spark golden when you're passionate about something.'

His thumbs brushed her lips, setting them tingling. 'How I only kissed you once in a bout of foolery, and how much I yearned to do it again. For the rest of my life.'

He kissed her, a soft, gentle melding of lips, a kiss of honesty, of hope. Her heart unfurled beneath it, filled with a burgeoning sense of infinite possibilities.

'Will you be my wife, Tasha? Be by my side, facing the future together?'

A vivid image of the two of them in bridal finery flashed before her eyes, a romantic picture to go with the romantic fairy-tale ending she'd never envisaged for herself.

Until now.

'I promise you everyone in Calida will come to love you as much as I do.'

Suddenly, her fantasy bubble popped, and reality set in with a vengeance.

She couldn't marry Dante, no matter how much she loved him.

They came from different worlds, a monstrous gulf of protocols and class and propriety separating them. She'd never been a snob, but she'd worked with his class of people her entire life, had seen the differences, the subtle ways which separated them from everyone else.

For some, like Dante, it wasn't a conscious thing, it was part of who he was, a birthright.

She would never fit in.

No matter how many etiquette lessons she had, no matter how hard she tried to blend in, she would never be good enough, and she'd had a gutful of having her self-esteem trampled, of feeling second best.

Dante loved her and that should've been enough.

But it wasn't. She'd heard about his mother, she'd seen the pushy, over-confident woman Gina was, and she couldn't stand up to that type of barrage long term. At the start, in the honeymoon period maybe, but sooner or later she'd find herself on the outside, and the thought of Dante's love turning to despair when he looked at his out-of-place wife made her want to run out the door that second and never look back.

'I'm sorry, I can't,' she said, stepping out of the comforting circle of his arms, cold loneliness replacing the warmth of his body.

His eyes widened with shock, his mouth a perfect O, as if he'd never dreamed she'd refuse him.

'Your answer is no?'

Natasha almost capitulated right then, hating the pain slashing his proud features, knowing it must reflect her own.

She had no choice.

She had to make the logical decision, the safe decision, for the both of them.

'Dante, listen to me. You're an incredible man, but we're too different. We're worlds apart in every way, and I don't think I'm the right woman for you. Your bride, the future queen of your country, needs to be someone in sync with you, with your family, and unfortunately I don't fit the bill. I'm sorry.'

The words caught in her throat, her refusal every bit as painful as losing him had been. However, this time would be worse, so much worse, when he exited her life for now she knew he loved her.

Her heart turned over, warring with her head, urging her to throw every common sense reason why they shouldn't be together out the window and follow him to the ends of the earth if needed. But she'd never been the frivolous type, never would be. Life consisted of responsibilities, and she couldn't change how she thought, just like Dante couldn't change his birthright.

'I understand your concerns,' he said, not appearing fazed in the slightest at her refusal.

If anything, he'd squared his shoulders, stood taller, and the corners of his too-kissable mouth twitched as if he knew the punchline of some upcoming joke.

'You've made some valid points. Yes, we're different, and yes, our worlds are so far apart, but these obstacles can be overcome by one thing. And, as it happens, it's the one thing you haven't mentioned.'

'What's that?'

His eyes twinkled and he actually smiled, the familiar action setting her pulse racing double-time when it had barely slowed to an acceptable rate after that sizzling kiss.

'Love,' he said, pronouncing it with all the importance of bestowing a title on her. 'You've mentioned connections and the like, I've said I love you, but you haven't said you love me.'

'What makes you think I do?'

She avoided his gaze, looking anywhere but at those all-seeing eyes which wouldn't let her get away with anything let alone a blatant lie like that.

Silence descended, a taut, tension-fraught silence which stretched on for endless moments, the type of uncomfortable silence neither of them wished to break.

'If you say you don't love me, I'll leave. It's as simple as that,' he said, his low voice compelling, urgent, tugging at her heartstrings, until she finally raised her eyes to his, knowing she couldn't do it.

She'd always been honest, brutally so at times, and now, when her future depended on a big, fat lie, she couldn't do it.

'Tasha?'

'I can't,' she said, shaking her head, knowing her answer would only complicate matters for both of them.

'You can't love me?'

For an impressive, macho guy, his tone wavered, and she captured his hands in hers, needing the physical contact to ground her, to get her through this.

'I can't lie to you,' she murmured, beseeching him to understand with her eyes, squeezing his hands for support. 'Of course I love you. Why do you think I came by your hotel that night? Why do you think I made a fool of myself there? I fell in love with you way too fast, and even now it scares me beyond belief. But love can't conquer all, Dante. Real life doesn't work like that. Being in love may get us through the early tough times, but you're a prince, soon to be king. Do you really think I'll be accepted into your world? Do you really think it isn't going to matter?'

She released one of his hands to reach up and caress his cheek, savouring the slight rasp of stubble against her palm. Though she appreciated his clean-shaven look, she liked the bad-boy unshaven look more.

'I'm a simple girl from Melbourne. I love my job, I love my friends, I love my family. It just wouldn't work out. As for Clay, I owed him money, money he once gave me for the hotel. What you saw was his pathetic attempt at asserting control over me, what you missed was me shoving him away.'

'You love me.'

He breathed the words on a breath of awe, sending a wave of pride over her that a guy like him loved a girl like her. 'Nothing else matters. Nothing. We can face the future, whatever it holds, together. You won't lose your friends or family. They can visit, and we'll spend more time in Melbourne.'

He pulled her close, locking his hands around her waist like he'd never let her go.

She wished.

'We can accomplish anything we want. Together. It has to be us together, always. I love you. I'll always love you.'

He rested his forehead on hers as if trying to transfer his thoughts by osmosis and she didn't move, content to be joined in some contact with the man she loved, the man she would always love.

The man she would always love…

There was her answer.

Rather simplistic, considering all the barriers she'd erected between them, all the perfectly legitimate excuses she'd made, but once the phrase lodged in her head she knew what she had to do.

Pulling away slightly, she slid her arms around his waist, enjoying their perfect fit.

'Dante?'

'Yes?'

She smiled. He never said 'yeah' like other guys, but a formal 'yes' that she could imagine him uttering to dignitaries across the world.

'You ever seen a movie called *The Princess Bride*?'

'No.'

Confusion warred with a tiny flicker of hope in his eyes, and she laughed, a purely happy sound for the first time in for ever.

'In that case, why don't we create our own version with me in the starring role?'

Realisation turned his eyes a startling blue and he let out a whoop of joy. 'Does that mean what I think it means?'

'It means you're about to be stuck with me for better or worse.'

He picked her up and swung her around, till they both staggered in a dizzy embrace.

She slid down his body, joy bubbling within her, spreading its incredible heat through her body like warm treacle. Or that could've been the obvious evidence of just how happy her future husband was with her declaration.

'We're going to live happily ever after in a big castle. You know that, don't you?'

Natasha smiled and traced her fiancé's lips with her fingertip. 'I know that I love you. I know that you're a wonderful guy. And I know that I finally believe in fairy tales.'

'So how does *The Princess Bride* end?' he whispered, kissing his way from her hand to her arm and slowly upwards, his lips trailing across her neck to the soft skin beneath her ear as she gasped in delight.

'Stick with me and you'll find out,' she said, smiling as his lips finally settled over hers, and she lost herself in the magic of his kiss, looking forward to creating a happy ending all of their own.

* * * * *

HER ROYAL
WEDDING WISH

BY
CARA COLTER

In memory of Hunter
1997–2007
Beloved.

CHAPTER ONE

JAKE Ronan took a deep, steadying breath, the same kind he would take and hold right before *the* shot or *the* assault or *the* jump.

No relief. His heart was beating like a deer three steps ahead of a wolf pack. His palms were slick with sweat.

He was a man notorious for keeping his cool. And in the past three years that notoriety had served him well. He'd taken a hijacked plane back from the bad guys, jumped from ten thousand feet in the dead of night into territory controlled by hostiles, rescued fourteen school-children from a hostage taking.

But in the danger-zone department nothing did him in like a wedding. He shrugged, rolled his shoulders, took another deep breath.

His old friend, Colonel Gray Peterson, recently retired, the reason Ronan was here on the tiny tropical-island paradise of B'Ranasha, shifted uneasily beside him. Under his breath he said a word that probably had never been said in a church before. "You don't have your *sideways* feeling, do you?" Gray asked.

Ronan was famous among this tough group of men, his comrades-in-arms, for the *feeling,* a sixth sense that warned him things were about to go wrong, in a big way.

"I just don't like weddings," he said, keeping his voice deliberately hushed. "They make me feel uptight."

Gray contemplated that as an oddity. "Jake," he finally said reassuringly, his use of Ronan's first name an oddity in itself, "it's not as if you're the one getting married. You're part of the security team. You don't even know these people."

Ronan had never been the one getting married, but his childhood had been littered with his mother's latest attempt to land the perfect man. His own longing for a normal family, hidden under layers of adolescent belligerence, had usually ended in disillusionment long before the day of yet another elaborate wedding ceremony, his mother exchanging starry-eyed "I do's" with yet another temporary stepfather.

Ronan had found a family he enjoyed very much when he'd followed in his deceased father's footsteps, over his mother's strenuous and tear-filled protests, and joined the Australian military right out of high school. Finally, there had been structure, predictability and genuine camaraderie in his life.

And then he'd been recruited for a multinational military unit that was a first-response team to world crises. The unit, headquartered in England, was comprised of men from the most elite special forces units around the world. They had members from the British Forces SAS, from the French Foreign Legion, from the U.S. SEALs and Delta Force.

His family became a tight-knit brotherhood of warriors. They went where angels feared to go; they did the work no one else wanted to do; they operated in the most dangerous and troubled places in the world. As well as protecting world figures at summits, conferences, peace talks, they dismantled bombs, gathered intelligence, took back planes, rescued hostages, blew up enemy weapons caches. They did the world's most difficult work. They did it quickly, quietly and anonymously. There were few medals, little acknowledgment, no back-patting ceremonies.

But there was: brutal training, exhausting hours, months of deep cover and more danger than playing patty-cake with a rattlesnake.

When Ronan had been recruited, he had said a resounding yes. A man knew exactly when his natural-born talents intersected with opportunity, and from his first day in the unit, code-named Excalibur, he had known he had found what he was born to do.

A family, other than his brothers in arms, was out of the question. This kind of work was unfair to the women who were left at home. A man so committed to a dangerous lifestyle was not ready to make the responsibilities of a family and a wife his priority.

Which was a happy coincidence for a man who had the wedding *thing* anyway. Ronan's most closely guarded secret was that he, fearless fighting man, pride of Excalibur, would probably faint from pure fright if he ever had to stand at an altar like the one at the front of this church as a groom. As a man waiting for his bride.

So far, no one was standing at it, though on this small island, traditions were slightly reversed. He'd been briefed to understand that the bride would come in first and wait for the groom.

Music, lilting and lovely, heralded her arrival, but above the notes Ronan heard the rustle of fabric and slid a look down the aisle of the church. A vision in ivory silk floated slowly toward them. The dress, the typical wedding costume of the Isle of B'Ranasha, covered the bride from head to toe. It was unfathomable how something so unrevealing could be so sensual.

But it was. The gown clung to the bride's slight curves, accentuated the smooth sensuality of her movements. It was embroidered in gold thread that caught the light and thousands of little pearls that shimmered iridescently.

The reason Ronan was stationed so close to the altar was that this beautiful bride, Princess Shoshauna of B'Ranasha, might be in danger.

Since retiring from Excalibur, Gray had taken the position as head of security for the royal family of B'Ranasha. With the upcoming wedding, he'd asked Ronan if he wanted to take some leave and help provide extra security. At first Gray had presented the job as a bit of a lark—beautiful island, beautiful women, unbeatable climate, easy job, lots of off-time.

But by the time Ronan had gotten off the plane, the security team had intercepted a number of threats aimed directly at the princess, and Gray had been grim-faced and tense. The colonel was certain they were generating from within the palace itself, and that a serious security breach had developed within his own team.

"Look at the lady touching the flowers," Gray said tersely.

Ronan spun around, amazed by how much discipline it took to take his eyes off the shimmering vision of that bride. A woman at the side of the church was fiddling with a bouquet of flowers. She kept glancing nervously over her shoulder, radiating tension.

There it was, without warning, that sudden downward dip in his stomach, comparable to a ten-story drop on a roller coaster.

Sideways.

Surreptitiously Ronan checked his weapon, a 9mm Glock, shoulder holstered. Gray noticed, cursed under his breath, tapped his own hidden weapon, a monstrosity that members of Excalibur liked to call the Cannon.

Ronan felt himself shift, from a guy who hated weddings to one hundred percent warrior. It was moments exactly like this that he trained for.

The bride's gown whispered as she walked to the front.

Gray gave him a nudge with his shoulder. "You're on her," he said. "I'm on the flower lady."

Ronan nodded, moved as close to the altar as he could without drawing too much attention to himself. Now he could smell the bride's perfume, tantalizing, as exotic and beautiful as the abundant flowers that bloomed in profusion in every open space of this incredible tropical hideaway.

The music stopped. Out of the corner of his eye, he saw the flower lady duck. *Now,* he thought, and felt every muscle tense and coil, *ready.*

Nothing happened.

An old priest came out of the shadows at the front of

the chapel, his golden face tranquil, his eyes crinkled
with good humor and acceptance. He wore the red silk
robe of a traditional B'Ranasha monk.

Ronan felt Gray's tension beside him. They exchanged glances. Gray's hand now rested inside his
jacket. His facade of complete calm did not fool Ronan.
His buddy's hand was now resting on the Cannon.
Despite the unchanging expression on Gray's face,
Ronan felt the shift in mood, recognized it as that *itching*
for action, battle fever.

The sideways feeling in Ronan's stomach intensified.
His brain did a cool divide, right down the middle. One
part of him watched the priest, the bride. The groom
would arrive next. One part of him smelled perfume and
noted the exquisite detail on her silk dress.

On the other side of the divide, Ronan had become
pure predator, alert, edgy, ready.

The bride lifted her veil, and for just a split second
his warrior edge was gone. Nothing could have prepared
Jake Ronan for the fact he was looking into the delicate,
exquisite perfect features of Princess Shoshauna of
B'Ranasha.

His preparation for providing security for the wedding had included learning to recognize all the members
of the royal families, especially the prospective bride
and groom, but there had never been any reason to meet
them.

He had been able to view Shoshauna's photographs
with detachment: young, pretty, pampered. But those
photos had not prepared him for her in the flesh. Her
face, framed by a shimmering black waterfall of straight
hair, was faintly golden and flawless. Her eyes were

almond shaped, tilted upward, and a shade of turquoise he had seen only once before, in a bay where he'd surfed in his younger days off the coast of Australia.

She blinked at him, then looked to the back of the room.

He yanked himself away from the tempting vision of her. It was very bad to lose his edge, his sense of mission, even for a split second. A warning was sounding deep in his brain.

And in answer to it, the back door of the church whispered open. Ronan glanced back. Not the prince. A man in black. A hood over his face. A gun.

Long hours of training had made Ronan an extremely adaptable animal. His mission instantly crystallized; his instincts took over.

His mission became to protect the princess. In an instant she was the focus of his entire existence. If he had to, he would lay down his life to keep her safe. No hesitation. No doubt. No debate.

The immediate and urgent goal: remove Princess Shoshauna from harm's way. That meant for the next few minutes, things were going to get plenty physical. He launched himself at her, registered the brief widening of those eyes, before he shoved her down on the floor, shielding her body with his own.

Even beneath the pump of pure adrenaline, a part of him *felt* the exquisite sweetness of her curves, felt a need beyond the warrior's response trained into him—something far more primal and male—to protect her fragility with his own strength.

A shot was fired. The chapel erupted into bedlam.

"Ronan, you're covered," Gray shouted. "Get her out of here."

Ronan yanked the princess to her feet, put his body between her and the attacker, kept his hand forcefully on the fragile column of her neck to keep her down.

He got himself and the princess safely behind the relative protection of the stone altar, pushed her through an opening into the priest's vestibule. There Ronan shattered the only window and shoved Princess Shoshauna through it, trying to protect her from the worst of the broken glass with his own arm.

Her skirt got caught, and most of it tore away, which was good. Without the layers of fabric, he discovered she could run like a deer. They were in an alleyway. He kept his hand at the small of her back as they sprinted away from the church. In the background he heard the sound of three more shots, screams.

The alley opened onto a bright square, postcard pretty, with white stucco storefronts, lush palms, pink flowers the size of basketballs. A cabdriver, oblivious to the backdrop of firecracker noises, was in his front seat, door open, slumbering in the sun. Ronan scanned the street. The only other vehicle was a donkey cart for tourists, the donkey looking as sleepy as the cabdriver.

Ronan made his decision, pulled the unsuspecting driver from his cab and shoved the princess in. She momentarily got hung up on the gearshift. He shoved her again, and she plopped into the passenger seat. He then jumped in behind her, turned the key and slammed the vehicle into gear.

Within seconds the sounds of gunfire and the shouted protests of the cabdriver had faded in the distance, but he kept driving, his brain pulling up maps of this island as if he had an Internet search program.

"Do you think everyone's all right back there?" she asked. "I'm worried about my grandfather."

Her English was impeccable, her voice a silk scarf— soft, sensual, floating across his neck as if she had actually touched him.

He shrugged the invisible hand away, filed it under *interesting* that she was more worried about her grandfather than the groom. And he red-flagged it that the genuine worry on her face made him feel a certain unwanted softness for her.

Softness was not part of his job, and he liked to think not part of his nature, either, trained out of him, so that he could make clinical, precise decisions that were not emotionally driven. On the other hand he'd been around enough so-called important people to be able to appreciate her concern for someone other than herself.

"No one was hit," he said gruffly.

"How could you know that? I could hear gunfire after we left."

"A bullet makes a different sound when it hits than when it misses."

She looked incredulous and skeptical. "And with everything going on, you were listening for that?"

"Yes, ma'am." Not listening for that *exactly,* but listening. He had not heard the distinctive *ka-thunk* of a hit, nor had he heard sounds that indicated someone badly hurt. Details. Every member of Excalibur was trained to pay attention to details that other people missed. It was amazing how often something that seemed insignificant could mean the difference between life and death.

"My grandfather has a heart problem," she said softly, worried.

"Sorry." He knew he sounded insincere, and at this moment he was. He only cared if one person was safe, and that was her. He was not risking a distraction, a misdirection of energy, by focusing on anything else.

As if to challenge his focus, his cell phone vibrated in his pocket. He had turned it off for the wedding, because his mother had taken to leaving him increasingly frantic messages that she had *big* news to share with him. Big news in her life always meant one thing: a new man, the proclamation it was *different* this time, more extravagant wedding plans.

Some goof at Excalibur, probably thinking it was funny, had given her his cell number against his specific instructions. But a glance at the caller ID showed it was not his mother but Gray.

"Yeah," he answered.

"Clear here."

"Here, too. Aurora—" he named the princess in Sleeping Beauty, a reference that was largely cultural, that might not be understood by anyone listening "—is fine."

"Excellent. We have the perp. No one injured. The guy was firing blanks. He could have been killed. What kind of nutcase does that?"

He contemplated that for a moment and came up with *one who wants to stop the wedding.* "Want me to bring her back in? Maybe they could still go ahead with the ceremony."

Details. The princess flinched ever so slightly beside him.

"No. Absolutely not. Something's wrong here. Really wrong. Nobody should have been able to penetrate the security around that wedding. It has to be someone within the palace, so I don't want her back here until I know who it is. Can you keep her safe until I get to the bottom of it?"

Ronan contemplated that. He had a handgun and two clips of ammunition. He was a stranger to the island and was now in possession of a stolen vehicle, not to mention a princess.

Despite circumstances not being anywhere near perfect, he knew in his business perfect circumstances were in short supply. It was a game of odds, and of trust in one's own abilities. "Affirmative," he said.

"I can't trust my phone, but we can probably use yours once more to give you a time frame and set a rendezvous."

"All right." He should have hung up, but he made the mistake of glancing at her pinched face. "Ah, Gray? Is her grandfather all right?"

"Slamming back the Scotch." Gray lowered his voice, "Though he actually seems a little, er, pleased, that his granddaughter didn't manage to get married."

Ronan pocketed his phone. "Your grandfather's fine."

"Oh, that's wonderful news! Thank you!"

"I can't take you back just yet, though."

Some finely held tension disappeared from her shoulders, as if she allowed herself to start breathing after holding her breath.

Eyes that had been clouded with worry, suddenly

tilted upward when she smiled. If he was not mistaken, and he rarely was, given his gift with details, a certain mischief danced in their turquoise depths.

She did not inquire about the groom, and now that her concerns for her grandfather had been relieved, she didn't look anything like a woman who had just had her wedding ceremony shattered by gunfire, her dress shredded. In fact, she looked downright happy. As if to confirm that conclusion, she took off her bridal head-dress, held it out the window and let the wind take it. She laughed with delight as it floated behind them, children chasing it down the street.

The wind billowing through the open window caught at the tendrils of her hair, and she shook it all free from the remaining pins that held it, and it spilled down over the slenderness of her shoulders.

If he was not mistaken, Princess Shoshauna was very much enjoying herself.

"Look, Your Highness," he said, irritated. "This is not a game. Don't be throwing anything else out the window that will make us easy to follow or remember."

She tossed her hair and gave him a look that was faintly mutinous. Obviously, because of her position, she was not accustomed to being snapped at. But that was too bad. There was only room for one boss here, and it wasn't going to be her.

With the imminent danger now at bay, at least temporarily, his thought processes slowed, and he began to sort information. His assessment of the situation wasn't good. He had been prepared to do a little wedding security, not to find himself in possession of a princess who had someone trying to kill her.

He didn't know the island. He had no idea where he could take her where it would be secure. He had very little currency, and at some point he was going to have to feed her, and get her out of that all-too-attention-grabbing outfit. He had to assume that whoever was after her would be sophisticated enough to trace credit card use. Ditto for his cell phone. They could use it once more to arrange a time and place for a rendezvous and then he'd have to pitch it. On top of that, he had to assume this vehicle had already been reported stolen; it would have to be ditched soon.

On the plus side, she was alive, and he planned to keep it that way. He had a weapon, but very little ammunition.

He was going to have to use the credit card once. To get them outfitted. By the time it was traced, they could be a long way away.

"Do you have any enemies?" he asked her. If he had one more phone call with Gray, maybe he could have some information for him. Plus, it would help him to know if this threat was about something personal or if it was politically motivated. Each of those scenarios made for a completely different enemy.

"No," she said, but he saw the moment's hesitation.

"No one hates you?"

"Of course not." But again he sensed hesitation, and he pushed.

"Who do you think did this?" he asked. "What's your gut feeling?"

"What's a gut feeling?" she asked, wide-eyed.

"Your instinct."

"It's silly."

"Tell me," he ordered.

"Prince Mahail was seeing a woman before he asked me to marry him. She's actually a cousin of mine. She acted happy for me, but—"

Details. People chose to ignore them, which was too bad. "Your instincts aren't silly," he told her gruffly. "They could keep you alive. What's her name?"

"I don't want her to get in trouble. She probably has nothing to do with this."

The princess wasn't just choosing to ignore her instincts, but seemed *determined* to. Still, he appreciated her loyalty.

"She won't be in trouble." *If she didn't do anything.* "Her name?"

"Mirassa," she said, but reluctantly.

"Now tell me how to find a market. A small one, where I can get food. And something for you to wear."

"Oh," she breathed. "Can I have shorts?" She blinked at him, her lashes thick as a chimney brush over those amazing ocean-bay eyes.

He tried not to sigh audibly. Wasn't that just like a woman? Even a crisis could be turned into an opportunity to shop!

"I'm getting what draws the least attention to you," he said, glancing over at her long legs exposed by her torn dress. "I somehow doubt that's going to be shorts."

"Am I going to wear a disguise?" she asked, thrilled.

She was determined not to get how serious this was. And maybe that was good. The last thing he needed was hysteria.

"Sure," he said, going along, "you get to wear a disguise."

"You could pretend to be my boyfriend," Princess Shoshauna said, with way too much enthusiasm. "We could rent a motorcycle and blend in with the tourists. How long do you think you'll have to hide me?"

"I don't know yet. Probably a couple of days."

"Oh!" she said, pleased, determined to perceive this life-and-death situation as a grand adventure. "I have always wanted to ride a motorcycle!"

The urge to strangle her was not at all in keeping with the businesslike, absolutely emotionless attitude he needed to have around her. That attitude would surely be jeopardized further by pretending to be her boyfriend, by sharing a motorcycle with her. His mind went there—her pressed close, her crotch pressed into the small of his back, the bike throbbing underneath them.

Buck up, soldier, he ordered himself. *There's going to be no motorcycle.*

"I'll cut my hair," she decided.

It was the first reasonable idea she had presented, but he was aware he wasn't even considering it. Her hair was long and straight, jet-black and glossy. Her hair was glorious. He wasn't letting her cut her hair, even if it would be the world's greatest disguise.

He knew he was making that decision for all the wrong reasons, and that his professionalism had just slipped the tiniest little notch. There was no denying the *sideways* feeling seemed to have taken up permanent residence in his stomach.

Shoshauna slid the man who was beside her a look and felt the sweetest little dip in the region of her stomach. He was incredibly good-looking. His short hair was auburn, burnt brown with strands of red glinting as the sun struck it. His eyes, focused on the road, were topaz colored, like a lion's. As if the eyes were not hint enough of his strength, there was the formidable set of his lips, the stubborn set of his chin, the flare of his nostrils.

He was a big man, broad and muscled, not like the slighter men of B'Ranasha. When he had thrown her onto the floor of the chapel, she had felt the shock first. No man had ever touched her like that before! Technically, it had been more a tackle than a touch. But then she had become aware of the hard, unforgiving lines of him, felt the strange and forbidden thrill of his male body shielding hers.

Even now she watched as his hands found their way to his necktie, tugged impatiently at it. He loosened it, tugged it free, shoved it in his pocket. Next, he undid the top button of his shirt, rubbed his neck as if he'd escaped the hangman's noose.

"What's your name?" she asked. It was truly shocking, considering how aware she'd felt of him, within seconds of marrying someone else. She glanced at his fingers, was entranced by the shape of them, the faint dusting of hair on the knuckles. Shocked at herself, she realized she could imagine them tangling in her hair.

Of course, she had led a somewhat sheltered life. This was the closest she had ever been, alone, to a man who was not a member of her own family. Even her meetings with her fiancé, Prince Mahail of the neighboring island, had been very formal and closely chaperoned.

"Ronan," he said, and then had to swerve to miss a woman hauling a basket of chickens on her bicycle. He said a delicious-sounding word that she had never heard before, even though she considered her English superb. The little shiver that went up and down her spine told her the word was naughty. Very naughty.

"Ronan." She tried it out, liked how it felt on her tongue. "You must call me Shoshauna!"

"Your Highness, I am not calling you Shoshauna." He muttered the name of a deity under his breath. "I think it's thirty lashes for calling a member of the royal family by their first name."

"Ridiculous," she told him, even though it was true: no one but members of her immediate family would even dare being so familiar as to call her by her first name. That was part of the prison of her role as a member of B'Ranasha's royal family.

But she'd been rescued! Her prayers had been answered just when she had thought there was no hope left, when she had resigned herself to the fact she had agreed to a marriage to a man she did not love.

She did not know how long this reprieve could possibly last, but despite Ronan telling her so sternly this was not a game, Shoshauna intended to make the very most of it. Whether she had been given a few hours or a few days, she intended to be what she might never be again. Free. To be what she had always wanted most to be.

An ordinary girl. With an ordinary life.

She was determined to get a conversation going, to find out as much about this intriguing foreigner as she could. She glanced at his lips and shivered. Would making the most of the gift the universe had handed her include tasting the lips of the intriguing foreigner?

She knew how *wrong* those thoughts were, but her heart beat faster at the thought. How was it that imagining kissing Ronan, a stranger, could fill her with such delirious curiosity, when the thought of what was supposed to have happened tonight, between her and the man who should have become her husband, Prince Mahail, filled her with nothing but dread?

"What nationality are you?"

"Does it matter? You don't have to know anything about me. You just have to listen to me."

His tone, hard and cold, did not sound promising in the kiss department! Miffed, she wondered how he couldn't know that when a princess asked you something, you did not have the option of not answering. Even though she desperately wanted to try life as an ordinary girl, old habit made her give him her most autocratic stare, the one reserved for misbehaving servants.

"Australian," he snapped.

That explained the accent, surely as delicious sounding as the foreign phrase he had uttered so emphatically when dodging the chicken bicycle. She said the word herself, out loud, using the same inflection he had.

The car swerved, but he regained control instantly. "Don't say that word!" he snapped at her, and then added, a reluctant afterthought at best, "Your Highness."

"I'm trying to improve my English!"

"What you're trying to do is get me a one-way ticket to a whipping post for teaching the princess curse words. Do they still whip people here?"

"Of course," she lied sweetly. His expression darkened to thunder, but then he looked hard at her, read the lie, knew she was having a little fun at his expense. He made a cynical sound deep in his throat.

"Are women in Australia ever forced to marry men they don't love?" she asked. But the truth was, she had not been *forced*. Not technically. Her father had given her a choice, but it had not been a *real* choice. The weight of his expectation, her own desperate desire to please him, to be of *value* to him had influenced her decision.

Plus, Prince Mahail's surprise proposal had been presented at a low point in her life, just days after her cat, Retnuh, had died.

People said it was just a cat, had been shocked at her level of despair, but she'd had Retnuh since he was a kitten, since she'd been a little girl of eight. He'd been her friend, her companion, her confidante, in a royal household that was too busy to address the needs of one insignificant and lonely little princess.

"Turn here, there's a market down this road."

He took the right, hard, then looked straight ahead.

"Well?" she asked, when it seemed he planned to ignore her.

"People get married all over the world, for all kinds of reasons," he said. "Love is no guarantee of success. Who even knows what love is?"

"I do," she said stubbornly. It seemed her vision of what it was had crystallized after she'd agreed to marry the completely wrong man. But by then it had been too late. In her eagerness to outrun how terrible she felt about her cat, Shoshauna had allowed herself to get totally caught up in the excitement—preparations underway, two islands celebrating, tailors in overtime preparing gowns for all members of both wedding parties, caterers in overdrive, gifts arriving from all over the world—of getting ready for a royal wedding.

She could just picture the look of abject disappointment on her father's face if she had gone to him and asked to back out.

"Sure you do, Princess."

His tone insinuated she thought love was a storybook notion, a schoolgirl's dream.

"You think I'm silly and immature because I believe in love," she said, annoyed.

"I don't know the first thing about you, what you believe or don't believe. And I don't want to. I have a job to do. A mission. It's to keep you safe. The less I know about you *personally* the better."

Shoshauna felt stunned by that. She was used to interest. Fawning. She could count on no one to tell her what they really thought. Of course, it was all that patently insincere admiration that had made her curl up with her cat at night, listen to his deep purring and feel as if he was the only one who truly got her, who truly loved her for exactly what she was.

If even one person had expressed doubt about her upcoming wedding would she have found the courage to call it off? Instead, she'd been swept along by all that gushing about how wonderful she would look in the dress, how handsome Prince Mahail was, what an excellent menu choice she had made, how exquisite the flowers she had personally picked out.

"There's the market," she said coldly.

He pulled over, stopped her as she reached for the handle. "You are staying right here."

Her arm tingled where his hand rested on it. Unless she was mistaken, he felt a little jolt, too. He certainly pulled away as though he had. "Do you understand? Stay here. Duck down if anyone comes down the road."

She nodded, but perhaps not sincerely enough.

"It's not a game," he said again.

"All right!" she said. "I get it."

"I hope so," he muttered, gave her one long, hard, assessing look, then dashed across the street.

"Don't forget scissors," she called as he went into the market. He glared back at her, annoyed. He hadn't said to be quiet! Besides, she didn't want him to forget the scissors.

She had wanted to cut her hair since she was thirteen. It was too long and a terrible nuisance. It took two servants to wash it and forever to dry.

"Princesses," her mother had informed her, astounded at her request, "do not cut their hair."

Princesses didn't do a great many things. People who thought it was fun should try it for a day or two. They should try sitting nicely through concerts, building openings, ceremonies for visiting dignitaries. They should try shaking hands with every single person in a receiving line and smiling for hours without stopping. They should try sitting through speeches at formal dinners, being the royal representative at the carefully selected weddings and funerals and baptisms and graduations of the *important* people. They should try meeting a million people and never really getting to know a single one of them.

Shoshauna had dreams that were not princess dreams at all. They were not even big dreams by the standards of the rest of the world, but they were her dreams. And if Ronan thought she wasn't taking what had happened at the chapel seriously, he just didn't get it.

She had given up on her dreams, felt as if they were being crushed like glass under her slippers with every step closer to the altar that she had taken.

But for some reason—maybe she had wished hard enough after all, maybe Retnuh was her protector from another world—she had been given this reprieve, and she felt as if she had to try and squeeze everything she had ever wanted into this tiny window of freedom.

She wanted to wear pants and shorts. She wanted to ride a motorcycle! She wanted to try surfing and a real bathing suit, not the swimming costume she was forced to wear at the palace. A person could drown if they ever got in real water, not a shallow swimming pool, in that getup.

There were other dreams that were surely never going to happen once she was married to the crown prince of an island country every bit as old-fashioned and traditional as B'Ranasha.

Decorum would be everything. She would wear the finest gowns, the best jewels, her manners would have to be forever impeccable, she would never be able to say what she really wanted. In short order she would be expected to stay home and begin producing babies.

But she wanted so desperately to sample life before she was condemned to that. Shoshauna wanted to taste snow. She wanted to go on a toboggan. She felt she had missed something essential: a boyfriend, like she had seen in movies. A boyfriend would be fun—someone to hold her hand, take her to movies, romance her. A husband was a totally different thing!

For a moment she had hoped she could talk Ronan into a least pretending, but she now saw that was unlikely.

Most of her dreams were unlikely.

Still, a miracle had happened. Here she was beside a handsome stranger in a stolen taxicab, when she should have been married to Prince Mahail by now. She'd known the prince since childhood and did not find him the least romantic, though many others did, including her silly cousin, Mirassa.

Mahail was absurdly arrogant, sure in his position of male superiority. Worse, he did not believe in her greatest dream of all.

Most of all, Shoshauna wanted to be educated, to learn glorious things, and not be restricted in what she was allowed to select for course material. She wanted to sit in classrooms with males and openly challenge the stupidity of their opinions. She wanted to learn to play chess, a game her mother said was for men only.

She knew herself to be a princess of very little consequence, the only daughter of a lesser wife, flying well under the radar of the royal watchdogs. She had spent a great deal of time, especially in her younger years, with her English grandfather and had thought one day she would study at a university in Great Britain.

With freedom that close, with her dreams so near she could taste them, Prince Mahail had spoiled it all, by choosing her as his bride. Why had he chosen her?

Mirassa had told her he'd been captivated by her hair! Suddenly she remembered how Mirassa had looked at her hair in that moment, how her eyes had darkened to black, and Shoshauna felt a shiver of apprehension.

Before Mahail had proposed to Shoshauna, rumor had flown that Mirassa was his chosen bride. He had flirted openly with her on several occasions, which on these islands was akin to publishing banns. Shoshauna had heard, again through the rumor mill, that Mirassa had asked to see him after he had proposed to Shoshauna and he had humiliated her by refusing her an appointment. Given that he had encouraged Mirassa's affection in the first place, he certainly could have been more sensitive. Just how angry had Mirassa been?

Trust your instincts.

If she managed to cut her hair off before her return maybe Prince Mahail would lose interest in her as quickly as he had gained it and Mirassa would stop being jealous.

Being chosen for her hair was insulting, like being a head of livestock chosen for the way it looked: not for its heart or mind or soul!

The prince had taken his interest to her father, and she had felt as if her father had noticed her, *really* seen her for the very first time. His approval had been drugging. It had made her say yes when she had needed to say no!

Ronan came back to the car, dropped a bag on her lap, reached in and stowed a few more on the backseat. She noticed he had purchased clothing for himself and had changed out of the suit he'd worn. He was now wearing an open-throated shirt that showed his arms:

rippling with well-defined muscle, peppered with hairs turned golden by the sun. And he was wearing shorts. She was not sure she had ever seen such a length of appealing male leg in all her life!

Faintly flustered, Shoshauna focused on the bag he'd given her. It held clothing. A large pair of very ugly sunglasses, a hideous hat, a blouse and skirt that looked like a British schoolmarm would be happy to wear.

No shorts. She felt like crying as reality collided with her fantasy.

"Where are the scissors?" she asked.

"Forgot," he said brusquely, and she knew she could not count on him to make any of her dreams come true, to help her make the best use of this time she had been given.

He had a totally different agenda than her. To keep her safe. The last thing she wanted was to be safe. She wanted to be *alive* but in the best sense of that word.

She opened her car door.

"Where the hell are you going?"

"I'm going the *hell* in those bushes, changing into this outfit, as hideous as it is."

"I don't think princesses are supposed to change their clothes in the bushes," he said. "Or say *hell,* for that matter. Just get in the car and I'll find—"

"I'm changing now." *And then I'm going into that market and buying some things I want to wear.* "And then I'm going into that market and finding the restroom."

"Maybe since you're in the bushes anyway, you could just—"

She stopped him with a look. His mouth snapped

shut. He scowled at her, but even he, as unimpressed with her status as he apparently was, was not going to suggest she go to the bathroom in the bushes.

"Don't peek," she said, ducking into the thick shrubbery at the side of the road.

"Lord have mercy," he muttered, whatever that meant.

CHAPTER TWO

RESIGNED, Ronan hovered in front of the bushes while she changed, trying to ignore the rustling sound of falling silk.

When she emerged, even he was impressed with how good his choices had been. Princess Shoshauna no longer looked like a member of the royal family, or even like a native to the island.

The women of B'Ranasha had gorgeous hair, their crowning glory. It swung straight and long, black and impossibly shiny past their shoulder blades, and was sometimes ornamented with fresh flowers, but never hidden.

The princess had managed to tuck her abundant locks up under that straw hat, the sunglasses covered the distinctive turquoise of those eyes, and she'd been entirely correct about his fashion sense.

The outfit he'd picked for her looked hideous in exactly the nondescript way he had hoped it would. The blouse was too big, the skirt was shapeless and dowdy, hanging a nice inch or so past her shapely knees. Except for the delicate slippers that showed off the daintiness of her tiny feet, she could have passed for an overweight British nanny on vacation.

As a disguise it was perfect: it hid who she really was very effectively. It worked for him, too. He had effectively covered her curves, made her look about as sexy as a refrigerator box. He knew the last thing he needed was to be too aware of her as a woman, and a beautiful one at that.

He accompanied her across the street, thankful for the sleepiness of the market at this time of day. "Try not to talk to anyone. The washrooms are at the back."

His cell phone vibrated. "Five minutes," he told her, checked the caller ID, felt relieved it was not his mother, though not a number he recognized, either. He watched through the open market door as she went straight to the back, then, certain of her safety, turned his attention to the phone.

"Yeah," he said cautiously, not giving away his identity.

"Peterson."

"That's what I figured."

"How did Aurora take the news that she's going to have to go into hiding?"

"Happily waiting for her prince to come," he said dryly, though he thought a less-true statement had probably never been spoken.

"Can you keep her that way for Neptune?"

Neptune was an exercise that Excalibur went on once a year. It was a week-long training in sea operations. Ronan drew in his breath sharply. A week? Even with the cleverness of the disguise she was in, that was going to be tough on so many levels. He didn't know the island. Still, Gray would never ask a week of him if he didn't absolutely need the time.

Surely the princess would know enough about the island to help him figure out a nice quiet place where they could hole up for a week?

Which brought him to how tough it was going to be on another level: a man and a woman holed up alone for a week. A gorgeous woman, despite the disguise, a healthy man, despite all his discipline.

"Can do." He let none of the doubt he was feeling creep into his tone. He hoped the colonel would at least suggest where, but then realized it would be better if he didn't, considering the possibility Gray's team was not secure.

"We'll meet at Harry's. Neptune swim."

Harry's was a fish-and-chips-style pub the guys had frequented near Excalibur headquarters. The colonel was wisely using references no one but a member of the unit would understand. The Neptune swim was a grueling session in ocean swimming that happened at precisely 1500 hours every single day of the Neptune exercise. So, Ronan would meet Gray in one week, at a British-style pub, or a place that sold fish and chips, presumably close to the palace headquarters at 3 p.m.

"Gotcha." He deliberately did not use communication protocol. "By the way, you need to check out a cousin. Mirassa."

"Thanks. Destroy the phone," the Colonel said.

Every cell phone had a global positioning device in it. Better to get rid of it, something Ronan had known all along he was going to have to do.

"Will do."

He hung up the phone and peered in the market. The princess had emerged from the back, and was now going through racks of tourist clothing, in a leisurely manner, hangers of clothing already tossed over one arm. Thankfully, despite the darkness of the shop, she still had on the sunglasses.

He went into the shop, moved through the cluttered aisles toward her. If he was not mistaken, the top item of the clothing she had strung over her arm was a bikini, bright neon green, not enough material in it to make a handkerchief.

A week with that? He was disciplined, yes, a miracle worker, no. This was going to be a challenging enough assignment if he managed to keep her dressed like a refrigerator box!

He went up beside her, plucked the bikini off her arm, hung it up on the closest rack. "We're not supposed to attract attention, Aurora. That doesn't exactly fit the bill."

"Aurora?"

"Your code name," he said in an undertone.

"A code name," she breathed. "I like it. Does it mean something?"

"It's the name of the princess in 'Sleeping Beauty.'"

"Well, I'm not waiting for my prince!"

"I gathered that," he said dryly. He didn't want to feel interested in what was wrong with her prince. It didn't have anything to do with getting the job done. He told himself not to ask her why she dreaded marriage so much, and succeeded, for the moment. But he was aware he had a whole week with her to try to keep his curiosity at bay.

"Do you have a code name?" she asked.

He tried to think of the name of a celibate priest, but he wasn't really up on his priests. "No. Let's go."

She glanced at him—hard to read her eyes through the sunglasses—but her chin tilted in a manner that did not bode well for him being the boss. She took the bikini back off the rack, tossed it back over her arm.

"I don't have to wear it," she said mulishly. "I just have to have it. Touch it again, and I'll make a scene." She smiled.

He glanced around uneasily. No other customers in the store, the single clerk, thankfully, far more interested in the daily racing form he was studying than he was in them.

"Let's go," he said in a low voice. "You have enough stuff there to last a year."

"Maybe it will be a year," she said, just a trifle too hopefully, confirming what he already knew—this was one princess not too eager to be kissed by a prince.

"I've had some instructions. A week. We need to disappear for a week."

She grabbed a pair of shorty-shorts.

"We have to go."

"I'm not finished."

He took her elbow, glanced again at the clerk, guided her further back in the room. "Look, Princess, you have a decision to make."

She spotted a bikini on the rack by his head. "I know!" she said, deliberately missing his point. "Pink or green?"

Definitely pink, but he forced himself to remain absolutely expressionless, pretended he was capable of ignoring the scrap of material she was waving in front of his face. Unfortunately, it was just a little too easy to imagine her in that, how the pink would set off the golden tones of her skin and the color of her eyes, how her long black hair would shimmer against it.

He took a deep breath.

"This is about your life," he told her quietly. "Not mine. I'm not going to be more responsible for you than you are willing to be for yourself. So, if you want to take chances with your life, if you want to make my life difficult instead of cooperating, I'll take you back to the palace right now."

Despite the sunglasses, he could tell by the tightening of her mouth that she didn't want to go back to the palace, so he pressed on.

"That would work better for me, actually," he said. "I kind of fell into this. I signed up for wedding security, not to be your bodyguard. I have a commanding officer who's going to be very unhappy with me if I don't report back to work on Tuesday."

He was bluffing. He wasn't taking her back to the palace until Gray had sorted out who was responsible for the attack at the church. And Gray would look after getting word back to his unit that he had been detained due to circumstances beyond his control.

But she didn't have to know that. And if he'd read her correctly, she'd been relieved that her wedding had been interrupted, delirious almost. The last thing she wanted to do was go back to her life, pick up where she'd left off.

He kept talking. "I'm sure your betrothed is very worried about you, anxious to make you his wife, so that

he can keep you safe. He's probably way more quali-
fied to do that than I am."

He could see, *clearly,* that he had her full attention,
and that she was about as eager to get back to her prince
as to swim with crocodiles.

So he said, "Maybe that's the best idea. Head back,
a quick secret ceremony, you and your prince can get
off the island, have your honeymoon together, and this
whole mess will be cleared up by the time you get
home."

His alertness to detail paid off now, because her body
language radiated sudden tension. He actually felt a
little bit sorry for her. She obviously didn't want to get
married, and if she had feelings for her fiancé they were
not positive ones. But again he had to shut down any
sense of curiosity or compassion that he felt. That
wasn't his problem, and in protection work, that was the
priority: to remember his business—the very narrow
perimeters of keeping her safe—and to not care
anything about what was her business.

Whether she was gorgeous, ugly, unhappy at love,
frustrated with her life, none of that mattered to him. Or
should matter to him.

Still, he did feel the tiniest little shiver of unwanted
sympathy as he watched her getting paler before his
eyes. He was glad for her sunglasses, because he didn't
want to see her eyes just now. She put the pink bikini
back, thankfully, but turned and marched to the counter
as if she was still the one in charge, as if he was her
servant left to trail behind her—and pay the bills.

Apparently paying had not occurred to her. She had
probably never had to handle money or even a credit

card in her whole life. She would put it on account, or some member of her staff would look after the details for her.

She seemed to realize that at the counter, and he could have embarrassed her, but there was no point, and he certainly did not want the clerk to find anything memorable about this transaction.

"I got it, sweetheart," he said easily.

Though playing sweethearts had been her idea, she was flustered by it. She looked everywhere but at him. Then, without warning, she reached up on tiptoe and kissed him on the cheek.

"Thanks, Charming," she said huskily, obviously deciding he needed a code name that matched hers.

But a less-likely prince had never been born, and he knew it.

He hoped the clerk wouldn't look up, because there might be something memorable about seeing a man blushing because his supposed lady friend had kissed him and used an odd endearment on him.

Ronan didn't make it worse by looking at her, but he felt a little stunned by the sweetness of her lips on his cheek, by the utter softness, the sensuality of a butterfly's wings.

"Oh, look," she said softly, suddenly breathless. She was tapping a worn sign underneath the glass on the counter.

"Motorcycles for rent. Hour, day, week."

It would be the last time he'd be able to use this credit card, so maybe, despite his earlier rejection of the idea, now was the time to change vehicles. Was it a genuinely good idea or had that spontaneous kiss on the cheek rattled him?

He'd already nixed the motorcycle idea in his own mind. Why was he revisiting the decision?

Was he losing his edge? Finding her just too distracting? He had to do his job, to make decisions based solely on what was most likely to bring him to mission success, which was keeping her safe. Getting stopped in a stolen car was not going to do that. Blending in with the thousands of tourists that scootered around this island made more sense.

Since talking to Gray, he wondered if the whole point of the threats against the princess had been to stop the wedding, not harm her personally.

But he knew he couldn't let his guard down because of that. He had to treat the threat to her safety as real, or there would be too many temptations to treat it lightly, to let his guard down, to let her get away with things.

"Please?" she said softly, and then she tilted her sunglasses down and looked at him over the rims.

Her eyes were stunning, the color and depth of tropical waters, filled at this moment with very real pleading, as if she felt her life depended on getting on that motorcycle.

Half an hour later, he had a backpack filled with their belongings, he had moved the car off the road into the thick shrubs beside it and he was studying the motorcycle. It was more like a scooter than a true motorcycle.

He took a helmet from a rack beside the motorcycles. "Come here."

"I don't want to wear that! I want to feel the wind in my hair."

He had noticed hardly anyone on the island did wear motorcycle helmets, probably because the top speed of these little scooters would be about eighty kilometers an hour. Still, acquiring the motorcycle felt a bit like giving in, and he was done with that. His job was to keep her safe in every situation. Life could be cruelly ironic, he knew. It would be terrible to protect her from an assassin and then get her injured on a motorbike.

"Please, Charming?" she said.

That had worked so well last time, she was already trying it again! It served him right for allowing himself to be manipulated by her considerable charm.

She took off her sunglasses and blinked at him. He could see the genuine yearning in her eyes, but knew he couldn't cave in. This was a girl who was, no doubt, very accustomed to people jumping to make her happy, to wrapping the whole world around her pinky finger.

"Charming isn't a good code name for me," he said.

"Why not?"

"Because I'm not. Charming. And I'm certainly not a prince." To prove both, he added, sternly, "Now, come here and put on the helmet."

"Are you wearing one?"

He didn't answer, just lifted his eyebrow at her, the message clear. She could put on the helmet or she could go home.

Mutinously she snatched the straw hat from her head.

He tried not to let his shock show. In those few un-supervised minutes while he had talked to Gray on the phone, she had gone to the washroom, all right, but not for the reason he had thought or she had led him to believe. Where had she gotten her hands on a pair of scissors? Or maybe, given the raggedness of the cut, she had used a knife.

She was no hairdresser, either. Little chunks of her black hair stood straight up on her head, going every which way. The bangs were crooked. Her ears were tufted. There wasn't a place where her hair was more than an inch and a half long. Her head looked like a newly hatched chicken, covered in dark dandelion fluff. It should have looked tragic.

Instead, she looked adorable, carefree and elfish, a rebel, completely at odds with the conservative outfit he had picked for her. Without the distraction of her gorgeous hair, it was apparent that her bone structure was absolutely exquisite, her eyes huge, her lips full and puffy.

"Where's your hair?" he asked, fighting hard not to let his shock show. He shoved the helmet on her head quickly, before she had any idea how disconcerting he found her new look. His fingers fumbled on the strap buckle, he was way too aware of her, and not at all pleased with his awareness. The perfume he'd caught a whiff of at the wedding tickled his nostrils.

"I cut it."

"I can clearly see that." Thankfully, the mysteries of the helmet buckle unraveled, he tightened the strap, let his hands fall away. He was relieved the adorable mess of her hair was covered. "What did you do with it after you cut it?"

Her contrite expression told him she had left it where it had fallen.

"So, you did it for nothing," he said sternly. "Now, when we're traced this far, and we will be, they'll find out you cut your hair. And they'll be looking for a bald girl, easier to spot than you were before."

"I'm not bald," she protested.

"I've seen better haircuts on new recruits," he said. She looked crestfallen, he told himself he didn't care. But he was aware he did, just a little bit.

"I'll go back and pick up my hair," she said.

"Never mind. Hopefully no one is going to see you."

"Does it look that bad?"

He could reassure her it didn't, but that was something Prince Charming might do. "It looks terrible."

He hoped she wasn't going to cry. She put her sunglasses back on a little too rapidly. Her shoulders trembled tellingly.

Don't be a jerk, he told himself. But then he realized he might be a lot safer in this situation if she did think he was a jerk.

When had his focus switched from her safety to his own?

Rattled, he pushed ahead. "I need you to think very carefully," he said. "Is there a place on this island we can go where no one would find us for a week?"

He tried not to close his eyes after he said it. A week with her, her new haircut and her new green bikini stuffed in the backpack. Not to mention the shorty-shorts, and a halter top that had somehow been among her purchases.

He could see in her eyes she yearned for things that were forbidden to her, things she might not even be totally aware of, things that went far beyond riding on motorcycles and cutting her hair.

Things her husband should be teaching her. Right this minute. He had no right to be feeling grateful that she had not been delivered into the hands of a man she'd dreaded discovering those things with.

Instead she'd been delivered into his hands. One mission: keep her safe. Even from himself.

Still, he was aware he was a warrior, not a saint. The universe was asking way too much of him.

He turned from her swiftly, got on the motorcycle, persuaded it to life. He patted the seat behind him, not even looking at her.

But not looking at her didn't help. She slid onto the seat behind him. The skirt hiked way up. Out of his peripheral vision he could see the nakedness of her knee. He glanced back. The skirt was riding high up her thigh.

It was a princess like no one had ever seen, of that he was certain. On the other hand, no one would be likely to recognize her looking like this, either.

"Hang on tight," he said.

And then he felt her sweet curves pull hard against him. Oh, sure. For once she was going to listen!

"I know a place," she called into his ear. "I know the perfect place."

His cell phone vibrated in his pocket. He slowed, checked the caller ID. His mother. He wrestled an impulse to answer, to yell at her, Don't do it! Instead he listened to her leave yet another voice mail.

"Ronan, call me. It's so exciting."

They were crossing over a bridge, rushing water below, and he took the phone and flung it into the water.

He was in the protection business; sometimes it felt as if the whole world was his responsibility. But the truth was he could not now, and never had been able to, protect his own mother from what she most needed protecting from.

Herself.

Shoshauna pressed her cheek up against the delicious hardness of Ronan's shoulder. His scent, soapy and masculine, was stronger than the scent of the new shirt.

Alone with him for a week. In a place where no one could find them. It felt dangerous and exciting and terribly frightening, too. She pressed into him, feeling far more endangered than she had when the gun had gone off in the chapel.

Some kind of trembling had started inside her, and it was not totally because he had hurt her feelings telling her her hair looked terrible. It wasn't totally because of the vibration of the motorbike, either!

"Go faster," she cried.

He glanced over his shoulder at her.

"It doesn't go any faster," he shouted back at her, but he gave it a hit of gas and the little bike surged forward.

Her stomach dropped, and she squealed with delight.

He glanced back again. His lips were twitching. He was trying not to smile. But he did, and his smile was like the sun coming out on the grayest of days. That glimpse of a smile made her forget she had only a short time to squeeze many dreams into, though a week was more than she could have hoped for.

Still, it was as if his smile hypnotized her and made
her realize maybe there was one dream he could help
make come true. A dream more important than wearing
shorts or riding astride or touching snow. A dream that
scorned people who pretended all the time.

She had only a few days, and she wanted to be with
someone who was real, not kowtowing. Not anxious to
please. Not afraid of her position. Someone who would
tell her the truth, even if it hurt to hear it.

*I'm not going to be more responsible for you than you
are willing to be for yourself,* he had told her. She
shivered. In that simple statement, as much as it had
pained her to hear it, was the truth about how her life
had gone off track so badly. Could Ronan somehow
lead her back to what was real about herself?

When she was younger, there'd been a place she had
been allowed to go where she had felt real. Relaxed. As
if it was okay to be herself.

Herself—something more and more lost behind the
royal mask, the essential facades of good manners, of
duty. Something that might be lost forever when she was
returned to Prince Mahail as his bride.

"There's an island," she called over the putter of the
engine. "My grandparents have a summer place on a
small island just north of the mainland. No one is ever
there at this time of year."

"No one? No security? No groundskeeper?"

"It's a private island, but not the posh kind. You'd
have to know my grandfather to understand. He hates
all the royal fuss-fuss as he calls it. He likes simplicity.

"The island is almost primitive. There's no electricity, the house is like a cottage, it even has a thatched roof."

"Fresh water, or do we have to bring our own?"

"There's a stream." Ronan thought like a soldier, she realized. All she could think about was it would be such a good place to try on her new bikini, such a wonderful place to rediscover who she really was! But, given the strange trembling inside her, how wise would that be? Given the reality of his smile, the pure sexiness of it, was it possible she was headed into a worse danger zone than the one she was leaving?

"Bedding? Blankets?"

His mind, thankfully, a million miles from bikinis, on the more practical considerations. "I think so."

"How do you get to it?"

"My grandfather keeps a boat at the dock across the bay from it."

"Perfect," he said. "Show me the fastest way to the boat dock."

But she didn't tell him the shortest way. She directed him the longest way possible, because who knew if she would ever ride a motorcycle again, her arms wrapped so intimately around a man with such an incredible, sexy smile?

She *loved* the motorcycle, even if she had been deprived of feeling the fingers of the wind playing with her hair. She could still feel the island breeze on her face, playing with the hem of her skirt, touching her legs. She could feel the kiss of warm sunshine. She had a lovely sensation of being connected to everything around her. The air was perfumed, birds and monkeys chattered in the trees. She didn't feel separate from it, she felt like a part of it.

And she could feel the exquisite sensation of being connected to him—her arms wrapped around the hard-muscled bands of his stomach, her cheek resting on the solid expanse of his back, her legs forming a rather intimate vee around him.

Her mother, she knew, would have an absolute fit. And her father wouldn't be too happy with her, either. She could only imagine how Mahail would feel if he saw her now!

Which only added to the delectable sense of dancing with danger that Princess Shoshauna was feeling: free, adventurous, as if anything at all could happen.

Just this morning her whole life had seemed to be mapped out in front of her, her fate inescapable. Now she had hair that Prince Mahail would hate, and she didn't think he'd like it very much that she had spent a week alone with a strange man, either!

"Can you go faster?' she called to Ronan over the wind.

The slightest hesitation, and then he did, opening the bike up so that they were roaring down the twisting highway, until tears formed in her eyes and she could feel the thrill to the bottom of her belly.

She refused to dwell on how long it would last, or if this was the only time she would ever do this.

Instead she threw back her head and laughed out loud for the sheer joy of the moment, at her unexpected encounter with the most heady drug of all—freedom.

CHAPTER THREE

RONAN cut the engine of the motorboat, letting it drift in to the deserted beach. He glanced at the princess, asleep in the bottom of the boat, exhausted from the day, and decided there was no need for both of them to get wet. He stood up, stepped off the hull into a gentle surf. The seawater was warm on his legs as he dragged the boat up onto the sand.

It was night, but the sky was breathtaking, star-studded. A full moon frosted each softly lapping wave in white and painted the fine beach sand a bewitching shade of silver.

From a soldier's perspective, the island was perfect. Looking back across the water, he could barely make out the dark outline of the main island of B'Ranasha. He could see the odd light flickering on that distant shore.

He had circled this island once in the boat, a rough reconnaissance. It was only about eight kilometers all the way around it. Better yet, it had only this one protected bay, and only the one beach suitable for landing a boat.

Everywhere else the thick tropical growth, or rocky cliffs, came right to the water's edge. The island was too small and bushed in to land a plane on. It would be a nightmare to parachute in to, and it would be a challenge to land a helicopter here. Planes and helicopters gave plenty of warning they were arriving, anyway.

It was a highly defensible position. Perfect from a soldier's perspective.

But from a personal point of view, from a man's perspective, it couldn't be much worse. It was a deserted island more amazing than a movie set. The sand was white, fine and flawless, exotic birds filled the night air with music, a tantalizing perfume rode the gentle night breeze. Palm trees swayed in the wind, ferns and flowers abounded.

At the head of the beach was a cottage, palm-frond roof, screened porch looking out to the sea. It was the kind of retreat people came to on holidays and honeymoons, not to hide out. Which was a good thing. He highly doubted anyone would think to look for the princess here.

He gave the rope attached to the boat another pull, hauled it further up on the sand until he was satisfied it would be safe, even from the tide, which, according to the tide charts he had purchased at a small seaside village, would come up during the night.

Only then did he peer back at Aurora, his very own Sleeping Beauty. The princess, worn down from all the unscheduled excitement of her wedding day, was curled up in the bottom of the boat, fast asleep on a bed of life jackets.

The silver of the moon washed her in magic, though

he felt the shock of her shorn head again, followed by a jolt of a different kind—the short hair did nothing but accentuate her loveliness. Right now he was astonished by the length and fullness of her lashes, casting sooty shadows on the roundness of her cheeks. Her lips moved, forming words in her sleep, something in her own language, *ret-nuh*.

He'd insisted on a life jacket, but the skirt was riding high up her legs, he caught a glimpse of bridal white panties so pure he could feel a certain dryness in his mouth. He reached out and gave the skirt a tug down, whether to save her embarrassment or to save himself he wasn't quite sure.

A deserted island. A beautiful woman. A week. He was no math whiz, but he knew a bad equation when he came across it.

He'd done plenty of protection duty, and though it wasn't his favorite assignment, Ronan prided himself on doing his work well. He'd protected heads of states and their families, politicians, royalty, CEOs.

The person being protected was known amongst the team as the "principal." The team didn't even use personal names when they discussed strategy, formulated plans. The cardinal rule, the constant in protection work, was maintaining a completely professional, arm's-length relationship. Emotional engagement compromised the mission, period.

But the very circumstances of those other assignments made maintaining professionalism easy. The idea of forming any kind of deeper relationship or even a friendship, with the principal had been unthinkable. There was always a team, never just one person. There was always an environment conducive to maintaining preordained boundaries.

Ronan was in brand-new territory, and he didn't like it. So, before he woke her up, he looked to the stars, gathered his strength, reminded himself of the mission, the boundaries, the *rules*.

"Hey," he called softly, finally, "wake up."

She stirred but didn't wake, and he leaned into the boat and nudged her shoulder with his hand. She was slender as a reed, the roundness of her shoulder the epitome of feminine softness.

"Princess." It would be infinitely easy to reach in and scoop her up, to carry her across the sand to that cottage, but that brief contact with her shoulder was fair warning it would be better not to add one little bit of physical contact to the already volatile combination.

A bad time to think of her lips on his cheek earlier in the day, her slight curves pressed hard against him on that motorcycle.

"Wake up," he said louder, more roughly.

She did, blinked—that blank look of one who couldn't quite place where they were. And then she focused on him and smiled in a way that could melt even the most professional soldier's dedication to absolute duty.

She sat up, looked around and then sighed with contentment. She liked being here. She had liked the entire day way too much! He had not been nearly as immune to her laughter and her arms wrapped around him as he had wanted to be, but thankfully she didn't have to know that!

She shrugged out of the life jacket and then stretched,

pressing the full sensuous roundness of her breasts into the thin fabric of the ill-fitting blouse. Then she stood up. The boat rocked on the sand, and the physical contact he wanted so badly not to happen, happened anyway. He caught her, steadied her as the boat rocked on the uneven ground. She took one more step, the boat pitched, and she would have gone to her knees.

Except his hands encircled her waist nearly completely, the thumb and index finger of his right hand nearly touching those of his left. He lifted her from the boat, swung her onto the sand, amazed by her slightness. She didn't weigh any more than a fully loaded combat pack.

"You're strong!" she said.

He withdrew from her swiftly, not allowing himself to preen under her admiration. A week. They had to make it a week.

"It's beautiful, isn't it?" she asked, hugging herself, apparently oblivious to his discomfort. "I love it here. My grandfather called it Naidina Karobin—it means something like *my heart is home.*"

Great.

"Isn't that pretty?"

"Yeah, sure." Real men didn't use words like *pretty.* Except maybe in secret, when they looked at a face like hers, washed in moonlight, alive with discovery. *Mission.*

He reached into the boat and grabbed the knapsack. As he followed her across the sand toward the cottage, he noted that the trees in the grove around it were loaded with edible fruits, coconuts, bananas, mangos.

He'd landed in the Garden of Eden. He only hoped he could resist the apple. *Boundaries.*

As they got closer, the princess jacked her skirt up and ran, danced really, across the sand. She looked like some kind of moonlit nymph, her slender legs painted in silver. *Rules, duty, professionalism.*

He followed her more slowly, as if he could put off the moment when they set up housekeeping together and everything intensified yet more.

Becoming part of Excalibur, Ronan's endurance, physical strength, intellectual assets, ability to cope with stress had all been tested beyond normal limits. One man in twenty who was recruited for that unit made it through the selection process. Membership meant being stronger, faster, tougher in mind and spirit than the average man.

And yet to share the space of that cottage on this island with a real-live sleeping beauty seemed as if it would test him in ways he had never been tested before.

Ronan had been in possession of the princess for less than twenty-four hours and he already felt plenty tested!

He drew a deep breath as he followed her up wide steps to the screen door that he thought had been a screened-in veranda. As his eyes adjusted to the lack of moonlight inside, he saw he had been mistaken.

It was not a screened porch, but a screened-in house. A summer house, she'd said, obviously designed so that it caught the breeze from every angle on hot summer nights. The huge overhang of the roof would protect it from the rare days of inclement weather these islands experienced.

White, sheer curtains lifted and fell in the breeze, making the inside of the house enchanting and exotic. The main room had dark, beautiful wooden floors, worn smooth from years of use, moonlight spilling across them. Deeply cushioned, colorful rattan furniture was grouped casually around a coffee table, a space that invited conversation, relaxation.

Intimacy.

At the other end of the room was a dining area, the furniture old, dark, exquisitely carved and obviously valuable. That such good furniture would be left out in an unlocked cottage should have reassured him how safe the island was. But Ronan was a little too aware that the dangers here could come from within, not without.

The screens as walls gave a magnificent illusion of there being no separation between the indoor living space and the outdoors.

He spied a hurricane lamp and lit it, hoping the light would chase away the feeling of enchantment, but instead, in the flickering golden light, the great room became downright romantic, soft, sultry, sensual.

The light was soft on her face, too, her expression rapt as she looked around, her eyes glowing with the happiness of memories.

Ronan would have liked it a lot better if she was spoiled rotten, complaining about spiderwebs and the lack of electricity.

To distance himself from the unwanted *whoosh* of attraction he felt, Ronan went hurriedly across the room to investigate a door at the back of it. It led to an outdoor kitchen, and he went out. The outdoor cooking space was complete with a huge wood-fired oven and a grill.

Open shelves were lined with canned goods. A person could camp out here, on this island, comfortably, for a year.

Beyond that, in a flower- and fern-encircled grove was an open-air shower, and the *whoosh* he'd been trying to outrun came back.

He reentered the house reluctantly, thankful he didn't see her right away. He finished his inventory of the main house: there were two rooms off the great room, and he entered the first. It was the main bedroom, almost entirely taken up by a huge bed framed with soaring rough timbers, dark with age, more sheer white curtains flowing around the bed, surrounding it. Again the screens acting as outer walls made the bed seem to be set right amongst the palms and mango trees. The perfume of a thousand different flowers tickled his nose. There was no barrier to sound, either. The sea whispered poetry. He backed hastily out of there.

Princess Shoshauna was in the smaller of the bedrooms, looking around and hugging herself.

"This is where I always stayed when I was a child! Look how it feels as if you are right outside! My grandfather designed this house. He was an architect. That's how he came to be on B'Ranasha. I'll have this room."

He would have much preferred she take the bigger room, act snotty and entitled so he could kill the *whoosh* in his stomach.

"I think you should take the bigger room," he suggested. "You are the princess."

"Not this week I'm not." She smiled, delighted to have declared herself not a princess.

If she wasn't a princess, if she was just an ordinary

girl…he cut off the train of his thought. It didn't matter if she was a wandering gypsy. She was still the *principal,* and it was still his mission to protect her.

He reached into his pocket, took out a pocketknife and cut the cord that kept the mattress rolled up. He found the bedding in a tightly closed trunk under the bed. A floral sachet had been packed with it, and the white linen sheets smelled exotic.

He laid them quickly on the bed, then watched, bemused, when she eyed the pile of bedding as though it were an interesting but baffling jigsaw puzzle.

"You don't know how to make a bed," he guessed, incredulous, then wondered why it would surprise him that a princess had no idea how to make a bed.

The truth was, it would be way too easy to forget she was a princess, especially with her standing there with shorn hair, and in a badly rumpled and ill-fitting dress.

But that was exactly what he had to remember, to keep his boundaries clear, his professionalism unsullied, his duty foremost in his mind. She was a princess, a real one. He was a soldier. Their stations in life were millions of miles apart. And they were going to stay that way.

"My mother would never have allowed it," she said, sadly. "She had this idea that to do things that could be done by servants was *common.* Of course, she was a commoner, and she never quite overcame her insecurity about it."

She didn't know how to make a bed.

Every soldier had been tormented, at one time or another, with making a bed that could satisfy a drill sergeant who had no intention of being satisfied. Ronan could make a bed—perfectly—anywhere, anytime.

To focus on the differences between them would strengthen his will. To perceive her as pampered and useless would go a long way in erasing the memory of her slender curves pressed into his back as they rode that motorcycle together.

"I'd be happy to make it for you, Princess," he said.

She glared at him. "I don't want you to make it for me! I want you to show me how to make it."

He was tired. He had not had the benefit of a two hour nap in the bottom of the boat. She had slept for an hour or so before that, as well, while they had waited, hidden, for it to get dark enough to take her grandfather's boat from the dock and cross the water without being seen.

It would be easier for him to make the bed himself, but he had to get through a full week, and that wasn't going to be easy if he argued with her over little things.

His eyes went to the full puffiness of her lips, and he felt his own weariness, his resolve flickering.

He had to get though a full week without kissing her, too.

Making a bed together didn't seem like a very good starting point for keeping things professional and distant. Neither did fighting with her.

He had the uneasy feeling he'd better adjust to being put in no-win positions by the princess.

He separated the sheets from the blankets, found the bottom sheet and tossed it over the mattress.

"First you tuck this under the mattress," he said.

"I'll do it!" she said, when he reached out to demonstrate.

He held up his hands in surrender, stood back, tried not to wince at her sloppy corners, the slack fabric in the center of the bed. He didn't offer to help as she grunted over lifting the corners of the mattress.

He handed her the second sheet, tried to stay expressionless as she shoved it under the bottom of the mattress in such a bunched-up mess that the mattress lifted.

She caught the tip of her tongue between her teeth as she focused with furious concentration on the task at hand. He folded his arms firmly over his chest.

She inserted the pillows in the cases with the seams in the wrong places and fluffed them. Then he handed her the top blanket, which she tossed haphazardly on top of the rest of her mess.

The bed was a buck private's nightmare, but she smiled with pleasure at her final result. To his eye, it looked more like a nest than a well-made bed.

"See?" she said. "I can do ordinary things."

"Yes," he said, deadpan. "I can clearly see that."

Something in his tone must have betrayed him, because she searched his face with grave suspicion.

A drill sergeant would have had the thrill of ripping it apart and making her do it again, but he wasn't a drill sergeant. In fact, at the moment he was just an ordinary guy, trying to survive.

"Okay," he said, "if you have everything—"

"Oh, I'll make yours, too. For practice."

"What do you need practice making a bed for?" he asked crankily. He didn't want her touching his bedding.

He was suddenly acutely aware of how alone they were here, of how the dampness of the sea air was making the baggy dress cling to her, of how her short hair was curling slightly from humidity, and there seemed to be a dewy film forming on her skin. He was aware of how her tongue had looked, caught between her teeth.

Ignoring him, she marched right by him into his room. He trailed behind her reluctantly, watched as she opened the trunk where the linens were kept and began tossing them on his bed.

"I'm going to do all kinds of ordinary things this week," she announced.

"Such as?" He didn't offer to help her make the bed, just watched, secretly aghast at the mess she was making.

"Cooking!" she decided.

"I can hardly wait."

He got the suspicious look again.

"Washing dishes. Doing laundry. You can show me those things, can't you?"

She sounded so enthused he thought she must be pulling his leg, but he could tell by the genuine eager expression on her face she really wasn't.

How did a man maintain professional distance from a princess who wanted nothing more than to be an ordinary girl, who was enthralled at the prospect of doing the most ordinary of things?

He nodded cautiously.

"I would like to learn how to sew on a button," she decided. "Do you know how to do that?"

Sewing buttons, insignia, pant hems, was right up there with making beds in a soldier's how-to arsenal, but she didn't wait for him to answer.

"And I can't wait to swim in the ocean! I used to swim here when I was a child. I love it!"

He thought of that bikini in their backpack, closed his eyes, marshaling strength.

"You don't happen to know how to surf, do you?" she asked him. "There used to be a surfboard under the cottage. I hope it's still there!"

His boyhood days had been spent on a surfboard. It was probably what had saved him from delinquency, his love of the waves, his *need* to perfect the dance with the extraordinary, crashing power of them.

"This bay doesn't look like it would ever get much in the way of surf," he told her. "It's pretty protected."

She looked disappointed, but then brightened. "There's snorkeling equipment under there, too. Maybe we can do that."

We, as if they were two kids together on vacation. Now would be the time to let her know he had no intention of being her playmate, but he held his tongue.

She gave his bed a final, satisfied pat. "Well, good night Ronan. I can't wait for tomorrow." She blew him a kiss, which was only slightly better than the one she had planted on his cheek earlier in the day.

He rubbed his cheek, aggravated, as if the kiss had actually landed, an uncomfortably whimsical thought for a man who prided himself on his pragmatic nature. He listened for her to get into her own bed, then went on silent feet and checked each side of the cabin.

The night was silent, except for the night birds. The ocean was dark and still, the only lights were from the moon and stars, the few lights on the mainland had winked out.

He went back into his bedroom. He knew he needed to sleep, that it would help him keep his thinking clear and disciplined. He also knew he had acquired, over the years, that gift peculiar to soldiers of sleeping in a state of readiness. Any sound that didn't belong would awaken him instantly. His highly developed sixth sense would guard them both through the night.

He shrugged out of his shirt but left the shorts on. He certainly didn't want her to ever see him in his underwear, and he might have to get out of bed quickly in the night. He climbed into bed. It had to be his imagination that her perfume lingered on the sheets. Still, tired as he was, he tossed and turned until finally, an hour later, he got out of the bed, remade it *perfectly*. He got back in and slept instantly.

Shoshauna awoke to light splashing across her bed, birdsong, the smell and sound of the sea.

She remembered she was on her grandfather's island and thought to herself, my heart *is* home. She remembered her narrow escape from marriage, the unexpected gifts yesterday: riding the motorcycle, buying the daring bathing suit and shorty-shorts.

Kissing Ronan on the cheek. Feeling the muscles of his back as they shared the motorcycle, feeling his hands encircle her waist.

Ronan was a gloriously made man, all hard muscle, graceful efficiency of movement, easy, unconscious strength, a certain breathtaking confidence in his physical abilities. Add to that the soft, firm voice, his accent. And his eyes! A soldier's eyes to be sure, stern, forbidding even. But when the mask slipped, when they glinted with laughter, she felt this uncontrollable—and definitely wicked—shiver of pure wanting. He made her feel such an amazing mixture of things: excited and shy, aggravated, annoyed, *alive*.

Shoshauna knew it was wrong to be thinking like that. She was promised to another. And yet…if you could pick a man to spend a week on a deserted island with, you would pick a man like Ronan.

She gave her head a shake at the naughty direction of her own thoughts and realized her head felt unnaturally light and then remembered she had cut her hair.

She had glimpsed her hair in the mirror of the motorcycle. Now she hopped out of bed and had a good look in the mirror above the dressing table.

"Oh!" she said, touching her fingers to it. It looked awful, crushed in places from sleep, standing straight up in others. Despite that, she decided she loved it. It made her look like a girl who would never back down from an adventure, not a princess who had spent her life in a tower, at least figuratively speaking! In fact, she felt in love with life this morning, excited about whatever new gifts the day held. Excited about a chance to get to know Ronan better.

But wasn't that a betrayal of the man she was promised to?

Not necessarily, she told herself. This was her opportunity to be ordinary!

She realized she had not felt this way—happy, hopeful—since she had said yes to Prince Mahail's proposal. Up till now she had woken up each and every morning with a knot in her stomach that shopping for the world's most luxurious trousseau could not begin to undo. She had woken each morning with a growing sense of dread, a prisoner counting down to their date with the gallows.

Her stomach dipped downward, reminding her that her reprieve was probably temporary at best.

But she refused to think of that now, to waste even one precious moment of her freedom.

Ronan had left the backpack in her room, and she pawed through it, found the shorty-shorts and a red, spaghetti-strapped shirt that hugged her curves. She put on the outfit and twirled in front of the mirror, her sense of being an *ordinary* girl increased sweetly.

Her mother would have hated both the amount of leg showing and the skimpiness of the top, which made Shoshauna enjoy her outfit even more. She liked the way lots of bare skin against warm air felt: free, faintly sensual and very comfortable.

She went out her door, saw his bedroom was already empty. She stopped when she saw his bed was made, hesitated, then went in and inspected it. The bedding was crisp and taut. She backed out when she realized the room smelled like him: something so masculine and rich it was nearly drugging.

She went back to her own room, tugged the rumpled bedding into some semblance of order, declared herself and the room perfectly wonderfully ordinary and went in search of Ronan.

He was at the outdoor kitchen, a basket of fruit beside him that he was peeling and cutting into chunks. She watched him for a moment, enjoying the pure poetry of him performing such a simple task, and then blushed when he glanced at her and lifted an eyebrow. He had known she stood there observing him!

Still, there was a flash of something in his eyes as he took in her outfit, before it was quickly veiled, a barrier swiftly erected. And there was no hint of that *flash* in his voice.

"Princess," he said formally, "did you sleep well?"

It was several giant steps back from the man who had laughed with her yesterday. She wanted to break down the barrier she saw in his eyes. What good was being an ordinary girl if it was as if she was on this island alone? If her intrigue with this man was not shared?

"You must call me Shoshauna," she said.

"I can't."

She glared at him. "I command it."

He actually laughed out loud, the same laugh that had given her her first glimpse yesterday of just how real he could be, making her yearn to know him, know someone real.

"Command away, Princess. I'm not calling you by your first name."

"Why?"

"It's too familiar. I'm your bodyguard, not your buddy."

She felt the sting of that. Her disappointment was acute. He wanted the exact opposite of what she wanted! She wanted to feel close to another human being, he wanted to feel distant. She wanted to use this time together to explore his mysteries, he was just as determined to keep them secret.

It was frustrating! Her mother would approve of his attitude, a man who knew his *place* and was so determined to keep their different positions as a barrier between them.

But so would her grandmother love him. Her grand-mother said soldiers made the best husbands, because they already knew how to obey. Not that he was showing any sign of obeying Shoshauna!

And not that she wanted to be thinking of this hand-some man and the word *husband* in the same sentence. She had just narrowly missed making marriage her fate.

Still, she wanted him to participate in the great adventure she was on. How could she forget she was a princess, forget her obligations and duties for a short while, if he was going to insist on reminding her at every turn by using a formal title?

"How about my code name, then?" she asked.

He hesitated, glanced at her, shrugged. She couldn't tell if it was agreement or appeasement, though which-ever it was, she sensed it was a big concession from him, he suddenly refused to look at her, took an avid interest in the fruit in front of him.

"I'll do that," she said, moving up beside him. Did he move a careful step away from her? She moved closer. He moved away again and without looking at her, passed her a little tiny knife and a mango.

"Don't cut your fingers off," he said dryly.

She watched for a moment as his own fingers han-dled the knife, removed a fine coil of peel from the fruit. He caught her watching him, *again,* put down the knife and turned away from her to put wood in the oven.

"What are we going to make in there?" she asked eagerly.

"*I'm* going to make biscuits."

"I want to learn!"

"What for?"

"It seems like it would be a useful skill," she said stubbornly.

"It is a useful skill. For someone like me, who frequently finds himself trying to make the best of rough circumstances. But for a princess?" He shook his head.

"I want to know useful things!"

"What is useful in your world and what is useful in mine are two very different things," he said almost gently.

Rebelliously she attacked the mango with her knife. Ten minutes later as she looked at the sliver of fruit in front of her, what was left of her mango, she realized he was probably right. Domestication at this late date was probably hopeless. She felt sticky to the elbow, and had managed to get juice in her eye. The mango was mangled beyond recognition.

She cast him a look. Ronan was taking golden-brown biscuits off a griddle above the stove. The scent of them made her mouth water.

"Here," she said, handing him the remnants of her mango. He took it wordlessly, his face a careful blank, and added it to the plate of fruit he had prepared.

She thought they'd take the food inside to the dining table, but he motioned her over to a little stone bench, set the plate down between them, lifted his face to the morning sun as he picked up a piece of fruit.

She followed his example and picked up a slice of fruit and a biscuit with her fingers.

Shoshauna had dined on the finest foods in the world. She had eaten at the fanciest tables of B'Ranasha, using the most exquisite china and cutlery. But she felt as if she had never tasted food this fine or enjoyed flavor so much.

She decided she loved everything, absolutely everything, about being an ordinary girl. And she hadn't given up on herself in the domestic department yet, either!

CHAPTER FOUR

AFTER a few minutes Shoshauna couldn't help but notice that her pleasure in the simplicity of the breakfast feast seemed to be entirely one-sided.

Ronan, while obviously enjoying the sunshine and eating with male appetite, seemed pensive, turned in on himself, as anxious not to connect with her as she *was* to connect with him.

"Are you enjoying breakfast?" she asked, craving conversation, curious about this man who had become her protector.

He nodded curtly.

She realized she was going to have to be more direct! "Tell me about yourself," she invited.

He shot her a look, looked away. "There's nothing to tell. I'm a soldier. That means my life is ninety-nine percent pure unadulterated boredom."

She supposed you didn't learn to make a bed like that if you led a life of continuous excitement, but she knew he was fudging the truth. She could tell, from the way he carried himself, from the calm with which he had handled things yesterday that he dealt with danger as comfortably as most men dealt with the reading of the morning paper.

"And one percent what?" she asked when it became apparent he was going to add nothing voluntarily.

"All hell breaking loose."

"Oh!" she said genuinely intrigued. "All hell breaking loose! That sounds exciting."

"I wish you wouldn't say that word," he said, ignoring her implied invitation to share some of his most exciting experiences with her.

"Hell, hell, hell, hell, hell," she said, and found it very liberating both to say the word and to defy him. Her society prized meekness in women, but she had made the discovery she was not eager to be anyone's prize!

He shot her a stern look. She smiled back. He wasn't her father! He didn't look more than a few years older than she was. He couldn't tell her how to behave!

He sighed, resigned, she hoped, to the fact he was not going to control her. She'd been controlled quite enough. This was her week to do whatever she wanted, including say *hell* to her heart's content.

"What's the most exciting thing that ever happened to you?" she pressed, when he actually shut his eyes, lifted his chin a bit higher to the sun, took a bite of biscuit, apparently intent on pretending he was dining alone and ignoring her questions.

He thought about it for a minute, but his reluctance to engage in this conversation was palpable. Finally he said, without even opening his eyes, "I ran into a grizzly bear while in Canada on a mountain survival exercise."

"Really?" she breathed. "What happened?" It was better than she could have hoped. Better than a movie!

She waited for him to tell her what she could picture so vividly—Ronan wrestling the primitive animal to the ground with his bare hands…

"It ran one way and I ran the other."

She frowned, sharply disappointed at his lack of heroics. "That doesn't sound very exciting!"

"I guess you had to be there."

"I think I would like to go to the mountains in Canada." Yes, even with bears, or maybe because of bears, it sounded like an adventure she'd enjoy very much. "Are the mountains beautiful? Is there snow?"

"Yes, to both."

"What's snow like?" she asked wistfully.

"Cold."

"No, what does it *feel* like." Again, he was trying to disengage, but he was the only person she'd ever met who had experienced snow, and she *had* to know.

"It's different all the time," he said, giving in a little, as if he sensed her needing to know. "If it's very cold the snow is light and powdery, like frozen dust. If it's warmer it's heavy and wet and sticks together. You can build things with it when it's like that."

"Like a snowman?"

"Yeah, I suppose. I built a snow cave out of it."

"Which kind is better for sledding?"

"The cold, dry kind. What do you know about that?"

"Nothing. I've seen it on television. I've always had a secret desire to try it, a secret desire to see different things than here, more beautiful."

"I don't know if there's anything more beautiful than this," he said. "It's a different kind of beauty. More rugged. The landscape there is powerful rather than gentle. It reminds a person of how small they are and how big nature is." He suddenly seemed to think he was talking too much. "I'm sure your husband will take you there if you want to go," he said abruptly.

It was her turn to glare at him. She didn't want to be reminded, at this moment, that her life was soon going to involve a husband.

"I'm fairly certain Prince Mahail," she said, "is about as interested in tobogganing in snow as he is in training a water buffalo to tap dance."

"He doesn't like traveling? Trying new things?" He did open his eyes then, lower his chin. He was regarding her now with way too much interest.

She felt a sensation in her stomach like panic. "I don't know what he likes," she said, her voice strangled. She felt suddenly like crying, looked down at her plate and blinked back the tears.

Her life had come within seconds of being linked forever to a man who was a stranger to her. And despite the fact the heavens had taken pity on her and granted her a reprieve, there was no guarantee that linking would not still happen.

"Hey," Ronan said, "hey, don't cry."

After all the events of yesterday, including being shot at, this was the first time she'd heard even the smallest hint of panic in that calm voice!

"I'm not crying," she said. But she was. She scrubbed furiously at the tear that worked its way down her cheek. She didn't want Ronan to be looking at her like that because he felt sorry for her!

She reminded herself she was supposed to be finding out about Ronan, not the other way around!

"What made you want to be a soldier?" she asked, trying desperately for an even tone of voice, to change the subject, to not waste one precious second contemplating all the adventures she was not going to have once she was married to Mahail.

Something flickered in his eyes. Sympathy? Compassion? Whatever it was, he opened up to her just the tiniest little bit.

"I had a lousy home life as a kid. I wanted routine. Stability. Rules. I found what I was looking for." He regarded her intently, hesitated and then said softly, "And you will, too. Trust me."

He would be such an easy man to trust, to believe that he had answers.

"Isn't it a hard life you've chosen?" she asked him, even though what she really wanted to say was *how? How will I ever find what I'm looking for? I don't even know where to look!*

He shrugged, tilted his chin back toward the sun. "Our unit's unofficial motto is Go Hard or Go Home. Some would see it as hard. I see it as challenging."

Was there any subtle way to ask what she most wanted to ask, besides *How will I ever find what I'm looking for?* It was inappropriate to ask him, and too soon. But still, she was not going to find herself alone on a deserted island with an extremely handsome man ever again.

She had to know. She had to know if he was available. Even though she herself, of course, was not. Not even close.

"Do you have a girlfriend?" She hoped she wasn't blushing.

He opened his eyes, shot her a look, closed them again. "No."

"Why not?"

His openness came to an abrupt end. That firm line appeared again around his mouth. "What is this? Twenty questions at the high school cafeteria?"

"What's a high school caff-a-ter-ee-a?"

"Never mind. I don't have a girlfriend because my lifestyle doesn't lend itself to having a girlfriend."

"Why?"

He sighed, but she was not going to be discouraged. Her option was to spend the week talking to him or talking to herself. At the moment she felt her survival depended on focusing on his life, rather than her own.

Maybe her desperation was apparent because he caved slightly. "I travel a lot. I can be called away from home for months at a time. I dismantle the odd bomb. I jump from airplanes."

"Meeting the grizzly bear wasn't the most exciting thing that ever happened to you!" she accused.

"Well, it was the most exciting thing that I'm allowed to talk about. Most of what I do is highly classified."

"And dangerous."

He shrugged. "Dangerous enough that it doesn't seem fair to have a girlfriend or a family."

"I'm not sure," she said, thoughtfully, "what is unfair about being yourself?"

He looked at her curiously and she explained what she meant. "The best thing is to be passionate about life. That's what makes people really seem alive, whole, isn't it? If they aren't afraid to live the way they want to live and to live fully? That's what a girlfriend should want for you. For a life that makes you whole. And happy. Even if it is dangerous."

She was a little embarrassed that she, who had never had a boyfriend, felt so certain about what qualifications his girlfriend should have. And she was sadly aware that passion, the ability to be alive and whole, were the very qualities she herself had lost somewhere a long the way.

As if to underscore how much she had lost or never discovered, he asked her, suddenly deciding to have a conversation after all, "So, what's the most exciting thing you've ever done?"

Been shot at. Cut my hair. Ridden a motorcycle.

All the most exciting events of her life had happened yesterday! It seemed way too pathetic to admit that, though it increased her sense of urgency, this was her week to live.

"I'm afraid that's classified," she said, and was rewarded when he smiled, ever so slightly, but spoiled the effect entirely by chucking her under her chin as if she was a precocious child, gathered their plates and stood up.

Shoshauna realized, that panicky sensation suddenly back, that she had to squeeze as much into the next week as she possibly could. "I'm putting on my bathing suit now and going swimming. Are you coming?"

He looked pained. "No. I'll look after the dishes."

"We can do the dishes later. Together. You can show me how."

He said another nice word under his breath.

She repeated it, and when he gave her *that* look, the stern, forbidding, don't-mess-with-me look, she said it again!

When he closed his eyes and took a deep breath, a man marshaling his every resource, she knew beyond a shadow of a doubt that he was dreading this week every bit as much as she was looking forward to it.

"How about if we do the dishes now?" he said. "In this climate I don't think you want to leave things out to attract bugs. And then," he added, resigned, "if you really want, I'll show you how to make biscuits."

She eyed him suspiciously. He didn't look like a man who would be the least bothered by a few bugs. He'd probably eaten them on occasion! And he certainly did not look like a man who wanted to give out cooking lessons.

So that left her with one conclusion. He didn't like the water. No, that wasn't it. And then, for some reason, she remembered the look on his face when he'd put that pink bikini back on the rack in the store yesterday.

And she understood perfectly!

Ronan did not want to see her in a bikini. Which meant, as much as he didn't want to, he found her attractive.

A shiver went up and down her spine, and she felt something she had not felt for a very long time, if she had ever felt it at all.

Without knowing it, Ronan had given her a very special gift. Princess Shoshauna felt the exquisite discovery of her own power.

"I'd love to learn to make biscuits instead of going swimming," she said meekly, the perfect B'Ranasha princess. Then she smiled to herself at the relief he was unable to mask in his features. She had a secret weapon. And she would decide when and where to use it.

* * *

"Hey," Ronan snapped, "cut it out."

The princess ignored him, took another handful of soap bubbles and blew them at him. Princess Shoshauna had developed a gift for knowing when it was okay to ignore his instructions and when it wasn't, and it troubled him that she read him so easily after four days of being together.

He had not managed to keep her out of the bathing suit, hard as he had tried. He'd taken her at her word that she wanted to learn things and had her collecting fruit and firewood. He'd taught her how to start a decent fire, showed her edible plants, a few rudimentary survival skills.

Ronan had really thought she would lose interest in all these things, but she had not. Her fingers were covered in tiny pinpricks from her attempts to handle a needle and thread, she was sporting a bruise on one of her legs from trying to climb up a coconut tree, she gathered firewood every morning with enthusiasm and without being asked. Even her bed making was improving!

He was reluctantly aware that the princess had that quality that soldiers admired more than any other. They called it "try." It was a never-say-die, never-quit determination that was worth more in many situations than other attributes like strength and smarts, though in fact the princess had both of those, too, her strength surprising, given her physical size.

Still, busy as he'd tried to keep her, he'd failed to keep her from swimming, though he'd developed his own survival technique for when she donned the lime-green handkerchief she called a bathing suit.

The bathing suit was absolutely astonishing on her. He knew as soon as he saw it that he had been wrong thinking the pink one he'd made her put back would look better, because nothing could look better.

She was pure, one-hundred-percent-female menace in that bathing suit, slenderness and curves in a head-spinning mix. Mercifully, for him, she was shy about wearing it, and got herself to the water's edge each day before dropping the towel she wrapped herself in.

His survival technique: he went way down the beach and spearfished for dinner while she swam. He kept an eye on her, listened for sounds of distress, kept his distance.

He was quite pleased with his plan, because she was so gorgeous in a bathing suit it could steal a man's strength as surely as Delilah had stolen Sampson's by cutting off his hair.

Shoshauna blew some more bubbles at him.

"Cut it out," he warned her again.

She chuckled, unfortunately, not the least intimidated by him anymore.

It was also unfortunately charming how much fun she was having doing the dishes. She had fun doing everything, going after life as if she had been a prisoner in a cell, marveling at the smallest things.

Hard as it was to maintain complete professionalism in the face of her joie de vivre, he was glad her mood was upbeat. There had been no more emotional outbursts after that single time she had burst into tears at the very mention of her fiancé, her husband-to-be.

Ronan could handle a lot of things, up to and including a mad mamma grizzly clicking her teeth at him and rearing to her full seven-foot height on her hind legs. But he could not handle a woman in tears!

Still he found himself contemplating that one time, in quiet moments, in the evenings when he was by himself and she had tumbled into bed, exhausted and happy. How could Shoshauna not even know if her future life partner liked traveling, or if he shared her desire to touch snow, to toboggan? The princess was, obviously, marrying a stranger. And just as obviously, and very understandably, she was terrified of it.

But all that fell clearly into the none-of-his-business category. The sense that swept over him, when he saw her shinny up a tree, grinning down at him like the cheeky little monkey she was, of being protective, almost furiously so, of wanting to rescue her from her life was inappropriate. He was a soldier. She was a princess. His life involved doing things he didn't want to do, and so did hers.

But marrying someone she didn't even really know? Glancing at her now, bubbles from head to toe, it seemed like a terrible shame. She was adorable—fun, curious, bratty, sexy as all get-out—she was the kind of girl some guy could fall head over heels in love with. And she deserved to know what that felt like.

Not, he told himself sternly, *that he was in any kind of position to decide what she did or didn't deserve. That wasn't part of the mission.*

He'd never had a mission that made him feel curiously weak instead of strong, as if things were spinning out of his control. He'd come to *like* being with her, so much so that even doing dishes with her was weakness, pure and simple.

It had been bad enough when she waltzed out in shorts every morning, her legs golden and flawless, looking like they went all the way to her belly button. Which showed today, her T-shirt a touch too small. Every time she moved her arms, he saw a flash of slender tummy.

It was bad enough that when he'd glanced over at her, hacking away at the poor defenseless mango or pricking her fingers with a needle, he felt an absurd desire to touch her hair because it had looked spiky, sticking up all over the place like tufts of grass but he was willing to bet it was soft as duck down.

It was bad enough that she was determined to have a friendship, and that even though he knew it was taboo, sympathy had made him actually engage with her instead of discouraging her.

I had a lousy home life as a kid. That was the most personal information he'd said to anyone about himself in years. He *hated* that he'd said it, even if he'd said it to try and make her realize good things could come from bad.

He hated that sharing with her that one stupid, small sentence had made him realize a loneliness resided in him that he had managed to outrun for a long, long time. He'd said he didn't have a girlfriend because of his work, but that was only a part truth. The truth was he didn't want anyone to know him so well that they could coax information out of him that made him feel vulnerable and not very strong at all.

He was a man who loved danger, who rose to the thrill of a risk. He lived by his unit's motto, Go Hard or Go Home, and he did it with enthusiasm. His life was about intensely masculine things: strength, discipline, guts, toughness.

After his mother's great love of all things frilly and froufrou, he had not just accepted his rough barracks existence, he had embraced it. He had, consciously or not, rejected the feminine, the demands of being around the female of the species. He had no desire to be kind, polite, gentle or accommodating.

But in revealing that one small vulnerability to Shoshauna, he recognized he had never taken the greatest risk of all.

Part of the reason he was a soldier—or maybe most of the reason—was he could keep his heart in armor. He'd been building that armor, piece by meticulous piece, since the death of his dad. But when he'd asked her, that first day together, "Who knows what love is?" he'd had a flash of memory, a realization that a place in him thought it knew exactly what love was.

There was a part of him that he most wanted to deny, that he had been very successfully denying until a few short days ago, but now it nibbled around the edges of his mind. Ronan secretly hoped there was a place a man could lay his armor down, a place he could be soft, a place where there was room to love another.

Shoshauna, without half trying, was bringing his secrets to the surface. She was way too curious and way too engaging. Luckily for him, he had developed that gift of men who did dangerous and shadowy work. He was taciturn, wary of any interest in him.

In his experience, civilians thought they wanted to know, thought a life of danger was like adventure movies, but it wasn't and they didn't.

But Shoshauna's desire to know seemed genuine, and even though she had led the most sheltered of lives, he had a feeling she could handle who he really was. More than handle it—embrace it.

But these were the most dangerous thoughts—the thoughts that jeopardized his mission, his sense of professionalism and his sense of himself.

But what had his choices been? To totally ignore her for the week? Set up a tent out back here? Pretend she didn't exist?

He was no expert on women, but he knew they liked to talk. It was in his own best interests to keep the princess moderately happy with their stay here. Hell, part of him, an unfortunately large part, *wanted* to make her happy before he returned her to a fate that he would not have wished on anyone.

Marriage seemed like a hard enough proposition without marrying someone you didn't know. Ask his mother. She'd made it her hobby to marry people she didn't really know.

A renegade thought blasted through his mind: if he was Shoshauna's prince, he'd take her to that mountaintop just because she wanted to go, just to see the delight in her face when she looked down over those sweeping valleys, to see her inhale the crispness of the air. He'd build snowmen with her and race toboggans down breathtakingly steep slopes just to hear the sound of her laughter.

If he was her prince? Cripes, he was getting in bigger trouble by the minute.

There had been mistakes made over the past few days. One of them had been asking her about the most exciting thing in her life. Because it had been so pathetically evident it had probably been that motorcycle ride and all of *this*.

From the few words she'd said about passion he'd known instantly that she regretted the directions of her own life, *yearned* for more. And he'd been taken by her wisdom, too, when he'd told her that the dangerous parts of his job kept him from a relationship.

Was there really a woman out there who understood that caring about someone meant encouraging her partner to pursue what made him whole and alive? Not in his experience there wasn't! Beginning with his mother, it was always about how *she* felt, what *she* needed to feel safe, secure, loved. Not that it had ever worked for her, that strangling kind of love that wanted to control and own.

The last thing he wanted to be thinking about was his mother! Even the bathing suit would be better than that. He was aware the thought of his mother had appeared because he had opened the door a crack when he admitted he had a lousy childhood. That was the whole problem with admissions like that.

He was here, on this island, with the princess, to do a simple job. To protect her. And that meant he did not—thank God—have the luxury of looking at himself right now.

Still, he knew he had to be very, very careful because he was treading a fine line. He'd already felt the uncomfortable wriggle of emotion for her. He didn't want to be rude, but he had to make it very clear, to himself and to her, this was his job. He wasn't on vacation, he wasn't supposed to be having fun.

He couldn't even allow himself to think the thoughts of a normal, healthy man when he saw her in that bathing suit every day.

But now he was wondering if he'd overrated that danger and underrated this one. Because in the bathing suit she was sexy. Untouchable and sexy, like a runway model or a film actress. He could watch her from a safe distance, up the beach somewhere, sunglasses covering his eyes so she would never read his expression.

With soap bubbles all over her from washing dishes, she was still sexy. But cute, too. He was not quite sure how she had managed to get soap bubbles all over the long length of her naked legs, but she had.

She put bubbles on her face, a bubble beard and moustache. "Look!"

"How old are you?" he asked, putting duty first, pretending pure irritation when in fact her enjoyment of very small things was increasingly enchanting.

"Twenty-one."

"Well, quit acting like you're six," he said.

Then he felt bad, because she looked so crestfallen. *Boundaries,* yes, but he was not going to do that again: try to erect them by hurting her feelings. He'd crossed the fine line between being rude and erecting professional barriers. Ronan simply expected himself to be a better man than that.

Against his better judgment, but by way of apology, he scooped up a handful of suds and tossed them at her. She tossed some back. A few minutes later they were both drenched in suds and laughing.

Great. The barriers were down almost completely,

when he had vowed to get them back up—when he knew her survival depended on it. And perhaps his own, too.

Still, despite the fact he knew he was dancing with the kind of danger that put meeting a grizzly bear to shame, it occurred to him, probably because of the seriousness of most of his work, he'd forgotten how to be young.

He was only twenty-seven, but he'd done work that had aged him beyond that, stolen his laughter. The kind of dark, gallows humor he shared with his comrades didn't count.

Even when the guys played together, they played rough, body-bruising sports, the harder hitting the better. He had come to respect strength and guts, and his world was now almost exclusively about those things. There was no room in it for softness, not physical, certainly not emotional.

His work often required him to be mature way beyond his years, required him to shoulder responsibility that would have crippled any but the strongest of men. Life was so often serious, decisions so often involved life and death, that he had forgotten how to be playful, had forgotten how good it could feel to laugh like this.

The rewards of his kind of work were many: he felt a deep sense of honor; he felt as if he made a real difference in a troubled world; he was proud of his commitment to be of service to his fellow man; the bonds he had with his brothers in arms were stronger than steel. Ronan had never questioned the price he paid to do the work before, and he absolutely knew now was not the time to start!

Sharing a deserted island with a gorgeous princess who was eager to try on her new bikini, was absolutely the wrong time to decide to rediscover those things!

But just being around her made him so aware of *softness,* filled him with a treacherous yearning. The full meltdown could probably start with something as simple as wanting to touch her hair.

"Okay," he said, serious, trying to be very serious, something light still lingering in his heart, "you want to learn how to make my secret biscuit recipe?"

Ronan had done many different survival schools. All the members of Excalibur prided themselves in their ability to produce really good food from limited ingredients, to use what they could find around them. He was actually more comfortable cooking over a fire than he was using an oven.

An hour later with flour now deeply stuck on her damp skin, she pulled her biscuit attempt from the wood-fired oven.

Ronan tried to keep a straight face. Every biscuit was a different size. Some were burned and some were raw.

"Try one," she insisted.

Since he'd already hurt her feelings once today and decided that wasn't the way to keep his professional distance, he sucked it up and took one of the better-looking biscuits.

He took a big bite. "Hey," he lied, "not bad for a first try."

She helped herself to one, wrinkled her nose, set it down. "I'll try again tomorrow."

He hoped she wouldn't. He hoped she'd tire soon of

the novelty of working together, because it was fun, way more fun than he wanted to have with her.

"Let's go swimming now," she said. "Could you come with me today? I thought I saw a shark yesterday."

Was that pure devilment dancing in the turquoise of those eyes? Of course it was. She'd figured out he didn't want to swim with her, figured out her softness was piercing his armor in ways no bullet ever had. She'd figured out how badly he didn't want to be anywhere near her when she was in that bathing suit.

In other words, she had figured out his weakness.

He could not let her see that. One thing he'd learned as a soldier was you never ran away from the thing that scared you the most. Never. You ran straight toward it.

"Sure," he said, with a careless shrug. "Let's go."

He said it with the bravado of a man who had just been assigned to dismantle a bomb and didn't want a single soul to know how scared he was.

But when he looked into her eyes, dancing with absolute mischief, he was pretty sure he had not pulled it off.

She was not going to be fooled by him, and it was a little disconcerting to feel she could see through him so completely when he had become such an expert at hiding every weakness he ever felt.

CHAPTER FIVE

SHOSHAUNA stared at herself in the mirror in her bedroom and gulped. The bathing suit was really quite revealing. It hadn't seemed to matter so much when Ronan was way down the shoreline, spearfishing, picking up driftwood, but today he was going to swim with her! Finally.

She could almost hear her mother reacting to her attire. "Common." Her father would be none to pleased with this outfit, either, especially since she was in the company of a man, completely unchaperoned.

But wasn't that the whole problem with her life? She had been far to anxious to please others and not nearly anxious enough to please herself. She had always dreamed of being bold, of being the adventurer, but in the end she had always backed away.

She remembered the exhilarating sense of power she had felt when she realized Ronan didn't want to see this bathing suit, when she'd realized, despite all his determination not to, he found her attractive. Suddenly she wanted to feel that power again. She was so aware of the clock ticking. They had been here four days. There was three left, and then it would be over.

Suddenly nothing could have kept her from the sea, and Ronan.

At the last minute, though, as always, she wrapped a huge bath towel around herself before she stepped out of the house.

Ronan waited outside the door, glanced at her, his expression deadpan, but she was sure she saw a glint of amusement in his eyes, as if he *knew* she was really too shy to wear that bikini with confidence, with delight in her own power when there was a man in such close quarters.

"Look what I found under the porch," he said.

Two sets of snorkels and fins! No one could look sexy or feel powerful in a snorkel and fins! Still, she had not snorkeled since the last time she had been here, and she remembered the experience with wonder.

"Was the surfboard there?"

"Yeah, an old longboard. You want me to grab it? You could paddle around on it."

"No, thank you," she said. Paddle around on it, as if she was a little kid at the wading pool. She wanted to surf on it—to capture the power of the sea—or nothing at all. Just to prove to him she was not a little kid, *at all,* she yanked the towel away.

He dropped his sunglasses down over his eyes rapidly, took a sudden interest in the two sets of snorkels and fins, but she could see his Adam's apple jerk each time he swallowed.

She marched down the sand to the surf, trying to pretend she was confident as could be but entirely aware she was nearly naked and in way over her head without even touching the water. She plunged into the sea as quickly as she could.

Once covered by the blanket of the ocean, she turned back, pretending complete confidence.

"The water is wonderful," she called. "Come in." It was true, the water was wonderful, warm, a delight she had been discovering all week was even better against almost-naked skin.

Suddenly she was glad she'd found the courage to wear the bikini, glad she'd left the towel behind, glad she was experiencing how sensuous it was to be in the water with hardly anything between it and her, not even fabric. Her new haircut was perfect for swimming, too! Not heavy with wetness, it dried almost instantly in the sun.

She looked again at the beach. Ronan was watching her, arms folded over his chest, like a lifeguard at the kiddy park.

She was going to get that kiddy-park look off his face if it killed her!

"Come in," she called again, and then pressed the button she somehow knew, by instinct, he could not stand to have pressed. "Unless you're scared."

Not of the water, either, but of her. She felt a little swell of that feeling, *power,* delicious, seductive, pure feminine power. She had been holding off with it, waiting, uncertain, but now the time felt right.

She watched as Ronan dropped the snorkeling gear in the sand, pulled his shirt over his head. She felt her mouth go dry. This was how she had hoped he would react to her. A nameless yearning engulfed her as she stared at the utter magnificence of his build.

He was pure and utter male perfection. Every fluid inch of him was about masculine strength, a body honed to the perfection of a hard fighting tool.

Shoshauna had thought she would feel like the powerful one if they swam together, but now she could see the power was in the chemistry itself, not in her, not in him.

There was a universal force that called when a certain woman looked at a certain man, when a certain man looked at a certain woman. It pulled them together, an ancient law of attraction, metal to magnet, a law irresistible, as integral as gravity to the earth.

Shoshauna became aware that the "power" she had so wanted to experiment with, to play with, was out of her control. She felt a kind of helpless thrill, like a child who had played with matches and was now having to deal with a renegade spark that had flared to flame.

Impossible to put this particular fire out. Ronan was all sleek muscle and hard lines, not an ounce of superfluous fat or flesh on his powerful male body. His chest was deep, his stomach flat, ridged with ab muscles, his shoulders impossibly broad. His legs were long, rippling with muscle.

He dove cleanly into the water, cutting it with his body. Two powerful strokes carried him to her, another beyond her. She watched, mesmerized, as his strong crawl carried him effortlessly out into the bay. He stopped twenty or thirty yards from her, trod water, shook diamond droplets of the sea from his hair.

Watching him, she realized what she had been doing could not even really be called swimming. She was paddling. No wonder he treated her as if she belonged in the kiddy pool! Bathing suit aside, in the water she was an elephant trying to keep pace with a cheetah!

Ronan flipped over on his back, spread his arms like a star and floated. It looked so comfortable, so relaxing that she tried it and nearly drowned. She came up sputtering for air.

"Are you okay?"

And what if she wasn't? Would he swim over here, gather her in his arms, maybe give her mouth-to-mouth resuscitation?

"I'm fine," she squeaked.

He did swim back over, but did not come too close. "You're about as deep as you should go," he told her. "I've noticed over the past few days you are not a very strong swimmer."

"In my mother's mind swimming in the ocean was an activity for the sons and daughters of fishermen."

"It seems a shame to live in a place like this, surrounded by water and not know how to swim. It seems foolish to me, unnecessarily risky, because with this much water you're eventually going to have an encounter with it." Hastily he added, "Not that I'm calling your mother foolish."

"Plus, she has this thing about showing skin." And that was with a *regular* bathing suit.

Ronan eyed her. "I take it she wouldn't approve of the bathing suit."

He *had* noticed.

"She'd have a heart attack," Shoshauna admitted.

"It's having just about the same effect on me," he said with a rueful grin, taking all her power away by admitting he'd noticed, a man incapable of pretense, *real,* just as she'd known he was.

"That's why your mom doesn't want you wearing stuff like that. Men are evil creatures, given to drawing conclusions from visual clues that aren't necessarily correct."

Back to the kiddy pool! He was going to turn this into a lecture. But he didn't. He left it at that, yet she felt a little chastened anyway.

As if he sensed that, he quickly changed the subject. "So, I've got you out here in the water. Want to—"

Was she actually hoping he was going to propose something a little evil?

"Want to learn how to swim a little better?"

She nodded, both relieved and annoyed by his ability to treat her like a kid, his charge, nothing more.

"You won't be ready to enter the Olympics after one lesson, but if you fall out of a boat, you'll be able to survive."

It had probably been foolish to suggest teaching Shoshauna to swim. But the fact of the matter was she lived on an island. She was around water all the time. It seemed an unbelievable oversight to him that her education had not included swimming lessons.

On the other hand, what did he know about what skills a princess needed? Still, he felt he could leave here a better man knowing that if she did fall off a boat, she could tread water until she was rescued.

Probably he was kidding himself that he was teaching her something important. If a princess fell overboard, surely ten underlings jumped in the water after her.

But somehow it was increasingly important to him that she know how to save herself. And maybe not just if she fell off a boat. All these things he had been teaching her this week were skills that made no sense for a princess.

But for a woman coming into herself, learning the power of self-reliance seemed vital. It felt important that if he gave her nothing else, he gave her a taste of that: what her potential was, what she was capable of doing and learning if she set her mind to it.

Because Ronan was Australian and had grown up around beaches and heavy surf, he had quite often been chosen to instruct other members of Excalibur in survival swimming.

Thankfully, he could teach just about anybody to swim without ever laying a hand on them.

She was a surprisingly eager student, more willing to try things in the water than many a seasoned soldier. Like the things she had been doing on land, he soon realized she had no fear, and she learned very quickly. By the end of a half hour, she could tread water for a few minutes, had the beginnings of a not bad front crawl and could do exactly two strokes of a backstroke before she sank and came up sputtering.

And then disaster struck, the kind, from teaching soldiers, he was totally unprepared for.

She was treading water, when her mouth formed a startled little *O*. She forgot to sweep the water, wrapped her arms around herself and promptly sank.

His mind screamed *shark* even though he had evaluated the risks of swimming in the bay and decided they were minimal.

When she didn't bob right back to the surface, he was at her in a second, dove, wrapped his arm around her waist, dragged her up. No sign of a shark, though her arms were still tightly wrapped around her chest.

Details. Part of him was trying to register what was wrong, when she sputtered something incomprehensible and her face turned bright, bright red.

"My top," she sputtered.

For a second he didn't comprehend what she was saying, and when he did he was pretty sure the heart attack he'd teased her about earlier was going to happen for real. He had his arms around a nearly naked princess.

He let go of her so fast she started to sink again, unwilling to unwrap her arms from around her naked bosom.

Somehow her flimsy top had gone missing!

"Swim in to where you can stand up," he ordered her sharply.

He knew exactly what tone to use on a frightened soldier to ensure instant obedience, and it worked on her. She headed for shore, doing a clumsy one-armed crawl—her other arm still firmly clamped over her chest—that he might have found funny if it was anyone but her. As soon as he made sure she was standing up on the ocean bottom, he looked around.

The missing article was floating several yards away. He swam over and grabbed it, knew it was the wrong time to think how delicate it felt, how fragile in his big, rough hands, what a flimsy piece of material to be given so much responsibility.

He came up behind her. She was standing up to her
shoulder blades in water and still had a tight wrap on
herself, but there was no hiding the naked line of her
back, the absolute feminine perfection of her.

"I'll look away," he said, trying to make her feel as
if it was no big deal. "You put it back on."

Within minutes she had the bathing suit back on, but
she wouldn't look at him. And he was finding it very difficult to look at her.

Wordlessly she left the water, spread out her towel
and lay down on her stomach. She still wouldn't even
look at him and he figured maybe that was a good thing.
He put on the snorkeling gear and headed back out into
the bay.

He began to see school after school of butterfly fish,
many that he recognized as the same as he would see in
the reefs off Australia: the distinctive yellow, white and
black stripes of the threadfin, the black splash of color
that identified the teardrop.

Suddenly, Ronan didn't want her to stay embarrassed
all day, just so that he could be protected from his own
vulnerability around her. He didn't want her to miss the
enchantment of the reef fish.

Her embarrassment over the incident was a good
reminder to him that she had grown up very sheltered.
She had sensed the bikini would get his attention, but
she hadn't known what to do with it when she succeeded.

In his world, girls were fast and flirty and knew
exactly what to do with male attention. Her innocence
in a bold world made him want to share the snorkeling
experience with her even more.

They would focus on the fish, the snorkeling, not each other.

"Shoshauna! Put on a snorkel and fins. You have to see this."

He realized he'd called her by her first name, as if they were friends, as if it was *okay* for them to snorkel together, to share these moments.

Too late to back out, though. She joined him in the water, but not before tugging on her bathing suit strings about a hundred times to make sure they were secure.

And then she was beside him, and the magic happened. They swam into a world of such beauty it was almost incomprehensible. Fish in psychedelic colors that ranged from brilliant orange to electric blue swam around them. They saw every variety of damselfish, puffer fish, triggerfish, surgeonfish.

He tapped her shoulder. "Watch those ones," he said, pointing at an orange band. "It's a type of surgeonfish, they're called that because their spines are scalpel sharp."

Her wonder was palpable when a Moorish idol investigated her with at least as much interest as she was giving it! A school of the normally shy neon-green and blue palenose parrot fishes swam around her as if she was part of the sea.

He was not sure when he lost interest in the fish and focused instead on her reaction to them. Ronan was not sure he had seen anything as lovely as the awed expression on her face when a bluestripe snapper kissed her hand.

He was breaking all the rules. And somehow it seemed worth it. And somehow he didn't care. Time evaporated, and he was stunned when he saw the sun going down in the sky.

They went in to shore, dried the saltwater off with towels. He saw she was looking at him with a look that was both innocent and hungry.

"I'm going to cook dinner," he said gruffly. Suddenly breaking the rules didn't seem as great, it didn't seem worth it, and he did care.

He cared because he felt something, and he knew it was huge. He felt the desire to *know* someone. He *wanted* to know her better. He *wanted* things he had never wanted and that, in this case, he knew he could never have.

These four days together had created an illusion that they were just two normal people caught up together. These days had allowed him to see her as real, as few people had ever seen her. These days had allowed him to see her, and he had liked what he had seen. It was natural to want to know more, to explore where this affinity he felt for her could go.

But the island was a fantasy, one so strong it had diluted reality, made him forget reality.

He was a soldier. She was a princess. Their worlds were a zillion miles apart. She was promised to someone else.

With those facts foremost in his mind, he cooked dinner, refusing her offer to help, and he was brusque with her when she asked him if he knew the name of a bright-yellow snout-nosed fish they had seen. She took the hint and they ate in blessed silence. Why did he miss being peppered with her questions? Did she, too, realize that a dangerous shift had happened between them?

Still, getting ready for bed, he was congratulating himself on what a fine job he'd done on reerecting the barriers, when he heard an unmistakable whimper from her room.

Surely she wasn't that embarrassed over her brief nude scene?

He knew he had to ignore her, but then she cried out again, the sound muffled, as if she had a blanket stuffed in her mouth. It was the sound being stifled that made him bolt from his room, and barge through her door.

She was alone, in bed. No enemy had crept up on him while he'd been busy playing reef guide instead of doing his job.

"What's the matter?" He squinted at her through the darkness.

The sheet was pulled up around her, right to her chin.

"I hurt so bad."

"What do you mean?"

He lit the hurricane lamp that had been left on a chair just inside her door, moved to the side of her bed and gazed down at her. She reluctantly pulled the sheet down just enough to show him her shoulders. That's why she had been quiet at dinner.

Not embarrassed, not taking the hint that he didn't want to talk to her, but in pain. Even in the light of the lantern he could clearly see she was badly sunburned. Cursing himself silently, he wondered how close she had come to heat exhaustion.

White lines where her bikini straps had been were in sharp contrast to her skin.

Because her skin tones were so golden it had never occurred to him she might burn. It had not seemed scorchingly hot out today. On the other hand he should have known breezes coming off the water could make it seem cooler than it was. It had never occurred to him that someone who lived in this island paradise might not avail themselves of the outdoors.

He remembered, too late, what she had said about her mother. "Has your skin ever seen the sun before?" he asked her.

She shook her head, contrite. "Not for a long time. I was allowed to come here until I was about thirteen, but then my mother thought I was getting to be too much of a tomboy. She thought skin darkened by the sun was—"

"Let me guess," he said dryly. "Common."

He was rewarded with a weak smile from her. Selfish bastard that he was he thought, *At least I'm not going to have to see her in a bikini again for the three days we have left here on the island.*

But there was another test he had to pass right now. He was going to have to administer first aid to her burns. She'd exposed her back to the sun while they snorkeled. The water beading on it had drawn the sun like a magnet. Though her shoulders were very red looking, most of that burn was going to be on her back where she couldn't reach it herself.

Having grown up in Australia, he was cautious of the sun, but his skin was also more acclimatized to sun than that of most of the people he worked with. He did not have fair coloring, his skin seemed to like the sun.

But many times after long training days in the sun, especially desert training, soldiers were hurting. Ronan had learned lots of ways to ease the sting with readily available ingredients: either vinegar or baking soda added to bath water could bring relief. Unfortunately, just as when he was in the field, they didn't have a bath here.

What they did have was aspirin, he had seen that in a cabinet in the outdoor kitchen, and powdered milk, an ingredient he'd used before to field dress a sunburn.

He knew, though, there was going to be a big difference between placing soothing dressings cooled with freshly made milk onto her back, and slapping it onto a fellow soldier's.

All day he'd struggled to at least keep the physical barriers between them up, since the emotional ones seemed to be falling faster than he could reerect them. When she'd lost the top, and he'd wrapped his arms around her to pull her back to the water's surface, he'd known he had to avoid going to that place again at all costs, skin against skin.

But here he was at that place again. It almost felt as if the universe was conspiring against him.

But she was his charge. He had no choice. He felt guilty that she'd gotten burned on his watch in the first place. It was proof, really, he could not be trusted with softer things, more tender things, things that required a gentle touch.

It was proof, too, that he was preoccupied, missing the details that he had always been so good at catching.

"Come on out to the kitchen," he said gruffly. "I'll put something on that that will make it feel better."

"I can't get dressed," she told him, and blushed. "My skin feels like its shrinking. I don't think I can move my arms. I don't want to put anything on that touches my skin."

Oh well, just run out there naked then.

He yanked the sheet out from the bottom of the bed and tucked it around her right up to her chin. "Come on."

She wobbled out behind him to the kitchen, the sheet draped clumsily over her, him uncomfortably and acutely aware that underneath it she was probably as naked as the day she was born. The outfit was somehow as dangerous—maybe more so—than the bikini had been.

And the night was dangerous—the stars like jewels in the night sky, the flowers releasing their perfume with a gentle and seductive vengeance.

"Sit," he said, swinging a chair out for her. He took a deep breath, prayed for strength and then did what had to be done. He lifted the sheet away from her back, forced himself to be clinical.

Her back looked so tender with burn that he forgot how awkward this situation was. The marks where her bikini strings had been tied up dissected it, at her neck and midback, white lines in stark contrast to the rest of her. Her skin was glowing bright red on top of her copper tones.

"I hate to be the bearer of bad news," he said, his sympathy genuine, his guilt acute even though he knew how hard it was to spot a burn as it was happening in the full sunlight, "but in the next few days your skin is going to be peeling. It may even blister."

"Really?" she asked.

She couldn't possibly sound, well, *pleased,* rather than distressed.

He had to make it a bit clearer. "Um, you could probably be lizard lady at the sideshow for a week or two."

"Really?" she said, again.

No doubt about it. Definitely pleased.

"Is there some reason that would make you happy?" he asked.

"Between my new hair and lizard lady, Prince Mahail will probably call off the wedding. Indefinitely."

Now there was no mistaking the pleasure in her voice.

Don't ask, Ronan. "Is he really that superficial?"

"He chose me for my hair!"

Well, he'd asked. Now he had to deal with the rush of indignation he felt. A man chose a wife for her *hair?*

It was primitive and tyrannical. It was not what she deserved. Wasn't he in the business of protecting democracy? Of protecting people's freedoms and right to choose? If she was being forced into this, then what? Cause an international incident by imposing his values on B'Ranasha, by rescuing the princess from her fate?

"Are you being forced to marry him?" he asked.

"Not exactly."

"What does that mean?"

"Nobody forced me to say yes, but there was enormous pressure, the weight of everybody's expectations."

He turned from her quickly to stave off the impulse to shake her. Here he'd been thinking he had to rescue her when the aggravating truth was she had not, as far as he could see, made a single move to rescue herself. She seemed to just be blindly trusting *something* was going to happen to get her out of her marriage. And much as he hated to admit it, so far that had worked not too badly for her.

But her luck was going to run out, and for a take-charge kind of guy, relying on luck to determine fate was about the worst possible policy.

Rather than share that with her, or allow her to see the fury he felt with her, Ronan busied himself mixing a solution of powdered milk and water in a big bowl. He tore several clean tea towels into rags and submerged them in the mixture.

Then, his unwanted surge of emotion under control, a gladiator who had no choice but the ring, he turned back to her, lifted the sheet off her back.

"Hold that up for me."

He laid the first of the milk-soaked rags flat on her naked back, smoothed it on with his hands. She seemed unbelievably delicate. Her skin was hot beneath the dressing. And, for now anyway, before the inevitable peeling, it felt incredibly smooth, flawless beneath his fingertips. He didn't know of any other way to bring her comfort, but touching her like this was intimate enough to make him feel faintly crazy, a purely primitive longing welling up within him.

He thought she might flinch, but instead she gave a little moan of pleasure and relief as the first cool, milk-soaked dressing adhered to her back, a sound that could have easily been made in another context.

"Oh," she breathed. "That feels so good. I don't think I've ever felt anything that good."

His wicked male mind wondered just how innocent that made her. Plenty innocent. And it was his job to keep it that way.

He thought about a man he had never seen, whom he knew nothing about, becoming her husband, being trusted with her delicacy, and he felt another unwanted stab of strong emotion.

Not jealousy, he told himself, God forbid, not jealousy, just an extension of his job. Protectiveness.

But he knew it wasn't exactly a part of his job to wonder, was that man whom she had almost married, worthy of her? Would her prince be able to make her pleasure as important as his own when the time came? Would he be tender and considerate? Would he stoke the fire that burned in her eyes, or would he put it out?

Ronan, he reprimanded himself. *Stop it!* By her own admission, she was not being forced into anything. It was her problem not his.

Still, the feeling of craziness intensified, he felt a sudden primitive need to *show* her what it *should* feel like, all heat and passion, tenderness and exquisite pleasure. If she'd ever experienced what was *real* between a man and a woman she wouldn't accept a substitute, no matter how much pressure she thought she felt.

She was seriously going to pay with her life to relieve a little temporary pressure from her folks?

He gave himself a fierce mental shake. His thinking was ludicrous, totally unacceptable, completely corrupted by emotion. He had known her less than a full week, which really meant he did not know her at all!

He was not dating her, he was protecting her. Imagining his lips on her lips was not a part of the mission.

Who would have thought he would end up having to protect the princess from himself?

"Leave those dressings on there for twenty minutes,"

he said, his voice absolutely flat, not revealing one little bit of his inner struggle, the madness that was threatening to envelope him. "Unfortunately in this heat the residue of the milk will start to sour if you leave it on overnight. You're going to have to rinse off in the shower before you go back to bed." He passed her some aspirin and a glass of water.

"This will take the sting out." He sounded as if he was reading from a first-aid manual. "Drink all the water, too, just in case you're a bit dehydrated. I think you'll sleep like a baby after all this."

She probably would, too, but he was wondering if he was ever going to sleep again!

Fixing her up had taken way too long, even with him trying to balance a gentle touch with his urgency to get this new form of torture over with.

"I'll head back to bed, I'll leave this lamp for you. You can peel those dressings off by yourself in twenty minutes or so. Don't forget to shower."

"All right."

"You should be okay for a few hours. If the pain comes back, starts bugging you, wake me up. We'll do it all again." He had to suck it up to even make that offer. He didn't want to touch her back again, have her naked under a sheet, the two of them alone in a place just a little too much like paradise.

No wonder Adam and Eve had gone for the apple!

"Ronan?" Her voice was husky. She touched his arm.

He froze, aware he was holding his breath, scared of what could happen next, if she asked him to stay with her. Scared of the physical attraction, scared of the thoughts he had had earlier.

"What?" He growled.

"Thank you so much."

What was he expecting? She was burned to a crisp. The last thing on her mind was, well, the thing that was on his mind. Which was her lips, soft and pliable, and how they would feel underneath his, how they would taste.

"Just doing my job."

She glanced over her shoulder at him. Her eyes met his. There was no mistaking the heat and the hunger that changed their color from turquoise to a shade of indigo. He realized it wasn't the last thing on her mind after all. That one small push from the universe and they'd be all over each other, burn or no burn. The awareness that sizzled in the air between them put that burn on her back to shame.

He sucked in a deep breath, then ducked his head, turned abruptly and walked quickly away from her.

It took more discipline to do that than to do two hundred push-ups at the whim of a aggravated sergeant, to make a bed perfectly for the thousandth time, to jump out of an airplane from twenty thousand feet in the dead of the night. Way more.

He glanced at his watch to check the date. He had to get control over this situation before it deteriorated any more.

But when he thought of her shaking droplets of water from the jagged tips of her hair, laughing, the tenderness of her back underneath the largeness of his hands, he felt a dip in the bottom of his belly.

He focused on it, but it wasn't that familiar warning, his *sideways* feeling. It was a warmth as familiar as the sun and as necessary to life.

What had happened to his warning system? Had it become dismantled? Ronan wondered if he had lost some part of himself that he *needed* in the turquoise depths of her eyes.

Isn't that what he'd learned about love from his mother? That relationships equaled the surrender of power?

"You are not having a relationship with her," he told himself sternly, but the words were hollow, and he knew he had already crossed lines he didn't want to cross.

But tomorrow was a new day, a new battle. He was a warrior and he fully intended to recapture his lost power.

CHAPTER SIX

SHOSHAUNA took a deep breath, slid a look at Ronan. He was intense this morning, highly focused, but not on her. She could not look at him—at the dark, neat hair, his face freshly shaven, the soft gold brown of his eyes, the sheer male beauty of the way he carried himself—without feeling a shiver, remembering his hands on her back last night.

"Are you mad at me?"

"Princess?" he asked, his voice flat, as if he had no idea what she was talking about.

"Yesterday you called me Shoshauna," she said.

He said nothing; he did not look at her. He had barely spoken to her all morning. She'd gotten up and managed to get dressed, a painful process given the sunburn. Still, she had been more aware of something hammering in her heart, a desire to see him again, to be with him, than of the pain of that burn.

But Ronan had been nowhere to be found when she had come out of her bedroom. He'd left a breakfast of fresh biscuits and cut fruit for her, not outside on the bench where she had grown accustomed to sharing casual meals with him, but at the dining room table, at a place perfectly set for one.

Shoshauna had rebelled against the formality of it and taken a plate outside. As she ate she could hear the thunk of an ax biting into wood in the distance. Just as she was finishing the last of the biscuits, he dragged a tree into their kitchen clearing.

Watching him work, hauling that tree, straining against it, that *awareness* tingled through her, the same as she had felt yesterday when she had watched him strip off his shirt before swimming. She felt as if she was vibrating from it. Ronan was so one hundred percent man, all easy strength and formidable will.

Even to her inexperienced eye it looked as if he was bringing in enough wood to keep the stove fired up for about five years.

"Good morning, Ronan." Good grief, she could hear the *awareness* in her voice, a husky breathlessness.

She knew how much she had come to live for his smile when he withheld it. Instead, he'd barely said good morning, biting it out as if it hurt him to be polite. Then he was focusing on the wood he'd brought in. After using a handsaw to reduce the tree to blocks, he set a chunk on a stump chopping block, swung the ax over his head, and down into the wood.

The whole exercise of reducing the tree to firewood was a demonstration—entirely unconscious on his part—of pure masculine strength, and she could feel her heart skip a beat every time he lifted the ax with easy, thoughtless grace. She remembered again the strength in those hands, tempered last night, and shivered.

But today his strength was not tempered at all. He

certainly *seemed* angry, the wood splintering into a thousand pieces with each mighty whack of the ax blade, tension bunching his muscles, his face smooth with a total lack of expression.

He had not even asked her how her sunburn felt, and it felt terrible. Could she be bold enough to ask him to dress it again? She felt as if she was still trembling inside from the way his hands had felt pressing those soothing cloths onto her back last night. But he looked angry this morning, remote, not the same man who had been so tender last night.

"Ronan?" she pressed, even though it was obvious he didn't want to talk. "Are you angry about something?"

Actually, something in him seemed to have shifted last night when he had questioned her about her marriage. He had gone very quiet after she had admitted she wasn't being forced to marry anyone.

"No, ma'am, I'm not angry. What's to be angry about?"

"Stop it!"

He set down the ax, wiped the sweat off his forehead with a quick lift of his shirt collar, then folded his arms over his chest, looked askance at her.

"I didn't mean chopping the wood," she said, knowing he had misunderstood her deliberately.

"What did you mean then, Princess?"

"Why are you being so formal? You weren't like this yesterday."

"Yesterday," he said tightly, "was a mistake. I forgot myself, and it's not going to happen again."

"Having fun, going snorkeling was forgetting yourself?"

"Yes, ma'am."

"If you call me ma'am one more time, I'm going to throw this coconut right at your large, overweight head!"

"I think you might mean my big, fat head."

"That's exactly what I meant!"

He actually looked as though he might smile, but if he was amused he doused it quickly.

"Princess," he said, his patience elaborate and annoying, "I'm at work. I'm on the clock. I'm not here to have fun. I'm not here to teach you to swim or to identify yellow tangs for you. My job is to protect you, to keep you safe until I can get you back to your home."

"I could have been assassinated while you were out there chopping down the jungle," she said, aware her tone was growing snippy with impatience. How could he possibly not want more of what they'd had yesterday?

Not just the physical touch, though that had filled her with a hunger that felt ravenous, a tiger that needed to be fed, but the laughter, the easy camaraderie between them. It was that she found herself craving even more. How could it be that he did not want the same things?

"I think," he said dryly, "if assassins had arrived on the island, I would have heard a boat. Or a helicopter. I was only a few seconds away."

He was deliberately missing the point! "Bitten by a snake, then!"

He didn't answer, and she hated that he was treating her like a precocious child, though for some reason his attitude was making her act like one.

"Eaten by a tiger," she muttered. "Attacked by a monkey."

He sent her one irritated look, went back to the wood.

"I'm making a point! There is no danger here. None. No assassins, no snakes, no tigers, no mad monkeys. It would be perfectly fine for you to relax your vigilance."

Crash. The wood splintered. He gathered the splinters, tossed them in a pile, wouldn't look at her. "I relaxed yesterday. You got a large, overweight sunburn because of it."

"You are not feeling responsible for that, are you?" His lack of a response was all the answer she needed. "Ronan, it wasn't your fault. It's not as if it was life threatening, anyway. A little sunburn. I can hardly feel it today." Which was a lie, but if it got rid of that look from his face—a look of cool professional detachment—it would be a lie worth telling.

He said nothing, and she knew this was about more than a sunburn.

"Are you mad because I *agreed* to get married?"

Bull's-eye. Something hard and cold in his face shook her. "That falls squarely in the none-of-my-business category."

"That's not true. We're friends. I want to talk to you about it." And suddenly she did. She felt that if she talked to Ronan, all the chaos and uncertainty inside her would subside. She felt that the terrible loneliness that had eaten at her ever since she said yes to Prince Mahail would finally go away.

She felt as if she would know what to do.

"My cat died," she blurted out. "That's why I agreed to marry him."

It felt good to say it out loud, though she could tell

by the look on his face he now thought she was certifiably insane.

"But you have to understand about the cat," she said in a rush.

"No," he said, holding up his hand, a clear stop signal. "No, I don't have to understand about the cat. I don't want you telling me about your personal life. Nothing. No cat. No marriage. Not what is on or off your mother's approval list, though we both know that what isn't on it is cavorting in the ocean in a bathing suit top that is unstable with a man you barely know."

"I do know you," she protested.

"No you don't. We can't be friends," he said quietly. "Do you get that?"

She had thought they were past that, that they were already well on their way to being friends, and possibly even something more than friends. These last few days she had shared more with him than she could remember sharing with anyone. She had felt herself opening around him, like a flower opening to sunshine.

He made her discover things about herself that she hadn't known. Being around him made her feel strong and competent. And alive. It was *easy* to be herself with him. How could he say they could not be friends?

"No," she said stubbornly. "I don't get it."

"Actually," he said tersely, "it doesn't really matter if you get it or not, just as long as I get it."

She felt desperate. It was as if he was on a raft and she was on shore, and the distance between them was growing. She needed to bring him back, any way she could. "Okay, I won't tell you anything about me. Nothing."

He looked skeptical, so she rushed on, desperate. "I'll put a piece of tape over my mouth. But I can't go out in the sun today. I was hoping you'd teach me how to play chess. My mother felt chess was a very masculine game, that girls should not play it."

Even though he'd specifically told her not to mention her mother to him, she took a chance and believed she had been right to do so, because something flickered in his eyes.

He *knew* she'd be a good chess player if she got the chance, but if he'd realized that, he doused the thought as quickly as his smile of moments ago. He was silent, refusing the bait.

"Do you know how to play chess?" If she could just get him to sit down with her, spend time with her, soon it would be easy again and fun. She wanted to know so much about him. She wanted him to know so much about her. They only had a few days left! He couldn't spoil it. He just couldn't.

He took up the ax and put another piece of wood on the stump he was using as a chopping block. He hit it with such furious strength she winced.

"Are you going to ignore me?"

"I'm sure as hell going to try."

Shoshauna was a princess. She was not used to being ignored. She was used to people doing what she wanted them to do.

But this felt different. It felt as if she would die if he ignored her, if they could not get back to that place they had been at yesterday, swimming in the magical world of a turquoise sea and rainbow-hued fish, his hands on her back strong, cool, filled with confidence, the hands of a man who knew how to touch a woman in ways that could steal her breath, her heart, her soul.

Her sense of desperation grew. He was holding the key to something locked inside of her. How could he refuse to open that secret door? The place where she would, finally, know who she was.

"If I told my father you had done something inappropriate," she said coolly, "you'd spend the rest of your life in jail."

He gave her a look so fearless and so loaded with scorn it made her feel about six inches high. And that was when she knew he was immovable in his resolve. She knew it did not matter what she did—she could threaten him, try to manipulate him with sweetness— he was not going to do as she wanted. He had drawn his line in the sand.

And over such a ridiculously simple thing. She only wanted him to play chess with her!

Only, it wasn't really that simple, and he knew it, even if she was trying to deny it. Getting to know each other better would have complications and repercussions that could resound through both their lives.

But why worry about that today? They had so little time left. Couldn't they just go on as they had been? Couldn't they just pretend they were ordinary people in extraordinary circumstances?

But even as she thought it, she knew he would never like pretending. He was too real for that. And when she slid another look his way, she could tell by the determined set of his jaw that he intended to worry about *that* today, and she could tell something else by the set of his jaw.

She was completely powerless over him.

"I'm sorry I said that," she said, feeling utterly defeated, "about my father putting you in prison. It was a stupid thing to say, very childish."

He shrugged. "It doesn't matter." As if he *expected* her to say things like that, to act spoiled and rotten if she didn't get her own way. She had not done one thing—not one—to lead him to believe such things of her.

Unless you included saying yes to marrying a man she did not love.

That would speak volumes about her character to a man like Ronan, who wore his honor and his integrity as part of the armor around him.

"I would never do something so horrible as tell lies about you. I'm not a liar." But hadn't she lied to herself all along, about Mahail, her marriage, her life?

"I said it didn't matter," he said sharply.

"Now you really are mad at me."

He sighed heavily.

Shoshauna, looking at herself with the brutal assessment she saw in his eyes, burst into tears, ran into the house, slammed her bedroom door and cried until she had no tears left.

Shoot, Ronan thought, was she ever going to stop crying? Bastard. How hard would it have been to teach her to play chess?

It wasn't about teaching her how to play chess, he told himself sternly. It was about the fact that things were already complicated so much that she was in there crying over something as tiny as the fact he'd refused to teach her to play chess.

Though, dammit, when she had said her mother didn't want her to play chess, that it was *masculine,* something in him had just itched to give her the rudiments of the game. She had such a good mind. He bet she'd be a better-than-average player once she got the fundamentals down, probably a downright formidable one.

She didn't come out of that room for the rest of the day. When he told her he had lunch ready, she answered through the closed door, her voice muffled, that she wasn't hungry.

Now it was the same answer for supper. He should have been relieved. This was exactly what *he* needed to keep his vows. Distance. Space. Instead he felt worried about her, guilty about the pain he'd caused.

"Come on," he said, from the other side of the door, "you have to eat."

"Why? To make you feel like you've fulfilled your obligation to look after me? Is providing a nutritious menu part of protecting me? Go away!"

He opened the door a crack. She was sitting on her bed cross-legged in those shorty-shorts that showed way too much of her gorgeous copper-toned legs. She looked up when he came in, looked swiftly back down. Her eyes were puffy from crying. Her short, boyish hair was every which way. She'd taken her bra straps off her burned shoulders, and they hung out the arms of her T-shirt.

"I told you to go away."

"You should eat something." He stepped inside the door a bit.

"You know what? I'm not a little kid. You don't have to tell me to eat."

He was already way too aware she was not a little kid. He'd seen the damned bikini once too often! He'd seen what was under the bikini, too.

He was also aware this was becoming a failure of major proportions. He was going to take her back safe from threat but damaged nonetheless: hair chopped off, sun-burned, starving, puffy-eyed from crying. Though they still had two days and a couple of hours to get through before he could cross back over that water with her, deliver her to Gray. She couldn't possibly cry that long.

His stomach knotted at the thought. Could she? He studied her to see if she was all done crying.

She'd found a magazine somewhere, and she was avoiding his eyes. The magazine looked as if it had been printed in about 1957, but she was studying it as intently as if she could read her future on the pages. Her eyes sparkled suspiciously. More tears gathering?

"Look," he said uncomfortably, shifting his weight from one foot to the other, "I'm not trying to be mean to you. I'm just telling you the way things have to be."

"Is that right?" she snapped, and threw down the magazine. She regarded him with spitting eyes, and he could see clearly it was fury in them, not tears. "As it happens, I'm sick and tired of people telling me how it's going to be. Why are you the one who decides how it's going to be? Because you're a man?"

She had him there.

"Because I'm the one with the job to do," he said, but he heard the wavering of his own conviction. If ever a woman was born to be his equal it was this one.

She hopped off the bed. Instinct told him to get away from her. A stronger instinct told him to stay.

She stopped in front of him, regarded him with challenge. He, foolishly, held his ground.

She reached up on tiptoe, and she took his lips with her own.

He was enveloped in pure and sweet sensation. Her kiss was as refreshing and clean as rainwater. Her lips told him abut the polarities within her: innocence and passion, enthusiasm and hesitancy, desire and doubt.

He had heard there were drugs so strong a man could be made helpless by them after one taste.

He had never believed it until this moment. He willed himself not to respond, but he did not have enough will to move away from her, from the sweetness of her quest.

The hesitancy and the doubt suddenly dissolved. Her arms reached out, tangled themselves around his neck, drew him closer to her. Her scent wrapped around him, feminine, clean, intoxicating. Through the thinness of her shirt he could feel the warmth radiating off her skin. Her curves, soft, sensual, womanly, pressed into him.

Temptation was furious within him. Pure feeling tried to swamp rational thought. But the soldier in him, highly disciplined, did the clean divide between the emotion he was feeling and what he *needed* to do.

If he continued this, if he accepted the invitation of her lips, the growing urgency of her kiss, if he allowed it to go where it wanted to go, it would be like a wild horse that had broken free, allowed to run. There would be no bringing it back under rein once it had gone too far.

The soldier wanted control; the man wanted to lose control.

The soldier insisted on inserting one more fact. If this

carried to its natural conclusion, Princess Shoshauna would be compromised. The wedding would be off. Her wedding. Again, she wouldn't have made a *choice,* just allowed herself to be carried along by forces she considered out of her control.

It was not what Ronan wanted for her.

He didn't want her to get married to anyone but—

But who?

Him? A soldier. A soldier who didn't believe in marriage? Who *hated* it? This must be a genetic flaw in his family, the ability to convince oneself over a very short period of time, before reality had a chance to kick in, that a marriage could work. He yanked himself away from her.

This was the difference between him and his mother: he didn't have to follow the fantasy all the way through to the end. He already knew the end of every love story.

The soldier won—fact over fiction, practical analysis over emotion, discipline over the wayward leanings of a man's heart.

But he was aware it was a slim victory at best. And he was aware that aggravating word, *love,* had popped up again, banished from his vocabulary since around his thirteenth birthday. It was suddenly presenting itself in his life with annoying frequency.

Ronan made himself hold Shoshauna's gaze, fiery with passion, soft with surrender. He tried to force all emotion from his tone. But the magnitude of his failure to do so—the cold fury of his voice—even took him by surprise. Of course, he really wasn't angry at her, but at himself, at his own vulnerability, his own weakness, his sudden crippling wistfulness.

Hope—a sudden ridiculous wish to regain his own innocence, a desire to be able to believe in things he had long since lost faith in.

"Are you using me to buy your freedom?"

She reeled back from him. If he was not mistaken the tears were back in her eyes, all the proof he needed that insanity had grabbed him momentarily, that moment when he had contemplated her and himself and marriage in the same single thought.

The truth was much more simple. He was a soldier, rough around the edges, hardened, not suitable for the company of a princess or anyone sensitive or fragile.

But there was nothing the least bit fragile about Shoshauna when she planted both her little hands on his chest and shoved him with such amazing strength that it knocked him completely off balance. He stumbled backward, two steps, through her bedroom doorway, and she rushed forward and slammed the door behind him with the force of a hurricane.

As he contemplated the slammed door, he had the politically incorrect thought that it was a mistake that hurricanes weren't still named exclusively after women: volatile, completely unpredictable, even the strongest man could not hope to hold his balance in the fury.

"Just go straight to hell!" she yelled at him through the door. She followed that with a curse that was common among working men and soldiers, a curse so *common* her mother surely would have had heart failure hearing it come from her princess daughter's refined lips.

So he was returning Shoshauna a changed woman. No hair, sunburned, starved *and* she was going to be able to hold her own in a vocabulary contest with a construction crew.

He turned away, muttering to himself, "Well, that didn't go particularly well."

But outside, contemplating a star-studded night, black-velvet sky meeting inky-black ocean, he rethought his conclusions.

Maybe it had gone well. Shoshauna was a woman who needed to discover the depths of her own power, who needed to know how to utilize the hurricane forces within her, so she would not be so easily buffeted by the forces outside of her. In the past it seemed that every shift of wind had made her change direction.

She'd made the decision to get married because her cat died? Only his mother could come up with a fruitier reason than that!

But from the way Shoshauna had shoved him and slammed that door, she was nearly there. Could she hold on to what she was discovering about herself enough to refuse a marriage to a man she did not love? Could she understand she had within her the strength to *choose* the life she wanted for herself?

Despite the peaceful serenity of the night, contemplating such issues made his head hurt. One of the things he appreciated most about his military lifestyle was that it was a cut-and-dried world, regulated, no room for contemplation, few complexities. You did what you were trained to do, you followed orders: no question, no thought, no introspection.

He scrubbed his hand across his lips, but he had a feeling what had been left there was not going to be that easy to erase.

After a long time he looked at his watch. It was past midnight. Just under forty-eight hours to go, and then they were leaving this island, meeting Gray.

What if her life was still in danger?

Well, if it was, if the situation was still not resolved, Gray had to have come up with a protection plan for her that did not involve Ronan.

But was he going to trust anyone else with her protection if she was still in danger? Would he have a choice? If he was ordered back to Excalibur, he was going to have to go, whether she was in danger or not.

He hoped it was a choice he was never going to have to make. Which would he obey? The call of duty or the call of his own heart?

Jake Ronan had never had to ask himself a question like that before, and he didn't like it one little bit that he had asked it now.

The fact that he had asked it meant something had shifted in him, changed. He cared about someone else as much as he cared about duty. Once you had done that, could you ever go back to the way you were before?

That's what he felt over the next twenty-four hours. That he was a man trying desperately to be what he had been before: cool, calm, professional, a man notorious for being able to control emotion in situations gone wild.

He almost succeeded, too.

It wasn't fun, and it wasn't easy, that he was managing to keep the barriers up between them. She was using the kitchen at different times than him. She refused to eat what he left out for her. He found her burnt offerings all over the kitchen, along with mashed fruit.

He didn't know if she was trying to torment him by washing her underthings and stringing them on a line by the outdoor shower, but torment him it did, especially since she had managed to turn her bra from pure white to a funny shade of pink.

Of course, he could show her how to do laundry. He *wanted* to, but to what end? Nothing about her life included needing an ability to do laundry without turning her whites to pink.

And nothing about his life needed the complication of inviting her back into it.

No, this might be painful: these silences, the nose tilted upward every time she had to pass him, the hurt she was trying to hide with pride and seething silence, but in the end it was for the best. Even when he found an aloe vera plant and knew how it would soothe her sunburn, bring moisture and coolness and healing to her now badly peeling skin, he would not allow himself to make the offer.

When he saw her sitting at the dining room table by herself, moving chess pieces wistfully, he would not allow himself to give in to the sudden weakness of *wanting* to teach her how to play.

It only led to other wantings: wanting to make her laugh, wanting to see her succeed, wanting to see her tongue stuck between her teeth in concentration, wanting to touch her hair.

Wanting desperately to taste her lips again, just one more time, as if he could memorize how it felt and carry it inside him forever.

But he didn't give in to any of that. He applied every

bit of discipline he had ever learned as a soldier to do what was right instead of what he wanted to do.

And he would have made it.

He would have made it right until the end, except that the wind came up.

The surf was up in the bay. And Princess Shoshauna, clad in a T-shirt to cover her burns, was running toward it, laughing with exhilaration and anticipation, the old surfboard they'd uncovered tucked under her arm.

"Hey," he yelled from the steps of the cottage, "you aren't a good enough swimmer for that water."

She glanced back. If he was not mistaken she stuck out her tongue at him. And then she ran even faster, kicking up the sand in her bare feet.

With a sigh of resignation and surrender, Ronan went after her.

CHAPTER SEVEN

SHOSHAUNA found the waves extraordinarily beautiful, rolling four feet high out in the water where they began their curl, breaking on the beach with a thunderous explosion of white foam and fury.

Her foot actually touched the hard pack of wave-pounded sand, when his hand clamped down on her shoulder with such strength it spun her.

Even though she had spent way too much time imagining his touch, it was not satisfactory in that context! She faced him, glaring. "What?" she demanded.

"You're not a strong enough swimmer for that surf."

"Well, you don't know everything! You said the surf would never even come up in this bay and you were wrong about that!"

"I'm not wrong about this. I'm not letting you go in the water by yourself."

He had that look on his face, fierce; the warrior not to be challenged.

But Shoshauna had been counting days and hours. She knew this time of freedom was nearly over for her. Tomorrow they would be gone from here. And she knew something else. She was responsible for her own life and her own decisions.

She stood her ground, lifted her chin to him.

"I have a lifelong dream of doing this, and I'm doing it."

He looked totally unimpressed with her newfound resolve, indifferent to her discovery of her own power, immune to the sway of her life dreams. He folded his arms over his chest, set his legs, a man getting ready to throw her over his shoulder if he had to.

As delicious as it might be to be carried by him kicking and screaming up to the cottage, this was important to her, and she suddenly had to make him see that.

"It's my lifelong dream, and the waves came. Don't you think you have to regard that as a gift from the gods?"

"No."

"Ronan, all my life people have made my decisions for me. And I've let them. Starting right here and right now, I'm not letting them anymore. Not even you."

Something in him faltered. He looked at the waves and he looked at her. She could see the struggle in his face.

"Ronan, its not that I want to. I *have* to. I have to know what it feels like to ride that kind of power, to leash it. I feel if I can do that, conquer those waves, it's just the beginning for me. If I can do that, I can do anything."

And suddenly she knew she had never spoken truer words. Suddenly she realized she had made a crucial error the other night when she had thought he held the key to the secrets locked away within her.

When they had started this adventure, she remembered saying she didn't know how to find what she was looking for because she didn't know where to look.

But suddenly she knew exactly where to look.

Every answer she had ever needed was there. Right inside herself. And part of that was linked to these waves, to *knowing* what she was capable of, to tapping her sense of adventure instead of denying it. She could not ask Ronan—or anyone else—not her mother or her father or Mahail to accept responsibility for her life. She was in charge. She was taking responsibility for herself. He did not hold the key to her secrets; she did.

She knew that what she was thinking must have shown in her face, because Ronan studied her, then nodded once, and the look on his face was something she would take back with her and cherish as much, maybe more, than the satisfaction of riding the wave.

She had won Ronan's admiration—reluctant, maybe, but still there. He had looked at her, long and hard, and he had been satisfied with what he had seen.

She turned and stepped into the surf, laughed as she leaped over a tumbling wave and it crashed around her, soaking her in foam and seawater.

Then, when she was up to her knees, she placed the board carefully in front of her and tossed herself, belly down, on top of it. It was as slippery as a banister she had once greased with butter, and it scooted out from underneath her as if it was a living thing. A wave pounded over her, awesome in its absolute power, and then she got up and ran after the board.

Drenched, but deliriously happy, she caught the board, shook water from herself, tried again. And then again. It was discouraging. She couldn't even lie on it without getting dumped off. How was she ever going to surf?

Her arms and shoulders began to hurt, and it occurred to her this was going to be a lot harder than she'd been led to believe by watching surfers on TV. But in a way she was glad. She wanted it to be challenging. She wanted to test her spunk and her determination and her spirit of adventure. Life-altering moments were not meant to be easy!

Ronan came and picked her up out of the sand after she was dumped for about the hundredth time, grabbed the board that was being dragged out to sea. She grabbed it back from him.

He sighed. "Let me give you a few tips before you go back out there. The first is this: you don't *conquer* that water. You work with it, you read it, you become a part of it. Give me the board."

It was an act of trust to hand the board to him, because he could just take it and go back to the cottage, but somehow she knew he was now as committed to this as she was. There was nothing tricky about Ronan. He was refreshing in that he was such a what-you-see-is-what-you-get kind of guy.

"You're lucky," he said, "it's a longboard, not a short one, a thruster. But it's old, so it doesn't have a leash on it, which means you have to be very aware where it is at all times. This board is the hardest thing in the water, and believe me, it hurts when it clobbers you."

She nodded. He tossed the board down on the sand.

"Okay, get on it, belly down."

She recognized the gift he was giving her: his experience, and recognized her chances of doing this were better if she listened to him. And that's what he'd said. True power wasn't about conquering, it was about working *with* the elements, reading them.

And that's what Ronan was like: one of the elements, not to be conquered, not to be tamed. To be read and worked with.

When she was down on her belly, he gave her tips about positioning: how to hold her chin, where to have her weight on the board—dead center, not too far back or too far forward.

And so she learned another lesson about power: it was all about balance.

He told her how to spot a wave that was good to ride. "Nothing shaped like a C," he warned her sternly. "Look for waves shaped liked pyramids, small rollers to start with. We'll keep you here in the surf, no deeper than your hips until you get the hang of it."

He said that with absolute confidence, not a doubt in his mind that she would get the hang of it, that she would be riding waves.

"So, practice hopping up a couple of times, here on the sand. Grab the rails."

"It doesn't have rails!"

"Put your hands on the edges," he showed her, positioning her hands. She tried not to find his touch too distracting! "And then push up, bend your back and knees to start, get one leg under you, and pop up as fast as you can. If you do it slow, you'll just tip over once you're in the water."

Under his critical eye, she did it about a dozen times. If he kept this up she was going to be too tired to do it for real!

"Okay," he finally said, satisfied, peeling off his shirt and dropping it in the sand. "Let's hit the water."

They didn't go out very far, the water swirling around his hips, a little higher on her, lapping beneath her breastbone.

"This is the best place to learn, right here." He steadied the board for her while she managed to grace-lessly flop on top of it.

"Don't even try to stand up the first couple of times, just ride it, get a sense for how your surfboard sleds."

"Sleds? As in snow?"

"Same word," he said, and she smiled thinking this might be as close as she got to sledding of any kind. Maybe she would have to be satisfied to look after two dreams with one activity!

"Okay, here it comes. Paddle with those arms, not too fast, just to build momentum."

Shoshauna felt the wave lift the board, paddled and then felt the most amazing thing: as if she was the masthead at the head of that wave. The board was moving with its own power now and it shot her forward with incredible and exhilarating speed. The ride lasted maybe a full two seconds, and then she was tossed onto the sand with such force it lifted her shirt and ground sand into her skin.

"Get up," he yelled, "incoming."

Too late, the next wave pounded down on top of her, ground a little more sand into her skin.

He was there in an instant hauling her to her feet.

She was laughing so hard she was choking. "My God, Ronan, is there anything more fun in the entire world than that?"

He looked at her, smiled. "Now, you're *stoked*," he said.

"Stoked?"

"Surfer word for *ready,* so excited about the waves you can barely stand it."

"That's me," she agreed, "stoked." And it was true. She felt as if she had waited her whole life to feel this: excited, alive, tingling with the awareness of possibility.

"Ready to try it standing up?"

"I'm sooo ready," she said.

"You would have made a hell of a soldier," he said with a rueful shake of his head, and she knew she had just been paid the highest of compliments.

"I want to do it myself!"

"Sweetheart, in surfing that's the only way you *can* do it."

Sweetheart. Was it the exhilaration of that offhanded endearment that filled her with a brand-new kind of power, a brand-new confidence?

She went back out, got on the board, carefully positioned herself, stomach down. She turned, watching over her shoulder for just the right wave.

She floated up and over a few rolling waves, and then she saw one coming, the third in a set of three. She scrambled, but despite her practice runs, the board was impossibly slippery beneath her feet. It popped out from under her. The wave swallowed her, curled around her, tossed her and the board effortlessly toward the shore.

She popped up, aware Ronan was right beside her,

waiting, watching. But the truth was, despite a mouth full of seawater, she loved this! She loved feeling so part of the water, feeling so challenged. There was only excitement in her as she grabbed the board, swam back out and tried again. And again. And again.

Ronan watched, offered occasional advice, shouted encouragement, but he'd been right. There was only one way to do this. No one could do it for you. It was just like life. He did not even try to retrieve the board for her, did not try to help her back on it after it got away for about the hundredth time. Was he waiting for her to fail? For exhaustion and frustration to steal the determination from her heart?

But when she looked into the strong lines of his face, that was not what she saw. Not at all. She saw a man who believed she could do it and was willing to hold on to that belief, even while her own faith faded.

It was his confidence in her, the look on his face, that made her turn the board back to shore one last time, watch the waves gathering over her shoulder. It was the look on his face that made Shoshauna feel as if she would die before she quit.

Astonishingly, everything worked. The wave came, and the crest lifted her and the board. She found her feet; they stuck to the board; she crouched at exactly the right moment.

She was riding the sea, being thrust with incredible power toward the shore.

She rode its fabulous power for less than a full second, but she rode it long enough to feel its song beneath her, to feel her oneness with that power, to taste it, to know it, to want it. Her exhaustion disappeared, replaced by exhilaration.

She was really not sure which was more exhilarating, riding the wave or having earned the look of quiet respect in Ronan's face as he came up to her, held up his hand. "Slap my hand," he told her.

She did, and felt his power as surely as she had felt that of the wave.

"That's a high five, surfer lingo for a great ride," he told her.

She achieved two more satisfactory rides before exhaustion made her quit.

He escorted her to shore. She was shivering with exhaustion and exertion and he wrapped her in the shirt he had discarded there in the sand.

"I did it!" she whispered.

"Yes, you did."

She thought of all the things she had done since they had landed on this island and felt a sigh of contentment within her. She was a different person than she had been a few short days ago, far more sure of herself, loving the glimpse she'd had of her own power, of what she was capable of doing once she had set her mind to it.

"I want to see what you can do," she said. She meant surfing, but suddenly her eyes were on his lips, and his were on hers.

"Show me," she asked him, her voice a plea. *Show me where it all can go. Show me all that a person can be.*

He hesitated, looked at her lips, then looked at the waves, the lesser of two temptations. She saw the longing in his eyes, knew he was *stoked*. She caught a glimpse of the boy he must have once been, before he had learned to ride his power, tame it, leash it.

And then he picked up the board and leaped over the crashing waves to the water beyond. He lay down on the board, paddled it out, his strength against the surging ocean nothing less than amazing. He scorned the surf that she had ridden, made his way strongly past the breakers, got up into a sitting position, straddling the board and then waited.

He rode up and over the swells, waiting, gauging the waves, patient. She saw the wave coming that she knew he would choose.

He dropped to his chest, paddled forward, a few hard strokes to get the board moving, glanced back just as the top of the wave picked up the back of his board. She saw the nose of the board lift out of the water, and then, just when she thought maybe he had missed it, in one quick snap, he was up.

He rode the board sideways, one hip toward the nose of the board, the other toward the tail, his feet apart, knees bent, arms out, his position slightly crouched. She could see him altering his position, shifting his weight with his body position to steer the board. He was actually cutting across the face of the wave, down under the curl, his grace easy, confident and breathtaking. He made it look astonishingly easy.

This was where it went, then. When a person exercised their power completely, it became a ballet, not a fight with the forces, but a beautiful, intricate dance with the elements. Ronan rode that wave with such certainty.

Shoshauna had walked all her life with men who

called themselves princes, but this was the first time she had seen a man who truly owned the earth, who could be one with it, who was so comfortable with his own power and in his own skin.

There was another element to what he was doing, and she became aware of it as he outran the wave, dropped back to his stomach, moved out to catch another. He was not showing her up, not at all.

Showing *off* for her, showing her his agility and his strength and his grace in this complex dance with the sea.

He may have been mastering the sea, but he was giving in, surrendering, to the chemistry, the sizzle that had been between them from the very moment he had first touched her, dragged her to the ground out of harm's way, a mere week ago, a lifetime ago.

Ronan was doing what men had been doing for woman since time began: he was preening for her, saying, without the complication of words: *I am strong. I am fearless. I am skilled. I am the hunter, and I will hunt for you. I am the warrior, and I will protect you.*

It was a mating ritual, and she could feel her heart rising to the song he was singing to her out there on the waves.

Finally he came in, tossed the board down, then threw himself down on his stomach and lay panting in the sand beside her.

She wanted to taste his lips again, but knew she was in the danger zone. He questioned her motives, he would never allow himself to be convinced that it was about *them,* not about her looking for convenient ways to escape her destiny.

To even try to convince him might be to jeopardize the small amount of time they had left.

Tomorrow, hours away from now, they would leave here.

As if thinking the same thought, he told her his plan for the day. They would take the boat back across the water, find where the motorcycle was stashed in the shrubbery. Did she know of a fish-and-chips-style pub close to the palace? She told him that almost certainly it was Gabby's, the only British-style pub on the island that she was aware of.

"We'll meet Colonel Peterson there at three," he said.

"And then?"

"If it's safe, you'll go home. If it isn't, you'll most likely go into hiding for a little longer."

"With you?"

"No, Shoshauna," he said quietly. "Not with me."

She would have tonight, then one more ride on that motorcycle, and then, whatever happened next, *this* would be over.

Sadness threatened to overwhelm her, and she realized she did not want to ruin one moment of this time she had left contemplating what was coming. She suspected there was going to be plenty of time for sadness.

Now was the time for joy. For connection. He knew they were saying goodbye, it had relaxed his guard.

Shoshauna looked at the broadness of Ronan's shoulders as he lay in the sand beside her, how his back narrowed to the slenderness of his waist, she looked at how the wet shorts clung to the hard-muscled lines of his legs and his buttocks.

She became aware he was watching her watching

him, out of the corner of his eye, letting it happen, maybe even enjoying it.

She reached out and rested her hand on the dip of his spine between his shoulders. For a minute his muscles stiffened under her touch, and she wondered if he would deprive her of this moment, get up, head to the cottage, put distance between them. She wondered if she had overplayed.

But then he relaxed, closed his eyes, let her touch him, and she thought, *See? I knew I would be a good chess player.* Still, she dared not do more than that, for fear he would move away, but she knew he was as aware as she was that their time together was very nearly over. That was the only reason he was allowing this. And so she tried to memorize the beauty of his salt- and sand-encrusted skin beneath her fingertips, the wondrous composition of his muscle and skin. She felt as if she could feel the life force flowing, vibrating, throbbing through him with its own energy, strong, pure, good.

Night began to fall, and with it the trade winds picked up and the wind chilled. She could feel the goose bumps rising on his flesh and on her own. The waves crashed on the shore, throwing fine spray droplets of water up toward them.

Still, neither of them made a move to leave this moment behind.

"Do you think we could have a bonfire tonight," she asked, "right here on the beach?"

Silence. Struggle. It seemed as if he would never answer. She was aware she was holding her breath.

"Yeah," he said, finally, gruffly. "I think we could."

She breathed again.

* * *

Ronan slid a glance at Shoshauna. She had changed into a striped shirt and some crazy pair of canvas slacks she had found in the cottage, lace-up front with frayed bottoms that made her look like an adorable stowaway on a pirate's ship.

Despite the outfit, she was changed since the surfing episode, carrying herself differently. A new confidence, a new certainty in herself. He was glad he'd let down his guard enough to be part of giving her that gift, the gift of realizing who she would be once she went back to her old world.

Surely, he thought looking at her, at the tilt of her chin, the strength in her eyes, the fluid way she moved, a woman certain of herself, she would carry that within her, she would never marry a man for convenience, or because it would please others. He remembered her hand resting on his back. Surely, in that small gesture, he had felt who she was, and who she would be.

Tonight, their last night together, he would keep his guard down, just a bit, just enough.

Enough to what? he asked himself.

To have parts of her to hold on to when he let her go, when he did not have her anymore, when he faced the fact he would probably never look at her face again.

Then he would have this night: the two of them, a bonfire, her laughter, the light flickering on her skin, the sparkle in her eyes putting the stars to shame.

In the gathering darkness they hauled firewood to the beach. As the stars came out, they roasted fish on sticks, remembered her antics in the water, laughed.

Tomorrow it would be over. For tonight he was not going to be a soldier. He was going to be a man.

And so they talked deep into the night. When it got colder, he went and got a blanket and wrapped it around her shoulders, and then when it got colder still and she held up a corner, he went and sat beneath the blanket with her, shoulder to shoulder, watching the stars, listening to the waves and her voice, stealing glimpses of her face, made even more gorgeous by the reflection of the flame that flickered across it.

At first the talk was light. He modified a few jokes and made her laugh. She told him about tormenting her nannies and schoolteachers.

But somehow as the night deepened, so did the talk. And he was hearing abut a childhood that had been privileged and pampered, but also very lonely.

She told him about the kitten she had found on a rare trip to the public market, and how she had stuck it under her dress and taken it home. She smiled as she told the story about a little kitten taking away the loneliness, how she had talked to it, slept with it, made it her best friend.

The cat had died.

"Silly, maybe to be so devastated over a cat," she said sadly, "but I can't tell you how I missed him, and how the rooms of my apartment seemed so empty once he was gone. I missed all his adorable poses, and his incredible self-centeredness."

"What was his name?"

"Don't laugh."

"Okay."

"It was Retnuh. In our language it means Beloved."

He didn't laugh. In fact, he didn't find it funny at all. He found it sad and lonely and it confirmed things about her life that she had wanted to tell him all along but that he had already guessed anyway.

"Prince Mahail's proposal came very shortly after my Beloved died. Ronan, it felt so much easier to get swept along in all the excitement than to feel what I was feeling. Bereft. Lonely. Pathetic. A woman whose deepest love had been for a cat."

But he didn't see it as pathetic. He saw it as something else: a woman with a fierce capacity to love, giving her whole heart when she decided to love, giving it her everything. Would the man who finally received that understand what a gift it was, what a treasure?

"Will you tell me something about you now?"

It was one of those trick questions women were so good at. She had shared something *deep,* meaningful. She wasn't going to be satisfied if he talked about his favorite soccer team.

"I wouldn't know where to begin," he said, hedging.

"What kind of little boy were you?" she asked him.

Ah, a logical place to begin. "A very bad one," he said.

"Bad or mischievous?"

"Bad. I was the kid putting the potatoes in the tailpipes of cars, breaking the neighbors' windows, getting expelled from school for fighting."

"But why?"

But why? The question no one had asked. "My Dad died when I was six. Not using that as an excuse, just some boys need a father's hand in their lives. My mother seemed to know she was in way over her head with me. I think wanting to get me under control was probably motivation for most of her marriages."

"*Marriages?* How many?" Shoshauna whispered, wide-eyed. This would be scandalous in her country where divorce was nearly unheard of. It had been scandalous enough in his own.

"Counting the one coming up? Seven?"

"You can't be responsible for that one!"

Still, he always felt vaguely responsible, a futile sense of not being able to protect his mother. When he was younger it was a sense of not being enough.

"What was that like for you growing up? Were any of her husbands like a father to you?" Shoshauna asked.

And for some reason he told her what he had never told anyone. About the misery and the feelings of rejection and the rebellion against each new man. He told her about how that little tiny secret spark of hope that someday he would have a father again had been steadily eroded into cynicism.

He didn't know why he told her, only that when he did, he didn't feel weaker. He felt lighter.

And more content than he had felt in many years.

"What was your mother's marriage to your father like?" she asked softly.

He was silent, remembering. Finally he sighed, and he could hear something that was wistful in him in that sigh. He had thought it was long dead, but now he found it was just sleeping.

"Like I said, I was only six when he died, so I don't know if these memories are true, or if they are as I wish it had been."

"Tell me what you think you remember."

"Happiness." He was surprised by how choked he sounded. "Laughter. I remember, one memory more vivid than any other, of my dad chasing my mom around the house, her running from him shrieking with laughter, her face alight with life and joy. And when he caught her, I remember him holding her, covering her with kisses, me trying to squeeze in between them, to be a part of it. And then he lifted me up, and they squeezed me between them so hard I almost couldn't breathe for the joy of it."

For a long time she was silent, and when she looked at him, he saw what the day had given her in her face: a new maturity, a new ability to be herself in the world.

And he heard it in her voice, in the wisdom of what she said.

She said, "Once your mother had that, what she had with your father, I would think she could not even imagine trying to live without it. By marrying all those men, she was only trying to be alive again. Probably for you, as much as for herself. It wasn't that she wanted those men to give you something you didn't have, it was that she wanted to give you what she had been before, she saw you grieving for her as much as for him."

It was strange, but when he heard those words, he felt as if he had searched for them, been on a quest that led him exactly to this place.

A place where, finally, he could forgive his mother.

Ever since he'd left home, it was as if he had tried desperately to put a lid on the longing his earliest memories had created. He had tried to fill all the spaces within himself: with discipline, with relentless strength, with purpose, with the adrenaline rush of doing dangerous things.

But now he saw that, just like Shoshauna, he had

been brought to this place to find what was really within himself.

He was a man who wanted to be loved.

And deserved to be loved.

A man who had come to know you could fill your whole world, but if it was missing the secret ingredient it was empty.

With the fire warm against their faces and the blanket wrapped around them, they slept under the winking stars and to the music of the crashing waves. He had not felt so peaceful, or so whole, for a long, long time.

But he awoke with a fighting man's instinct just before dawn.

For a moment he was disoriented, her hair, soft as eiderdown, softer than he could have ever imagined it, tickling the bottom of his chin, her head resting on his chest, her breath blowing in warm puffs against his skin.

The feeling lasted less than half a second.

He could hear the steady, but still far off, *wop-wop-wop* of a helicopter engine, beneath that the steady but still-distant whine of powerboats.

He sat up, saw the boats coming, halfway between the island and the mainland, three of them forming a vee in the water, the helicopter zooming ahead of them to do reconnaissance.

The fire, he thought, amazed at his own stupidity. He'd been able to see the lights of the mainland from here, how could he have taken a chance by lighting that fire?

Because he'd been blinded, that's how. He'd forgotten the number-one rule of protection, no not forgotten it, been lulled into believing, that just this once it would be okay to set it aside. But he'd been wrong. He'd broken the rule he knew to be sacred in his business, and now he was about to pay the price.

He knew that emotional involvement with the principal jeopardized their well-being, their safety. And he had done it anyway, putting his needs ahead of what he knew was right.

He'd acted as if they were on a damn holiday from the moment they'd landed on this island. Instead of snorkeling and surfing, he should have spent his time creating a defensible position: hiding places, booby traps, a fallback plan.

He felt the sting of his greatest failure, but there was no time now for self-castigation. There would probably be plenty of time for that later.

He eyed their own boat, the tide out, so far up on the sand he didn't have a chance of getting it to the water before the other boats were on them, and he didn't like the idea of being out in the open, sitting ducks. He could hear the engines of those other boats, anyway. They were far more powerful than the boat on the beach.

"Wake up," he shouted at her, leaping to his feet, his hand rough on her slender shoulder.

There was no time to appreciate her sleep-ruffed hair, her eyes fluttering open, the way a line from his own chest was imprinted on her cheek. She was blinking at him with sleepy trust that he knew himself to be completely unworthy of.

He yanked her to her feet. She caught his urgency instantly, allowed herself to be pushed at high speed toward the cottage. He stopped there only briefly to pick up the Glock, two clips of ammo, and then he led the way through the jungle, to where he had chopped down the tree earlier.

He tucked her under the waxy leaves of a gigantic elephant foot shrub. "Don't you move until I tell you you can," he said.

"You're not leaving me here!"

He instantly saw that her concern was not for herself but for him. This was the price for letting his barriers down, for not maintaining his distance and his authority. She thought listening to him was an option. She did not want to understand it was his job to put himself between her and danger.

She did not want to accept reality.

And his weakness was that for a few hours yesterday he had not accepted it either.

"Princess, do not make me say this again," he said sharply. "You do not move until you hear from me, personally, that it's okay to do so."

Three boats and a helicopter. He had to assume the worst in terms of who it was and what their intent was. That was his job, to react to worst-case scenarios. There was a good chance she might not be hearing from him, personally, ever again. He might be able to outthink those kind of numbers, but their only chance was if she cooperated, stayed out of the way.

"*My* life depends on your obedience," he told her, and saw, finally, her capitulation.

He raced back to the tree line, watched the boats coming closer and closer, cutting through the waters of the bay. His mind did the clean divide, began clicking through options of how to keep her safe with very limited resources. Not enough rounds to hold off the army that was approaching.

The boats drew closer, and suddenly he stood down. His adrenaline stopped pumping. He recognized Colonel Gray Peterson at the helm of the first boat, and he stepped from the trees.

Ronan moved slowly, feeling his sense of failure acutely. This was ending well, but not because of his competence. Because of luck. Because of that thing she had always seemed to trust and he had scorned.

Gray came across the sand toward him.

"Where's the princess?" he asked.

"Secure."

Of course she picked that moment to break from the trees and scamper down the beach. She must have left her hiding place within seconds of Ronan securing her promise she would stay there.

"Grandpa!" She threw herself into the arms of a distinguished-looking elderly man.

Ronan contemplated her disobedience—the complete disintegration of his authority over her—with self-disgust.

Gray looked at her, his eyebrows arched upward. "Good grief, man, tell me that's not the princess."

"I'm afraid it is."

But Gray's dismay was not because she had broken cover without being given the go-ahead.

"What on earth happened to her hair?"

The truth was Ronan could only vaguely remember what she had looked like before.

"She's safe. Who cares about her hair?"

Gray's look said it all. People cared about her hair.

Ronan was glad she had cut it if it made her less of a commodity.

"She is safe, isn't she?" Ronan asked. "That's why you're here? That's why you didn't wait for me to come in?"

"We made an arrest three days ago."

"Who?" He needed to know that. If it was some organized group with terror cells all over the place, she would never be safe. And what would he do then?

Peterson lowered his voice. "You gave us the lead. Princess Shoshauna's cousin, Mirassa. She was an old flame of Prince Mahail's. You've heard that expression 'Hell hath no fury like a woman scorned,' but in this case it was more like high school high jinx gone very wrong."

Ronan watched Shoshauna, felt her joy at being with her grandfather and felt satisfied that her instincts had been so correct. If she had that—her instincts—and now the ability to capture the power of the wave, she was going to be all right.

"You went deep," Gray said, "if I could have found you I would have pulled you out sooner."

Oh, yeah, he'd gone deep. Deep into territory he had no right going into, so deep he felt lost even now, as if he might never make his way out.

"But when one of the villagers saw the fire last night and reported it to her grandfather he knew right away she'd be here." Gray glanced down the beach at her, frowning. "She doesn't look like the same person, Ronan."

Ronan was silent. She was the same person. But now she had a better idea of who that was, now, he hoped she would not be afraid to let it show, to let it shine.

He was aware of Gray's sudden scrutiny, a low whistle. "Anything happen that I should know about?"

So, the changes were in him, too, in his face.

"No, sir." Nothing anybody should know about. He would have to live with the fact his mistakes could have cost her her life. Because they hadn't, no one else had to know. Ronan watched the other two boats unload. Military men, palace officials, bodyguards.

"Where's Prince Mahail?' he asked grimly.

"Why would he be here?"

"If I was going to marry her and she'd disappeared, I'd sure as hell be here." But only her grandfather had come. Not her mother. Not her father. Not her fiancé. And suddenly he understood exactly why she had loved a cat so much, the loneliness, the emptiness that had driven her to say yes instead no.

But she knew herself better now. She knew what she was capable of. As far as gifts went, he thought it was a pretty good one to give her.

Gray was looking at him strangely now, then he shook it off, saying officiously, "Look, I've got to get you out of here. Your commanding officer is breathing down my neck. Your Excalibur team is on standby waiting to be deployed. I've been told, in no uncertain terms, you'd better be back when they pull the plug. I'm going to signal the helicopter to drop their ladder."

Ronan was a soldier; he trained for the unexpected; he expected the unexpected. But somehow it caught him completely off guard that he was not going to be able to say goodbye.

The helicopter was coming in low now in response

to Gray's hand signals, sand rising around it. The ladder dropped.

Don't think, Ronan told himself and grabbed the swaying rope ladder, caught it hard, pulled himself up to the first rung.

With each step up the ladder, he was aware of moving back toward his own life, away from what had happened here.

Moments later, hands were reaching out to haul him on board.

He made the mistake of looking down. Shoshauna was running with desperate speed. She looked as if she was going to attempt to grab that ladder, too, as if she was going to come with him if she could.

But the ladder was being hauled in, out of the way of her reaching hands. Had he really been holding his breath, *hoping* she would make it, hoping by some miracle she could come into his world. Was he really not ready to let go? But this was reality now, the chasms between them uncrossable, forces beyond either of their control pulling them apart.

She went very still, a small person on a beach, becoming smaller by the second. And then, standing in the center of a cyclone of dust and sand, she put her hand to her lips and sent a kiss after him. He heard the man who had hauled him in take in a swift, startled gasp at the princess's obvious and totally inappropriate show of affection for a common man, a soldier no different from him.

But he barely registered that gasp or the startled eyes of the crew turning to him.

Jake Ronan, the most pragmatic of men, thought he

felt her kiss fly across the growing chasm between him and touch his cheek, a whisper of an angel's wings across the coarseness of his whiskers, as soft as a promise.

CHAPTER EIGHT

SHOSHAUNA looked around her bedroom. It was a beautiful room: decorated in turquoises and greens and shades of cream and ivory. Like all the rooms in her palatial home, her quarters contained the finest silks, the deepest rugs, the most valuable art. But with no cat providing lively warmth, her space seemed empty and unappealing, a showroom with no soul.

She was surrounded by toys and conveniences: a wonderful sound system; a huge TV that slid behind a screen at the push of a button; a state-of-the-art laptop with Internet access; a bathroom with spa features. But today, despite all that luxury, all those things she could occupy herself with, her room felt like a prison.

She longed for the simplicity of the island, and she felt as if she had been *robbed* of her last few hours with Ronan. She had thought they would at least have one more motorcycle ride together. No, she had even been robbed of her chance to say goodbye, and to ask the question that burned in her like fire.

What next?

The answer to that question lay somewhere in the six

days of freedom she had experienced. She could not go back to the way her life had been before, to the way she had been before.

Where was Ronan? She still felt shocked at the abruptness of his departure. After that final night they had shared, she had wanted to say goodbye. No, *needed* to say goodbye.

Goodbye? That isn't what she wanted to say! *Hello. I can't wait to know you better. I love the way I feel when I'm with you. You show me all that is best about myself.*

There was a knock on her door, and she leaped off her bed and answered it, but it was one of the maids and a hairdresser.

"We've come to fix your hair," the maid said cheerfully, "before you meet with Prince Mahail. I understand he's coming this afternoon."

Shoshauna did not stand back from the door to invite them in. She said quietly but firmly, "I happen to like my hair the way it is, and if Prince Mahail would like to see me he will have to make an appointment to see if it's convenient *for me.*"

And then she shut the door, her maid's mouth working soundlessly, a fish gasping out of water. For the first time since she had come back to this room, Shoshauna felt free, and she understood the truth: you could live in a castle and be a prisoner, you could live in a prison and be free. It was all what was inside of you.

A half hour later there was another knock on her door, the same maid, accompanied by a small boy, a street ragamuffin.

"He said," the maid reported snippily, "he has something that he is only allowed to give to you. Colonel Peterson said it would be all right."

The boy shyly held out the basket he was carrying and a book.

Shoshauna took the book and smiled at him. She glanced at the book. *Chess Made Simple.* Her heart hammering, she took the basket, heard the muted little whimper even before she rolled back the square of cloth that covered it.

An orange kitten stared at her with round green eyes.

She felt tears film her eyes, knew Ronan was gone, but that he had sent her a message.

Did he know what it said to her? Not "Learn to play chess," not "Here's a kitten to take the edge off loneliness."

To her his message said he had seen the infinite potential within her.

To her his message said, "Beloved." It said that he had heard her and seen her as no one else in her life ever had.

But then she realized this gift was his farewell gift to her. It said he would not be delivering any messages himself. Had he let his guard down so completely on that final day together because he thought he would never see her again?

Never see him *again?* The thought was a worse prison than this room—a life sentence.

She wanted to just slam her bedroom door and cry, but that was not the legacy of her week with Ronan. She had learned to be strong. She certainly had no intention of being a victim of her own life! No, she planned from this day forward to be the master of her destiny! To take charge, to go after what she wanted.

And to refuse what she didn't want.

"Tell Prince Mahail I will see him this afternoon after all," she said thoughtfully.

She realized she had to put closure on one part of her life before she began another. She did not consult her father or her mother about what she had to say to Mahail.

He was waiting for her in a private drawing room, his back to her, looking out a window. When she entered the room, she paused for a moment and studied him. He was a slight man, but handsome and well dressed.

She saw the boy who had said to her, years ago, as he was learning to ride a pony at his family's compound, "Girls aren't allowed."

He turned and smiled in greeting, but the smile faltered when he saw her hair. She deliberately wore short sleeves so he could see the chunks of skin peeling off her arms, too.

He regained himself quickly, came to her and bowed, took both her hands.

"You are somewhat worse the wear for your adventure, I see," he said, his voice sorrowful, as if she had survived a tsunami.

"Not at all," she said, "I've never *felt* better."

Of course he didn't get that at all—that how she felt was so much more important than how she looked.

"I understand you have been unaccompanied in the presence of a man," he said. "Others might see that as a smirch on your character, but of course, I do not. I understand the man's character is unimpeachable."

She knew she should be insulted that the *man's* character was unimpeachable, but in fact it *had* been Ronan who had exercised self-control, not her. Still!

"How big of you," she said. "Of course that man saved me from a situation largely of your making, but why think of that?"

"My making?" the prince stammered.

"You were cruel and thoughtless to Mirassa. She didn't deserve that, and she retaliated. I'm not excusing what she did, but I am saying I understand it."

The prince was beginning to look annoyed, not used to anyone speaking their mind around him, especially a woman. What kind of prison would that be? Not being able to be honest with the man you shared the most intimate things in the world with?

"And that man, whom *others* might see as having put a smirch on my character, was absolutely devoted to protecting me. He was willing to put my well-being ahead of his own." *To refuse everything I offered him, if he felt it wasn't in my best interests.*

"How noble," the prince said, but he was watching her cautiously. She wasn't supposed to speak her mind, after all, just toss her hair and blink prettily.

"Yes," she agreed, "noble." Ronan, her prince, so much more so than this man who stood in front of her in his silk and jewels, the aroma of his expensive cologne filling the room.

What would he say if she said she would rather smell Ronan's sweat? She smiled at the thought, and Mahail mistook the smile for a change in mood, for coy invitation.

"Are you well enough, then, to reschedule the day of our marriage?" he asked formally.

So, despite the hair, the skin, her new outspokenness, he was not going to call it off, and suddenly she was glad, because that made it her choice, rather than his— that made it her power that had to be utilized.

She needed to *choose.*

"I've decided not to marry," she said firmly, with no fear, no doubt, no hesitation. A bird within her took wing.

"Excuse me?" Prince Mahail was genuinely astonished.

"I don't want to get married. I have so many things I want to achieve first. When I marry I want it to be for love, not for convenience. I'm sorry."

He glared at her, put out. "Have you consulted your father about this?"

Of all the maddening things he could have said, that about topped her list!

"It's my choice," she said dangerously, "not his."

Prince Mahail looked at her, confused, irritated, annoyed. "Perhaps it is for the best," he decided. "I think I might like your cousin, Mirassa, better than you after all."

"You would," Shoshauna muttered as he marched from the room.

And yet the next day, when she met with her father, she felt terrible trepidation, aware her legs were shaking under her long skirt.

Meetings with him always had a stilted quality, formal, as if his children were more his subjects than his blood.

"I understand," he said, without preamble, "that you have told Prince Mahail there will be no wedding."

"Yes, Father."

"Without consulting me?" he asked with a raised eyebrow.

Shoshauna took a deep breath and told him who she was. She did not tell him she was the girl he wanted her to be, meek, docile, pliable, but she told him of longing for education and adventure…and love.

"And so you see," she finished bravely, "I cannot marry Mahail. I am prepared to go to the dungeon first."

Her father's lips twitched, and then he laughed. "Come here," he said.

As she stepped toward him, he stood up and embraced her. "I want for you what every father wants for his daughter—your happiness. A father thinks he knows best, but you have always been a strong-spirited girl, able, I think, to find your own way. Do you want to go to school?"

"Yes, Father!"

"Then it will be arranged, with my blessing."

As she turned to go, he called her back.

"Daughter," he said, laughing, "we don't have a dungeon. If we did I suspect your poor mother would have locked you away in it a long time ago. I will explain this, er, latest development to her."

"Thank you."

Funny, she thought walking away, her whole life she had sought her father's love and approval. And she had gotten it, finally, not when she had tried to please him, but when she had been brave enough to please herself, brave enough to be herself.

This was news she had to share with Ronan. She asked Colonel Peterson where he was.

He looked at her carefully. "He's been deployed," he said, "even if I knew where he was, I wouldn't be able to tell you."

And then she realized that was the truth Ronan had tried to tell her about his life.

And she recognized another truth: if you were going to be with a man like that, you had to have a life—satisfying and fulfilling—completely separate from his. If Ronan was going to be a part of her life, she had to come to him absolutely whole, certainly able to function when his work called him to be away.

She renewed her application for school and was accepted. In two months she would be living one more dream. She would be going to study in Great Britain.

And until then?

She was going to learn to surf! There was no room in a world like Ronan's for a woman who was needy or clingy. She needed to go to him a woman confident in her ability to make her own life.

And then she would be a woman who could make a life with him.

An alarm was going off, and men were pouring through the doors of an abandoned warehouse, men in black, their faces covered, machine guns at the ready. Ronan was with Shoshauna, his body between her and the onslaught, but he felt things no soldier ever wanted to feel—outnumbered, hopeless, helpless. He couldn't protect her. He was only one man...

Ronan came awake, drenched in sweat, grateful it wasn't real, perturbed that after six months he was still having that dream, was unable to shake his sense of failure.

Slowly he became aware that the alarm from his dream was really his phone ringing. He'd picked up the phone, along with a whole pile of other things he needed, when he'd moved off base a few months ago. Next time he bought a phone, he'd know to test the damned ringer first. This one announced callers with the urgency of an alarm system announcing a break-in at the Louvre.

He got up on one elbow and looked at the caller ID window.

"Hi, Mom," he said.

"Are you sleeping? It's the middle of the day."

"We're just back from a deployment. I'm a little turned around."

Six months ago he wouldn't have imagined voluntarily giving his mother that information, but then, six months ago she would have been asking all kinds of questions about what he'd been up to, trying to get him to quit his job, do something safer.

Interestingly, Ronan found he wasn't enjoying the emergency call-outs the way he once had. He recognized that adrenaline had become his fix, his drug, it had filled something in him.

It didn't work anymore. Not since B'Ranasha. He'd felt something else then, softer, kinder, ultimately more real.

Adrenaline had been a substitute, a temporary solution to a permanent problem. Loneliness. Yearning.

He'd been asked if he would consider taking an

instructor's position with Excalibur. Maybe he was just getting older, but the idea appealed.

Now his mother didn't even ask a single detail about the deployment, which was good. Even though she now had her own life and it had made her so much more accepting of his, Ronan thought it might set their growing trust in each other back a bit if he told her he'd just been behind the lines in a country where a military coup was in full swing rescuing the deposed prime minister.

Or, he thought, listening to the happiness in her voice, maybe not.

The big news that she had been trying to reach him about when he'd taken the wedding security position on B'Ranasha, amazingly, had nothing to do with another wedding, or at least not for her. No, she'd had an idea.

She'd wanted to know if he would invest in her new company.

But of course, that wasn't really what she had been asking. Sometime, probably in that week with Shoshauna, Ronan had developed the sensitivity to know this.

She was *really* asking for an investment in her. She was asking him, fearfully, painfully, *courageously,* to believe in her. One last time, despite it all, *please.*

And isn't that what love did? Believed? Held the faith even in the face of overwhelming evidence that to believe was naive?

The truth was he had all kinds of money. He'd had a regular paycheck since leaving high school. Renting this apartment was really the first time he'd spent any significant amount of it. His lifestyle had left him with little time and less inclination to spend his money.

Why not gamble it? His mother wanted to start a wedding-planning service and a specialized bridal boutique. Who, after all, was more of an expert on weddings than his mother? There was no *sideways* feeling in his stomach—not that he was at all certain it worked anymore—so he'd invested. When she'd told him she'd decided on a name for their new company, he'd expected the worst.

"'Princess,'" she said, "the *princess* part in teeny letters. That's important. And then in big letters 'Bliss.'"

Into his telling silence she had said, "You hate it."

That was putting it mildly. "I guess I just don't understand it."

"No, you wouldn't, but Ronan, trust me, every woman dreams of being a princess, if only for a day. Especially on *that* day."

And then Ronan had been pleasantly surprised and then downright astounded at his mother's overwhelming success. Within a few months of opening, Princess Bliss had been named by *Aussie Business* as one of the top-ten new businesses in the country. His mother had been approached about franchising. She was arranging weddings around the globe.

"Kay Harden just called," his mother told him breathlessly. "She and Henry Hopkins are getting married again."

"Uh-huh," Ronan said.

"Do you even know who they are, Jacob?"

"No, ma'am."

"Don't call me that! Jacob, you're hopeless. Movie stars. They're both movie stars."

He didn't care about that, he'd protected enough important people to know the truth. One important person in particular had let him know the truth.

All people, inside, were the very same.

Even soldiers.

"We're going to have a million-dollar year!" his mother said.

Life was full of cruel ironies: Jake Ronan the man who hated weddings more than any other was going to get rich from them. He'd told his mother he would be happy just to have his initial investment back, but she was having none of it. He was a full, if silent, partner in Princess Bliss, if he liked it or not. And when he saw how happy his mother was, for the first time in his memory since his father had died, he liked it just fine.

"Mom," he said. "I'm proud of you. I really am. Please, don't cry."

But she cried, and talked about her business, and he just listened, glancing around his small apartment while she talked. This was another change he'd made since coming home from B'Ranasha.

After a month back at work he had decided to give up barrack life and get his own place. The brotherhood of his comrades was no longer as comfortable as it once had been. After he'd gotten back from B'Ranasha he had felt an overwhelming desire to be alone, to create his own space, a life separate from his career.

If the apartment was any indication, he hadn't really succeeded. Try as he might to make it homey, it just never was.

Try as he might to never think about *her* or that week on the island, he never quite could. He was changed. He was lonely. He hurt.

The apartment was just an indication of something else, wanting *more,* wanting to have more to life than his work.

And all that money piling up in his bank account, thanks to his partnership in Bliss, was an indication that something *more* wasn't about money, either.

He'd contacted Gray Peterson once, a couple of days after leaving B'Ranasha. He'd been in a country so small it didn't appear on the map, in the middle of a civil war. Trying to sound casual, which was ridiculous given the lengths he'd gone to, to get his hands on a phone, and hard to do with gunfire exploding in the background, he'd asked if she was all right.

And found out the only thing he needed to know: the marriage of Prince Mahail and Princess Shoshauna had been called off. Ronan had wanted to press for details, called off for what reason, by *whom,* but he'd already known that the phone call was inappropriate, that a soldier asking after a princess was not acceptable in any world that he moved in.

Ronan heard a knock on his door, got up and answered it. "Mom, gotta go. Someone's at the door."

Was it Halloween? A child dressed as a motorcycle rider stood on his outside step, all black leather, a helmet, sunglasses.

And then the sunglasses came off, and he recognized eyes as turquoise as the sunlit bay of his boyhood. His mouth fell open.

And then she undid the motorcycle helmet strap, and struggled to get the snug-fitting helmet from her head.

He had to stuff his hands in his pockets to keep from helping her. Finally she had it off.

He studied her hair. Possibly, her hair looked even worse than it had on the island, grown out considerably but flattened by the helmet.

"What are you doing here?" he asked gruffly, as if his heart was not nearly pounding out of his chest, as if he did not want to lift her into his arms and swing her around until she was shrieking with laughter. As if he had not known, the moment he had recognized her, that she was the something *more* that he yearned for, that filled him with restless energy and a sense of hollow emptiness that nothing seemed to fill.

This was his greatest fear: that with every moment he'd dedicated to helping her find her own power, he had lost some of his own.

"What am I doing here?" she said, with a dangerous flick of her hair. "Try this—'Shoshauna, what a delightful surprise. I'm so glad to see you.'"

He saw instantly she had come into her own in ways he could not even imagine. She exuded the confidence of a woman sure of herself, sure of her intelligence, her attractiveness, her power.

"I'm going to university here now."

That explained it. Those smart-alec university guys were probably all over her. He tried not to let the flicker of pure jealousy he felt show. In fact, he deliberately kept his voice remote. "Oh? Good for you."

She glared at him, looked as if she wanted to stamp her foot or slap him. But then her eyes, smoky with heat, rested on his lips, and he knew she didn't want to stamp her foot or slap him.

"I didn't get married," she announced in a soft, husky purr.

"Yeah, I heard." No sense telling her he had celebrated as best he could, with a warm soda in one hand and his rifle in the other, watching the sand blow over a hostile land, *wishing* he had someone, something more to go home to. Feeling guilty for being distracted, wondering if he was just like his mother. Did all relationships equal a surrender of power? Wasn't that his fear of love?

"But I have dated all kinds of boys."

"Really." It was a statement, not a question. He tried not to feel irritated, his sense of having given her way too much power over him confirmed! Seeing her after all this time, all he wanted to do was taste her lips, and he had to hear she was dating guys? *Boys.* Not men. Why did he feel faintly relieved by that distinction?

"I thought I should. You know, go out with a few of them."

"And you stopped by to tell me that?" He folded his arms more firmly over his chest, but something twinkled in her eyes, and he had a feeling his defensive posture was not fooling her one little bit. She knew she had stormed his bastions, taken down his defenses long ago.

"Mmm-hmm. And to tell you that they were all very boring."

"Sorry."

"And childish."

"Males are slow-maturing creatures," he said. Had she kissed any of them, those boys she had dated? Of course she had. That was the way things worked these days. He remembered all too well the sweetness of her kiss, felt something both possessive and protective when he thought of another man—especially a childish one—tasting her.

"I didn't kiss anyone, though," she said, and the twinkle in her eyes deepened. Why was it she seemed to find him so transparent? She had always insisted on seeing who he really was, not what he wanted her to see.

He wanted to tell her he didn't care, but he had the feeling she'd see right through that, too, so he kept his mouth shut.

"I learned to surf last summer. And I can ride a motorcycle now. By myself."

"So I can see."

"Ronan," she said softly, "are you happy to see me?"

He closed his eyes, marshaled himself, opened them again. "Why are you here, Shoshauna?"

Not princess, a lapse in protocol that she noticed, too. She beamed at him.

"I want to play you a game of chess."

He didn't move from the doorway. A game of chess. He tried not to look at her lips. A game of chess was about the furthest thing from his poor, beleaguered male mind. "Why?" he croaked.

"If I win," she said softly, "you have to take me on a date."

He could have gotten her killed back there on that island. She apparently didn't know or didn't care, but he was not sure he'd ever be able to forgive himself or trust himself either.

"I can't take you on a date," he said.

"Why not? You aren't in charge of protecting me now."

If he was, she sure as hell wouldn't be riding a motorcycle around by herself. But he only said, "Good thing, since I did such a crack-up job of it the first time."

"What does that mean?"

"Don't you ever think what could have happened if those boats that arrived that day hadn't been the colonel and your grandfather? Don't you ever think of what might have happened if it hadn't been your cousin, if it had been a well-organized terror cell instead?"

There it was out, and he was glad it was out. He felt as if he had been waiting months to make this confession. Why was it always so damned easy to show her who he really was? Flawed, vulnerable, an ordinary man under his warrior armor.

"No," she said, regarding him thoughtfully, *seeing* him, "I don't. Do you?"

"I think of the possibilities all the time. I didn't do my job, Shoshauna, I just got lucky."

"The boys at school use that term sometimes," she said, her voice sultry.

"Would you be serious? I'm trying to tell you something. I can't be trusted with you. I've never been able to protect the people I love the most." The look wouldn't leave her face, as if she thought he was adorable, and so he rushed on, needing to convince her, very sorry the word *love* had slipped out, somehow. "I have this thing, this *sideways* feeling, that tells me what to do, an instinct, that warns of danger."

"What's it doing right now?" she asked.

"That's just it. It doesn't work around you!"

She touched his arm, looked up at him, her eyes so full of acceptance of him that something in him stilled. Completely.

"You know why it doesn't work around me, Ronan? Because nothing is wrong. Nothing was wrong on the island. You were exactly where you needed to be, doing exactly what you needed to do. And so was I."

"I forgot what I was there to do and, Shoshauna, that bugs the hell out of me. I didn't do a good job of protecting you. I didn't do my job, period."

"I seem to still be here, alive and kicking."

"Not because of anything I did," he said stubbornly.

She regarded him with infinite patience. "Ronan, there are some things that are bigger than even you. Some things you just have to surrender to."

"That's the part you don't get! *Surrender* is not in any soldier's vocabulary!"

She sighed as if he was being impossible and childish just like those boys she had dated. "Thank you for the kitten, by the way. I was able to bring him with me. He's a monster. I called him Hope."

He wasn't really done discussing his failures with her, but he said reluctantly, "That sounds like a girl's name." The name said it all, named the thing within him that he had not been able to outrun, kill, alter.

He *hoped.* He hoped for the life he saw promised in her eyes: a life of connection, companionship, laughter, *love.*

"You know what I think, Ronan?"

"You're going to tell me if I want to know or not," he said.

"Just like I want someone to see me for who I am, someone I don't have to put on the princess costume for, you want someone to see you without your armor. You want someone to know there is a place where you are not all strength and sternness. You want someone to see you are not all warrior."

"No, I don't!"

"Now," she said, casually, as if she had not ripped off his mask and left him feeling trembling and vulnerable and on the verge of surrendering to the mightiest thing of all, "let's play chess. I told you the terms—if I win you have to take me on a date."

"And if I win?" he asked.

She smiled at him, and he saw just how completely she had come into herself, how confident she was.

"Ronan," she said softly, her smile melting him, "why on earth would you want to win?"

CHAPTER NINE

"I can't believe you'd ever accept anything but my very best effort," he said, though the truth was he already knew he was lost.

She contemplated him. "That's true. So if you win?"

"I haven't even agreed to play yet!"

"Well, we've stood at this point before, haven't we, Ronan? Where you have to decide whether or not to let me in."

They had stood at this point before. On the island he'd refused to play chess with her, and he'd made her cry. But then he had only been doing his job, and in the end that barrier had not been enough to keep him from caring about her.

Without that barrier where would it go?

A single word entered his mind. And oddly enough, it was not surrender. *Bliss.*

He stood back from his door, an admission in his heart. He was powerless against her; he had been from the very beginning. Princess Shoshauna of B'Ranasha walked into his humble apartment, took off the black jacket and tossed it on his couch as if she belonged here.

The form-fitting white silk shirt and black leather pants were at least as sexy as that bikini she had nearly driven him crazy in, and his feeling of powerlessness increased.

She looked around his place with interest. He shoved a pair of socks under the couch with his foot. She looked at him.

"I want to live in a cute little place just like this, one day."

His mother had claimed that every girl wanted to be a princess, but somehow, someway he had lucked into something very different. A girl who had already been a princess and who wanted to be ordinary.

He got his chess set out of a cabinet, set it up at the small kitchen table.

"Why didn't you call me?" she asked, sitting down, taking a black and a white chess piece and holding them out to him, closed fist.

He chose. Black, then. Let her lead the way.

He snorted. "Call you? You're a princess. You're not exactly listed in the local directory."

"You knew how to get ahold of me, though, if you'd wanted to."

"Yes."

"So you didn't want to?"

He was silent, contemplating her first move, her opening gambit. He made a defensive move.

"I couldn't. I still dream about what could have happened on that island. I failed you. There I was snorkeling and surfing, when really I should have been setting up defenses."

"I'd been protected all my life. You didn't fail me.

You gave me what I needed far more than safety. A wake-up call. A call to live. To be myself. You gave me a gift, Ronan. Even when you didn't call it that, it was a gift."

He waited.

"I needed to choose and I have. I've chosen."

"To play chess with a soldier?"

"No, Ronan," she said gently. "It was never about the chess."

"So I see." He was surrendering to her, just as he had on the island, even though he didn't want to, even though he knew better. *Bliss.* It unfolded in him like a sail that had finally caught the wind, it filled him, it carried him forward into a brand-new land.

She beat him soundly at chess, though he might have been slightly distracted by the scent of her, by the pure heaven of having her in the same room again, by the sound of her voice, the light in her eyes, the way she ran her hand through the disaster that was her hair.

"Do you know why I dated those other boys?" she asked.

He shook his head.

"So that you wouldn't have one single excuse to say no to me. So that you couldn't say, 'You only think you love me. You don't know anyone else.'"

"Love?" he said.

She sighed. "Ronan, I made it perfectly clear it wasn't about the chess game."

That was true, she had.

"So," he said, "what do you want to do for that date?"

What would a princess want to do? The opera? Live theater? Was he going to have to get a new wardrobe?

"Oh," she said, " I want to go to a pub for fish and chips and then to a movie after. Just like an ordinary girl."

His mother had been so wrong. Not every girl wanted to be a princess, not at all. Still, when he looked at her and smiled, he knew there was no hope she would ever be an ordinary girl, either.

And suddenly it came to him, a truth that was at the very core of humanity. A truth that was humbling and reassuring at the very same time.

Love was more powerful than he was.

He got up from his chair, came around to hers and tugged her out of it. Shoshauna came into his arms as if she was coming home.

"I guess," he whispered against her hair, "it's time for you to start calling me Jake."

He picked her up for their first official date three nights later. He felt like a teenager getting ready. He wore jeans and a T-shirt, trying for just the right note of casual.

As he approached her address, he was aware that for a man who had done the most dangerous things in the world with absolute icy calm, his heart was beating faster, and his palms were sweat-slicked.

She lived on campus in what looked to be a very ordinary house until he went to the front door, rang the bell and was let in.

There were girls everywhere, short girls, tall girls, skinny girls, heavy girls. There were girls dressed to go to nightclubs and girls in their pajamas. There were girls with their hair in rollers and girls hidden behind frightening facial masks of green creams and white creams. And it seemed when he stood in that front foyer, every single one of them stopped and looked at him. Really looked.

"Sexy beast," one of them called out. "Who are you here for?"

The last time he had blushed was when Shoshauna had kissed him on the cheek and called him Charming in that little market in B'Ranasha. She was determined to put him in predicaments that stretched him! At least now he knew a little blush wouldn't kill him.

"I'm here for Shoshauna." There were groans and calls of "lucky girl," and he found himself blushing harder.

But when he saw her, coming down the steps, two at a time, flying toward him, all thought of himself, of his wild discomfort at finding himself, a man so used to a man's world, so surrounded by women, was gone.

There was a look on her face when she saw him that he knew he would never forget, not if he lived to be 102.

It was unguarded and filled with tenderness.

A memory niggled at him, of a moment a long, long time ago. His father coming up the steps from work, in combat uniform, his mother running to meet him, a look just like the one on Shoshauna's face now in her eyes. And he remembered how his father had looked at her. Despite the uniform, in that moment his father had not been a warrior. No, just a man, filled with wonder, gentled by love, amazed.

In the next few weeks, even though Ronan had to run the gauntlet of her housemates every time he saw her, he spent every moment he could with her. Every second they could wangle away from hectic schedules, they were together. Simple moments—a walk, holding hands, eating pizza, playing darts at the pub—simple moments became infused with a light from heaven.

Ronan was aware that, left to his own devices, he would have performed his duties perfectly on B'Ranasha. He would have been a perfect professional, he would never have allowed himself to become personally involved with the principal.

And he would have missed this: the tenderness, the sweetness of falling head over heels in love. But somehow, some way, a kind universe had taken pity on him, given him what he needed the most, even though he had been completely unaware of that need. Even though he had strenuously denied that need and tried to fight against it.

Falling in love with Shoshauna was like waking from a deep hypnotic state. When he woke in the morning, his first thought was of her. He felt as if he was living to make her laugh, to feel the touch of her hand, to become aware of her eyes resting on his face, something in them so unguarded and so breathtakingly, exquisitely beautiful.

For some reason he, a rough soldier, had come to be loved by a woman like this one. He planned to be worthy of it.

Shoshauna looked around, let the trade winds lift her hair. There was a flower-laced pagoda set up on the beach, the royal palace of B'Ranasha white and beautiful in the background. They had tried to keep things small, but even so the hundred chairs facing the wedding

pagoda were filled. The music of a single flute inter-
twined with the music of the waves that lapped gently
on the sand.

Jake's mother, Bev, had managed to get over her disappointment that, despite the fact it was a royal wedding, her first, they wanted nothing elaborate. Now
Shoshauna saw why her mother-in-law's business was
so successful: she had read their hearts and given them
exactly what they wanted—simplicity—the beauty
provided by the ocean, the white-capped waves in the
blue bay the perfect backdrop to the day.

Shoshauna wore a simple white sheath, her feet were
bare, she had a single flower in her hair.

She watched from the tree line as Jake made his way
across the sand and felt the tears rise in her eyes.
Beloved.

He was flanked by Gray Peterson, just as he had
been the first time she had seen him, but this time Jake
looked calm and relaxed, a man at ease despite the formality of the black suit he was wearing, the people
watching him, the fact it was his wedding day.

It had been almost a year since she had first laid eyes
on him, six months since she had won her first date with
him in that chess match.

Since then there had been so much laughter as they
discovered a brand-new world together—a world seen
through the viewfinder of love.

They had ridden motorcycles, gone to movies,
walked hand in hand down rain-filled streets, played
chess and done nothing at all. Everything was equally
as astounding when she did it with him.

He was so full of surprises. Who would have ever

guessed he had such a romantic nature hidden under that stern exterior? The kitten as a gift should have been her first clue! He was constantly surprising her with heart-felt or funny little gifts: a tiara he'd gotten at a toy store; a laser pointer that drove the kitten, Hope, to distraction; a book of poems; a pink bikini that she would use now, for the first time, on her honeymoon.

And the stern exterior was just that. An exterior. She'd always thought he was good-looking, but now the hard lines on his face were relaxed around her, and the stern mask was gone from his eyes. The remoteness was gone from him and so was his need to exercise absolute control over everything. Jake Ronan seemed to have enjoyed every second of letting go of control, seeing where life—and love—would take them, if they gave it a chance.

It had taken them to this day and this moment. He stood at the pagoda, his eyes searched the tree line until they found her.

And he smiled.

In his smile she saw such welcome and such wonder—and such sensual promise—that her own heart beat faster.

Of course, there was one thing they had not done, one area where he had maintained every ounce of his for-midable discipline. Jake Ronan had proven to be very old-fashioned when it came to the question of her virtue.

Oh, he had kissed her until she had nearly died from wanting him, he had touched her in ways that had threat-ened to set her heart on fire, but always at the last moment he had pulled away. He had told her his honor was on the line, and she had learned you did not question a warrior's honor!

But tonight she would lie in his arms, and they would discover the breathtaking heights of intimacy. After the reception, they would take her grandfather's boat, and they would go to *their* island, Naidina Karobin, *my heart is home*. The island would be once again inhabited only by them.

Last night, even though he wasn't supposed to see her until today, Jake had managed to charm his way past all her girlfriends and her cousins and aunts.

"I brought you a wedding present."

"You're not supposed to be here," she told him, but not with a great deal of conviction. She loved seeing him.

"I know. I couldn't stay away. Knowing you were here, just a few minutes away from me, I couldn't not be with you. Shoshauna, that's what you do to me. Here I am, just about the most disciplined guy in the world, and I'm helpless around you. Worse," he moved closer to her, touched her cheek with the familiar hardness of his hands, "I like being helpless. You make me want to be with you all the time. You make everything that is not you seem dull and boring and like a total waste of time.

"You make me feel as if all those defenses I had, had kept me prisoner in a world where I was very strong but very, very alone. You rescued me."

Her eyes filled with tears. "Ronan, you could not have given me a more beautiful gift than those words."

He smiled, a little bit sheepishly. "There's still enough soldier in me that I don't see words as any kind of gift." He opened the door and brought in what he had left in the hallway.

She burst out laughing. That's what he did to her, and for her—took her from tears to laughter and back again in the blink of an eye.

A brand-new surfboard, and she had been delighted, but at the same time she rather hoped, much as she was *stoked* about surfing, that the waves would never come up. She rather hoped they would never get out of bed! Not for the whole two weeks. That she could touch him until she had her fill of the feel of his skin under her fingertips, until she had her fill of the taste of his lips, and she already knew she was never going to get her fill of that!

Shoshauna was still blushing from the audacity of her own thoughts when her mother and her father came up beside her, not a king and a queen today but proud parents. Each of them kissed her on the cheek and then took their seats.

Her father in particular was very taken with Jake. Her mother had been more slow to come around, but no one who truly got to know Jake could do anything but love him.

Her mother had also been appalled by the simplicity of the wedding plans, but she and Bev had managed to console each other and had become quite good friends as they planned the wedding of their children.

Her grandfather came to her side, linked his arm through hers, smiled at her, though his eyes were wet with tears of joy.

And then Shoshauna was moving across the sand toward her beloved, toward Jake Ronan, and she could see the whole future in his eyes. Her grandfather let her go, and she walked the last few steps to him on her own, a woman who had chosen exactly the life she wanted for herself.

Jake watched Shoshauna move toward him across the fineness of the pure white sand.

She had chosen the simplest of dresses, her feet were bare, but when you were as beautiful as she was, even his mother had agreed that simplicity was the best way to let her true beauty shine through.

His mother and his wife-to-be, here together.

And in him the most wonderful surrender. He would protect them with his life, if he ever had to, and they both knew that.

Someday he would have children with Shoshauna, and he could feel the fierce protectiveness within himself extend to them, but something new was there, too.

A trust, that he would do whatever he could do, but when his strength ran dry, then there would be *something* else there to step in, *something* that seemed to have a better plan for him than anything he could have ever planned for himself, if the woman walking over the sand toward him was any indication.

He knew that *something* went by a great many names. Some called it the Universe, the life force, God.

He had come to call it Love, and to recognize it had been running the show long before he'd come along, and would be running it long after.

There came a point when a man had to realize that there were things he did not control, and that he would only exhaust himself, drain away his strength and his soul, if he continued to think the whole world would fall apart if he was not running it.

Ronan had come to believe that he could trust the protection and care of a force larger than himself.

It was the same force that brought a certain man and a certain woman together, against impossible odds, across cultural and social differences, the force that made one heart recognize another.

And it was that force that would protect them and see their children into the world.

Once upon a time Jake Ronan had thought if he ever had to stand where he was standing today, he would probably faint.

And yet the truth was, he had never felt so calm, so strong, so *right*. And the strangest thing of all was that, even as Ronan admitted he was powerless in the face of this thing called love, with each day of his surrender he felt more powerful, more alive and more relaxed, more grateful, more everything.

This was the something *more* he had longed for all his life: to be a part of the magnificent mystery that flowed around him and in him as surely as it flowed through the waves on the sea. He longed to ride that incredible energy with the ease and joy with which he could ride the most powerful of waves. Not to conquer but to feel connected.

He watched Shoshauna move toward him, and he almost laughed out loud.

For one thing he had come to know that this thing he chose to call Love had the most delicious sense of humor.

And for the longest time he had thought it was his job to rescue the princess.

But now he saw that wasn't it at all.

That she had come to rescue him. And that allowing himself to be rescued had not made him a weaker man but a better one.

She reached him, looked him in the face, his equal, the woman who would be the mother of his children, his companion, his friend, his lover through all the days of his life.

"Beloved," she said, her voice hushed with reverence of what they stood in the presence of, that Force greater than all things. "Retnuh."

And he said to her, his eyes never leaving her face, in her own language, a greeting and a vow, "My heart is home."

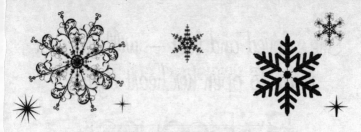

Wrap up warm this winter with Sarah Morgan...

Sleigh Bells in the Snow

Kayla Green loves business and hates Christmas.

So when Jackson O'Neil invites her to Snow Crystal Resort to discuss their business proposal... the last thing she's expecting is to stay for Christmas dinner. As the snowflakes continue to fall, will the woman who doesn't believe in the magic of Christmas finally fall under its spell...?

4th October

www.millsandboon.co.uk/sarahmorgan

She's loved and lost — will she ever learn to open her heart again?

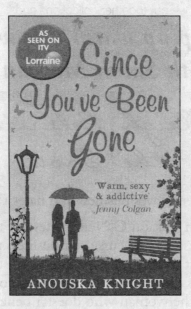

From the winner of ITV Lorraine's Racy Reads, Anouska Knight, comes a heart-warming tale of love, loss and confectionery.

'The perfect summer read — warm, sexy and addictive!'
—Jenny Colgan

For exclusive content visit:
www.millsandboon.co.uk/anouskaknight

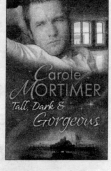